Immolation

VOLUME I

Immolation

Volume I

S.D. Diastrefo

Cover Art:
Garland, John Bingley. *Durenstein!* 1854, scrapbook, Harry Ransom Center, The University of Texas at Austin, USA.
www.hrc.utexas.edu/
Arranged by S.D. Diastrefo

Second Edition 2026

A zealous Archbishop grapples for control over a city that's being slowly but steadily overrun. While his loyal hunters can cull the undead threat, they cannot halt the encroaching ideals of a secular empire: ideals that condemn the righteous hunt as unjust.

*To my friends and patrons for their support
throughout this project.*

Dramatis Personae

PRINCIPAL CHARACTERS

CYRIL STACY, Hunter and Archbishop of Windermere

BRONTË TACHRAN, novice and Hugo's apprentice

BENJAMIN SAVA, Cleric and Bishop

SERGE GABOURY, Cleric, head of infirmary, Philip's uncle

HUGO SIWARD, clergy's head baker and cellar keeper

PHILIP GABOURY, Hunter, Serge's nephew, Jael's hunt partner

MADDOC PARNELL, Hunter, Deacon, Miriam's husband

ROYAL GUARD

DOMINGO CASTILLEJO, Captain of the Royal Guard

LEVI STERLING, Sergeant

IRMA ALLERMANE, Sergeant

CLERGY

FLORENCE MOREAU, Huntress and Bishop

SYBIL REGABI, Huntress and Bishop

BEATRICE PEMBLY, Cleric and Mara's principal caretaker

GEMMA CLEMENTINE, Cleric and Mother Superior

JAMES TRILLMOT, Cleric

JAEL BAHADIR, Huntress, Emre's twin sister, Philip's hunt partner

LAYFOLK

MARA STACY, Cyril's Mother

MIRIAM PARNELL, clergy's head cook, Maddoc's wife

NOBILITY

VIDAL SINCLAIR, Lord Governor of Visimund

ISABEL SINCLAIR, Lady Governor of Visimund

CITIZENS

THOMAS GREER, Owner, Millerton-Greer Grocery
FREDERICA COVINGTON, Proprietress of the Warbling Wren
GEORGIANA HACKETT, cobbler, daughter of a dead addict
EMRE BAHADIR, Lamplighter, Jael's twin brother
HEZEKIAH MACMILLAN, Huntsman, husband to Lucia
LUCIA MACMILLAN, wife to Hezekiah
BLAIR MACMILLAN, daughter of Lucia and Hezekiah
TICHE PAHARAN, apprentice to Ambrose, employed at Ashgrove Lane Apothecary

VAMPIRES

ZEMIRAH, Pureblood Vampire, Esther's older sister
ESTHER, Pureblood Vampire, Zemirah's younger sister
NOEL MCGOWAN, Vampire, Esther's bodyguard
AMBROSE DEBAUVE, Vampire, Doctor and owner of Ashgrove Lane Apothecary
THOMASINA, Vampire Thrall

GENTRY

AOIFE FOLVILLE, Heiress, Folville Trading Co.
ERWIN FOLVILLE, Aoife's half-brother
FINLAY GERRING, Erwin's Valet
DARCIE VADAMERCA, Aoife's Butler
HEVA SUNDERMAN, Owner, Sunderman Farms

A glossary of story-relevant terms is available
at the back of the book.

BOOK I
The Lady

1

BOOK II
The Thief

219

BOOK III
The Addict

370

Prologue

NO ONE TRULY KNEW WHERE SHE HAD COME FROM. She cut an elegant, if intimidating, figure – all dressed in black and adorned with trappings of gold. She was so very tall, too. She had this way of looking down on others that some might perceive as judgmental. When she spoke, her voice was of brilliant bronze. It demanded attention and admiration, a sound utterly unique in its tone and its beauty.

Yet, for each harsh look or steel-sharp edge, she hid just as much softness. If one was to listen long enough, behind the commanding bronze they might catch the softer, psalm-sweet notes of brass chimes in her voice. Her long shadow cast a welcome shade in the summer, her arms a sanctuary of warmth and light in the frozen winters.

She had stood for centuries – calm and resolute through snow and storm, through drought and famine, through peace and war. Some speculated her very heart had been built for war. That, deep down in her foundations, she was a keep of the old warriors, those knights from some several thousand years past. Others said she was only ever a cathedral: a holy place the saints had constructed atop the dust and rubble of ruins, mending the scars war had left behind.

Her architecture was indeed a love letter to those fabled days, grand and ornate and imposing. Every inch of her was guarded by loyal saints and messengers carved of stone. Her body was crafted of sooty, gray-black granite and capped with a bouquet of gilt domes and high spires that rose to pierce the heavens. Her walls, though dusty and stained with the stories of a hundred seasons' worth of rainwater, would catch the sun at dawn and dusk in dazzling hues of peach and violet.

She was adored by the people – and so it was fitting she be named thus: Our Beloved Lady.

Here she stood, since time immemorial, surveying her dominion. From the rolling hills, blanketed with thick forests and smothered by fog, to the inky-black waters of the twin rivers that sliced like knives through her dear city, raging cold and pure at her feet.

Now, as the seasons marched onward as they are ever wont to do, she waited. Waited for two of her treasured faithful to return to her, to be safe once more within her arms. The world was, after all, quite a cruel place beyond her embrace.

BOOK I
The Lady

1

THE SUMMER COUNTRYSIDE GLITTERED GREEN AND GOLD as it flew by outside the train window. Inside one of the compartments, two figures sat in comfortable silence, barely illuminated by candles flickering behind blown glass. The pair practically vanished into the dark, oily-black habits melting into the green velvet benches, save for those bits of gold trim around the hems, gilt crosses borne at the breast, and the bleached, crisp white at their throats – the lady her coif, and the gentleman his clerical collar.

The nun had a warm, hazelnut complexion; her face dusted with precious few freckles, high on her cheekbones. Her eyes were a soft brown, dotted with flecks of gold. Her features were sharp, with angular brows and steely lips. Despite her intensity, she had a gentleness about her. Her hair could not be seen beneath her veil, but her eyebrows boasted a darker lavender that betrayed the color lurking beneath her coif.

The man across from her was darker in complexion. His skin was a deep, olive bronze. Hair grew a cold brown against his skin, fading into a silvery seafoam color the longer it grew. The sides of his head were shaved down to a velvety fuzz, kept neat and tidy – much like the short, narrow beard on his chin. Only the thick hair atop his head grew long enough to be pulled back into the silk-wrapped tail between his shoulder blades. He had no handsome freckles like his companion, but had similarly angular, intense features. High cheekbones, a stiff lip, and sharp edges only softened by time – by wrinkles that had begun to appear in the corner of his eye.

The steam rail line was the most comfortable, and arguably the safest, route through the patches of dense forest, rolling hills, and steep cliffs of the countryside. But it was far from the fastest, what with her meandering path and her occasional stops. Both of the passengers knew this, but the priest hadn't been fond of the decision. He preferred the more direct path, on horseback, as the crow flies, to save precious time. Even now, the nun couldn't help but pity the poor man fidgeting in his seat across from her, crossing and uncrossing his ankle over the opposite knee restlessly, a small book of poetry thumbed open to occupy himself.

"She will be alright for one more night." She said.

"I know." He replied. "I know that."

Diamond panes of heavily frosted glass only allowed vague silhouettes to be seen from inside the candlelit cabin. Rowdy, raucous youths shuffled past, freshly aboard from the recent stop. A fair few brought the stench and demeanor of excess alcohol with them, along with the common clatter of steel weapons rattling in scabbards, the jingle of ill-fitting armor, the flutter of skirts and cloaks, the thudding and inevitable trailing of dirt from well-worn shoes and boots.

One young man who liked the sound of his own voice just a bit too much bounced his way down the corridor, pressing his flushed face up to the glass, eyes cupped with his hands in an attempt to peek inside at his fellow travelers.

His actions were rewarded with a sharp inhale from the priest, who swiftly picked up the cane rested against his leg and rapped it on the opposite side of the glass. It had the desired effect, spooking the young man back a pace and making him shuffle off quickly down the hall, giggling in embarrassment. The priest huffed and settled back in his seat, shaking his head before going back to reading. The train jostled as a few low-hanging branches were snapped off, sending twigs and acorns tumbling over the roof above them. The train jostled again.

"We're slowing down." He said.

"Probably to put less stress on the bridge."

He squinted out the window at the woods. "We are not so near the bridge yet."

A thump just a little too heavy to be foliage sounded on the roof above them. His brow furrowed in dismay and he looked at the woman across from him. A knowing glance was exchanged between the two. She'd heard it as well.

The priest shut his book, tossing it aside on the bench and gripping his cane as he rose to his feet. He unlatched the door and slid it open. The nun fell in step behind him, and they both strode swiftly to the rear of their car, polished boots padding quietly along the wool carpet of the corridor.

He went first, elbowing the door open and stepping out between the rattling train cars. The ground passed beneath his feet at a dizzying speed as he gripped the ladder's cold metal and climbed up as quietly as was possible. She followed suit, nimbly scaling the ladder and shuffling up beside him.

Crouching low until the train was clear of the remaining branches, the pair crept forward, only standing when she broke from the forest cover and sped about the curve of a grassy knoll. Wind whipped through the loose, billowing folds of their pleated habits, revealing the form-fitting uniforms of the Order of the Sacred Heart's Hunters as each of them stood – two black silhouettes staring down the three ragged figures crouched together on the next car's rooftop.

At a passing glance, they might have looked utterly average, unimpressive, even. One stood slightly taller than the other two, and was far better dressed. The lesser two, though, had the familiar look to them. The sunken features, the ruddy tinge in their skin, the awful, milky-blue clouds in their eyes – clouds that caught the fading sunlight in such a horrible way as they slowly turned around. Tattered shirts clung to their shoulders as the breeze threatened to tear them off. The tallest of the three, the one with clear eyes and better-fitting garments, had a suspiciously clean rapier tucked into her belt. Adventurers or simple travelers at a glance, stowaways or petty thieves, most likely, given their chosen method of arrival aboard and the condition of their clothes. But to two experienced Hunters, there was no doubt – these two knew vampires when they saw them.

Smoke churned and steam hissed as the priest took a single step forward. His boot hitting the roof of the car rang out like a warning bell. The sound made their leader turn around in a start, but it was the nun who spoke first, shouting her words above the wind and the rhythmic pitter-patter of the engine that otherwise would have drowned her out.

"If you are dead men walking, go with god and peace to you. I will pray for you. Only do no harm here."

An angry shriek cut her off as it tore from the throat of one of the two dead men; so loud and so piercing, it stung the ear more than the brutally loud steam whistle as the engine thundered over a dirt crossing. The two men with dead eyes darted towards them.

"They have strayed too far to hear you, Sister." The priest turned his cane over in his hand. "Let us be quick about it."

Quick as they were, the woman in black was quicker still. She overtook even her comrade in arms, dashing out in front of him and sliding underneath the bony knees of their attackers as they leaped forward. A blinding flash, a burst of heat, and she summoned a gold spear. A firm swipe of the glittering stave knocked the two white-eyed monsters down. She immediately raced towards the third, who drew her own rapier.

The two vampires that had crashed hard into the roof struggled to reorient themselves. They looked up just in time to see the priest meander toward them at a much more relaxed pace than his Huntress companion. One vampire was swifter than the other, scrambling to its feet and screeching as it brought both tooth and claw to bear against him. A hard slash aimed for the man's belly swiped through the air a hair's breadth from his gilded sash. The momentum of the failed blow paired with a nasty kick from the man sent the creature reeling forward awkwardly – another descent face-first into the roof of the car only halted by the priest's gloved hand gripping their silvery hair.

A sickening snap sounded as the priest pulled the vampire's head back by the scalp, jamming his knee up into his back at the same time, spine folding back fast like wet paper. The monster yelped, flailing clawed hands in desperation. At the same time, the other vampire had finally recovered and pulled itself up, and was dashing precariously along the roof toward the man.

The Hunter flung the convulsing vampire from him, sending their damaged body tumbling off the side of the car. He'd done so not a moment too soon, hopping nimbly out of range of the closed fist that came arching his direction. Far more controlled and collected than the other, this scrawny figure set their feet properly and kept their hands up to guard a gnarled face.

On the roof of the next car, the rapier came crashing down to meet the nun's braced stave. The metal sent gold sparks flying and made the magicked weapon ripple like shattering glass. The Huntress swatted out against her opponent with the far end of her weapon, delivering a bone-shattering blow to the ribs that made the vampire curse into the wind. She was weak, slow – her energy and effort spent on raising the dead men. But she still had her sword arm and skill to spare.

The Huntress was forced back, boots scraping against the metal roof, by the vampire spinning around and thrusting the rapier toward her. She caught the nun in the hand, slicing open a grisly wound along her forearm as it slithered up the sleeve of her habit. The nun sucked in air through her teeth at the pain and shuffled back as blood dripped from her hand.

In the gap this created, the vampire dropped to one knee and held her shattered side. She reached into her pocket, yanking the cork from a tiny glass vial of blood with her teeth. She downed it in a hurry and smashed the bottle into the roof, growling in pain and frustration as she forced herself back to her feet. Her head twitched, and the Huntress wisely adopted a defensive stance. The vampire lunged with a newfound strength. Her wild, piercing strikes quickened. Each of them smashed out a loud, reverberating note as metal met metal. Her jaw opened wide and her mangled, overgrown teeth flashed bright in the early night as she fought for her life against the Huntress.

The train plunged from the open meadows into the trees, and gradually the sound of roaring water told all aboard they were nearing the falls. Craggy boulders appeared, greater in number and size the further she ventured, stationary between the trees like guards standing watch as they whisked by in the night.

This vampire seemed to have enough of his own mind still intact to see the priest was missing an eye. He sought to use this to his own advantage, maneuvering into the priest's blind spot. Unfortunately, with age and injury often comes wisdom, and the priest did not allow the creature to loiter on his right side very long, matching each movement with a lazy sway of his shoulders and quick shuffles of his feet.

The nun's steps were light and her movements swift, countering the rapier as the flurry of lunges and swipes attempted to pierce her defenses. One blow punched through, a hard kick from the enraged vampire that sent her stumbling awkwardly back, nearly slipping between the cars as the train raced through the forest. She caught her breath and moved quickly enough to hop to the next car, the vampire following close on her heels, angry and hungry, and perhaps no longer thinking straight.

The cane that the older Hunter carried had yet to strike a blow, grasped in his hand where it rested atop the other leisurely behind his back. Hooks and jabs flew from the vampire, a few kicks thrown in for good measure. But the man in the cassock was quick. He moved no more than was absolutely necessary, with an expression bordering on boredom as he twisted his shoulders and leaned his head just far enough as the pair danced further and further back. Any fighter worth their salt could tell the priest was trying to force the vampire closer, and with one tiny misstep, he got what he wanted. His knee came up to catch the fist flying for him, the hard crack of knuckles crashing into the joint making the vampire grimace. The priest kicked that leg out and sent the poor soul floundering about, finally whipping out his cane from behind his back.

The gilt handle of the cane hooked into the vampire's mouth, blessed metal burning the skin and sending blood spluttering and steam hissing from their maw. A hard pull tore a hole through their cheek, exposing overgrown yellow teeth. Their ear hung down from the side of their head, dangling by a thin, mangled strip of flesh. A monstrous, ungodly screech erupted from their throat as they doubled over, choking on their own blood. A hard kick from the priest flung them off into the passing forest, body crashing hard and wrapping around the trunk of a birch tree, gurgling as it was swiftly left behind.

The vampire with the rapier saw the body tumble into the trees and groaned at the loss. The nun's opening presented itself, and she took it. She plunged her spear straight through the vampire's stomach, ripping it out to one side with a violent twist that sent blood spraying in the wind. She screamed out a pitiful wail, tottering clumsily to and fro as the Huntress spun around and landed a hard kick. The blow sent her careening off the roof, bloody body tumbling into the saplings and shrubbery beside the tracks, smearing blood over the forest floor and across a small boulder.

Her arm still bleeding and throbbing in pain, the Huntress gripped her lance firmly and leaped back across to the previous car. The train abandoned the cover of the forest once again, winding a path between craggy boulders to where the river waters tumbled over and down into a ravine. As she dashed toward her fellow Hunter, her eyes strained in the dark and noticed movement. Claws curled up over the lip of the roof as a twitching, mangled figure pulled itself up the side of the car, barreling toward the priest while his back was turned.

All the man heard was a worried "Father!" from his fellow before he felt the impact of the vampire, slamming into him with enough force to cast them both from the roof and out into the open air.

A metallic snap sounded as his cane extended, whipping up and catching its barbs fast into the metal of the train. His quick reflexes were enough to prevent his untimely demise, but did nothing to help with the vampire latched onto him. Spindly limbs wrapped about him, even as the blessed fabric of his cassock made the monster's skin hiss and steam. It howled, baring a mouth full of deformed fangs and attempting to find purchase, be it with teeth or claws. The Hunter grunted as the two of them dangled precariously before summoning enough strength to pull himself up.

He braced his feet against the side of the car, kicking himself and the mangled mess out and away, before using that momentum to swing back toward the car and fling the vampire underneath. There was a split second where the poor sod's humanity returned, and it let out a genuine, terrified squeal; a cry abruptly silenced as it was caught under the wheels and splattered into nothing over the rails.

The Huntress offered a hand and the man pulled himself up. Their chests heaved and hearts raced as they took a few moments to collect themselves. Unperturbed, the train sped north, toward the taller evergreen forests and vast, rolling hills rising in the distance.

The night sky was brilliant this far away from Windermere, natural beauty undimmed by the pollution of a hundred thousand guttering candles in streetlamps or fires burning in hearths, pouring their light out from every window. Serene and silent and forgiving of the bloodshed she'd witnessed, the evening gifted the Hunters a passing meteor as it plummeted from the heavens toward the horizon – leaving a bright trail as it etched out its last few moments in an explosive flash through the clouds.

Come morning, the good Hunters would be back in the arms of their Lady.

2

𝔄 PAIR OF MISMATCHED ELVES WERE HOVERING over a shared newspaper. A Brother and Sister of the Order. Both were dressed in neatly pleated black robes with gold sashes worn high at the waist, heavy metal rosary beads strung through them. In addition, the two wore wool cloaks this cool morning, cut to allow free movement of the arms. Despite this thick outer layer, they still huddled near the crackling brazier for warmth. Though identical at their three-and-twenty years of age, there was a decent disparity in height between the two.

Philip, the taller of the two, wore the summer colors of a southern elf: their textbook golden skin and their thick, wavy hair. His hair was a deep, chocolate brown, combed in a part down the middle. Sharp ears pointed slightly up and out from his head. He had blue eyes dotted with gold, and a darling pair of dimples etched into his face: an ever-present symptom of his chronic smiling. He almost always wore some form of a grin. Except for at this moment, as he winced and felt at the bandage secured to his head, just above his right eyebrow.

Jael, meanwhile, was practically Philip's opposite. She was a dusky, gray-skinned northeastern night elf with bright moonlight eyes, softer features, and a much shorter stature than her companion. She only came up to Philip's shoulder, and her shoulders were only just as broad as his waist. Her straight dark hair and pointed ears were both concealed beneath her coif and veil. The latter she had a habit of pulling forward over her shoulder and stroking, as if finger-combing her hair instead.

For now, her fingers were occupied elsewhere. Stained and smudged black from the still-drying ink of the newspaper, which she tilted toward the flame to allow Philip to read better. Her silver eyes needed no such help, but Philip's blue strained to make out the article she underscored with her thumb.

"Stop fiddling with your bandage," she muttered. "You'll irritate the stitches. Look, says here the new captain is some sort of war hero."

Philip grumbled about his wound being itchy, but leaned in to see better, huffing sparks and smoke from the brazier out of his way. An artist's rendition of the man in question had been printed beside a small introduction. He was touted as a veteran of battles, a champion and commander, a brilliant strategist ... All in all, he seemed grossly overqualified to oversee the local guard of a sleepy city on the outskirts of the empire.

Philip's voice trilled out somewhere between admiration and annoyance. "That's an awfully accomplished fellow to be sent to us. Probably just like the last, though. Keen to ride out a few more easy years before retiring."

"Probably. I'll bet this sketch of him makes him look thirty years younger than he is."

The pair of big, dappled gray horses harnessed to the carriage behind the two nickered. One of them pawed the ground impatiently, snorting and chewing at her bit. Woken up early, and for what? To idle away while these two youngsters babbled on, and without a bite of breakfast! Neither oat nor apple, nor even a stray tuft of grass!

"He'll probably come shambling in to introduce himself on a cane –"

"Good morning." Both Jael and Philip straightened to attention as a voice came from behind, interrupting their gossip.

Benjamin's brown eyes were, as always, hidden behind a round pair of rosy-colored spectacles. He wore these on a gold chain that dangled from the lenses to loop about his neck. Fair skin and steely-blond hair gave him an aura of being spun from silver in the low morning light – and in any other light. While only a decade or so older than both Jael and Philip, Benjamin was adorned in the trappings of a full-fledged priest: a long, gilt sash hanging from the customary wrap at his waist, the ornate, embroidered trim decorating his otherwise plain cassock, and the raw magical power that seemed to radiate from the rosary carried at his belt.

Clean shaven and pink from the tip of his nose to his comparatively stubby human ears, only Benjamin's hands were protected from the cold, nestled inside the warm folds of his sleeves. A blessing provided by the larger, billowy outer sleeves that his uniform touted, rather than the fitted sleeve cuffs worn by the other two.

Most importantly and in yet more contrast to the two young Hunters, Benjamin was a Cleric. A dedicated pacifist. He and his fellows dealt with the living and the dead, but never the undead.

"Are we ready to depart?"

Benjamin had a gentle but no-nonsense voice. Philip, for his part, adopted a more formal tone, carrying himself a bit taller: chest back, head up.

"Yes, Brother."

"Excellent. Then let us away."

Philip opened the door to the carriage and Benjamin picked up his robes, climbing neatly inside, but not before swiping Jael's copy of the morning paper. One swift final check of the harnesses, and Philip climbed up beside Jael, placing his pointed hat on his head as she clicked her tongue and urged the horses on. They crept leisurely toward the gatehouse, and the pair of Hunters guarding the gate saluted their fellows before unbarring and pushing the massive creaking gates open.

Twin lanterns hanging off the front of the carriage, each carrying a little flickering tongue of an unnaturally gold and unusually stable flame, offered little visibility in the low morning light and enveloping fog. Jael's night-attuned eyes missed little, though, and the carriage dashed nimbly across the arched cobblestone bridge. Over the stone path, between statues of long-dead clergy that lined the bridge and above the inky-black waters lurking beneath, they left the safety of Our Beloved Lady's walls, and ventured out into the still-sleeping town she called home.

Inside the carriage, Benjamin drew his cassock about him as he unfolded the newspaper, eyes naturally drawn to the many smudged fingerprints that littered it. He whispered a small incantation under his breath, creating a tiny bubble of gold light that hovered just beside his head, illuminating the page just enough to read as they traveled.

At the same time the black carriage was leaving the church grounds, another pair of horses were making their way toward that very place. Two of a sleek, athletic breed, nothing like the burly draft horses pulling the carriage, and certainly not native to these harsh lands. They were all dressed up in neatly kept military barding and meticulously polished tack, and bore a pair of equally well-kept riders. Engraved armor trimmed with gold flashed when the lampposts caught a glimpse of it, tucked beneath the fabric of the dress uniforms both riders wore.

It was not the first time these two trod this path, but as newcomers and foreigners, both of them, they were met with wary glares. Sleepy, superstitious eyes inspected them from behind still-drawn curtains and cracks in closed shutters. Both were officers, but one clearly held higher rank. He wore an ugly, unimpressed frown as he picked out yet more details in this strange, so-called holy city.

The church seemed to ... infect the very town, in his observation. Instead of street signs on the wide boulevards that made up the web of interconnected main roads, statues of venerated saints stood. The long lanes were named for whichever soul guarded it. The effigies all pointed the same way: toward the cathedral where she sat on a steep hill, the tallest within the city's walls, and overlooked the city from the northwest.

These saints stood on corners, in squares, at the center of fountains and within pavilions. As if the city radiated out from Our Lady, and as if one would simply find their way through her boroughs and alleys by this guidance alone. As the two knights rode over the bridge toward the cathedral, yet more saints greeted them – set in a line along the banisters, only interrupted by empty, blackened stones, whose saints must have eroded or toppled centuries ago.

One such saint even guarded the modest, but well-maintained train platform. The train whistled out her arrival and steam hissed loud as she slowed to a crawl, flooding the platform with yet more fog. The sea of white swallowed up the conductor as she walked alongside the metal beast, carrying both her key and lantern. Benjamin tilted his head to make out a familiar silhouette emerging from the steam and fog over the rim of his glasses.

Despite his best efforts, Cyril was easy to find in a crowd, if one knew what to look for. He stood a head or so taller than the average man, especially if one counted the pointed hat the Hunters wore, that sat naturally angled high on the back of his head and low in the front. Said hat only slightly obscured the seafoam hair he wore long and tied back. Thanks to the dreary weather, he had donned his long cloak, the smoky fur collar helping him retain some precious amount of anonymity by covering up that recognizable color.

He carried two modest leather suitcases, his cleaned cane tucked between the handles of one of them, over toward his black-robed fellow and stooped slightly to set them down. The bespectacled Brother wrinkled his nose in disgust, slipping his fingers under the hem of his inner sleeve and retrieving a folded, lightly perfumed cotton kerchief.

"Ugh, you reek of vampire blood. What, were you having it by the glass all night?"

"Hilarious." Cyril took the proffered handkerchief and attempted to wipe the remains of dried blood from his neck and jaw. Though he and his companion had both changed into fresh clothes, that vile magic loved to linger on the skin. It would require a proper bath and blessings to be completely rid of it.

Benjamin gestured, and Brother Philip rushed to fetch the suitcases. Out of consideration for the Archbishop's well-known desire not to draw attention to himself, Philip forsook the traditional greeting of kneeling and kissing his hand, instead bowing his head as he addressed him, trying and failing to contain his excitement beneath a more professional formality.

"Welcome back, Father."

He moved immediately to fetching the suitcases, only pausing to give the Father a moment to pull his cane from between the handles, and to return the greeting with a much more subtle, but still gracious, bow of his head.

"Thank you, Brother."

As Philip set about securing the two suitcases to the rear of the carriage, he couldn't help but smile. A rosy blush spread from his tawny cheeks to the tips of his pointed ears.

Jael elbowed him sharply. "Spend less time giggling and more time paying attention! These are not secure at all. You won't be grinning if Father's suitcase falls off on the road."

Philip chuckled awkwardly and rubbed the back of his head as she properly knotted the ropes about the luggage. Benjamin leaned over once more to look behind Cyril, expecting to see his traveling companion, but only seeing the string of civilian passengers disembarking. The Archbishop flicked his head off to a small crowd, where the Sister in question stood, surrounded by passengers and even the conductor, all thanking her profusely and praising her for her bravery and initiative.

The conductor, named Constance, was a slender, charming woman. Ruby-red lips and a neat pinstripe suit cut quite the figure, especially now as she fluttered her eyelashes and rather unabashedly flirted with the Sister.

"Sister Sybil, such a pleasure to finally meet you – what good fortune you happened to be aboard! I had no idea you were returning to Windermere so soon."

Poor Sybil was far too humble to accept such praise, bowing her head and doing her utmost to retain a demure, pleasant expression as both her hands were clasped by the conductor. "Please, there is no need to thank me."

To her relief, Benjamin strolled over and interjected that it was time to depart. He masterfully slipped his hand between Sybil's and Constance's, giving the conductor a smile and distracting her enough to allow the Sister to retract her own hand. As they strolled toward the carriage, Sybil thanked him under her breath, letting her forced smile unwind and flexing her cramping cheeks.

Cyril, for his part, was hiding on the far side of the carriage. Head bowed and obfuscated by his hat, lest he be subject to the same sort of reception. He offered his downturned hand,

and Sybil rested hers atop it to step up into the carriage, with Benjamin following just behind her in the same fashion. Before climbing up into the carriage himself, Cyril spoke to Philip. The young elf straightened up twice the amount he had for Benjamin, eager to hear the Archbishop's instructions.

"Before we go, extend my apologies to the conductor. Please tell her that I will arrange to pay for the damage to the car."

Philip nodded, though an inquisitive tilt of his head conveyed his confusion. Cyril didn't answer his curiosity, and the younger Brother was left to simply stare at the train itself, only noticing now the damaged metal and cracked windows on one of the cars, and the muddy brown splatter that he realized must have been dried blood.

On the far side of the train platform, an observant young man had noticed the clergy's presence immediately. His face was obscured, partially by the high collar of a black silk shirt, partially by a wide-brimmed leather hat common among working-class gentlemen, and partially by the paper-wrapped bundle of foliage he carried. The smell of herbs, heavy and medicinal, masked the sickly stench of his relatively weak, but still cursed, blood to even the most observant or sensitive. Constance saw him, though. She gave him an intense scowl through her narrow spectacles that made him heft his bundle and quickly stride off down a slip road.

Once finally inside the carriage and out of the public's immediate line of sight, Cyril sighed a deep breath and relaxed back against the seat. Sybil and Benjamin sat opposite him, facing forward toward the horses, while he rode in reverse.

Benjamin had already spied Sybil favoring her wounded arm, though she attempted to play it off as nothing until the Archbishop intervened.

"Sister's left arm, Brother. I stemmed the bleeding as much as I could, but I believe it needs more attention."

Sybil shot Cyril a petty glare, but allowed Benjamin to roll up her sleeve and inspect the wound as the carriage lurched forward. Slashed skin was stitched neatly together with wispy white threads. Barely there, like spider silk caught in sunlight. The magic served to keep the wound closed and halt bleeding, but was unable to do much else.

"I see. It is not severe, but we will need to disinfect and bind it properly at once."

Sybil sat back and let out an annoyed sigh.

"It won't take long," Benjamin reassured her. "I'll have you in and out of the infirmary before breakfast."

"You won't make me take any of your nasty tonics, will you?"

"Mention them again and I just might."

"No, please. You'll put me off my long-awaited breakfast," she moaned. "Do you know how long I've been looking forward to Miriam's cooking?"

Cyril chuckled quietly as they continued bickering, glancing out the window as the carriage made its way up the gently sloping cobblestone roads. He could see his Hunters patrolling the roads and rooftops – a few of the particularly observant recognized the carriage and saluted, even from considerable distance. A few houses – too many, for his liking – had those familiar upside-down, multi-tiered crosses typically used to mark illness, death, or worse. Some were proper metal casts, provided and sold by the church. Some were homemade, of wood or painted cloth stretched over twigs. Some were painted right on the door. Marks of pleas, of fear, of desperation.

Frustration furrowed the brow of the Archbishop. "I am counting more crosses than I would like. Have the Hunters grown docile in my absence?"

Benjamin folded his arms into his habit sleeves and shrugged. As a Cleric, he was a dedicated pacifist, and so preferred not to dwell on the more gruesome occupation of his fellows.

"I am not informed on the matter. Speak to Brother Maddoc about that."

A few younger boys crossing the road on their way to school noticed Cyril in the carriage and called out to him, waving. As the carriage picked up pace, a group of five or so of the schoolchildren raced along beside it, waving and hopping up, hoping to glimpse the Archbishop.

"Father's back, Father's back!"

Cyril gave a small wave of his own to the boys, who had to stop when the carriage traveled too fast for them, to prevent themselves from deviating too far from their path to school. A few of the older folk bowed their heads and kissed their hands in respect, now that the identity of the passenger had been thus revealed.

3

OUR BELOVED LADY WAS A CITY UNTO HERSELF. Even before one reached her walls, her influence was deeply felt. The worn stones of the road grew smoother where they were better maintained, in that borough closest to the church. Across one of the taller bridges, where river water rushed ice-cold as it diverged from the main body, only to rejoin it later, began the realm of the church's layfolk. The oldest part of the city, indeed considered by many to be the original city itself. Living so close to the Lady, and in such charming accommodations, was a privilege reserved for few families.

The sloping hills leading up to the cathedral's own walls had been chiseled into neatly kept tiers reinforced with stone. These slopes bore all manner of gardens and orchards, which were already buzzing with activity as tenant farmers saw to their care. Inside her walls was a scene much the same, as the many lay people emerged from their apartments, or trekked up on foot from their homes in the surrounding district, and began the myriad of daily tasks necessary to keep such a massive complex in operation. Skilled craftsmen and women of every inclination were eagerly making use of daylight. From stonemasons to coopers, from tinkers to beekeepers, every task was seen to under the ever-watchful eye of the clergy.

By circling to the southwest, the carriage could be spared the publicity, noise, and relative chaos of the public grounds. They crossed back over the bridge they had departed via, and were welcomed back into the restricted grounds where the clergy's private stables resided. This both spared the passengers the hassle of being subject to a throng of people, as well as enabled them a far more leisurely, pleasant path into the church proper. Upon departing the stables, one could wind through any one of many paths. Through one of the several orchards, the flower gardens, or even keeping to the paved cloisters, with their protective arches and glittering, ever-burning lanterns.

The distant, fragrant aroma of wood fires, smoked meat, and citrus taunted the Sister's appetite, and Sybil attempted to quietly divert her path from that of her two fellows. Benjamin noticed the shift in her steps and reached out, taking hold of her by the arm in the same way a parent would a wiggling child.

"Ah, ah. Infirmary, now."

"Drat."

Cyril chuckled at them yet again, shaking his head and glancing about the gardens as they continued on their way toward the main buildings. Sunlight was filtering through the fog, slicing lines through the foliage of the apple orchard. His steps slowed as he thought he noticed a familiar shape poking out from behind the trunk of a tree.

"Oh, and Father, I believe you have guests this morning ..." Benjamin's words trailed off as he realized Cyril had stopped to stare off into the orchard, and clearly was not listening.

"Hm? Oh ... yes. I will see to it. Thank you, Brother. Please, go on ahead, you two."

Benjamin and Sybil carried on in the direction of the infirmary as Cyril changed course. He descended the stone steps from the cloister that let out onto the garden's dirt paths, heading toward the apple orchard. He ducked his head under a branch to get a better look at the pair of feet sticking out ostentatiously from between fallen leaves and twisted roots.

Though swiftly approaching her twenty-fourth year, Brontë was still technically a novice. That being the case, her black dress and habit were slightly shorter in length than the fuller attire of the Sisters her age. The hem of her dress only approached her calves. This meant her legs – or, more accurately, her stockings – were subject to all the trials and tribulations she put them through by trouncing about the gardens without her shoes on. Already muddled with dirt, at least two fresh holes had been torn in them from snagging on wayward branches or splintering fence beams. Her novice veil, and the small amount of ebony hair that poked out from underneath it at her brow and temples, fared little better.

Brontë was relatively petite in build, short, and pleasingly plump. Everything about her was soft. The relatively sharp, angular bone structure of her face was tempered by fuller cheeks and a soft jawline. She had deep, chocolate-brown eyes that flickered with equal parts sincerity and mischief ... when they were open. The white marble statues scattered about the grounds rivaled her complexion. Her cheeks, though, were blotchy and flushed pink, either a symptom of the cold, or perhaps a symptom of whatever she had been reading, and perhaps was dreaming about as a result.

Her book was still open, now sprawled out page-down on her belly, with one hand resting atop it as she dozed. Cyril had to tilt his head to read what he could of the title through her fingers ... some romance novel. He sighed and cleared his throat in an attempt to wake her. When this achieved nothing, he took his cane and softly swatted at her foot.

Her toes curled and her eyelids fluttered open, half expecting to find a brave, overly curious squirrel or perhaps a bird pecking at her. The bleary, burly silhouette of Cyril looming over her – all dressed in black and with a fluffy fur pelt over his shoulders, breath puffing like dragon smoke in the cold morning – made for a startling surprise indeed. Brontë's cheeks went bright red and she leaped to her feet, frantically flinging her book behind the tree and brushing dirt from her skirts, as if that would somehow help her predicament.

"Father!"

Cyril's one eye followed the poor book as it fluttered off into the dirt, before coming back to rest on the mortified young lady. Stammered syllables of excuses were halfway out of her mouth when she remembered her manners, dropping to her knees and reaching for his hand to kiss it. He disentangled his hand after she'd done so, gesturing with two fingers for her to stand.

After an embarrassing few seconds of attempting to collect herself, she stood still with her stockinged feet together, hands clasped in front of her, head up smartly. Well, smartly save for the desperate puff she made out of one side of her mouth to try and coax a flyaway hair out of her face. *Of all people to find her like this!* She would have preferred Mother Superior found fault with her and twisted her ear right off.

"Welcome home! You've returned early? Is everything alright? Was there trouble? Are you well –?"

Cyril put a finger up before his lips to silence her.

"Good morning. Is this how you've been spending all of them, in my absence? Enjoying three months of idleness and storybooks?" His good eye blinked slowly as he surveyed her from head to toe and back up again, before fishing for his pocket watch and squinting at it. "Don't you have something useful you should be doing?"

She furrowed her brow and smiled awkwardly, rubbing her foot against the back of her opposite leg. His words stung, and so did her eyes as she fought back the bite of embarrassment.

She murmured in shame, "I don't join –"

"Speak up, girl. None of your mumbling."

"I don't join Brother Hugo in the bakery until six –!"

The loud chimes of the bells ringing out the hour silenced her. Cyril clicked his watch shut, stowing it in the folds of his sash. Brontë's already pink cheeks went progressively redder with each reverberation and she pursed her lips. Six o'clock.

"Exactly." He sighed and pinched the bridge of his nose. "Come along."

Brontë grabbed her book, and her shoes, hastily pulling one on and hopping awkwardly on one foot behind Cyril to wriggle the second on properly and still keep up with him. Cyril had been kind enough to slow his pace, and good thing, too – for every one of his long, lazy strides, Brontë had to take a rushed two of her own. He held out his arm in a gesture for her to walk alongside him once she caught up.

As they left the orchard, Cyril rolled his shoulder, sore from the previous night's exertions. His newfound walking companion, observant as ever, grew worried. Her own shame and embarrassment were momentarily forgotten as she leaned in a little closer, catching the scent of blood on him. Yes, yes ... of course it was common for Hunters to return wearing that familiar odor. But, to travel back all the way from Parrvon on such short notice? They *must* have taken the train – and there was no safer way to travel! Concern washed plain over her features and she took a few rushed steps out in front of Cyril, walking backward so she could face him as she spoke.

"Are you well, Father? Are you injured? Oh, perhaps you should go to the infirmary –"

"So many questions," he mused, interrupting her. "Watch your step, please."

Brontë didn't need his guidance, swaying and swerving nimbly around the turn in the cloister's path without even needing to turn around, and giving him a cheeky grin as she did so.

"You need not fret over me." He narrowed his one eye and gave her a pointed look. "If you are indeed concerned, you could etch fewer lines in my brow by attending faithfully to your *chores*, instead of loitering off in the gardens."

Her embarrassment returned and she fell back in step next to him, mumbling more of her mastered excuses. "It was only to read ..."

"Right." His unamused tone made her belly roil in shame. "Speaking of which, do be sure to return that storybook to the public library, where it belongs *oof* –"

His words were cut short as a gaggle of uniformed school children all tackled him at once, bursting from the manicured bushes with leaves in their hair and branches stuck in socks, reveling in their delight at catching the towering Hunter off guard. Five of them in total, with the oldest among them no older than four years. All combined, they threatened to knock the man down with their leaping and clinging.

His hat went fluttering off as one of the girls clambered up his bent back in an effort to reach his shoulders. He rushed to steady himself, lest she tumble down or he misstep and crush tiny fingers or toes. Brontë caught the leather hat and smiled as the poor Father had to take several moments to right himself. The girl atop his shoulders clasped sticky hands to his forehead while two more children grabbed his legs. The remaining two fought for his free hand, bouncing about him in a circle.

"We caught you!"

"Aye, indeed you did. Quick as the wind. I was no match."

"Did you fight any monsters while you were away, Father?"

"I bet you saw five monsters!" said the child at his right leg.

"I bet he saw ten!" replied the voice from his left, not to be outdone.

Cyril had to lean on his cane and swing each leg out carefully as he ambled along with the added weight of the two children, both of whom giggled with glee as they were carried forward on his boots.

"Oh, yes, terrible monsters. No less than twelve."

"Twelve is even more than ten!" said the girl atop his shoulders, leaning over to look down at him.

"It certainly is, you clever girl."

He finally reached the arched terrace of the courtyard and leaned his cane against a pillar. One of the Sisters responsible for wrangling the younglings came around the far corner of the courtyard, simultaneously relieved to find her escapees, and apologetic that they were troubling the Archbishop ... again. Cyril saw her and gave a reassuring gesture before reaching up with both hands to remove the child sitting on his shoulders and set her down.

"Now, what are we betting?"

There was a shuffle as the children freed themselves of him, huddling and holding a hushed conference before they turned around with determination in their eyes and hands on their hips. One boy, assumedly nominated by his peers, proudly held out precisely three buttons, a foil candy wrapper, a crumpled dandelion, and a pebble – all presented with a generous portion of pocket lint.

Cyril hummed and put a thoughtful hand on his chin, stroking the patch of facial hair that grew there. He leaned over, picking up one button, then the other, holding it up to the sky as if inspecting a precious metal or antique coin. There were murmurs of apprehension among the children and he gave them a suspicious look before turning around a moment, as if to shield the trinket from both the sunlight and their eyes for further inspection.

The children climbed over one another, eager to lean in or get a glimpse of whatever it was Father was doing. He abruptly turned back around, making half the group jump in surprise. He then knelt down – ushering the children in closer to hear his verdict.

He held the button up between his thumb and index finger before dropping it into his palm. A quick flick of his hand and he materialized in its place a small, sheer bag of chocolate-dusted almonds tied with a ribbon. The little satchel had five of the treats inside, exactly the amount for the children.

"One for each of you –"

A tried-and-true tactic for dispersing otherwise clingy children. They had swiped the sweets and were scampering off into the gardens for an informal picnic before he had even finished his words. They giggled with delight at their good fortune, wholly bedazzled by the magic with which the candy had been produced. All it took was Father and a button! They were so delighted by this event in their morning that they scrambled right past the Sister, who only sighed in exasperation and bowed to Cyril before she turned to follow them.

Brontë strolled up behind Cyril, offering him his hat as he stood. She had seen him turn around, indeed witnessed him fetching the candy from a pocket to make the sleight of hand possible. She could barely talk through her smile.

"Had you been saving those for yourself, or were you expecting the welcome?"

A small smile fluttered at the corner of his mouth a moment, replaced with his textbook stoicism the next. He shook his head to right his hair and set his hat back upon it.

"It never hurts to be prepared, though I do hope I gave them the chocolate ... and not the pepper ..." As he spoke, he pulled a second, identical little bag of the treats from his pocket and twirled it around his gloved finger. Brontë's mouth went wide before she threw a hand over it to stop herself from laughing.

"Father!"

4

REDERICA WAS SKITTISH AS A KITTEN and superstitious as they came in Windermere. Her cluster of freckles across her left cheek had made her so, and she compensated with a pair of teardrop-shaped silver earrings. Even her headscarf, which she wore tied behind her neck to keep her hair back, covered her ears and was embroidered with silver thread in a floral pattern.

She was busy checking each of the plants she kept behind the key counter, looking back and forth from the small book purchased from the church – a guide on how to keep a home, or business, as free from vampires as possible without a Cleric or Hunter present. She checked each leaf, each stalk, each color of every herb, every flower, every grass – all the necessary plants to craft the simplest remedies and preventatives, per the Archbishop's own writings.

The innkeeper checked that she had enough incense under the counter to put by the doorways at night. She checked for her valuable flasks of blessed oil, that precious commodity provided by the Lamplighter's Guild. She checked and rechecked for bottles of holy water. So engrossed was she in this inventory of her counter and cabinets she was startled half to death when her quiet was disturbed.

The double doors to the Warbling Wren were tossed open by two knights. Frederica clutched her rosary to her chest and leaped in fright at the unexpected noise, but relaxed slightly when she realized it was the Royal Guard. Her tension returned when a silhouette stepped inside from the foggy, sunlit morning

– a dark, intimidating woman with the empire's gold written all over her armor. She strolled past her knights with a grace befitting her station, one hand behind her back, the other swinging at her side. In that hand was the multi-tiered cross Frederica had hung upon the door.

"Good morning, ma'am," the knight said in a cold tone. She shoved the church's book aside and set down a document, sealed with wax and the captain's stamp, in its place. "Sergeant Allermane. I will be utilizing the premises henceforth." The knight then flung the metal cross down upon the counter, wiping her hands now that she was rid of it. "And you may put that thing away, you no longer need it."

Frederica's heart was still racing as Allermane gestured behind her to the knights, who began to file into the taproom in two neat lines. The woman snatched up the cross and held it to her chest, appalled and beside herself with indignation.

"I –" She stammered. "I beg your pardon, dame?"

"Consult the document before you trouble me with questions, ma'am." Allermane gave the flustered proprietress a judgmental look over her shoulder. "You *can* read, I trust?"

Frederica snatched up the document and began to read. The thing was a mess of references and long legal clauses that would confuse the average person, uneducated in their meanings and intricacies. Perhaps this was by design. But skimming the document was enough to find the confirmation: the Guard had the right to assume control of the premises, and to bar any Hunter from interfering.

"How long will you –?" Frederica stammered.

"Indefinitely."

"But, I –"

"You will be paid."

"I don't want your *money*, southerner." She frowned. "You invite death into my taproom alongside yourself, dame –"

Allermane rolled her eyes and sighed. She did her best to put on a slightly more empathetic tone, but it came out just as cold as usual. "You are quite safe, ma'am." Allermane eyed the book from the church. "By all means, say your prayers and burn your incense if it please you. Even call for a Cleric to bless the place, if that will soothe your troubled mind."

Frederica lifted her cross off the counter, as if intending to go right back outside and hang it up herself. "I need Hunters to –"

Allermane slapped her hand flat atop the cross, smacking it and Frederica's hands back to the countertop. "But no Hunters are to enter the premises so long as I am here. My answer on the matter is final. If you wish to complain, you may take it up with my captain."

5

ESPITE HER BIG-BONED STATURE, MARA WAS A THIN, wispy shell of a woman. She was reasonably broad-shouldered, and quite tall – not that you'd know it, as she had been confined to a wheelchair, or her bed, the greater part of the past fifteen or more years. Her health was a fickle thing, but she had the kind of attitude that made you feel silly for even inquiring if it was troublesome. *Pah!* she'd say, rolling her rosy eyes and grinning. She'd be more likely to wave your concern away with a wrinkled hand, or threaten to run over your toes with her chair, if you questioned her. Pity the fool who called her frail, and had to flee the woman down the hall as she wheeled after them.

But for all her brave words and brushing off concern, she was still frail and fragile. Much to her detriment, the only thing she suffered from in equal measure was vast overconfidence. Already once this month had she fallen, badly bruising her knees and hips. Thank goodness luck had been with her – that it had only been bruises, and not a broken bone or two. Alas, such luck only bolstered her overflowing overconfidence.

One of Mara's several skilled caretakers, a Sister named Beatrice, came through the open door to her bedroom to find the woman tottering precariously off the edge of her bed, reaching for her wicker wheelchair.

"Heavens, Mara! What do you think you're doing – you must stay abed!"

"Nonsense! I must wash and dress at once!"

"Stop that! You will fall and damage yourself again."

The exhausted Sister flung down the pile of folded linens she'd been carrying and pulled the wheelchair out of reach, before the elder's weak, spindly hands could claim it. Huffing with exertion but admitting defeat, Mara pouted like a schoolgirl and slowly resituated herself back in her bed while Beatrice put her hands on her hips and scolded her. She hissed through her teeth at the pain of moving, and a ragged cough interrupted further complaints. Hoarse and weak, her coughs made it that much harder to take a full breath – something she already struggled enough to do. The Sister shook her head at her charge.

"See, what did I tell you? You overexert yourself and –"

"I know, I know."

Mara sighed, clearly still terribly dejected about the verdict that she remain bedbound. Her voice was ragged, and just as shaky as her hands. And while she be in this state, her son – her son! – was to come home this very day! And how would she greet him? Shivering and sad, sore amidst her downy fortress of pillows, and depressed from being cooped up indoors. Though Mara's words sometimes failed her, her face often wore her emotions more plainly than any words could. Beatrice's expression softened as she saw Mara's lower lip quiver.

"How about some fresh tea, Miss Mara?"

"Oh, I suppose ..."

Both Mara and Beatrice perked up as a pair of familiar footsteps echoed from the lower floor of the apartment. The heavy, methodical click of polished boots prefaced the swish of oily-black fabric as the Archbishop abruptly rounded the corner of Mara's open bedroom door and made his way to her side. Beatrice took a few respectful steps back, curtsying as the Archbishop entered the room, though he hardly seemed to notice her.

"Cyril!"

Mara practically bounced with excitement to see her son, eagerly reaching out for him. He leaned his cane against the foot of her bed and tossed his hat on the duvet beside it. He held his cross to his chest to prevent it from bumping into her as he leaned over, giving her a tight but gentle hug and kissing her cheek. His voice dropped down into their native language, which Mara parsed much quicker and always preferred to speak to him in.

"Hello, mother."

Her dour mood dispersed all at once. Her trembling hands clasped about her son's ribs in a weak but equally delighted hug. She returned his kiss with a few of her own, peppered over his cheek. As he pulled away to straighten up, she beamed a grin, resting her spindly, bare hands in the sinewy, gloved palms of his.

"Welcome home!" She had to think and shift back to common speak, pushing words out past her accent. "Oh, oh … Sister!" Mara suddenly remembered Beatrice's offer of tea, looking over to her where the woman stood, on the opposite side of her canopied bed. "Could you – two cups, please?"

"Of course."

"Thank you, Sister." The Archbishop looked up at her briefly to convey both of their thanks before turning his attention back to his mother. Mara reached one hand up to cup his cheek, pressing her fingers to his forehead to feel his temperature, before finally setting her hand back in his.

"Are you well? Forgive me my state, would that I could be dressed properly for your return."

He held her hands daintily in his, leaning back on one leg to get as good a look at her as he could manage, what with her nestled in her pillows and still in her big, blousy nightgown and cap. Her silver hair hadn't even been brushed yet, and despite the twinkle in her eyes and the blush in her cheeks, he could feel the tremor in her hands, and could see the sickly pallor in her olive skin, hear the crack and crumble in her voice. If this observation made him feel any particular way, he didn't show it, idly leaning over to kiss her hands.

"How are you?"

"Quite well, quite well – you needn't fret over me."

When Sister Beatrice returned with tea a few minutes later, Mara had shuffled just enough to let Cyril sit up in bed next to her. He sat atop the covers, one ankle crossed over the other, holding one of Mara's hands in his, their fingers laced together as he leaned back against the mountain of pillows beside her. They paused in their discussion as the Sister set the tea tray down, the steaming pot smelling of delicious dandelion tea and accompanied by two overturned cups upon saucers.

"Brother Maddoc was looking for you, Father," Beatrice added as she straightened up. "He says he has guests waiting to speak with you."

"They can wait a few minutes longer."

Beatrice gave another quick curtsy and meandered off to leave the two to their former discussion, and likely to relay the news of the Archbishop being unavailable at the moment. Mara giggled like a schoolgirl and eagerly reached for the silver tray placed next to her, and Cyril pulled it closer on her behalf. She attempted to pour the tea herself, but her hands could barely grasp the little porcelain pot, much less lift it without trembling. So, he filled her cup for her, just about halfway, so that she could comfortably lift it. Mara continued the conversation in their native language.

"And you're certain you're not harmed? I could smell the blood on you from near downstairs."

"Not at all. I must apologize, I have not yet had time to dispel the blood properly."

"Nonsense, it does not upset me. But what of you? I know how it grates on you –"

A knock of knuckles against the open door came as a voice sought Cyril's attention.

"Father."

Cyril and Mara both glanced over to see the big, burly silhouette of Maddoc in the doorway.

Maddoc was hard to mistake and even harder to miss. A thick-boned bear of a man, he had a waist twice the size of the average man, comprised purely of solid muscle. Powdery blond hair was parted on one side of his head and combed quite tidily into place, at least this early in the day. By evening it'd be reduced to a rough, finger-combed mess as he always ran his hands through it to keep it out of his face. His skin had a small bit of sunshine to it, and his face was littered with pink scars. The marks crisscrossed his forehead, struck a line down his cheek, and one particularly gnarly specimen sliced through where his short beard grew.

"You have important guests waiting, Cyril." Maddoc dipped his head and gave Mara a salute with two fingers. "Ma'am."

"How important?" Cyril asked.

"The Royal Guard."

Cyril sighed. He took Mara's free hand in his own, bringing it up to his mouth to kiss the back of it, before uncrossing his ankles and rising to his feet. She pouted as he meandered around the foot of her bed and took up his cane. As he made to follow Maddoc out of the room, he stopped short as if remembering something.

"Ah." He turned and reached into his breast pocket, procuring a little sheer bag of candied almonds. Mara's eyes lit up when she recognized the little bag as the favors from the rail line.

It was a silly thing, but for some reason the little candies were a specific treat she enjoyed. Infrequent traveler as she was, though, she had no real opportunity to swipe the snack – not unless she could get regular customers to smuggle them to her. A small favor her son was happy to oblige. Cyril set the bag down on the tea tray for her.

"I'm afraid all I have are the pepper, but you were fond of them too, I recall." He leaned in to give her one more kiss on the forehead, whispering to her briefly as he did so. "We will speak of your state later. Be gentle with yourself until then, please."

She grabbed his arm, curling her skinny fingers into his sleeve. "Let's take breakfast together in the courtyard? Please, oh please?"

"*Cyril.*"

Cyril sighed as Maddoc grumbled behind him, and his mother fluttered her eyelashes and gave him a coy look, evidently not keen to release him until he bowed to her whims.

"Very well, as you wish."

"Give me your word?"

He sighed yet again and offered her his little finger. She beamed with delight, hooking her little finger – the one that still answered her – into his and released her hold on him. Cyril finally turned to accompany Maddoc out of the room and down the hall. Once the two men were safely out of earshot, Maddoc ventured a question.

"How is she?"

"Terrible," came the reply, without any hesitation. "I am shocked she can hold her head up at all."

6

HILE ONLY ONE OF MANY INFIRMARY KEEPERS, Brother Benjamin's knowledge of all manner of apothecary and mending magic was nearly unparalleled. He had a vast knowledge of herbs and salves, of spells and charms, and a distinct knack for blending the two together. And so, the Cleric immediately set to work tending to his patient.

With a careful incantation, he unstitched Cyril's temporary magic from Sybil's arm, allowing him free access to clean and disinfect the wound. His hands were steady with their work, grasping the thin pair of metal tongs and the wispy puff of cotton he'd soaked in a salve. Though the touch indeed stung like nothing else, the Clerics of Our Beloved Lady boasted exceptional skill in all manner of mending – both magic and mundane. The heavy-smelling herbs would clean and encourage healing, yes. But Benjamin had also laced the salve with a protective charm, warding off infection and driving any residual filth the rapier may have been carrying out of the wound. Especially the very real, and very dangerous, possibility of any vampire blood mingling with Sybil's own.

The infirmary was less one building and more a complex of several many-floored buildings. Strung together like beads on a chain, they formed a square, letting out at the ground floor into a sheltered cloister and beautifully manicured garden. Like the rest of the cathedral complex, each of the buildings had been built at different times, and for different purposes. While alike in their architecture, the inner chambers varied considerably.

Despite their subtle differences and specialties in the wounds they tended, each building was similar. The ground and first floors boasted the typical, high-occupancy hospital appointment. Soft beds lined each wall, with canopies of curtains for privacy between each of them. The upper floors hid private, sequestered rooms – typically for operations, for the severely wounded or ill, or for loyal layfolk approaching their eve of sleep.

In the corner closest to the cathedral's heart – where the infirmary was grafted to the rest of the complex proper - there was also the head of infirmary's office. It was through this office Benjamin had led Sybil to a currently vacant floor where only a few clergy were cleaning. Here, she could simply sit on one of the beds as he repaired her wounded arm.

So steady were Benjamin's hands that even the door being flung open downstairs and a familiar, raspy voice calling out did nothing to disturb his work. The head of the infirmary, Brother Serge, grumbled from behind his desk, not bothering to look up as the intruder dashed past him and up the stairs, disturbing him for the second time that morning.

"Mind your manners when barreling into my infirmary, Sister Florence," he called after her. Florence completely ignored him.

"Sister Sybil, welcome back!"

Sybil's face lit up at the voice, and she twisted around in an attempt to better see the speaker, much to Benjamin's annoyance.

"Or ..." Florence added in a singsong tone, "shall I call you *Abbess*?"

With Benjamin gripping her arm, the best Sybil could manage was to peek over her shoulder at Florence, who strode quickly up to her. Florence was all sunshine and shenanigans, and she dwarfed both Sybil and Benjamin. Granted, both Sybil and

Benjamin were relatively slender in build, but Florence was as tall as Cyril, and practically as wide as Maddoc. Broad, muscular shoulders rippled beneath her habit and she leaned down, beaming a grin before putting on an attitude of mock disappointment. She crossed her arms over her chest, scarred fingers tip-tapping against her bicep like a disappointed nanny.

"What's this, then? Gone and got yourself all sliced up? Did I not ask you to be especially careful?"

"I had done so well, nearly made it home unscathed. Not to worry, though. It's nothing serious, I'm sure Benjamin would give me some awful tonic if it was."

"Stay *still*, please."

"'Nothing serious', she says! Do you *hear* her, Brother! Why, I can practically see bone!"

Benjamin rolled his eyes but couldn't help but smile at Florence's typical theatrics. She had a way of forcing a genuine smile onto even Sybil's notoriously serious face. With the injury clean, Benjamin could re-stitch the wound with the same wispy, silklike threads that Cyril had originally employed. The threads were warm and painless, slithering about the air around his hand as he made sewing motions a few inches above her arm. He then placed a mundane wrap of cotton and linen over it, mostly to prevent the salve from dampening and sticking to her sleeve when she pulled it down.

"Remember to take the bandage off at night to let it breathe."

"I will. Thank you, Brother."

"And there were no other injuries on the train?"

"Eh, you got this on the train?" Florence interjected. Benjamin ignored her, looking over his glasses at Sybil and waiting for her reply.

"I would feel better, Brother, if you could at least inspect Father's right arm."

⁘

OUT WEST, AT THE VERY END OF THE RAIL LINE and final train platform, a poor employee was frantically counting and recounting the stock he was responsible for. He checked everything twice – thrice, even! Every stamped document, every seal, every ledger. Constance was tapping her foot impatiently, her pocket watch in her hand.

"Well? Come on, lad. I don't have all morning."

He bowed apologetically, giving her an awkward smile and mentally restarting his count. All around him, the farmers and millers had already loaded or unloaded their cargo, and were busy gossiping, puffing pipes of tobacco, or else dispersing to return to their work. This bustling platform was beyond the walls of the city proper. Situated on one of the few plots of flat land amidst the rolling hills of vineyards, orchards, and cereal crops. The plots and homesteads followed illogical curves, divided by lines that moved with the land. Cut up by the water that flowed naturally through ditches, around the edge of trees and thickets, and circumventing great boulders that would not be disturbed.

The Rotherdare sliced up these fertile plots of farmland. Delivering precious freshwater to the many irrigation canals and topping off wells. The water wove between the barns, warehouses, and windmills. There were many mills, of course, to manage the sheer amount of crop produced to not only feed the populace, but to feed the hungry ships that gobbled it up to take it downriver or across the sea. The blustery, constant winds that blew from the east powered the population of structures that dotted these rolling hills. There were many of them, the smaller, privately owned additions to homesteads, and the great, looming ones that belonged to long-standing businesses. The whitewashed towers and saffron-yellow blades of the Sunderman mills were well known by the locals, owned by one of the oldest and most respected lay families.

Perhaps it was this storied reputation that made the bumbling employee so nervous. The Lady Sunderman was known for her honesty, her piety! What would happen to him if she discovered he'd miscounted and given less than was paid for? Constance cleared her throat and slammed one of the doors to the cargo car, snapping him out of his stupor. She stood with her arms crossed in the bay of the other. He stomached his nerves and hoped only that blame would fall on another head, instead of his.

"All accounted for, ma'am!"

He hopped out of the car and she gave him a stern eye over the top of her shaded spectacles, clearly not believing him. She plucked the ledger from his hand just the same, though. It would not be her guilt, after all – she earned her coin either way. And he, plenty content to earn his pennies for his strong back, pulled his hat down on his head to cover his shame and departed back toward the fields.

As the morning rolled lazily on, the city and her surrounding hills would stir to busy life. The fog would burn off in the summer sun, save in those places it was clever enough to hug the churning waters, or keep to the cold shade. Carriages and cabs rumbled through the streets. The cathedral welcomed her faithful inside, out of the wind and blinding sun. Pilgrims paused along the path to pray to each of the saints that pointed the way. Children and adults brought pennies to wish in the fountain of Saint Lilian. Such was the natural pulse of life in Windermere. Here, tucked in a valley – between thick forests and bewilderingly tall mountains – she braved the seasons and superstition both.

7

IT WAS WELL PAST THE HOUR WHEN BRONTË came bumbling into the bakery. The baker, Brother Hugo, with a face full of flour and freckles, bellowed over his shoulder at her as she came scrambling through the door. He had thick, curly brown hair usually pulled back into a ponytail or bun on the back of his head. He had an equally curly short mustache that was kept neat with beeswax. He wasn't all that much older than Brontë – a handful of years, maybe – but he had the head and heart of a man thrice his age oftentimes. Brontë looked every which way for her apron as it was, of course, not hanging on the hook behind the door reserved for it. Instead, it loitered where it had been left last night: thrown over a stool now pushed in under the big mahogany worktable.

"Well, well, well!" Hugo's thick brogue did little to mask the smile in his voice. "How kind of you to show up, lass! I was beginning to think you'd left me on my own for breakfast."

Brontë threw her apron over her head and yanked the strings behind her, groaning in frustration as she realized, in her rush, she had failed to tie them properly and they had come completely undone. She took a deep breath as she slowed down to tie them again.

"I'm sorry, Hugo." She undid the button under her wrists that held her long sleeves in place and rolled them up, hurrying to the sink to wash her hands. "I had a busy morning."

"You, busy? That's a funny way to say 'overslept'." Hugo saw the color still fading from her cheeks and shook his head.

"Hah! I see – Father treated you to another one of his tongue-lashings, didn't he?"

She huffed indignantly. *Heaven forbid I have a hair out of place.* She moderated her reply better than she did her thoughts, though the same could not be said for her tone. She dried her hands on her apron. "He always has plenty for me, yes."

"They are seldom unearned."

"You aren't making me feel any better."

Hugo grinned. "I ain't here to make you feel better, lass! I'm here to make sure you're using that sharp mind of yours properly. But enough of that, get outside, tend the ovens. We have mouths to feed."

"Right away!"

"And take a cloak, it's chilly out there!"

Brontë was already prancing out the rear door and into the attached courtyard, braving the cool morning air once again to see to the row of masonry ovens that lined the ivy-covered far wall. Yet more embarrassment flooded her when she saw that Hugo had already set kindling and logs alight in each of them, performing what was indeed supposed to be her task, thanks to her tardiness.

The two bakers were responsible for crafting the bread served to the clergy, working to that end with clockwork-level precision. Or, they would, if Brontë wasn't often late, or with her head in the clouds, or nose-deep in a book. She was in the process of removing flaming scraps and scraping ashes when the pitter-patter of swift feet made her turn around.

Philip, still dusty from the road and wearing his pointed hat, skidded to a halt in the gravel at the entrance to the courtyard, beaming a grin and calling a greeting to Brontë. His thick cloak fluttered about him as he held out his arms to her.

"Good morning, Miss Brontë! My sweet, delightful, most talented of –"

"I don't have any pasties yet," she cut him off.

Philip frowned and his arms fell to his sides. "None? Not even leftovers?"

Brontë wagged her iron tongs at him, scolding him like one would a school babe. Playful as she was, exhaustion strained her voice. She had no desire to be the butt of her friend's jokes this morning, not after her horribly embarrassing encounter with the Archbishop. And as usual, Philip made no such subtle observations of her tone or mood.

"Not a one!" she said. "You *ate* all my leftovers, including the mushroom and leek I was saving."

"And it was delicious."

"Away with you! I have work to do."

"Since when do you take your chores so seriously?"

"Out, out!"

Hugo came outside bearing a tray of neatly prepared loaves on his shoulder, covered by a linen sheet, just in time to see Brontë wave her tongs at Philip, which he pretended to parry with a make-believe sword, making little swishing and clanging noises with his mouth as he did.

"Beautiful form, young lady –"

"Oi!" Hugo's voice carried across the courtyard, nearly as loud and long as the bronze bells. "Young Philip, you mind your manners! Act like the Brother you are now, you young scamp."

Philip and Brontë both attempted to suppress their laughter when the elder Brother spoke, with Philip winking at Brontë before greeting Hugo.

"Ah, Brother Hugo, always a pleasure! I was merely bidding the lovely maid a good –"

"Keep a latch on it, laddie! Don't you flirt with my apprentice. She's a proper lass, she is. She's too clever to mess about with a scheming Brother. One who's taken his vows and *should* know better, might I add! Off with you!"

As piercing – and correct – as Hugo's words were, they were always delivered with a sort of good-naturedness. Only Hugo had the exceptional ability to be simultaneously so serious and so lighthearted. Philip grinned and gave a low bow, backing out of the courtyard the direction he'd come.

"Right away, Brother. As you say, Brother –"

Philip caught the leftover half of a baguette that Hugo tossed to him, and the baker rolled his eyes and chuckled.

"Cheeky. Come on, back to work."

Thanks to the two bakers hard work, the courtyard would smell of golden, buttery bread before long.

8

THE DOORS TO THE ARCHBISHOP'S OFFICE OPENED swiftly, swinging back on whining hinges and announcing his arrival before even his loud voice came thundering into the room.

"Gentlemen of the Guard, I apologize for my tardiness."

Maddoc entered and closed the double doors behind the two of them as Cyril crossed the room toward his desk. Before said desk now lounged a dark, intense-looking man, flanked by a guard of lesser rank standing stiffly behind his chair. The man sitting down was unflinching at the sudden noise, though the slightly more slender and younger man with plum-chestnut hair hopped a little in surprise at Cyril's voice booming out behind him.

They both wore the deep Hunter-green of the Guard – neatly pressed, double-breasted uniforms worn over polished armor. The seated man bore the decorations of an accomplished officer, from the gold epaulets dangling from his shoulders to the braided cords looped under his arm to the subtle engraving in his armor. He wore a grizzled, tired expression on his narrow face. A handsome, hooked nose dominated his features, accentuated by the curly, well-kept auburn facial hair that grew to a point from his chin. He held his beret in his left hand, tucked under his arm, just beneath the silver crest of two stags emblazoned on his uniform – a symbol that any local would recognize to be a bastardization of Windermere's usurped military: the city guard that these royal guardsmen were meant to replace.

The officer rose leisurely, brushing aside his thick, fur-lined cloak over one shoulder and turning to face his tardy host. The hardened soldier made an effort to hide his surprise, limiting it to a suspicious squint, when he was faced with a man no older than himself. He had been informed that this Archbishop was unusually young for his station, but he had still expected a man at *least* some few years his senior. Not so – he estimated this priest could be no older than five and forty, rather close in age to himself. Cyril stopped a pace short of the royal guardsman, giving a small, but respectful, bow of his head.

"Cyril Stacy, Archbishop of Windermere. Honored to make your acquaintance."

"Captain Domingo Castillejo. A pleasure, Your Excellency."

A cold handshake was exchanged, both men quietly ascertaining the measure of the other. Domingo made a mental note that Cyril's hand, even while hidden beneath a glove, was alarmingly warm – as if he ran hot with magic. Cyril for his part, eyed Domingo's gnarled scars, lines raked over his left cheek, across his hooked nose, and down through his lips – proof of true battlefield experience that the previous, now-retired, captain had lacked.

"Please, do be seated," Cyril continued, disentangling his hand politely. "You will be more comfortable."

Domingo thanked him and sank back into the plush leather chair he'd been inhabiting before the Archbishop's arrival. His eyes followed the belt rosary that swung at the priest's hip briefly. It hummed with subtle power in a way that the other burly blond fellow's did not. Cyril circled to the opposite side of his desk as Maddoc leaned idly against the now latched double doors, arms crossed over his broad chest as he glared knives into the backs of the guardsmen. Domingo spoke first.

"Your reputation precedes you, Archbishop."

Cyril hooked his cane over the edge of his desk – a shiny indentation rubbed into the wood a telltale sign this was done often, and had been for many, many years. He remained standing as he addressed his company, a mannerism not lost on the captain.

"Is that so?"

"Youngest Archbishop in the province's history. Something of a controversial Cleric. Notorious vigilante."

Maddoc groaned aloud in exasperation at Domingo's last word and thunked his head back against the door behind him. Domingo turned to give him a glare over his shoulder, and Cyril sighed quietly, continuing the conversation as if Maddoc had not so rudely interrupted.

"That is one way to word it."

Cyril knew by the way Domingo spoke that he had done his due diligence in research. He was not naive – he knew that an enemy always sought to learn as much about his adversary as possible. But while this remained at the front of his mind, he could hear the tinge of respect that colored Domingo's words. Certainly, this man was a far cry from his now-retired predecessor. The previous captain had been an entitled, lazy man – the sort that was content to send orders down from his desk, and never once bothered to heft steel nor torch. Domingo was different. A hard, calculating man with intelligent blue eyes and a scarred face. Respectable as a captain, but damned to be a thorn in Cyril's side, and he knew it.

"You were a vigilante, before you were Archbishop, is that right?"

"We use the term 'Hunter' here, Captain."

"Of course, *Hunter*, excuse me." A sly smile could be heard in Domingo's voice as he accepted the correction, though his scarred lips displayed no flicker of it. "While I am plenty familiar with your church, I will confess I am far less familiar with your *order*. Albeit I do know of your ..." He chuckled dryly. "Righteous hunt."

Maddoc pushed himself away from the doors and made his way over to the side of Cyril's desk. The blond-haired behemoth of a man nonchalantly placed himself between the guards and the Archbishop, standing beside his desk. Domingo ignored him and continued speaking.

"It seemed only fitting and most prudent that, in this moment where I am to observe the formality of introducing myself as the new captain, I take the opportunity to remind you that vigilantism is illegal."

A sharp inhale sounded from Maddoc that made Domingo's eyes flick over to him. His fierce blue wordlessly challenged Maddoc's dusty gray. Domingo continued speaking without looking away from Maddoc.

"I would hate to be pedantic with you, Excellency –"

"No, please, by all means," Cyril cut him off coldly, a false politeness coloring his tone. "Speak plainly to me, Captain."

Domingo's eyes slowly slid back to Cyril. "While your vigilantism is illegal, *vampirism* – as you and yours call it – is not."

Maddoc's mouth fell open in shock at Domingo's words. Cyril was of half a mind to kick Maddoc's leg behind his desk. Despite this, he kept his own composure, listening in silence.

"*If* these so-called vampires commit such heinous acts as you and your Hunters constantly *claim* they do – then they are to be detained, tried, and punished in accordance with the law." Domingo narrowed his gaze. "Not executed at the whim of you, and your private army. I hope I am making myself understood."

"I understand your disbelief entirely, Captain Castillejo. You are not the first to doubt, and shall hardly be the last." He paused to consider his words. "But if you expect me to abandon my faithful – to leave the people of our city to suffer and die – I'm afraid you will be disappointed."

"And if you think I intend to let you purge the city of anyone your order deems a heretic," he snapped back. "You will be disappointed."

"You severely misunderstand the nature of our hunt, Captain."

"No, I don't think I do."

The reply was curt and immediate. Domingo stood, shoulders back and head high, clearly communicating the conversation was over. "Church and State are separate entities, Your Excellency. I shall remind you of this as often, and as bluntly, as I must. Good morning." Domingo gave a stiff bow of his head, turned on his heel, and brushed past his guard, who swiftly fell in step behind him. The plum-haired younger guard ran to open the door for his superior, and when he had passed, gave an awkward bow of his own to Cyril before shuffling away.

Maddoc blew air through his lips in exasperation before plopping down in Domingo's chair and propping up his feet on the desk. He ruined his hair by combing his fingers through it, his mouth still agape at the audacity of Domingo's parting remark. Cyril simply sat down in his chair and began rummaging through his desk – and the vast amount of paperwork that had accrued upon it during his absence.

"Close your mouth, Maddoc. You look like you've sat on yourself."

"Ugh."

"And get your feet off my desk."

"*Ugh.*"

Both heavy, booted feet thudded to the ground.

"Illegal!" Maddoc grumbled in his gravelly brogue, rolling his head back again in annoyance. "He may as well have threatened you with imprisonment! *Vigilantism*, he says – with that *cocky* look on his face. He's going to be a curse on our work."

"I don't doubt it," Cyril replied, eyeing a letter that bore a blue wax seal. "I take it he is the reason I saw so many crosses on doors riding up?"

"Aye. He's only been here two weeks, and he's already got the knights crawling all over the city like ants to honey, trying to limit where we can go."

"How efficient. Have there been any confrontations?"

"Not between us and them. Though some townsfolk have already voiced discontent."

"I suspect" – Cyril sliced a letter opener beneath the wax seal, unfolding the letter – "this particular Captain is plenty familiar with *quieting* discontent among civilians. You know how those Monocerian folk take pride in their fetters."

"Bah! He makes me miss the fat bastard what preceded him. What was his name? Callaghan?"

"Mind your language, Brother," Cyril said absentmindedly, smiling softly as he skimmed the letter. "Do not let him trouble you overmuch for the moment. I suspect Lord Sinclair has no intention of changing his policy of nonintervention toward us."

"I only worry more that his nonintervention will extend to the Guard."

"I would expect it. He's never been particularly involved. Though his wife is adamant in her support, she may hold some sway over his opinion. I may need to speak with her soon."

"Let the aristocrats bicker about it, then, says I. Heaven knows it's all they're good for."

Cyril folded up the letter and stood, tucking it into his sash and picking up his cane. "We'll speak more on the matter later. I am taking breakfast in the northwest courtyard. Find me there if you need me."

"Aye, aye."

Cyril opened the doors of his office, calling back to Maddoc. "And speak to Sister Sybil this morning, as soon as possible. I would have her relay her thoughts regarding the encounter on the train."

"Wait, what happened on the train?"

Cyril was already strolling swiftly down the hall in the direction of his own chambers by the time Maddoc had finished his question.

9

Ambrose cut a slender, perhaps one could even say dainty, figure. He had a ruddy complexion and stormy, green-blue eyes that were clear and alert. His hair was an earthy bronze, almost black when damp, as it was now. Black like the silky shirt he wore with a high collar and a brooch at the throat. A professional-looking waistcoat and overcoat were other constant companions. He carried a rapier in his belt, but one look at him gave the impression it was more for show and social rank than any true means of self-defense. An apothecary and doctor of modest income, he had few enemies, and little coin to loot, and so that rapier rarely left his hip.

He knew the conductor had seen him. She'd practically locked eyes with him, even as he hid behind his bundle. He was so flustered and filled with concern as he marched down the road that he failed to notice a woman coming down a small flight of stairs to the same path. She, too, was rather preoccupied with clutching her prayer beads, and was not anticipating someone barreling down such a sleepy road. Ambrose ran right into her and made her stumble, bumping into the tree that grew up from a granite planter wedged between flagstones. He was at once all apologies.

"Heavens! Forgive me, my good lady. Please, let me help you."

Ambrose had already mastered a subtlety of speaking and smiling that concealed his fangs. He helped the woman to right herself, brushing dirt from her hem and bowing his head and tipping his hat many more times. She was more surprised that a well-dressed man might pay her the courtesy of referring to her – a woman dressed in scratchy, woolen work clothes and with soil still under her fingernails – as a *lady*. She smiled and gave a small curtsy, along with her forgiveness. A final tip of his hat, and as quickly as he had entered her life, he exited it. He practically fled toward his business, fishing in his pocket for the brass key that unlocked the rear door to his shop.

The apothecary on Ashgrove Lane was a quaint, modest little shop. The rear door let Ambrose into the kitchen and workshop, where many empty bottles rested in linen-lined crates, and mundane medicament was stored in bulk, locked in brass-caged cabinets. Above this, accessed by a narrow, precarious flight of stairs, was his apartment – but he had no time to lounge there. He locked the door and raced toward the shop front, tumbling out from behind a swinging door that read Staff Only. He would have scared the daylights right out of his apprentice had the young man in question not felt his footsteps on the wood floor, or the slam of the door. Tiche turned to see Ambrose shuffle behind the counter, looking up from a book he'd been reading. He tossed the book aside to catch the paper-wrapped bundle of herbs, puffing the dangling leaves out of his face and peeking out from behind them with a curious look on his face. Ambrose spoke rapidly with his hands to his deaf employee.

"I'm going out. I will be gone some time. Tell any customers prescriptions will be delayed by a day."

He unlocked a cabinet beneath the counter and wrenched a pre-prepared briefcase from it. Without looking for a reply, he shoved his hat onto his head and flew back out the rear door, leaving his apprentice a bit dumbfounded and holding a bundle of herbs bigger than himself.

Ambrose had to walk a good portion of the way east before he could hail down a horse and cab willing to take him where he wanted to go – away from the shops and sunshine of central Windermere, and toward the bustling, fog-drenched port to the east. The twin rivers that intercepted one another within the city each had their own paths and purposes.

The winding, narrow Rotherdare River snaked in from the north, bringing clean, fresh water in from the snowmelt. The wider, slightly deeper Lusefil River meandered through the city from the west. They conjoined into a wider body within the city walls, slicing through it and carrying on east. This fuller body provided a path for the many water vessels. It was against the eastmost wall that the city's primary shipping port resided. For one could board a ship in Windermere, sail east down the river, and meet the ocean in only a few weeks' time. In the same vein, one could ride the winds up the river and into Windermere, as far as the bridges would allow, and fetch all manner of goods, or allow passengers and pilgrims alike to disembark.

The anatomy of the rolling hills and jagged stone Windermere ordinarily tried to force into submission worked in her favor here. The rivers had long since eroded a deep gash through the stone, allowing bridges to be built high and tall enough for ships to pass under, to reach the ports just beyond, where the elevation of the earth on either side became more agreeable. Here, both natural and man-made bays sheltered ships from the racing current, allowing them to dock safely.

Crossing the Rotherdare and ascending the sloped roads here may very well have felt like entering another world. A city within a city, not unlike the grounds of the Lady. Unlike the glistening silver district where those of the mercantile inclination gathered – with its long boulevards lined with inns for pilgrims and bespoke craftsmen peddling their custom – the roads here were narrow and claustrophobic. By comparison, it was a rather squalid and smelly borough. Houses were built in such a way as to overhang the streets, which left the whole place shaded and sunless. It made for a dark and dirty place. Make no mistake, it was here the murders and robberies occurred, as well as all those other sordid crimes that love the dark. Even the meticulously kept streetlamps seemed to gutter, gasping for breath at the end of their wicks, smothered by the oppressive atmosphere. The fog hung so thick here it was often hard to see the cathedral, looming far up in the distance, judging them all.

Instead of well-appointed shops and charming patisseries, there were cheap hostels and sleazy taverns – all of them overflowing with sailors and other working-class folk, or perhaps even the odd traveler willing to make sacrifices in safety in exchange for budget-friendly accommodation. Work songs bellowed by sailors and dockworkers drowned out the much gentler hymns often heard echoing from the cathedral. Even the Lady's commanding voice – her demands that all listen on the hour, or remember the precious liturgy – was dimmed here by the workman's clock chiming out the hour from a crumbling tower.

Windermere was a holy city, of this there was no doubt. But as much as she surpassed other cities in faith, within her walls lurked too, in the same vast amount, vice.

Ambrose thanked his driver and disembarked, polished boots sloshing in the mix of mud and river water that permeated the borough. He wove deftly through the morning crowd toward a small tavern perched up on an outcropping of rock.

The cobblestone steps leading up to the Cannoneer were perilously slippery. Perhaps intentionally, as it meant the obscenely drunk could not make the journey. Never mind how many departed by that route in such a state. Ambrose knocked in a particular pattern and was let swiftly inside. There was a sharp whisper exchanged between himself and the doorman, and yet more concern bubbled up in Ambrose's chest.

Barmaids were busy wiping down tables and fetching empty tankards. Ambrose marched past them for the doorway at the far side of the bar, rounding the corner and descending the stairs to the lower floor – where the great casks were stored and fewer, more private tables were still a mess from the previous night's patrons. A sprawling space, what to contain the sheer amount of ale and other foodstuffs required to sate the customer's appetites, but to loiter in a mere storeroom was not why Ambrose was here.

A small, reinforced door was tucked in a far corner, behind several casks that one would need to weave around in a rather particular pattern to make progress through them. Ambrose had the path well memorized. He pulled an oddly oval-shaped, engraved medallion from his pocket and slid it into the inconspicuous mechanism beside the door. It triggered a click, and the door opened for him. He rapidly shut it behind himself, taking the medallion from the little tray it fell into on the opposite side of the wall and putting it back in his pocket.

There was nothing behind this door except darkness and a gloomy staircase. His eyes needed no assistance navigating them, but a mere human might sign their death warrant going down these steps unlit as they were. They were original to the Cannoneer – or whatever building had stood here before – which meant they were uneven and deeply worn. Sleepy laughter and chatter could faintly be heard by the time he finally reached the second door at the foot of the spiral steps.

The stone floor was ice-cold this far below ground. So cold it seemed to seep through the soles of Ambrose's boots. This was only alleviated by the many blankets, furs, and rugs spread over the floor, along with a generous helping of various pillows.

Candles flickered and lanterns hung from the stone ceiling, illuminating the colorful, obscene illustrations woven into tapestries that hung from the walls. Most of the prostitutes were already awake, sitting and gossiping amongst themselves atop the cushions, or else lining up to make use of the washroom. His arrival earned a few delighted waves and greetings, which he returned in his usual polite fashion, touching the brim of his hat as he wove through the maze of privacy screens and curtains. Careful not to overturn any potted plants or empty drinking vessels, he ascended a set of stairs on the far side of the room to yet another nondescript door.

Ambrose threw open the door to the office and nearly cost himself an eye in the process. He inhaled sharply and leaned his head aside just in time. A steel dart strong enough to crucify a man embedded itself in the door just beside his cheek.

"My lady, *please* be careful," he whispered.

Esther's chest was heaving as she poked her head out from behind Noel, her bodyguard and current favorite, whom she'd dived behind to cower. Her curly hair and fluffy blouse bounced about her shoulders as she peeked. Noel, meanwhile, had not bothered to even draw her rapier, and was looking rather exasperated, standing resolutely still with her hands behind her back, head up, blonde hair braided back from her face. Ambrose dipped his head to her, and she barely acknowledged him with a nod in return.

"Dame Noel."

"Doctor Debauve."

Esther puffed her cheeks in embarrassment and glared at Ambrose, wrapping her arms around Noel's waist and standing up on her tiptoes so she could put her chin on her shoulder.

"Don't you ever *knock*, Doctor?" Esther said.

Like Ambrose, she had a red tint to her milky-brown skin, but clear and alert peach-pink eyes. Beneath her eyes was all puffy with a combination of worry, tears, and lost sleep. Her curly hair was long and tinted a forest green. Still, she apologized for her paranoia, graciously accepting the dart that Ambrose pulled from the door. She returned it to its place, back beneath her sleeve with its companions. When she realized he was alone, her expectant smile fell.

"Where is my sister? Why is she not with you?"

10

HE ARCHBISHOP'S CHAMBERS WERE A SANCTUARY of peace amidst the chaos of his daily routine. Situated in the northwest, on the far side of the cathedral from the public courtyards and gardens, he was gifted both precious solitude and quiet. Only the crackle of a warm fire in the hearth and the occasional settling of wooden beams above disturbed him here. He made a quick pass through his study, watering the collection of potted plants that had likely only been sporadically taken care of in his absence, and making a quick, visual sweep to ensure nothing was out of place, or missing.

Only just arrived home, he already had a pounding headache and a thorn in his side to deal with. A hot bath to cleanse himself of the blood and dust of traveling would soothe much of this, though, especially when followed by a hot cup of coffee with breakfast. Indeed, as he rewrapped the long, slim ponytail he wore and pulled on a clean pair of trousers, he felt quite refreshed.

He set a shirt aside and stood before the sink. Mara's right hand had shriveled while he was away, it had been rigid and cold when he'd held it, when he'd kissed it. First her legs, now her hands. She was in pain, too. Despite how she'd fought to hide it from him, it was obvious. So, the medicine he'd left to keep her stable had been insufficient. *What was he going to do with her?*

Cyril had only just wiped the first brush of lather over his jaw when a knock sounded on his chamber door. He sighed quietly, but the voice that came from the other side identified the visitor, and he called out in reply to bid him enter. A little click of the latch was all he heard, busying himself with leaning in closer to the washroom mirror and shaving away the stubble that had grown in.

"Good morning again, Father."

"Brother Benjamin." He paused as he scraped away stubble and suds from his jaw. "Good morning."

"When you are finished, please take a seat."

Cyril glanced over his shoulder, leaning back a bit to see Benjamin beyond the privacy screen and open doorway that separated them. Benjamin tossed aside a pillow on the sofa to clear a space. He wore his white linen infirmary sleeves, and carried his leather briefcase, into which he often had tucked a plethora of herbs, salves, and other medicaments or tools.

"Hm? Whatever for?"

"Sister Sybil informed me of your injury," he said as he set his case down and clicked it open.

"Her injury was more severe than my own."

"And hers has been tended to, while yours has not."

Cyril nonchalantly went back to shaving, but turning his back on the bespectacled Cleric did not have the desired effect of shooing him away.

"While full glad I am to see that your cassock performed its task, Father" – Benjamin's reflection hovered in the mirror behind Cyril as he finished and wiped suds from his razor – "protection from laceration is not synonymous with protection from blunt force, or overextension. Kindly sit *down*."

Cyril patted his face dry with a soft towel and sighed yet again, shuffling over to take a seat as Benjamin asked. The healer slid around to stand behind him, tossing the low ponytail the Father wore forward over his shoulder.

It was true that his cassock had defended him from being slashed apart by rotten claws. His skin was littered with subtle red marks where the vampire had latched onto him when they fell. Only faint lines had been left; hilariously, the sort of marks one might think were from a night of lovemaking. Not a single nail nor fang had broken the skin – thanks to those precious, wispy white strands of light keeping Sybil's wound closed. The same threads that could stitch skin back together and numb pain were employed in the construction of all the ordained clergy's garments. Such magic lent an unnatural strength to the fabric, making it incredibly resistant to puncture, and often serving as the only form of armor the Brothers and Sisters wore. Add a particularly potent blessing atop these woven threads, and the fabric would respond. It would rear its head and snap, delivering an awful, skin-melting burn to any vampire foolish enough to touch it.

Hardly invincible and far from impenetrable, but still a force to be reckoned with. Indeed, each black ensemble was a precious defense against the hungry maw and grimy claws of vampires, be the wearer a Cleric or a Hunter. But also true to Benjamin's words, even that blessed garment could only defend against broken skin. It could do very little to protect against strain or blunt force. Broken bones, torn ligaments, and dislocations were common injuries to the Hunters in their precarious line of work.

Benjamin's careful hands felt Cyril's shoulder as he lifted the Archbishop's arm and tested the movement. There was a slight click in the joint, some tension that rippled visibly through the muscle of his shoulder blade, betraying the strain it had endured. A cold compress would do the trick in one or two days' time. Benjamin set about preparing the required ingredients, nimbly weaving a light herbal salve between strips of linen and whispering charms to keep the wound cool as he did. In little time at all, he had fashioned a dressing that would, for the most part, not overly inhibit his patient's movement.

"Minor, but be careful. At your age, it may heal slower."

"Hah, 'at my age'." Cyril stood, looming over Benjamin. The Archbishop had at least a decade over him, and almost as many inches in height.

"At your age," Benjamin repeated matter-of-factly, picking up the pleated linen shirt that Cyril had set aside and holding it up for him. "Most Hunters are *retired*, not being hurled off the side of a moving steam train."

Cyril rolled his good eye, but turned around and allowed Benjamin to assist him, pulling his shirt up his arms. Benjamin circled around in front of him, observing Cyril carefully as he tested his shoulder's mobility to see if the bandages slipped about or loosened. He took a bit of pride in his skills when his work did not come undone, buttoning the cuff of Cyril's sleeve. He still slipped his hands beneath the shirt to make a few final tugs and tweaks to the dressing, for good measure. Cyril swatted his hand away.

"Oh, stop your fussing. I am not some bent-back old man."

Benjamin narrowed his eyes behind his glasses. He debated mentioning the silver sprouting at Cyril's temples and streaking through his long hair, or the soft wrinkles present underneath his eye and about his ever-furrowed brow, but resisted the urge.

"Fighting fit though you may be" – Benjamin pointed with his nose at Cyril's toned torso as he buttoned his shirt for him – "time is indiscriminate. So please, do be careful."

11

Breakfast at Our Beloved Lady was typically a rather solemn affair for the Brothers and Sisters. Clerics sat in carved mahogany chairs at long, ornate tables on one side of the room, while the Hunters sat across from them in an identical fashion. Both sides faced a long rug that ran through the hall's center, where layfolk or novices would walk with dishes and drink to set before the clergy. At the end of both tables was a raised dais, upon which the high table rested. Here, the Archbishop would typically sit, with the Mother Superior on his right side, and the other members of the Chapter, in order of importance after her, and on his left. He was absent this morning. Not that Mother Superior seemed to mind.

Mother Superior, called Gemma, was a striking snowy-colored woman, on account of the lack of pigment in her skin. She had soft pink eyes, a charming curl carved into her lips, and a little button nose – none of which at all matched her sometimes abrasive, intense personality. She could frighten anyone into obedience with a single glare over her brass spectacles. Like Cyril, she was young for her station. Unlike him, she was elected by her peers.

Gemma was hardly one for deep theology or philosophy the way many other clergy were. She instead was far better suited for the more logical duties: the myriad of managerial and financial tasks entrusted to her station. Where Cyril provided spiritual guidance, made the final decisions, and steered this ship of souls, she was the quartermaster that kept it running. Most of it, that is.

She never troubled herself with the gruesome pursuits of the Hunters, unless they cried for more bandages or more fresh horses than the budget allowed.

With Cyril absent, she stood, saying the usual grace quickly and quietly, rather eager to push her spectacles up on her nose and return to reading the ledgers she'd brought with her. With the grace spoken and everyone seated, it was then customary for the appropriate silence to settle over the refectory.

Maddoc did not have time for silence. He had seated himself deliberately next to Sybil, who really wasn't much in the mood for silence either this morning, already giggling and whispering to Sister Florence on her opposite side.

"You should have seen her ugly mug," Sybil whispered, shelling one of her eggs. "At *least* five extra teeth, all up in the roof of her mouth and poking out from underneath her tongue."

"I hope you knocked each of them right out."

"Sybil!" Maddoc interjected, whispering out of the side of his mouth as he pretended to take a drink. "What the hell happened on the train?"

"Did Father not tell you? They hopped aboard, just north of Meli."

At the high table, seated to the immediate left of Cyril's empty chair, Brother Serge was glaring at the trio of Hunters. With the crackling fire of the hearths, and the distance between their tables, he could not hear what was being said. He could only clearly see them side-eyeing one another and speaking behind forkfuls of food like naughty children.

"How many?"

"Three, though only one had her wits about her."

"Blast, one puppeteer and two poor souls, then? Did they give you much trouble?"

"The ringleader of their little act caught me just right and nicked my arm, but I was more in danger from the rust on the blade than the creature herself."

"Just a weakling, then?"

"I'd gather as much. She didn't even attempt magic."

"Oh." Maddoc frowned, mumbling more to himself than the two ladies. "Those puppets must have been fresh. A pity."

"And," Sybil continued after a bite. "She had to drink some blood or concoction to persuade herself to put up a decent fight."

"Hah," Florence chortled from behind a mouthful of salad. "She sounds like those boys in the fighting rings that can't go more than two rounds without the good ol' alchemical *nudge*."

"Were you able to get close enough to burn the witch?" Maddoc pushed for more details.

Sybil shook her head and sighed. "Not once she'd downed that vial. It was as if she suddenly remembered how to wield a sword. If I had been faster, perhaps ..."

"Attempting to get that close while on a moving train, too." Florence sounded simultaneously worried and relieved. "Thank goodness you weren't flung off the side."

"Well, I wasn't –"

"Was Cyril injured?" Maddoc muttered. "He looked in one piece, though he wore the stench of blood, that's for sure."

"I do fear for his arm, it held all his own weight when he fell –"

"He fell?" Both Florence and Maddoc hissed through their teeth in surprise, and Serge loudly cleared his throat across the room.

Sybil punched both of them in their thighs under the table. "Calm down! He recovered; caught himself with his cane. I just worry about carrying the additional weight of the vampire that had grabbed him –"

"He caught himself *and* a vampire?" Maddoc interrupted.

"Yes, now let me finish!"

"Could dislocate his arm, with a blow like that," Florence grumbled.

"Brother Benjamin said he would inspect the injury, there's nothing to worry about."

"And you said this was just north of Meli?" Maddoc asked.

"Aye, near the falls."

"I see."

Maddoc was still worried about Cyril, but already his mind was working. He exchanged a glance with Florence over the top of Sybil's head that told him she was of a similar mind. Someone would need to go back to find the felled witch. After all, real vampires like her always regenerated ... eventually. They wouldn't want her to come crawling back in some few years' time with a bone to pick.

12

THIS SUMMER MORNING BROUGHT A VISITOR to the Lord Governor's castle. Windermere boasted many parks, many patches of verdant green grass and open paths for walking and leisure. The largest and grandest of these, though, were the private grounds of the Dunrior Castle. As it was situated in the far south of the city, one had to walk or ride a good few minutes through meticulously well maintained meadow and forest to even see the lord's home through the trees. Unlike the other castles, she was clearly built for leisure and for pleasure, not for war. She had all the delicate detailing and gilt entrapments of nobility in her architecture.

Lord Vidal Sinclair wore his silver hairs like a crown. They were interspersed through his natural blend of earthy brown and dark pine hair, like snow on branches – mimicking the winter landscape of the domain he claimed lordship over. His slowly graying beard was kept neatly trimmed, close to his face. Lines from both time and stress were etched deep in his brow and around his eyes. But beside those eyes, and beneath his facial hair, one could spy the wrinkles that betrayed the fact he smiled often. Indeed, as Domingo followed the servant who escorted him into the lord's parlor, he was immediately greeted by a wide genteel smile.

"Ah, Captain Castillejo. A good morning to you. I take it you were able to meet with the Archbishop?"

"Yes, sir, I was."

"And how do you find him?"

"Perfectly intolerable, my lord."

Vidal laughed and leaned his head back in merriment. "Old Callaghan said the same. Come, come. Sit down."

Vidal poured two glasses of whiskey, placing one in Domingo's hand and clinking his own against it before sitting down opposite him. Both men wore their military decorations, though Vidal relinquished any color or design that might associate him with the capital. The lord wore the green-and-silver ensemble that denoted both his military rank and his bloodline's ownership. Domingo meanwhile only borrowed the Windermere colors. He wore them over his capital armor, a visual reminder of where his loyalty, ideals, and opinions really rested. In a way, this made him more honest than Vidal. Lord Sinclair was a local to Windermere, born and raised ... but educated in the capital. Educated in governance, military operation, and all things necessary to keep this annexed country under the empire's control. Some great-great-grandmother, somewhere, married into the local family had made this possible. Despite the serious tone of their conversation and of his position, Vidal had his typical jovial demeanor about him.

"You understand now why I feel at a loss with the Father?"

"I have an inkling."

"Decrees, democracy, and debate ... that I can do." He waved his beverage around emphatically, alcohol sloshing about in the glass. "But the church does not speak that sort of language. The Hunters do not. I need to speak to them in terms they understand."

"You need *me* to speak to them in terms they understand."

Vidal held up his glass, grinning. "I knew you were the man for the task, my old friend. We are of a like mind already."

He sat forward. "Their language. Real, tangible" – he tapped the table with his index finger – "pressure. A real presence."

"You can apply pressure well enough yourself."

Vidal ran his opposite hand through his hair. "The northern border requires my full attention. I cannot be everywhere at once."

"I thought your son was overseeing matters?"

Vidal opened his eyes a little wider in exasperation. "He's inexperienced. Brash. Eager to etch his name."

"And rather than assist you both at the northern border ... I am to oversee this sleepy, superstitious city?" Domingo drummed a finger against his own glass. "Impounding carriages parked at the church too long on Sundays? Hanging thieves up over the river? Tell me you're not assigning me to such doldrums."

The Lord Governor waved his hand dismissively. "She is not so sleepy, my friend. And even if she was, I fear this Archbishop seeks to wake her. Besides, your wits would be wasted on the oafs at the border. I can talk them down. I cannot talk down the Archbishop, despite my efforts to do so. I'm afraid he knows even our law too well."

"Why not amend the law?"

Vidal took a sip. And another.

Domingo continued speaking when he realized he'd get no reply. "Perhaps this new Archbishop requires new laws."

"Would that it was that simple." Vidal rubbed his hand through his hair again. "Even if I did write in an amendment, it would make no difference." He sat forward, pointing at Domingo with the hand that held his drink to once again emphasize his point. "This man, he does not care for laws. The way I hear it, that priest has defied even the most solemn oaths of his own order. *Our* laws mean nothing to him."

Domingo's mind was reeling at this information so casually revealed. "The Archbishop broke his own religious order's law? Then how in the world is he still –?"

Vidal held up his hands in defeat. "Hah! If you find the answer, I would love to learn. But let that be a reminder ... of the sort of man he is."

Domingo wasn't convinced the lord had revealed everything he knew, but already he was thinking. Brazen disregard for law like that meant enemies. *He must have enemies*, Domingo thought. *I would know them.* He knew very well how strictly the church adhered to its doctrine ... to its rules and regulations and its ultimate truths. The very idea that it would bend for one man, even for an Archbishop, was absurd. Then again, this particular order was alien to him. Indeed, no other order in the known world claimed to fight the undead plague of vampirism. He almost scoffed aloud at the thought. Vidal finished his drink and set it down on the coffee table. The clink of the glass brought Domingo back to his senses and out of his wonderings.

"I selected you for your talents, my good man. A competent strategist with an understanding of the more delicate social matters ... and with an exceptional ability for espionage, I might add."

"You flatter me," Domingo said dryly. "By mentioning it, am I to surmise that you are lending me your permission to utilize the latter?"

Vidal paused, thinking over the idea. "You ... have my permission to utilize whatever tools you deem necessary to deal with the church. Within *reason*. And with absolute confidentiality –"

"What talk is this concerning the church?"

A silky voice came from the far side of the parlor and both men promptly rose to their feet. Domingo turned to see perhaps the most striking woman he'd ever seen entering the room.

She wore a sleek dark gold gown trimmed with creamy lace and brown fur at the shoulders. Everything about how she carried herself – the high angle of her head, the effortless way she seemed to glide across the floor – it captivated Domingo in a way he immediately disliked. She had dark brown hair parted down the middle of her head and pulled into a neat, low bun – accentuating her strong nose and bare neck in equal measure. Long earrings dangled and swayed as she walked, gems catching the light and sending little sparks of refracted light glittering over her jaw. Her skin was a lovely dark brown color, almost identical to Domingo's; an observation that was not lost on him, nor was the soft sound present in her accent.

"Isabel, my dear –"

Vidal quickly walked over to meet her, offering both of his hands. She took them, smiling softly at her husband, but not without breaking that demure illusion for just a moment to glare at Domingo as Vidal kissed both her hands. The moment her husband looked up at her, though, she softened again. Her hand came up to cup his face, carefully manicured fingertips brushing over his cheek and lips, through the hair of his beard.

After a moment of whispered words, Vidal turned, holding his wife's hand in one of his own and outstretching the other to Domingo, bidding him approach.

"My dearest, may I present Captain Domingo Castillejo."

Domingo stood just barely close enough and gave her a formal bow, which she returned with a gracious nod of her head. She smirked at Domingo, holding out her hand, cooing softly at him.

"A pleasure to make your acquaintance."

Domingo removed his gauntlet and took her hand, pressing a quick kiss to the back of it and summoning all of his patience to murmur out a reply. "The pleasure is mine."

She seemed unimpressed with his greeting, but turned her attention back to her husband, now having looped her arm into the crook of his elbow. Her free hand meandered up from his chest to his jaw and back down again, brushing away wrinkles and straightening brocade. "You will pardon the intrusion. What talk is this that I heard? Nothing that will negatively impact my charity event come October, I hope?"

For a woman equal in age to the two men, Isabel had a subtle way of swaying her hips and batting her eyelashes that would put even the corner nymphs to shame. Somehow, despite the dichotomy between her almost bratty demeanor and the maturity of the soft wrinkles in her visage, the girlish playfulness she exhibited didn't seem out of place. Her soft lips curled into a coy pout as her husband melted under her caresses and her questions.

"Of course not, my dear."

"What a relief." She cupped her husband's face and pressed a kiss to his cheek.

Domingo quietly averted his eyes from the couple's affection, save for one moment when he flicked his gaze back to her to catch the glimmering cross she wore at her breast. It had been half-hidden, tucked beneath layers of lace, but he saw it. He then caught her cold gaze and corrected himself, sighing inwardly. The dawning realization settled over him that this battle of wit and strategy would be half fought with the church and half with the whims of the lady. *It was too early in the morning to be making this many enemies.*

The lord and lady were both busy figures, and both were set to depart to one of many aristocratic engagements that day.

Vidal seized the opportunity to pull Domingo aside and speak to him once more when his wife went upstairs to change.

"But, Captain, if I may ..."

Domingo, too, had matters of his own to attend – but stomached a groan and halted his steps toward the door to listen.

Vidal leaned in and mumbled to him, as if slightly ashamed to admit it. "My task is to keep the peace here. She is a remote city with a fierce population, close to the border. My lady, the Empress, she does not want nor *need* a second revolt from this province, nor another riot for independence. And the best way to negate this is to keep the townsfolk, all of them, happy. She has entrusted this most delicate task to me."

Domingo sighed as he realized he would be receiving very little help from the lord. "I understand, my lord."

"You know that you and I are of one mind concerning the church, but I must stress the caution and tact with which we must approach it. Pressure, yes, as I spoke of, but gentle pressure, for the time being." Vidal then smiled and clapped Domingo on the shoulder. "For a blessing, this Archbishop can't live forever. We need only contain his machinations for the foreseeable future, until another one of their peacekeeping Clerics assumes leadership again. This fire will die out naturally, then."

Domingo forced a smile in return and bowed. As he strode through the marble foyer, toward the footman waiting for him at the door, Lady Isabel came down the stairs. She now donned a form-fitting riding suit and netted hat. He bowed to her, and she gestured for him to accompany her outside, out into the gravel yard where the stable hands had brought each of their horses around.

His initial suspicions were confirmed as Lady Isabel muttered to him under her breath – her voice dropping down into the soft, rolling sound of their shared native language.

"Harm my church at your peril, my good man."

Domingo's scarred lips cracked a crooked smile and he eyed her. The intense look in his eyes did not match the polite, professional tone of his voice when he answered.

"I am but your humble servant, my lady."

13

BRONTË WAS SITTING IN THE SPACE SHE HAD LONG since claimed as her own. It was a small window alcove tucked into the side of the bakery, behind the great kegs and the massive spice rack that stretched from floor to ceiling and required a ladder to reach, even for Hugo. She had fashioned a small cushion from scrap fabric, and brought several blankets – and books – from different corners of the cathedral, from places they would not be missed. Each morning, after the rush to prepare breakfast, Hugo would go attend, and she'd be left to her own devices. Not being a Sister, she could not join Hugo, nor Philip, nor Father in the refectory for a traditionally quiet meal – so, instead, she observed one alone. Usually a small breakfast of bread, sliced cheese, and apples.

She sat with her ankles crossed and hands folded in her lap, gazing blankly out the window at the complicated, carefully sculpted roof of the building below, and the walled stable yard below that. Once again barefoot, her shoes were set side by side on the floor, just beneath her dangling feet.

Today, her appetite seemed to have vanished. Perhaps it was lost somewhere in the roiling of her belly that still stirred when she thought about how embarrassed she was to find Cyril standing over her this morning. She really had to be more careful

...

"Have you eaten today?"

Brontë squeaked and jumped in surprise, whipping her head around to see Cyril standing in the bakery's doorway. She cursed her luck and bit her tongue as he gave her a curious look. He held a small brown paper-wrapped parcel under his arm and a few letters, all tied with twine. Cyril's good eye drifted down to her once more bare feet. She practically felt his eye crawling over her. Self-consciousness flooded her again, and she frantically pulled her skirt down, as if it would ever be long enough to cover her feet entirely.

"No, I just – Did you need something, Father?" She surveyed him, eyeing the blank package and stack of letters he carried. He had bathed, in fact his hair still looked damp. The smell of vampire blood, too, had been cast away. In its place he now wore a familiar, medicinal smell that confirmed her earlier observations of his injury. The journey home must have been fraught, indeed.

"Oh." She realized the parcel and post under his arm must be for Hugo. "Brother Hugo is at breakfast."

"Still? Hm," he murmured, more to himself than to her and checked his watch. Cyril strolled over to the countertop and cabinets built into the masonry of the far wall, setting down the sealed parcel and pushing it back toward the wall for Hugo to open and read later.

"No matter, I will return for him." He paused in the doorway again, and repeated his first question. "Have you eaten?"

Brontë belatedly realized the subtle duality of his question and yet another wave of embarrassment flooded her.

"Oh! Yes." She folded her hands before her and gave a small bow of her head.

"Good." He glanced once more at his watch, brow furrowing as usual. "See me in my study tonight, nine o'clock. Bring your journal and your box."

"Yes, Father."

"And wipe your face, you have soot on your cheek again."

With that he strolled off, leaving Brontë to fall back into her alcove and cover her face to scream inwardly in frustration. *What an awful morning!*

DEEP WITHIN THE FORESTS SURROUNDING WINDERMERE, a fair way to the southwest, a scrappy little vixen was enjoying her good fortune! The forest itself bristled with life. Fog seeped heavy through the trees, clinging to bark and branches as it wafted forth, seeking solace from the sun so eager to burn it away. Insects scuttled about on leaves and blades of grass, mice and moles trundled through the underbrush, and birdsong mingled with the rushing water of the distant falls. A pleasant symphony, to accompany this mangy scavenger's feast!

Precious little meat was to be found on these bones, but what was there was fresh and lean. The linen shirt and corduroy waistcoat the vampire wore had quite conveniently been torn through – ripped from her body along with a generous portion of her entrails, which the fox now gnawed on. Her hair was a dark, earthy green – worn in a trio of loose braids that clung to her expressionless face like ivy. Her blood had soaked into the surrounding soil, killing the grass in a radius around her mangled corpse. The vixen shook the flesh in her mouth, trying to tear a piece out from underneath a blood-crusted patch of linen. The hand that moved to stop her was swift and silent.

A pained cry accompanied a crackle as the little bones in the fox's neck were broken. Tufts of hair flew every which way until Zemirah could sink teeth into skin without too much interference, tearing through until blood splattered over her lips. Pathetic sustenance, but it would do. Anything would do. She spat a curse out against the nun that had run her through, and sucked in a loud, pained breath. With no one else around to hear or judge her, she cried out in frustration.

She pinched her fingers into the fox, pulling a line of blood from it like a taut thread. She mumbled a hoarse spell and drew a glyph on her side, just above the grotesque wound. The thread followed the smeared line of her fingers, and she gritted her teeth as it stitched a mark into her skin in the same pattern. The blood in the soil around her began to flow in reverse, bubbling up to the surface and retracing its path back to her body.

She rolled over, then, feeling about blindly for the half-eaten flesh that had been pulled from her. She unceremoniously shoved it back inside of her, through her torn skin that had already begun to repair itself. With a grimace, Zemirah bit her sleeve and tore a long strip of linen from it, weakly binding it about her midsection to keep herself in relatively one piece.

Her rapier had suffered in the duel, bearing scars from Sybil's lance. It had landed not far from Zemirah, pierced into the earth. The beauty of the birdsong, the colorful canopy of summer above her head, the very miracle of being alive – all of it was lost on Zemirah as she snatched her sword from the earth and crawled her way into the deeper cover of the forest. Into the gentle, protective shade and out of that scalding sun. *Curse her luck and loss!* Her legs trembled as she tried to limp to her feet. Blood would only do so much to soothe her wounds, to keep her awake. She needed real healing; she needed her doctor.

14

The final toll of the nine o'clock hour had ceased some few minutes ago by the time a quiet knock came tap-tapping on Cyril's chamber door. Brontë stood in the corridor outside, and lamented that he arrived at the doors to let her in so quickly, as she hadn't yet recovered from her mad dash up the stairs, and was still puffing for breath at the effort. She clutched a small, simple book to her chest, along with a delicate, but plain, wooden box.

Brontë followed him through his chambers, past the marble knights carved into niches in the wall. She refused to make eye contact with them. She always felt like they glared at her, or as if their carved heads somehow swiveled to watch her every move. Luckily, those sculptures only inhabited the entryway of his chambers, and she was free from their judgmental gaze as soon as she stepped foot into the cozy study.

The study always smelled divine: a comforting blend of beeswax candles and smoldering frankincense. Thick rugs and brilliantly embroidered tapestries kept the warmth of the blazing hearth contained and the creeping cold evening air out. Tall, diamond-paned glass windows looked out over the city, barely visible through the thick fog and unnatural, clinging sludge of night in Windermere. His desk sat beneath one such window, and opposite it stretched a small personal library. It was composed of a few meticulously organized shelves, each holding copies of volumes in the archives below, for ease of access and reference.

Cyril had shed his oily-black cassock, instead donning a pleated, billowy-sleeved linen shirt with his clerical collar. Good thing, too – that pesky cassock always had the worst bite. If Brontë's bare hands strayed too close, the blessed fabric stung her like a nettle. Cyril took the book and box from Brontë, setting them down on his desk as she meandered off behind him. She checked on each of the many plants that inhabited the study. She had, after all, been their unofficial caretaker while he was away, and now she curiously inspected each one, observing where Cyril had watered or pruned them upon his return.

Cyril turned around to see her inspecting the plant with heart-shaped leaves that hung from a small woven pot, dangling from braided twine.

"Come here."

Brontë turned as Cyril pulled a hassock from under his desk with one foot. She did as he bid, kneeling to sit comfortably on the hassock, while he sunk into his chair.

"How are they?" she asked. "I didn't damage any of them, did I?"

Cyril was thumbing through the book she had brought him – a journal, containing her own notes and faithful documentation of when she took her prescribed medicament. Never mind the many scratched out mistakes that called into question the accuracy of her records. He flipped back a few pages before replying.

"Hm? No, no – not at all. Thank you."

Brontë straightened up quite contentedly and looked rather proud of herself, feeling just a tiny bit redeemed after her generous helping of embarrassment this morning. At least she'd done *something* right by Father, not that he seemed particularly appreciative.

He opened the box she'd brought. Thin pieces of wood divided the little chest into equal sections, and each square held exactly one tiny glass vial with a small stopper. His hand gestured over the, mostly empty, vials contained inside as he counted them.

"And you last ate three days ago?"

"Yes."

Cyril pulled out the only two vials that still held medicine – a minuscule amount of a gold, almost honey-like, liquid. He held the vial up to a candle between his fingers, twirling it over as he looked for impurities, any break in the seal, or some other detail that Brontë would not be able to notice. She watched him in silence until he shifted toward her in his chair.

"Up. Let me see."

Cyril held up one finger, and she dutifully lifted her head, keeping still while her eyes followed the movements his finger made in front of her. He inspected her chocolate-brown eyes, alert and curious, closely for any flicker, any hint of discoloration. They did not catch the light from the candle in any unnatural way, and he nodded, seemingly satisfied.

"No red in your eyes, not yet."

She breathed a deep sigh of relief, blinking rapidly to alleviate the sting from keeping her eyes open. She swallowed a noise as his fingertips slipped under her jaw. He tilted her chin up and carefully felt under her jaw and around her throat for any swelling or changes in temperature, feeling for her vein in her neck and pressing into it to count. *He's usually gentler than this*, she thought. She must have upset him more than she realized. He could feel how her throat tightened in embarrassment beneath his fingertips, though he didn't address it. She winced as his hands pressed too tight around her neck to be comfortable. A few more moments, and he released the pressure, content. One hand held her chin up.

"Let me see your teeth."

Brontë frowned, but did as he asked, opening her mouth just enough to let him see. To the casual observer, there was nothing interesting about her teeth – other than they were maybe a little crooked. Cyril knew better. Both her top and bottom canines, though of perfectly average human length, grew to a bit more of a point than normal. One would have to run their finger over her teeth, or perhaps be bitten by them, to truly discern their sharpness. His gloved thumb made a brief pass between her teeth. He bid her close her mouth and nodded.

"They do not appear to be growing. Good."

Yet more relief flooded her, and her heartbeat began to finally slow to the unnaturally lazy pace it preferred.

He turned back to her book and rubbed his forehead in thought. "It will take me some time to prepare more. Is this enough for the next few days?"

Brontë nodded quickly, and Cyril shut her journal, sliding it toward her, along with the two remaining vials of medicine.

"Very well. Off you go, then. I will return it to your room when it's ready."

Brontë took her journal and stood, and he did the same, tucking the hassock back under his desk. Brontë had already turned to leave before once again remembering her manners and kneeling before Cyril. A quick kiss on the back of his hand, and she shuffled off.

"Good night, Father."

With Brontë gone, Cyril breathed a deep, exhausted sigh and put his hands on his desk, leaning over it. Everything ached. After a few moments, he rummaged idly through the drawers for a little metal case, clicking it open with a thumb and retrieving a cigarette. As he collected himself and tapped his cigarette on the back of his hand, he spoke aloud.

"You can come down, now. Unless you intend to lounge up there all evening."

A little shuffle from the loft tucked up into the rafters of his study answered him. The soft pad of downy shoes and tinkling of metal beads were the only noises the red-robed clergy member made as they descended the staircase in the far corner, tucked into the wall behind a bookshelf. Dressed in red from head to toe, and with their face covered by a sleepy-eyed mask, they had to put a hand atop their wide-brimmed hat to keep it from getting bumped off on the way down, ducking beneath one of the many hanging plants.

"Thank you for indulging me with the privilege of eavesdropping. I'm glad to see my confidence was not misplaced," they said, upon reaching the floor.

There was no answer from Cyril.

"You handle her well," they continued. Genuine admiration colored their voice, though Cyril did not seem flattered.

"No thanks to you." Cyril snapped his lighter shut and flung it onto his desk, exhaling smoke as he turned around to look at the Cardinal. He crossed his arms and his ankles both, leaning back against his desk as he glared icicles at that gold mask. That sleepy, lazy, all-too-peaceful look that all the Cardinals wore. Gold mask, red coif and veil, even their hands were gloved in red. Nothing was visible of them beneath their trappings, and the silhouette of their robe did nothing betray whether they were man or woman. They meandered closer, straight fingertips together, as if in prayer – the way they always were, unless otherwise occupied. They tilted their head curiously, the strand of gold beads that hung from their hat clinking together melodically.

"Your treatment of the girl appears remarkably successful. Are you not pleased?"

"I should be treating the sinsick," he snarled around his cigarette. "Not wasting my time doctoring that thing."

"She is a child of the church – your church – in need of care, is she not?"

"You were always good at creating excuses to justify your decisions."

"Do not be bitter," said the voice behind the mask. "She is as much the consequence of my decision as she is yours."

Cyril groaned quietly and rolled his good eye, turning back around and busying himself with reorganizing the various notes and parchments scattered over his desk. After some silence, the Cardinal ventured to speak again – this time, sympathy tinged their words.

"I know she is a unique challenge for you –"

"She is a burden."

"But you show remarkable restraint with her, especially considering your ... nature toward v –"

"That will be all, Cardinal," Cyril interrupted, not bothering to turn around. "You may go."

They gave a slow bow, hands still pressed together, before strolling lazily out of the study. Red robes slithered across the floor behind them in near silence as they obeyed, leaving the Archbishop to his coveted solitude once more.

15

Of Ginger Cap was any sort of upright establishment, it would ban boxers in the ring from consuming vampire blood. But it was not such an establishment, and so one of the two young men brawling for coin and bragging rights both wore it heavy on his breath this evening. Patrons too queasy or too uptight to tolerate a bit of bloody fun had no reason to be at an underground fighter's ring anyway. The stench of alcohol, smoke, and sweat filled the Ginger Cap cellar as the crowd hollered from tables and cheered for their chosen fighter. Liquor sloshed about in bottles and tankards, and the tellers behind the betting counter were busy counting coin after coin.

While many patrons bet purely on Erwin as a fighter, still others used him – and his winning streak in the arena – in drunken debates over blood consumption. Erwin was a fine example of the exception to the rule. Everyone knew he drank vampire blood; the boy wasn't shy about it. Even if he had been possessed of enough sense to keep his mouth shut, his consumption was obvious the moment he stepped in the ring. Oh, he had skill enough to spare, as much skill as any scrappy, bare-knuckle fighter could have in an unregulated ring. His form was mostly correct, his stance solid; but that wasn't what revealed the blood. It was those swift reactions and deft footsteps that did the talking.

Every nerve of Erwin's body was alight with excitement. His senses were sharpened to near overstimulation. The crowd didn't trouble him. Their jeering shouts and drunken bellows he had long since learned to drown out. He instead heard every pant from his opponent, could hear every shuffle of his boots in the sand as they circled one another. There, just like that, his stance shifted again. Toying with blood magic in such a way meant Erwin could anticipate his opponent's maneuvers, and move to counter them. A little companion in the back of his head, a twitch on the back of his neck he'd learned to read. Be it ducking down or bringing up his arms to protect his face – he moved with a swiftness only granted by blood, and everyone knew it.

Erwin was living proof! Proof that those clergy folk were too uptight, too old-fashioned, too disconnected. Perched up high on their hill, behind their walls, sending down only judgment. The blood they decreed heretical, that they condemned as destructive and damning, did not undo this firecracker of a young man at all. He retained his presence of mind – no hallucinations or rambling – none of those terrifying symptoms the clergy preached would await those who drank.

Then again, these sleazy drinkers cared little for religion, cared little for guilt or sin. Sailors, whores, laborers – the east end of Windermere was suffused with such ilk. Unlike the placid middle-class folk or the well-to-do merchants, the spitfire lowborn cared little for the church's rules. These days, heresy could only get you in trouble if you were among the church's faithful – if you partook of their bread and wine. But who needed bread and wine to soothe one's soul when ale was cheap?

Like the patrons, Erwin wasn't religious in the slightest, and had no vested interest in pretending otherwise. A bastard child like him was to be ostracized either way in a place like Windermere, so wholly obsessed with pure bloodlines and unbroken marriages. He might as well indulge in pleasures without guilt. Already, his mind was distracted, taking more of an interest in which whore he could buy for the night with his winnings than in the still-standing opponent opposite him. A jab to Erwin's ribs was barely felt. A dangerous cocktail of blood and adrenaline had rendered him numb to much of the pain. Erwin knew his limits, and loved to dance right around them.

Finlay, meanwhile, was not paying anywhere near as much attention to his friend and employer in the ring as he should have been. He had a boyish look about him, not quite grown into his jawline yet. Sandy blond hair was neater than Erwin's, kept short and out of his face. Ordinarily, he'd be making note of the bruises already forming, of those injuries he would be responsible for treating and procuring medicament for. Instead, Finlay was overindulging the company of a flirty, intoxicated girl. A working-class young woman, not too dissimilar from himself; he'd had enough coin to buy her attention with an offered drink. More than a touch tipsy himself, he was now preoccupied with trying his own luck.

An older man, though – one with a little more money than he knew what to do with, and in desperate need of a sellsword or two – was very, very keenly aware of Erwin in the ring. Thomas Greer watched as the fighters traded blows. The ginger boy held his own, he thought, and held blood well enough to speak to a solid constitution. He'd need a sellsword that could keep his head on when around blood. He thanked his luck and meandered over to the betting counter, keen to learn more about the blood-drinking boy in the arena.

16

COLDWATER KEEP WAS THE ONLY STRUCTURE in Windermere that could compete, both in age and in grandeur, with Our Beloved Lady. She was a war-minded little sister or distant cousin to the cathedral. Domingo stood on the balcony of his new office, surveying the grounds below and the city sprawling out beyond. Where Our Beloved Lady was a city unto herself, Coldwater Keep was a village. No indulgent orchards or meditative gardens lay here; she instead was decorated with all the accoutrements of war, including the unwelcome cannons that now lined the thick walls, set near the more traditional ballistae.

Damn that church for infecting the very stone he stood on. Was there really nowhere in this entire city he could be rid of her influence? His eyes roved over the rooftops. Across the black river waters, over the rolling hills up toward that craggy plateau upon which the cathedral resided. From this perch atop Coldwater, he could see the way that color flowed down from the church. The lamps mimicked her, spreading a poor imitation of her gold through the streets. The roads stained with that color stretched out like veins through the city, bleeding into every crevice, every gutter, and even snaking across the river into his garrison. *She had to have her hand in everything.*

Domingo meandered back inside, out of the cold, and into the chaos of the office he had inherited. His antiquarian predecessor had hoarded every insignificant scrap of parchment he could get his hands on, and it now fell to Domingo's sergeant:

the same plum-haired young man who had accompanied him during his introductory visit to the Archbishop, to sort through it all.

Levi had thick, curly hair that fell to just about his jawline. A gentle, inquisitive – but equally intense and judgmental – face held a pair of matching mahogany eyes. He wasn't quite as dark as Domingo, but his skin had plenty of evidence of his birthplace being one of more temperate weather. He was smaller in stature, too. Remarkably so, for a knight. He barely scraped past the minimum height requirement, and wasn't particularly broad-shouldered or muscular to make up for it.

In their few weeks here, Levi had already made decent progress chipping away at the mess and slowly making sense of the inherited chaos on his superior's behalf.

"Well then," Domingo said as he closed the doors to the balcony. "What do you have for me?"

Levi stood at attention and saluted before reporting his findings of the day.

"I'm afraid I have found little of value to present on the existence of so-called 'vampires'. Nothing scientific, no research, only religious texts and other documents of similar bias."

"I am hardly surprised." Domingo huffed, the closest he'd probably ever come to laughing outright. He stroked the gold tags he wore, the symbol of his station and means of conducting magic both, habitually feeling for the engravings upon them. He shook his head as he stared off into space, pondering the matter.

"Superstitious nonsense. Vampires … ridiculous. Just another word for heretic. And what have you gathered about the Archbishop?"

"Very little. There are no real records regarding the Archbishop beyond what the church publicly offers, which is near nothing."

"Even the Herald's Office could not help you?"

Levi selected a tome he had ready and thumbed it open, flipping a few pages and removing a bookmark. He slid the book across the worktable, turning it about to face his superior. Domingo stared down at the record before him.

It was a genuine coat of arms, in fact it matched some of the stamps and plaques he'd seen on newer buildings or businesses built with the approval of, or sponsored by, the Archbishop in question. A typical shield of nobility, dressed with alternating colors of black and gold, stamped with heraldic symbols and a calligraphic letter *S*. It was hefted by two stags, a local custom that did not escape his notice, and was capped with a liturgical crown.

"The Herald did present me with this record," Levi said, "but it's practically brand new. Apparently, the Archbishop immigrated here when very young, though exactly *when* is unknown."

"Well, I suppose that much was obvious." Domingo gestured at his own face and hair, to insinuate he spoke of Cyril's instead of his own. "He sticks out like a sore thumb. He's clearly not born here."

The opposite page of the stamped and signed heraldic seal for the family only listed two individuals. Cyril Stacy and his mother: the presumably widowed Mara Stacy. No father was included, no grandparents, no bloodline at all. It was almost offensive to see such a grand record attributed to only two people. To a layperson, without the ability to research records, or any real understanding of what they were supposed to represent – that being the long, unbroken family lineage which tied people to a place or plot – it lent great legitimacy to an otherwise undeserving man.

"The record only includes him, and his mother," Levi continued. "It lists them as landowners, members of the gentry – though there is no actual plot or estate listed to their name. And there is no tie to, nor mention of, where they came from. They just suddenly exist on the record."

Domingo frowned and thumbed back a page, asking aloud even though he found the information right after saying it, "How long ago?"

"The record is approximately eight years old."

"It appears that the church was in a hurry to validate him when they made him Archbishop."

"Exactly my theory."

"So ... he's some unknown immigrant, a nobody, without connection or land ... that the church decided to set upon a pedestal. How intriguing. The locals are well known for despising anyone not tied to their land. He must have done well to ingratiate himself into their society."

"He is well received by a large swath of the population. But he is not without his doubters."

"Oh?" Domingo set his knuckles on the table and leaned forward, now quite interested.

"Sergeant Allermane has reportedly overheard many conversations regarding the Archbishop. The Archbishop being a Hunter, and not a Cleric, is apparently an odd anomaly."

"The Archbishop is usually one of their Clerics, then?"

"Always has been," Levi corrected. "Until this man, or so we have gathered."

"Why elect a Hunter then?"

"There is some speculation that it has to do with the practice of consuming vampire blood as a drug."

Levi had to swallow a chuckle at the idea to retain his composure. He had just as little belief in the whole supernatural affair as his captain, and it showed. Domingo scoffed at the idea, but ran one hand down his face in a way that betrayed the stress beneath it.

"And I suspect there is no evidence of this *unholy* concoction, either?"

"Not that I have yet laid hands on. And though they are known to confiscate it often, the church refused to provide a sample to me."

"Of course. It's just more religious nonsense for them to condemn. Will they start slaughtering those who partake of blood next?"

"Many of the townsfolk support the idea, yes. Enthusiastically. The church does condemn the practice as heretical, but their current prescribed punishment is only to flog and excommunicate. Neither is a death sentence."

"I suspect our new Archbishop will be keen to update that prescription." He retrieved a cigar from a box on a nearby table. "And the Hunters will do whatever he wills without question, I'm sure. What did you learn of them, their Order? They seem to operate like a private military."

"I believe their proficiency is due to the Deacon's handling of them, more than anything. He is apparently a notoriously harsh taskmaster. He may as well crack a whip, for the way he commands them."

"He did seem a rather rough character."

"What he lacks in formality or manners, he makes up for in volume and intensity."

"And his foul mouth."

"Yes ... yes, that too. Very much so."

"He seems more the type to be a mercenary or a sailor than a priest."

"I don't think he's a full-fledged priest. It seems he's some sort of quasi-clergy, perhaps a sellsword contracted to train the Hunters."

"The church loves its documentation. If he's somehow contracted to the church, there will be record of it. It would be useful to know just how these Hunters function."

Levi nodded. "I will look into the matter."

17

ENEATH ONE OF THE GREAT, GOLD-CAPPED DOMES of Our Lady was the Chapter House. Cyril stood on the mirrorlike marble floor, looking up at the Timekeeper ticking away the eons. A great astronomical clock with spindly, gilt hands pointing to the hour, the liturgy, to the constellations mapped on the inside of the dome.

"Hello, beautiful. It's been some time."

The Chapter House was empty this early in the morning, the many chairs and lecterns vacant of both body and book. As Cyril meandered about the center of the room, he trailed his fingertips along the edge of the shallow dish that stood in the middle of it. A relatively simple basin, comprised of blessed gold and hoisted upon the uplifted arms of three marble angels. It was the Order's most treasured relic. Rather, it was when it was not empty.

Now, it sat vacant – no flame burned from the dish. The embers within it were long dormant. Not even a flicker or a measly puff of smoke. See, this was perhaps the most unique facet of this order: the Sacred Heart – the very flame that burned away sin, purged poison, cauterized even the most serious of wounds – was not confined to the Chapter House.

Instead, it burned hot within the breast of the Archbishop. Not merely a token or a symbol, not merely the static, distant source of their magic. It was among them. It lived and breathed. It saw their struggles, heard their prayers, interceded on their behalf. It led them, through the man or woman of its choosing.

Here, unlike in other cathedrals, and even unlike in the Chapter itself, the Archbishop was not a role elected by their peers. The Heart had the only and final say. And, once it had nestled within the vessel best suited ... only death would part the two. Only then would that flame burn alone, appearing once again in the brazier, to deliberate within itself upon a new host. Thus had the Heart passed from person to person, from Cleric to Cleric, for centuries.

Until now. Until a Hunter – a bloodied, bitter, sadistic soul – became the object of its affection. And thus, was he raised far beyond his own station, up from Brother to Father. The Sacred Heart's say was final.

And so, even now, eight years later, scholars and theologians across the countryside still debated the meaning of this decision. Even as they traveled to pay deference to the Archbishop, even as they sought the Heart's blessing through him, even as they knelt to kiss the bloodied hands of a Hunter, they wondered and prophesied and deliberated. *Why him? Why now?* But theirs was a church of mysteries, and some answers never came.

Cyril, however, did not question the decision at all. Home again, back in the arms of his Lady, he was settling back into his comfortable routine. He went to pray in the orangery, he lit a candle at the niche for fallen Hunters, he pinned his cross – the mark of their god's constellation – in place over his chest.

The eastern chapel, the largest in the complex, was quiet and serene as Cyril contributed his piece to this long and storied tradition. He dropped to one knee at the foot of the dais before ascending the steps, approaching the altar and pulling a wrap of sooty-black linen from his sash. He unrolled it atop the altar and began the process of penning a document the Order simply referred to as the Second Table. He whispered a series of prayers in the church's old language, and with a few gestures and taps of his gloved fingers in the corners, the document inked the full prayers of mass and the liturgy of each hour in tiny gold print as he bid it, as if soaking up those sacred words from the altar beneath it. With this done, he sealed and signed the document in the same fashion.

The Second Table gave any Brothers or Sisters of appropriate rank permission to perform the mass in his stead. It gave them his blessing, and even lent them a small fraction of his own power while doing so. He stood quiet, resting his hand on the snowy-white linen draped over the altar. His other hand released his cane, letting it lean against his leg as he felt for his cross, pinned to the fourth button of his cassock.

Cyril did not doubt the Heart's decision. Now, the Clerics had to ask *his* permission to give the liturgy. He nearly smiled at the idea, his pride only tempered by the deep humility of his station and the very real reverence he felt for it.

Before, Cyril had been but the Brother entrusted to lead the Hunters. He had always been held back. Contained. *Lectured* by his peace-loving predecessor. Where was that old man, now? Rolling in his grave, perhaps, to see the very Hunter he tried to contain, to temper, become Father. *Those Clerics*, he thought, *so timid, so judgmental, but with no bite behind their bared teeth.* So content to hide behind the walls of Our Lady. To be coddled and comforted while the people of the city were picked through like market produce. While children were found half-devoured in alleys and lost loved ones were dug up from their graves to feed the undead's appetite. Content to look down from on high and pass their judgment, while the young and naive, the ill and the infirm, were bewitched and poisoned by blood.

Now, the Hunters had laid claim to the streets. No rooftop, no bridge, no crumbling cobblestone path was safe for a vampire. They would be driven out, burned out, never to terrorize the populace again, and they would take their sickness with them. Not even some war hero from the south would stop him. Every last abomination would be put down.

All except one, perhaps. The soft pad of nervous footsteps approaching – the subtle, but familiar and pleasant, smell of a certain line of blood – told Cyril who the encroaching visitor was without even needing to turn around: Brontë. That last vestige of his predecessor. His peace-loving, ever-forgiving nature made manifest in that annoying little prickle on the back of his neck whenever she was nearby. Even from beyond the grave his predecessor mocked him.

"Good morning, Father."

Cyril's hand curled a touch too hard into the linen on the altar. *Curse that girl for having such a pleasant voice.* It seemed to make all the tension in his body dissipate, but he told himself that was a deliberate act on his part, and not a consequence of her gentleness. He sighed quietly and turned around to look at her. Brontë stood just beside the closest pew, one hand resting atop it and the other fumbling about with the hem of her habit. Her damp hair had soaked through her cap and veil in a few places, and her eyes were still rather sleepy. It was early for her to be up, after all.

"Was there something you needed?" he said habitually, perhaps in a tone a bit too practiced, which made her brow furrow in worry.

"I'm sorry to disturb you."

He stepped halfway down the stone stairs, looming over her perhaps quite deliberately. "What do you need?"

"I ... was hoping ..." Her voice was barely a whisper.

Cyril cut her off. "Speak *up*, girl. Use your voice."

She corrected her tone at once. "I was hoping you might have time to hear my confession, Father."

Cyril already had his stole draped about his shoulders, and perhaps out of habit, or out of eagerness to hear her complaints and send her away, he gestured to the floor before him. As penance for troubling him so early, she would have to be content with the hard marble floor on her knees. It was only fair. He descended the other half of the steps as she sunk down, standing on her knees, even as the cold, hard floor felt like it was piercing right through her stockings.

"And how long has it been?"

"Three months, Father."

"You have not confessed since I left? You know I won't always be here to listen to you."

"I know."

Naturally no deep truth about what she was came out in confession. *That* secret remained deeply buried, spoken in shameful whispers behind closed doors. But, despite how he abhorred it, Cyril could not deny he understood her inclination to speak only to him. To the only priest who knew what she was. Rather, the only priest who knew and tolerated her in spite of it.

She knew it was only tolerance. Thinly veiled contempt, at most times, she was sure of it. She wasn't oblivious, hardly a fool. She saw the subtle shift in his jaw, the glow in his good eye, the way he always seemed to flex or find some other way to occupy his hands when near her – as if preventing himself from strangling the little life she had out of her. Or foul imitation of life, at least. It had always been that way. An ebb and flow between his hatred for her and forced pacifism; his abiding by that decree from his predecessor and an earnest attempt to see wisdom in it.

Cyril had begrudgingly accepted her existence as a child, even if he curled his lip when she passed by. It still embarrassed her to think about all the times she, oblivious and naive, had pestered him as a child. Taking him poorly made flower crowns during her school recesses and grabbing his little finger to walk with him to mass. Undoubtedly a consequence of the Archbishop's constant meddling and insistence, a younger Cyril had endured her antics with exceptional patience. It wouldn't do, after all, for a young man of the Order to be anything other than an absolute gentleman to a well-meaning child.

Brontë remembered fondly summers of being carried piggyback through the cloisters, of climbing up into his lap to peek at the big tomes full of words she couldn't understand when he was studying. He'd brushed and braided her unruly hair for her on Sundays, and even kissed her scraped knee when he found her alone and sniffling in the orchard after taking a fall. Such childhood innocence and affectionate privileges were long gone, now. They were both adults, and the cane that so often used to be pointed at him, to coerce him into gentility, was now wielded in his own hand. And she was hardly a child anymore. A proper young lady, well read and with a sharp wit to boot. She could endure his unvarnished opinions and blunt words, now. Indeed, had to. At least, she attempted to weather them with grace.

"Why are you crying?"

"I –" Brontë snapped back to attention. Her knees hurt. She put a hand up to her eye and realized with embarrassment both of them had welled up with tears.

"You seek me out only to wallow in silent self-pity? Will you waste my time this way, or will you speak up?"

Brontë rubbed her arms and tried to correct herself but – perhaps due to a combination of being a bit too tired, her mind a bit too scattered, and all of her a bit too overwhelmed by his hovering over her – no words came. She looked up at him apologetically, blinking back tears. Being this close to him, or probably more so his cassock and rosary, made her hair stand on end. Never mind the strange artifact left on her eyelids when she blinked. A consequence of the light, surely. It made a sort of ring appear to hover behind Cyril's head. She didn't like it.

He sighed and put a hand on her head, making her bow it and *stop staring up at him like that*. Pretty brown eyes full of tears and terror. He cleared his throat quietly and pushed the image from his mind.

"Perhaps you would benefit from speaking to another," he said. "I believe Sister Cecilia is awake, and could hear you. Or Brother Benjamin. Seek one of them out."

"I would ... rather not," she muttered.

"I know. That is one more reason why you should."

She huffed in dejection, before realizing that probably sounded incredibly rude. But before she could open her mouth to apologize, she heard footsteps behind her. She recognized them and frowned. Cyril withdrew his hand and bid her stand, turning his attention to Maddoc as he approached, thumbing a handful of documents. As Deacon, he wore his sash over his shoulder, rather than high across the waist the way other clergy did. His hair, too, was still damp from bathing, lying neatly above his scowling face as he glared at that particular novice.

That little brat was always assuming she had the right to be anywhere near the Archbishop. She'd follow him about like a lost puppy if he let her! And he usually did. Maddoc pointedly ignored her as he stopped before the altar, not even addressing her with so little as a nod of his head.

"Good morning, Father."

Cyril could tell Maddoc was being overly formal, by his standards. He tended to be around those of lesser rank, in an effort to reinforce Cyril's importance. Brontë pulled herself shakily to her feet, leaning heavily on the pew and away from Maddoc. She wasn't fond of him at all and gave an embarrassed warble as she found her footing and shuffled off. As soon as she was out of earshot, Maddoc's formality fell off. His voice dropped into his usual, rolling brogue and he addressed Cyril with an ease more befitting their friendship.

"Is it really proper to allow that brat to just come up to you whenever and wherever she pleases?"

Cyril set both of his hands atop his cane and shrugged.

"You spoil that girl, you know that?"

"And others say I spoil you." Cyril smiled. "But I don't see it that way."

18

NEWS TRAVELED FAST IN WINDERMERE. So too did fanciful gossip. Already, the markets and squares were bubbling with talk of the Archbishop's return. Not only had he returned, but the manner in which he had arrived defied all imagination! Cafés and coffeehouses alike were crowded to the brink with all manner of gossipers, eagerly leaning in to hear the account of a lucky handful who had been both aboard the train and awake at the time, or who were otherwise passing along the version of the story they had heard. A young woman spoke of hearing footsteps above her head. A young boy proudly bragged that he had touched one of the cracked windows of the passenger car. An elderly gentleman recounted a black shape fluttering past. Still another child said they saw a red-robed clergyman walk past their compartment. Many toasts and prayers were offered in gratitude to the Hunters for their steadfast protection.

The papers, too, had taken the story and run wild with it. They printed off all manner of fanciful retellings this cool summer morning.

In the midst of the excitement, a breathless, teary-eyed woman wailed in the street, attempting to make her voice heard above the celebratory laughter and elation of the throngs of people. In fog as thick as the crowd, it was hard to make sense of features or dress – but the familiar silhouette of a particularly pointed hat in the distance filled her with hope.

"Good Hunter, good Hunter!" she cried out. "I am in need of your aid!"

YET ONE MORE PART OF THE SPRAWLING COMPLEX called Our Beloved Lady, the Hunter's quarters boasted a spacious, segregated cloister, a gravel yard that often saw drills and duels both, as well as its own barracks, stables, smithy, and armory – all staffed by loyal layfolk, like the rest of the cathedral, to act as servants and keep things tidy. The faded tapestries and antique suits of armor lining the warming room spoke to a very different image of Hunters in seasons past, but those old things were just decoration now.

As Deacon, Maddoc was also the current head of the Hunters. A captain of sorts, in his own right. A position normally held by a *real* Brother of the Order, but one he suited well. What he lacked in decorum or charm he made up for in efficiency and command. It was he who set the patrols, he who guarded the map, he who ensured the Hunters were fit for fighting and developed the training regiments that kept them so. Every Hunter – even Cyril, sometimes – bemoaned the intensity of Maddoc's mandatory conditioning, but it served its purpose well, and that was all Maddoc was concerned with.

Maddoc was also the first to hear of any requests that came to the Hunters. And so it was that he stood quiet and listened to the two young clergy before his desk. The two had been out in the square, on their usual patrol, and now relayed the call for help they had received from a grieving young woman. Florence, too, happened to be present to hear the grim news. A man had perished in his bed with vampire blood still on his lips, and the family begged the church to accept him. As Maddoc dismissed the two Hunters to their respective tasks, he turned to Florence.

"Sister, are you preoccupied?"

"Not particularly, why?"

"Come with me, then. You and I should escort Brother Benjamin today."

"Eh? Jael and Philip are plenty capable of chasing off any corpse poachers."

"It's not poachers I'm worried about, I'll explain as we walk. Come on."

The grounds were all abuzz with their usual activity. The Hunter's courtyard was a wide, open space – with a walled cloister surrounding it. Florence and Maddoc crossed the distance in a hurry, Florence still not sure why she'd been requested to accompany him.

"Well? Don't leave me in suspense. What am I looking out for if not poachers?"

"It's the Guard. The new captain is hell bent on causing us trouble, I can feel it. I don't want him pushing around a soft-hearted healer."

"Has something happened? I knew he was pressuring us already, but –"

"Our local captain" – Maddoc groaned as he opened the door leading into the Hunter's dormitory and held it for Florence to walk through – "met the Archbishop yesterday morning."

Florence snorted a laugh, but it quickly quieted as she grew worried.

"Oh no ... did it go that poorly? Figures. He's been scratching at our doors to speak to Father ever since he arrived."

"Shows up and never takes no for an answer, that one. It went as well as you'd expect."

"Two men who won't back down, that bodes well."

"I only hope this fellow is much like the previous captain. You know the sort, just keen to earn his retirement."

"Aren't they all? Well, a bit of hope, then. We should only have to tolerate him for a few years at most."

19

SERGE WAS ENJOYING THE QUIET THAT HAD SETTLED over the small foyer. The space served as his office and one of the primary entries into the infirmary both. His office was the path taken by any hopeful visitor or new arrival – be they borne in on a stretcher or surrendering themselves to care. It was he who had say over who was admitted and who was discharged, he who chose if visits were acceptable, at what time, and for how long, and he who was always one of the first to hear news of injury, illness, or death.

Surrounded by tall cabinets that dangled scrolls and parchments like overgrown moss, his desk faced the center of the octagonally shaped room. The wooden doors behind him had square panes of spotless glass installed nearly top to bottom, which not only let one see out into the meticulously kept garden behind him, but let in warming sunlight. Serge made use of the morning light, poking through the fog now spilling over his shoulder as he carefully carved a small cross from a soft piece of wood, no bigger than his palm. The sunlight and the warm color of the wood matched his own sunshine complexion, though the tips of his pointy ears were pink from the cool morning. His features lacked most if not all of that sunshine. At his age, he wore a fair share of wrinkles – most of which accentuated his permanent frown. Said wrinkles in his face crinkled as he grew preemptively annoyed by the sound of quick footsteps approaching his office in the hallway beyond.

Jael rushed through the doors and he sighed as the quiet peace of the room was ruined, not to mention his rug soiled by her dirty boots. Clearly, she'd not even bothered to wipe them, much less rinse them of their dust and grime, as was the proper thing to do before entering the church. She huffed and puffed with the effort of running all the way across the grounds to reach the infirmary, chest rising and falling dramatically beneath her cloak.

"What now?" He adjusted the monocle he wore to magnify what his hands were doing, looking up over the lens in annoyance.

Jael slowed down enough to bow respectfully. "Brother Serge. A family has surrendered their deceased."

"Another sinsick?"

"Yes, Brother."

"Hmph. That's Brother Benjamin's business, not mine. Go find him."

"He sent me, Brother." She wheezed and swallowed as her lungs fought with her words to get the most air. "For the contract."

Serge reluctantly set down the carving he'd been working on and rose from his chair, stretching his fingers lazily before, in a similarly lazy fashion, fishing a small key from his gold sash to unlock a drawer in the cabinet. Though she was grateful for a chance to catch her breath, Jael paced back and forth impatiently as Serge licked his finger and slowly leafed through the documents stored there.

After what seemed an eternity, Serge procured the document. He set it down on his desk, placing another parchment atop it. With a mumbled charm and a gesture of his hand, he duplicated the document. He then held out the copy to

Jael, but snatched the paper away when she tried to take it, giving her a stern look.

"There's no hurry. The fool's already dead. The corpse won't be offended if you stop in the warming room to clean your boots. But *I* am very much alive, and will take offense. Do I make myself clear?"

"Yes, Brother. I apologize. It won't happen again."

He let her take the document and she practically fled the room, leaving a streak of dirt over the marble floor at the threshold.

⬦

PHILIP WIPED HIS BROW AND TOOK A FEW STEPS BACK to inspect his work, ensuring the two massive horses were properly harnessed to the simple hearse. It was a modest, utilitarian thing. A small cab compartment resided just behind the driver, and the concealed space for securing a coffin behind that. Philip tried and failed to stop from giggling when Brontë rounded the corner with a linen-covered basket on her hip.

"What?"

"You've got soot all over your face."

"Ah, drat ... again?"

Philip watched as Brontë, in an attempt to clean her face, smeared more soot over her opposite cheek. He laughed aloud and dunked a kerchief into a nearby bucket of cool water and offered it to her. She sighed, but thanked him and simply wiped her whole face. He took one of the apples from the basket she'd brought as payment, halving it and holding each half out in open palms to the two horses.

"Where's Jael?" Brontë asked as she wiped her hands of soot, finding the small lump that had lodged itself between her hand and her sleeve. "I brought breakfast for both of you."

"She went to fetch the contract from my uncle –"

As he spoke, Jael trotted around the far side of the barn. She smiled in relief when she saw Brontë, setting the document down inside the cab of the hearse before eagerly approaching and being served a rushed breakfast. Brontë provided each of them with a thick cut of yellow cheese dotted with walnuts, and a piping hot pasty stuffed with roasted vegetables and baked to a buttery, golden brown. She had also brought two sealed mugs of dandelion tea to wash down the whole affair. And two apples, originally – but now they had to suffice by splitting the remaining one. The hungry Hunters thanked her profusely and gobbled up their meal, Philip trying and failing magnificently not to burn his tongue in his eagerness.

It was a good thing they hurried, too, as the carpenter soon arrived, pulling a small handcart with an empty, simple wooden coffin. Brother Benjamin walked alongside her. The physical labor of loading and securing the coffin within the hearse was a task reserved for the two Hunters. Philip went about his task with the last slice of his apple hanging out of his mouth.

Brontë curled her lip at the grim task and hurried about returning the empty mugs to her basket. Even just the sight of the coffin – though it was yet empty, and Jael and Philip hoisted it so casually – made her wish to look away. She caught a glimpse of that ghastly mask the undertakers often wore when collecting these particular dead, tucked under Benjamin's arm, and decided she had seen enough. She said nothing, excusing herself and clutching her basket to her chest. She had only managed a few paces down the corridor before she rounded a corner and thumped against a warm body. She hopped in surprise, spitting out an apology before biting her tongue at her bad luck.

Maddoc glared at her and surveyed her basket. "Well, isn't this nice? Some among us get to lounge about and picnic, while the rest do our work?"

"Excuse me, Deacon."

"Aye, off with you. Go make use of yourself."

Florence had only caught the end of Maddoc's annoyed words as she caught up to him in the cloister, but knew very well the tone he typically took with Brontë. *Poor girl*, she thought, *it wasn't her fault she was sinsick.* She watched her walk away with her head down, oblivious to Florence's reassuring wave.

Florence fell in step with Maddoc around the corner, chastising him. "Would it kill you to be nice to the girl?"

"I have no patience for brats who forget their rank."

"Says the man who isn't even a monk."

"Aye, but I outrank her. And you. Come on."

20

The shade and comparative squalor of northeast Windermere smothered the clergy. Benjamin had only just tied tight the strings that held a small pouch of herbs in place when a knock on the cab door sounded. Florence's voice came from outside.

"I'm afraid this is as close as we can get you, Brother. The hearse won't fit down this road."

Benjamin removed his spectacles, letting them hang from the chain around his neck, and situated his mask over his face. He took a few deep breaths to settle it against his jaw and buckled the straps behind his head. The beak he now wore was stuffed with filters and the soft scent of herbs. When he spoke, it was muffled, but still plenty intelligible.

"Will the coffin fit?"

"Yes, Brother. The Deacon and I can bear it through without issue."

He opened the carriage door, and Sister Florence stepped aside, offering the Brother her hand. He took it as he disembarked, placing his round hat atop his head before turning to fetch his briefcase.

"Wait here while I tend to the man. I do not want them to see the coffin yet. Brother Maddoc, walk with me, please. I will send you back for the coffin when we need it."

The two nodded their acknowledgment, as did Jael, sitting up in the driver's seat of the hearse. Maddoc dismounted his horse, leaving Jael and Florence to guard the hearse, while the two Brothers slipped down the narrow road that departed from the only slightly wider avenue.

The house was not difficult to find, despite being tucked back through the older winding cobblestone streets. Streets so narrow they were half-obscured behind lines of washing draped between houses and gnarled old trees that had long since overgrown their granite planters and uprooted the flagstones.

A small crowd had amassed outside a door draped in black fabric, which bore an overturned, multi-tiered cross. Some good-hearted neighbors held small gifts of funeral biscuits or flowers. A few were rowdy, opportunistic street urchins with eyes and fingers set on unguarded coin purses. Others were simply morbidly curious passersby. At the sight of the masked Cleric and his bodyguard rounding the corner, the crowd murmured and shrunk away, half dispersing to give the men a clear path.

Maddoc had to make an effort not to curl his lip at the stench of vampire blood that reeked from the house. It soiled the very air, thick and heavy and sickly-sweet.

Benjamin was shown inside, while Maddoc turned his back to the door and put his hands on his hips to stand guard. One soul stood a touch too close and earned a hard stomp and a snarl from the mountain of a man.

"Away with you. Let 'em grieve in peace."

Inside, Benjamin was ushered into a rear room by a teary-eyed, breathless young woman who introduced herself as Georgiana. The bedroom was a cramped, crowded place. A terrifyingly thin man likely no older than sixty lay shriveled in his bed. His mouth hung wide and his eyes remained open, empty and unfocused, staring up at the ceiling. His family surrounded him, surviving siblings and children. His wife was at his side, a bowl and a damp rag the only tools she had to ease his suffering – besides her hand which he still clasped with his own malformed fingers, even in death. An old wooden rosary lay draped around his neck and down over his chest, covered in the still-wet blood and spittle he had hacked up.

His wife was dumbfounded, nonresponsive, staring at the strained face of her husband as if waiting for him to come to. Only when Georgiana softly shook her shoulder did she return to reality. As she turned, her eyes saw Benjamin standing in the bedroom doorway. The poor woman squeaked in fear at first. The undertaker's black robes and masked face made him look the very specter of death looming in the door, come to take her husband away.

"You brought the church here?" she hissed at Georgiana, half-angry, half-terrified.

"I am Brother Benjamin."

"You ... you can't take him away!" She stumbled to her feet from behind the bed, her free hand laid over her late husband protectively.

"Mother, please." Georgiana said. "You must let them."

"Not yet!"

"You shall have more time with him after, I promise." The Cleric's gentle voice served him well, rendering him a touch less intimidating.

Her daughter's reassuring hand on her shoulder seemed to soothe her further as Benjamin set his briefcase down on a table and fetched a few items. Tucked between his medical kit and the folded-up, blank contract, was a small vial of oil and a tin containing a small portion of blessed bread and wine.

As apprehensive as his wife had been of the church, the man had clearly been a believer. One gnarled hand, swollen at the joints and red with inflammation, clasped his well-loved wooden rosary. Benjamin set a small brass dish on his chest, and atop it a portion of the wine and bread. With another gesture, a dollop of consecrated oil on his forehead, and a whispered incantation, the man's rigid body relaxed. Benjamin worked with a practiced swiftness then to correct his posture, to render his deathbed something less terrifying. The Cleric closed his mouth and eyes, arranging the pillow behind his head and even fixing his messy hair. Another whisper and the body went rigid again, resuming the natural progression of death.

A quiet breath of relief seemed to release from the family all at once, no longer forced to see their loved one in such a pained state; instead, he lay as if he slept peacefully. Benjamin retreated then, as they crowded closer to their father. He pulled the contract and another tin from his briefcase, beckoning the deceased man's daughter to the dining room table in the front room. Georgiana had been the one to call for the church's aid and, with her mother in such a state, was the only one with enough presence of mind to tend to their father in his death.

The contract was a simple one. No superfluous terms or flowery legal language. Straightforward and clear, it detailed two things: one, that the church recognized the mortal sin of consuming vampire blood, that their involvement was not a pardon, and two, that the deceased would be embalmed in exchange for their surrender to the Order's undertakers. The service was a small blessing for those faithful whose loved ones damned their own souls by consuming vampire blood. If the deceased's soul could not be redeemed, at least their body could be spared. Only the church's embalming could prevent a vampire from raising that flesh to undeath.

The contract was stamped with the Archbishop's own seal and signature. It was his doing, after all. It was penned in the same, peculiar manner as the Second Table, and was just as binding – just as unbreakable. The lines at the bottom of the page were left free for both the grieving family and the undertaker acting on the Archbishops' behalf.

With some embarrassment, Georgiana asked him to read it to her. She patiently stood while he read her the document. When he had finished, he produced a small travel quill and ink from his tin. With some guidance from the benevolent brother, she signed it.

"You will take him away now, then?" she whispered, watching him fold up the signed contract and tuck it into his sash.

"We will, only for a few days. He will be embalmed and returned to you."

She nodded, rubbing her arms before reaching into her pocket. "Here, this is the last thing he drank."

She held out a small, mostly empty bottle, save for a dried drop of blood at the bottom. It was a peculiar thing – with an odd, gemlike shape and etching at the top and base – but such details hardly mattered at a time like this. Benjamin pulled his kerchief from his sleeve, opening it for her to set the vial in the palm of his hand. He then wrapped it up and tucked it into his sash as well.

"Is there anything else you can tell me now?"

She shook her head. "I am sorry, Brother. I didn't see what happened. I only heard my mother ... wailing."

When the door opened some portion of an hour later, a quick nod of Benjamin's head sent Maddoc back toward the hearse. He and Sister Florence returned, bearing the simple, lightweight coffin between them.

At the family's request, they lifted their own deceased off his bed. His wife cradled his head all the way from his pillow until he was at last set down inside the coffin. She leaned down and pressed a kiss to his forehead, then the lid was slid on and secured in place.

"I understand this interruption to your mourning is unpleasant," Benjamin said as he shut his briefcase. "Please be assured that we will take the utmost care with him, and he will be returned to you posthaste."

The coffin was then carefully removed from the home, feet first through the door, and carried between the two burly Hunters with surprising ease. As they departed, Benjamin turned the cross upon the door right-side up, indicating that the clergy had answered the call and done their task.

Benjamin heard the gentle commotion before he saw the cause of it. The townsfolk typically respected the perimeter around the hearse, so he was quite disgruntled to find a small crowd had amassed nearby. The hearse, however, was not the object of interest. Instead, what drew the attention was the Captain of the Guard and his horse, both adorned in the glittering trappings of their stations. The glistening armor at his shoulders and beneath his uniform matched the barding his warhorse wore. Benjamin sighed quietly and bid the Hunters load the deceased into the hearse, as he excused himself to speak to the captain.

Domingo had, thankfully, positioned himself a small distance from the hearse. All it took was a polite request from the Brother to disperse the curious crowd, barring a few particularly curious schoolboys more enamored with the stallion and his trappings than the rider sat astride him. He was an impressive thing, after all. A neck thick with muscle and slender, featherless legs. A soft, pink muzzle and blue eyes were only just visible beneath his metal champron and bridle. Benjamin cleared his throat and it was enough. The boys bowed to him and scuttled off, still glancing back over their shoulders a few times for good measure.

"Captain Castillejo, I presume?"

Domingo nodded, and Benjamin bowed his head. "I am Brother Benjamin. Is there something I can do for you, sir?"

Domingo could very clearly make out Benjamin's words, but that awful mask annoyed him. Surely, the polite thing to do would be to remove it when speaking to another. His eyes slid from beneath the shade of his beret to the hearse, where the coffin was being loaded up with the remains of a supposed addict. Retrieved, free of charge, by the church. To be taken back for … what? What grotesque science did they perform on those deceased? Such questions would have to wait, he supposed, if only because he would have no honesty here in the street. Witnessing their retrieval himself had answered several already anyway. Except for the one regarding that damn mask.

"Is the mask necessary?" Domingo asked.

"Yes," Benjamin replied in a bored, rehearsed tone. Clearly this was a question he received often.

"You undertakers wear them often, then?"

"When collecting the remains of the sinsick, yes."

"Right." Domingo didn't bother hiding the roll of his eyes.

"Vampire blood is remarkably addictive, sir. Even the scent of it may cloud the senses. Now, to you, or the average citizen, there is little danger at a small amount of exposure, such as a deceased addict. I, however, work with vampire blood and addicts regularly, and therefore take extra methods to protect myself from prolonged exposure." Benjamin paused as he heard the doors to the hearse behind him close, telling him they were ready to be on their way. "Does this answer satisfy you, Captain?"

Apparently, it didn't, because Domingo readjusted himself in his saddle and asked yet another question, flicking his head toward the hearse and the trio of clergy attending it. "Then why don't I see your Hunters wearing those masks?"

"The masks inhibit movement and visibility; therefore, it would be impractical for a Hunter. Instead, they employ certain blessings to protect themselves from exposure."

"Brother?" Benjamin turned around to see Maddoc already astride his own horse, and looking very pointedly at Domingo, whom he made no attempt to hide his contempt for. Benjamin knew he'd best cut this interaction short, lest the Deacon's patience run out and he let loose a string of colorful phrases unbefitting his rank.

"Then why don't you lot employ the same?" Domingo ignored Maddoc completely, eyes still fixed on Benjamin.

"So many questions ..." Benjamin turned over his shoulder and glared at Domingo through the round lenses of his mask, though Domingo heard rather than saw it. "We Clerics are quite different from Hunters, sir. We have our purpose, they have theirs; and we are each granted finite power to those ends. A Hunter cannot carry our shields, nor close wounds. A Cleric cannot call a weapon, nor summon a flame." Benjamin tilted his head, something that, with that mask and his hat together, ended up looking rather unsettling. "I wonder, Captain, if you grasp the enormity of the world you have entered. Good morning."

21

HE COUNTRYSIDE SURROUNDING WINDERMERE was dense with trees. Only once one was relatively close to the city did the valley open up and the trees begin to thin, making way for the lush farmland to her south and west, where the rivers roamed and hills rolled. It made for an impressive view, when approaching on foot. Be it day or night, the city stood proud atop the taller of the many hills. Her buildings and monuments rose up from behind her walls – spires and clock towers and apartments all stacked one atop the other on the hillside. The cathedral, of course, was the greatest presence. Sometimes the fog clung to the craggy plateau she sat on and made her look as if she was a second, smaller city floating upon a cloud.

Tumbling out of the forest, the dusty road began to straighten out. No longer forced to follow the whim of the trees, it widened and adhered to the lines cut by the waist-high drystone walls. It moved from point to point, meeting those tall weathered columns with much smaller, much simpler carvings of saints adorning them. These sculptures marked the pilgrim's path. The route was quite often taken on foot – either for spiritual reasons or by necessity – by many penitents. Worn down to hard dirt by seasons upon seasons of travelers – of horses and carriages and pedestrians all alike – it wasn't a hard path to walk, only tedious.

It was rendered far more bearable by the many homesteads that loitered near the paths. Private properties, yes, but home to many faithful. Or, if not faithful, at least friendly folk. A good sort, more than happy to let weary travelers rest their legs and fill their bellies. The valley was a place of abundance, after all. Crops took root and grew well here, and the forest bristled with life. All manner of game could be tracked and trapped, and a skilled huntsman was always in high demand.

One such young lady was very, very much awaiting a certain huntsman, right this moment! The sky was growing dark, a dusty blue-black canopy settling over the trees and rendering the stars just barely visible. Blair was no more than six years old. Her brown hair was tied up off her head in a length of blue ribbon her father had traded a rabbit pelt for. She practically bounced up and down, hands on the windowsill as she waited for him to arrive. Her hazel eyes scanned from one end of the path to the other – at least, what she could see of it, what with how the hills sloped and the stone walls curved.

"I see Papa!" Blair splayed her sticky hands out on the glass. "Oh, but where's Miss Attie?"

Her mother, Lucia, leaned back, looking out the window without lifting her ladle from the pot she was stirring. She could just barely see the silhouette of her husband coming down the path, wrapped up in his wool cloak. Attie – the hound her daughter inquired after – indeed wasn't trotting along beside him. She probably had been distracted by a rodent in the brush, or else had bounded up the path before him, rendering herself temporarily out of sight. That'd likely change when she came leaping in through the door, eager to claim her place on the rug before the fireplace, as she always did.

"Oh, I'm sure she'll be along." Lucia said. "Go upstairs and wash, then."

"Yes, Mama."

When the door opened, Lucia wiped her hands on her apron and turned around, smiling. Her mouth was half open to welcome her husband home when she froze. Her husband's cloak was draped over a slender, mean-looking woman with an awful smile on her face. Lucia was quick. She turned and grabbed the poker resting in the fire. She swung it straight for the intruder. The steel whistled before it clanged against Zemirah's rapier.

She snarled her annoyance, fangs glistening from the glow of the hearth. "Is this how you greet all your pilgrims?"

Lucia was no match for a skilled swordswoman. But with the end of that poker nearly red-hot, she didn't need to be. She hissed through her teeth as she swung again, swiping glowing orange lines through the air.

"Where is my husband, you monster? Get out of this house!"

It was all Zemirah could do to deflect the red-hot metal. It sparked and made an awful, hissing noise when it touched her rapier. Each collision had a strangely soft return that made Zemirah flinch. But a neat flourish at the right moment was all it took. Lucia yelled as Zemirah took control of her arm with a twist. It sent the poker flying. It struck a pelt on the far wall and clattered to the floor.

Blair screamed from behind the railing on the stairs. Zemirah whipped around to look at her. She temporarily lost interest in Lucia, darting toward Blair with her fangs bared. Lucia leaped at her from behind, before her teeth could clamp down around the petrified child. She wrapped her arm around the vampire's head, and Zemirah bit down on her forearm instead. Blood splattered over Blair and her mother cried out.

"Blair! Run, baby, run!"

Zemirah straightened up like an angry bear. She reached behind her, flailing. Her hand found purchase in Lucia's blouse. She tore through it as she flung the woman off her back and yelled in frustration. Lucia cracked hard into the oak dining table. Blair scrambled out the still-open door as fast as her little legs could take her. Her mother dove to follow her – to pick her up and run. Zemirah's hand grabbing her hair stopped her. Lucia's head snapped back far too quickly. Swaddled in her husband's cloak, she went limp. Both women slumped down to the floor, blood rushing from Lucia's neck as Zemirah's fangs sunk deep.

In the dense forest south of the homestead, Hezekiah's body was still warm. Stripped of his cloak, his now sightless eyes gazed up at the stars through the trees. His deerhound, unable to have defended him, limped to his side. Attie nudged his bloody cheek with her wet nose, whining when he didn't respond. A despondent howl echoed through the woods as she wept for her lost master.

22

SERGE SAT AT HIS DESK; HIS CHAIR TURNED SIDEWAYS as he sipped at a cup of coffee. He was preoccupied with looking out the glass-paned doors to the garden, making note of which beds needed tending later that morning, when it was a touch warmer. He groaned when he heard the door to the infirmary open, and turned back from the far more pleasant view of the garden to see Benjamin. He still wore his mask. Serge spoke as Benjamin set his briefcase down on a chair and began unbuckling his mask.

"You have finished your autopsy, then? And have you removed that sinner and his stench from my morgue?"

"Brother Benjamin!" Maddoc's voice echoed from down the hall. "Father's waiting!"

"I am very sorry, Brother Serge." Benjamin shook his hair out to let it settle into place naturally. "Could I request your assistance in preparing the man?"

Serge scoffed at the ask. "Absolutely not. I do not embalm addicts. Your faith can bend, if you like." He gave Benjamin a disapproving look from head to toe. "Mine will not."

Maddoc opened the door to Serge's office, about to shout for Benjamin again, only to look surprised and a bit offended that he was standing right before him but had not answered his calls. Maddoc dipped his head and saluted Serge with two fingers from his brow, the most formal greeting anyone who wasn't Cyril could really hope to receive from him, not that Serge appreciated it.

Benjamin tucked his mask under his arm and picked up his briefcase. "He needs only to be made presentable, Brother. I have done everything else. Please, do me this favor." Then Benjamin rushed off; the little glass vials of blood he'd taken from the deceased jingled in his briefcase as he strode swiftly in the direction of Cyril's office.

Maddoc watched the door close behind him, looking back to Serge – who had made no move to do as he'd been asked. "Well? You intend to just sit there, old timer?"

Serge sipped his coffee again. "I am not touching that filth. Complain to Father if you wish."

Maddoc clenched his fists and his lip curled in frustration. "Father expects each of us to contribute."

"And I do contribute. In my own ways." Serge put his cup back upon its saucer, spinning it around in a circle with a twirl of his finger against the handle. "Off you go, then. Go tattle if you wish. Father knows my convictions already. He respects them. You ought to learn to do the same."

Maddoc sighed in exasperation and turned on his heel to follow Benjamin. He easily caught up with him in the corridor, dwarfing the smaller gentleman as he walked alongside him. The two ascended the stairs leading toward Cyril's office.

"Anything odd with the man?" Maddoc asked.

"I am sure Father will share his findings with you."

"As am I, but I'm asking you right now."

Benjamin gripped his briefcase tighter in his hand. Luckily, he did not need to reply, as Cyril was waiting at the top of the stairwell. He looked up from his pocket watch, carrying a selection of tomes under one arm. Benjamin and Maddoc both bowed.

"Ah, here you are. Good. Brother Maddoc, could you dispatch a pair of Hunters to Doubury Lane this evening, please.

I would keep an eye on the man's family, lest they be harassed or targeted."

Maddoc simply nodded and turned to descend the stairs, leaving Benjamin and Cyril alone. They carried on to his office. Once inside, Cyril barred and sealed the door.

"Does Maddoc know your suspicions yet?" Cyril asked.

"No, Father," Benjamin replied from behind him. "I did not disclose them."

"Good. I would not invite a panic."

Rather than moving to his desk, or even to the soft chairs before the hearth, Cyril strode purposefully over to a pair of brass-gated doors opposite the fireplace. He unlocked the gate, and pulled the doors open. The private lift shaft and carriage were cold, and a bit blanketed with dust, on account of Cyril being the only operator. The two men slipped inside, closed the doors, and Cyril thumbed the lever that would deliver them down into the deeper floors of the cathedral. To the restricted libraries and, more importantly, to the space he'd claimed for his more delicate work.

A great underground octagonal rotunda that dipped bewilderingly deep into the frigid earth. The walls were drenched top to bottom in shelves that housed books of every kind. Each floor had a walkway, guarded by railing and supported by arched columns that reached up from the floor below. Spaced evenly between the shelves were wooden doors. Some of them were open, allowing a view into the warmly lit study rooms that had, perhaps at one point, welcomed many a student, lulled many a procrastinating theologian into a nap over some open textbook.

One such door, on the floor where the two men had arrived, was locked. Cyril opened it with a different key from his key ring, and a spell – whispered too quietly for even Benjamin beside him to hear – for good measure. This small study was rather cramped, but it was practical and serviceable. The air was thick and musty, and smelled heavily of frankincense.

A worktable fashioned of solid oak rested just off-center in the little room. Strewn all about were texts of every inclination. Some unfinished, being penned by none other than Cyril himself, adding his own research to the library, for future Mothers and Fathers to call upon, should they need it.

Cyril set the tomes he'd been carrying down, and gestured for Benjamin's briefcase, which was surrendered to him. Cyril set it down upon the worktable and clicked it open, pulling out the cuts of flesh and bottles of blood Benjamin had extracted from the corpse and arranging them in some particular order. Benjamin waited patiently as he began this work, his eyes roving about the room in wonder. That is, they would have roved, if they had not settled quite pointedly on a series of brilliant gold bottles resting in a small box on the table.

Benjamin always got an uneasy feeling at seeing the strange, golden potion occupying Cyril's desk. It radiated power. Far too much power for so little an amount of liquid. Not even vampire blood hummed with such energy. He could hardly pull his eyes away. He knew not what it was, nor what Cyril did with it – but that was not his business. Perhaps they were just more experiments. He had so many, after all. Many accrued, unsuccessful attempts to undo the plague of addiction that riddled the population. An issue quite dear to him, perhaps on account of his coming from the soggy, unkempt port streets of the east. It was there, after all, where much of the sinsickness was. Souls who would rather risk damnation for a temporary taste of power, chasing an addictive high – or even those unfortunate folk who turned to it to numb pain, having not the faith nor willingness to accept the Cleric's healing.

You wouldn't know it by looking at him. He seemed as well bred as any other gentleman, with mild manners and a formal demeanor that often put others to shame. But Benjamin knew better. He had seen the shift before, from Father back into Hunter, where his spitfire survival instincts served him well. It was likely this tumultuous childhood that made him such a formidable Hunter. He hadn't been born into comfort and trained in the safety of a guarded garrison. He'd been thrown to the wolves of the street, where only the strong or the wily survived. And survive he had … to be saddled with mountains of paperwork and expectations, locked in a dusty old library. The irony made Benjamin's mouth curve into a small smile.

"Something amuses you, Brother?"

Benjamin came out of his thoughts and corrected his expression. "No. Excuse me, Father. I was lost in thought."

Cyril looked at Benjamin as he clicked his briefcase shut. He held up the empty, oddly shaped bottle surrendered by the family. It had a distinct, irregular shape to it. The most common medicaments and tinctures were stored in flat-bottomed, cylindrical vials. These were easy to produce and easy to store. Not so this peculiar little specimen. It had a weirdly diamond-shaped silhouette. Pointed at the bottom, so it could not stand on its own, with little glass flourishes near the top. It even had a floral pattern in the throat, pressed or rolled into the glass during its creation. It was not the sort of craftsmanship that went into a cheap, regular dose of vampire blood.

"You confirmed that the deceased was indeed sinsick?"

"Yes, Father. His body had telltale signs of long-term consumption."

"Not just another victim that's been fed diluted blood?"

"No, certainly not." Benjamin almost smiled. "I think pig's blood would have done him less harm."

Cyril turned the strange vial over in his hand. "And he overindulged?"

"According to his daughter's description and the state of his body, that is what I surmise, yes."

"Doubury Lane ..." Cyril shook his head. "Was he wealthy?"

"Hardly. They're a poor family of cobblers."

"And they only gave you this? No more bottles?"

"Only that. And it was reportedly the only thing he ingested that day."

"I see."

Cyril rummaged about his worktable for a small bottle of holy water. He uncorked it and gave it a shake, wetting the tip of his finger with a single drop. He then let the drop fall from his fingertip into the odd vessel. The glass screeched out in defiance. Rather, the remaining contents did. The minuscule amount of dried blood lurking in the bottom of the vial bubbled violently at the touch of holy water, singing out in pain before fizzling out.

"Foul thing," Cyril snarled at it. "And you really suspect it to be pureblood?"

"It is my only hypothesis, Father. Even if he'd somehow hidden it from his family, a man of limited means could not have procured enough common blood to overindulge with such a small final amount. That single vial has to be what killed him. I know of nothing else more potent."

Cyril set the bottle down and sunk into his chair. He glared at the glass and brushed his finger over his lip in thought.

"They'd never sell pureblood to a lowly cobbler," he said. "They'd never sell it at all. This was some mistake; he should never have gotten his hands on it."

23

"GET OUT!"

A BATTERED MAN, WITH HIS CLOTHES FRESHLY torn and a few teeth already loose, was flung unceremoniously out the door of a modest inn in northwest Windermere. He skinned his hands as he slid across the stone. Despite his drunkenness, he caught himself with a concerning ease. Inside, the patrons hollered curses at him, prepared with knives or bottles in hand. A bloodier scene was only prevented by the brawny doorman standing in the way as he yelled.

"Filthy sinsick soul, keep your stench away from this place!"

Inside, the proprietor and his employees scrambled about. They pulled down lanterns and flung aside melted candles. They picked up ashtrays and washed them in a hurry. Anything suitable was filled instead with precious incense from the owner's stash. As the sorry addict carried himself off into the evening, nursing a swollen cheek and an inevitable black eye, the incense was strung up in lanterns to hang beside the door and set upon windowsills – a prayer to ward off vampires, and their half-prepared puppets. Away the addict went, squinting in the light of the boulevard, at the flames that made long lines streak through his vision. He grumbled and held his hand up to shield his eyes. *Damn the lamplighters and their efficiency.*

Any Windermere soul worth their salt knew to stay to the lamplighter's path. The diligent folk of that guild fought back against the dark just as much as the Hunters of Our Lady did, in their own, pacifist way. They kept the wide avenues and the winding streets both alight at night, as much as they were able. One lamplighter going about her route yawned as she raised her brass-tipped staff and lit the final lamp on the street. Garbed in the red scarf and cloak of her guild, she instinctively moved out of the road when she heard horseshoes on the cobblestone behind her.

The boulevards, with their candelabras of glass lanterns, were relatively safe – even in Windermere's pitch-black brand of night. The odd traveler on horseback through such well-lit routes was not uncommon. Imagine her surprise, though, to see a clergyman on horseback meandering by. A clergyman ... alone? The Hunters always worked in pairs. He tipped a familiar pointed hat, and she hastily bowed her respect in return. He went on without a word, black horse and cassock melting away as he departed the main boulevard eastward, toward the ports.

Any vampire with a lick of sense remaining knew to keep to the dark, to keep away from those annoying imitations. Oh, they were only imitations, true; mundane flames locked inside glass cages. Half-holy at most. They could do no true harm, trapped as they were. But an imitation was still a strain. A strain on those glassy eyes that so loved the dark, that yearned for it. Dead eyes that belonged in the comfort of a coffin, not up above wandering the streets.

Mundane as they were, those lanterns could reveal a monster, too. If the uncareful abomination dared lift their head too far – their milky eyes would reflect the light in a way more akin to an animal. A telling sign to the observant viewer, which the Hunters always were. That glint had been the downfall of many a foolish stiff. One of the many lifeless husks that had, in their undead confusion, wandered too near the light and life, then found themselves revealed for what they were in that pale light. Such was the fate of a spent puppet, of nobody's favorite.

The lamps grew fewer the further east one went. What flames did burn were gasping, coughing things that barely lent any light. No lamplighter was keen to venture into that shady, slimy borough; where the pickpockets roamed and the drunkards stumbled, where the street gangs tussled and sailors sang. It wasn't as if the lamps offered much benefit here anyway. Ever shrouded with fog churning up from the river, the black nights hung heavy here.

It was heavy enough to obscure the Hunter as he meandered through on his horse. Both black silhouettes, save where warm breath puffed to join the fog. The rush of water dampened the song of steel shoes on the street. The horse stopped at a tug on the reins, and another noise instead became clearer.

Scratching. Something scuttling about in the alleyway. One would be forgiven for thinking it a street dog. Some gnawing, gnashing thing scavenging for scraps, nudging over discarded crates or piles of rubbish. But street dogs did not speak. A certain whisper and the sound of fabric tearing. Desperate chewing as a vampire debated nonsense with itself.

Cyril dismounted his horse. As he wandered deeper into the alley, he had to duck under lines of damp laundry and twist his body to fit between rotting timbers. He kept himself low when he could, creeping forward with careful footsteps that avoided pebbles or puddles of filth. Now deep in the veins of unlit backstreets, he rolled up his sleeve. First, a small admonition, puffed under his breath. Then, ignoring the cold that made his skin prickle, he drew his knife and cut a line over his arm. Quick, shallow – it bled profusely and made him twitch his lip in discomfort. He waited.

A scratch, a choke, a string of confused syllables tumbling out from behind too many teeth and a rotten tongue. Cyril saw the flicker of confused, terrified eyes from behind an overgrown bush. Terrified, hungry, desperate. Just another masterless drifter and a starved moth to flame, unable to resist the pull of blood.

"There you are."

He dragged his thumb over his arm and murmured enough magic to close the wound. The vampire had enough sense to panic, and fled. Cyril darted after it. These backstreets were claustrophobic and narrow, but he knew them well enough. This vampire was an easy mark, weak and scrawny with nothing but a half-eaten burial shroud and rotten pair of trousers. Still, it was swift and skinny enough to fumble through gaps that forced his pursuer to take different paths.

Cyril kicked himself off a disused wagon and bounded up and over the building beside. As he slid down the opposite side of the roof, he caught sight of his mark again. He broke his fall with a roll and brandished his weapon. Not his cane, but a length of chain called up from his rosary. The chain snapped out like a serpent, coiling about the vampire's leg and tripping it. It howled in pain as it slammed into the ground. Overgrown, spindly fingers clawed lines in the grime as they were pulled backward, toward the Hunter.

The blessed metal burned through what little flesh was left on that leg. The pain made the already weak, decaying mess contort and cry. The writhing, confused vampire didn't hear the gentle words or the quiet hum of magic. To *it*, that candle in the priest's palm sounded like an angry furnace, the quiet voice like pealing bells. It whimpered in fear but could not escape as the flame grew closer, hotter.

⚜

THE SMALL OFFICE BENEATH THE CANNONEER WAS TENSE. The windows behind the desk opened up to dreary, cavernous nothingness. The crumbling foundations of long-abandoned buildings, eaten up by the earth over seasons upon seasons. Remnants of the original city, some small pieces of it, had tumbled into the chasm as the rivers cut and carved away her history. All long-settled, now. Any stone or soil that could be cut through had been worn down long ago. The city was stable as ever, even atop the cavernous graveyard of ancient ruins.

Zemirah hadn't arrived with the train as expected, and not any of the trains after that. There was nothing, not even a whisper of her. Noel stood quiet, bored, and watched while Esther practically twisted the tips of her hair into knots. Ambrose had taken to pacing back and forth, fingers interlocking and fidgeting.

"Will you *please* cease your pacing, doctor!" whined Esther. "My nerves worsen with every step!"

Ambrose bowed politely and took his fidgety self to a seat, though the tapping of his fingers and shaking of his knee were just as annoying and anxiety-inducing to Esther as his pacing had been. He had only been seated a moment when a door opened.

Zemirah staggered into the room with the dull-eyed huntsman behind her. She held her side and grimaced in pain, her shirt and doublet ragged and sticky with half-dried blood.

"Mother above!" Esther fumbled toward her sister to help her walk.

Ambrose was back on his feet immediately, pulling a chair toward the hearth and looking around for his briefcase. "Sit, sit!" he said.

With Esther's help, Zemirah sat down. Ambrose was quick to unfasten her ruined doublet and start peeling her shirt away from her hideous wound. Esther's face wrinkled in distress at the sight of the gash torn clean through her sister and she looked away. She seemed to only just notice the man her sister had brought in tow.

Hezekiah stood quiet. He was just a bit shy of Noel's height. A thick-boned build, thin dusting of freckles, and messy brunette hair beneath his hat. He had the typical garb of a huntsman: the leather and pelt ensemble that immediately told any viewer his trade and occupation. His crossbow was slung over his back. His eyes, frosted blue-gray in death, stared blankly at the floor. Esther was not impressed with him.

"Who is this?" she said.

"The only token I have for my troubles," Zemirah spat out as she winced.

"What?" Esther whipped her head around. "What about the twins?"

Ambrose didn't look up from his work as the two women spoke, busily wiping dirt and fraying threads from Zemirah's belly to survey the damage. Her side had been opened by some sort of dull instrument of the Hunters, he was sure. The flesh was torn, not sliced clean through, and partially cauterized by the heat of those accursed weapons the clergy carried. Scar tissue coated her inside and out, but thankfully she had begun to regenerate what was not scarred. An uncomfortable sentence, to be sure. Those scars would mean ongoing pain. But she would survive it. Had survived it. *Thank goodness.* His patient gritted her teeth as she lifted one leg to rest it on the chair opposite her.

"The twins are gone, wasted. Both of them," she answered her sister's question. "They didn't stand a chance against the Archbishop."

"He's back already –?" Ambrose began.

"You idiot!" Esther interrupted. "*Why* would you get on the train if the Archbishop was aboard? Do you *want* to join his collection?"

"He wasn't *supposed* to be." Zemirah hung her head backward off the chair and waved one hand dismissively. "He wasn't on the ledger. He was supposed to be in Parrvon until the end of the month." She sucked air in through her teeth and resituated herself on her chair. "Him *and* that damn Huntress –"

"There were *two* of them?"

"Of course there were," Ambrose mumbled as he pulled a tin of numbing salve from his briefcase, he looked back over his shoulder at Hezekiah. "And you still managed to raise this one? With your wound?"

"You play with fire, sister."

"I'm here, aren't I?" she snapped. "Get him cleaned up, he's a decent shot. I want him –" She grimaced as she tried to push herself up out of her chair and regretted it.

Ambrose's tone grew dark and serious. "My lady, *please* sit still. Half your belly and a rib are gone."

Esther frowned and almost wretched at Ambrose's words.

"McGowan." Zemirah winced as she shifted in her chair yet again as she addressed Noel. "The new captain, did you spy him?"

"I did, my Lady." Noel said.

"And? Another doubter like the last?"

"Deaf and blind as they come."

"Good, he'll trouble the bloodhounds for a time."

"Aye, but he has his own knights swarming about, now. I advised my Lady already to be careful."

"The knights are too afraid to go where the lamps don't burn."

Noel nodded. "Another thing, my Lady."

"Yes?"

"The captain carries death with him, I am sure of it."

Esther perked up. "Where? Does he wear a ring?"

"No rings that I have seen, but it's there."

Zemirah chewed her lip in thought. "On his person, you're sure of it?"

"Aye, my Lady. Even within the walls of Coldwater, in my observations, he wears it."

"It's bound to be some other piece of jewelry, then. Mourning pieces always are. Keep watching, that may prove useful."

A vague gesture towards Hezekiah indicated the conversation was over. Esther leaned in to give her sister a kiss on the forehead before marching off, perhaps intending to write a strongly worded letter to a certain conductor about accurate ledgers. Noel followed, taking Hezekiah by the sleeve and impatiently leading him out of the office, further into the maze of rooms underneath the Cannoneer. He followed without a word.

With them gone, Ambrose lowered his voice and spoke a bit softer. "You drank the blood you took with you, my lady?"

"I did. Just before ..." She gestured weakly at her side that he was smearing salve over. "This."

"Thank goodness. Was it the cane?"

"No, it was the Huntress, that soon-to-be Abbess," she snarled darkly, her face contorting at the thought of Sybil. Her patronizing tone, her attempt at diplomacy, her promise to pray. Ambrose saw her features wrinkle up in anger, but only felt relief.

"The Archbishop didn't get his hands on you? Not at all?"

Zemirah's face relaxed. Ambrose was looking up at her worriedly, expectantly. She almost smiled. "No, he didn't."

Ambrose breathed a deep sigh, wiping his hair back out of his face.

"You were lucky. I dread to think what that monster would have done if he'd had his way –"

"Please," she muttered. "I would ... rather not dwell on it."

Ambrose apologized and straightened up, intending to go wash his hands and continue treating her deep wound. She stopped him by grabbing hold of his arm. She wordlessly leaned her head against him. He stroked her hair as both of them silently processed her brush with death. No, not death, something perhaps worse.

24

THE WARBLING WREN WAS ABUZZ WITH ACTIVITY. Outside, the cold hung heavy, permeating every skinny alley, every cracked cobblestone. Inside, the hearth crackled and glowed, and the scent of burning cedar intermingled with the dusty smell of tobacco. Glasses clinked, cutlery clattered, and wooden furniture creaked as the patrons milled about. Some only meandered through the foyer, walking straight to the stairwell, to retire to their rooms above. Some staggered over to the counter, where two bartenders were rushing about, popping corks from bottles while apprentices hefted small kegs on shoulders up from the cellar to keep ale flowing.

One round corner table was particularly heavy with smoke. A group of well-dressed patrons were playing a game of cards, knocking knuckles against the table to signal their respective turns were over as they gambled what appeared to be red wax seals instead of copper or silver. One of them, a sleazy-looking man with several missing molars and a messy head of powdery brown hair, was thumbing his cards and sneering. Mister Thomas Greer was of middling age, with sparse facial hair and a soggy cigar teetering precariously out of his mouth. The sort of fellow who wore a nice shirt; but it didn't seem to fit him quite right. With a touch more money than he knew what to do with, he was keen to enjoy a little excitement. Especially if he could glean it at the cost of another. Preferably at the cost of the sellswords he hired for the day, to get their wages back in his own coin purse.

One by one, as more cards were revealed, the other opponents folded their hands. One player, however, remained confident. He had joined the game with silver coins, rather than wax, but was welcomed to the table anyhow. Erwin had a face speckled with freckles and brilliant sunset-orange hair that hung in ringlets from his brow, with the rest pulled back into a low ponytail. He was a bit better dressed than his opponent – certainly had better teeth – but even as he curled his lip and feigned confidence, he lacked the ease and nonchalance of Mister Greer.

"You bluff about as well as you drink, boy!" He threw his cards down victoriously, and his only remaining opponent in the game sighed and slapped his own cards down. Thomas cupped his hand around the silver the boy had brought and pulled it toward himself.

"Another round?"

"Hah!" Greer took his cigar from his mouth and puffed smoke. "With what money, boy? Your papa give you a bigger allowance this week?" The group of men laughed and slapped each other on the back.

"I don't have more silver, but I do have this ..." Erwin reached into his coat and retrieved a small glass vial, sealed with similar red wax and a cork. Dark, violently red blood sloshed around inside the tiny vessel, and the air around it seemed to ripple.

"Oi!" Thomas hissed quietly. "You keep that hidden. Pass him a seal, he'll bet with that."

A fresh hand was dealt – double Erwin's silver allowance against the little vial he kept in his breast pocket. Rowdy cheers and raucous laughter erupted in the tavern. Somewhere in the crowd, a creaky violin had begun to play – and a pair of young women had climbed up onto the tables to swirl their skirts about and sway their hips with the music and drinking songs.

This hand, Erwin seemed nervous. After all, something far more valuable than mere silver was on the line this time. Finlay, too, looked nervous at first, until he was distracted by a pretty brunette twirling about on the table.

Thomas gave a hard knock of his knuckles and tossed his cards down. "Go on, boy, hand it over." He gave Erwin a cocky grin. "It'll be safer with me, it will."

"Oh ..." Erwin sat up straighter and eyed his opponent's hand on the table. "Actually, sir ... it would appear, I win."

Erwin neatly set down his hand – having indeed lucked into a better hand than the older man.

Greer squinted and flopped back in his chair, throwing his arms up and waving the younger men away from him. "Pah! You spent your luck instead of your allowance, didn't you, boy?"

Erwin grinned and scraped his winnings toward himself, retrieving some of his silver and passing the grocer back the red wax seal he'd loaned for the match. "Maybe, sir!"

From the upper floor, in a corner opposite the smoking grocer, a knight was slumped in a chair at a table of her own. She drummed her fingers on the pad of parchment she'd been taking notes on. Greer really was a sleazy little man.

Erwin smiled and meandered into the Wren's stable with his companion, cackling and slipping up his sleeve to reveal the card he'd swapped out for his own. "That Greer isn't as sharp as he thinks, eh? Come on, Fin. There's a drop for both of us and enough silver to spend the night."

The boys mounted their horses and trotted off toward the docks, up into the claustrophobic, seedy borough that was eager to entertain and indulge their vices.

25

EVENINGS WERE PEACEFUL WITHIN THE CATHEDRAL grounds. The bells had ceased their toll of the hours and, in a gentler voice, the Lady bid her clergy to the final liturgy of the day. The clergy withdrew to their chapels, the Sisters disappearing into the southern wing, while the Brothers retreated to the north. Much like during breakfast, this meant Brontë was left to her own devices. And while she was plenty likely to curl up in her window nook with a book, she now and then indulged in a devious little pleasure.

The many winding stairwells and confusing hallways of Our Lady had long since revealed some of their secrets to Brontë. She knew there was a small passage, perhaps a long-forgotten servant's corridor or one of the many emergency paths for Clerics, tucked in a corner near the grand steps that led down toward the main hall. She knew the door was old and the latch rather weak. And so, with a bit of coaxing, she let herself through without any trouble and into the hallway beyond.

It conjoined with many other such narrow paths. Old, unfinished stones and uneven steps revealed just how ancient the hidden corridors were. The bare-flame torches that hung from chains had a unique design, making one wonder just how long those undying flames had been burning to keep the passages both warm and lit. Where the paths met was a spiral staircase of equally ancient stone. It had terribly narrow slits in the wall that allowed fresh air and little else in. Brontë counted the floors she ascended until she reached the number she knew from memory.

Another door, another old latch that was easy to open. Brontë held her breath and hoped the hinges wouldn't squeak to announce her. Luckily, it opened silently inward, and both gold light and the heavy smell of incense streamed into the passage. And so, she committed the sin of trespassing into not only the space reserved for clergy at this time, but also reserved for the Brothers.

As was the common design of the larger chapels, their high, vaulted ceilings held galleries up above. Pillars of stone and railings of iron filigree guarded this upper terrace. The space was often accessed –albeit by far newer, more accessible doors and stairs – to hook and drag the massive chandeliers and censers hung on chains aside for cleaning and repair. The wooden hooks for that task and many, many boxes of incense were stored up here – up where the smoke wafted and the light from the chandeliers was the brightest. Brontë had to blink several times to adjust her eyes.

The men's voices could be heard below, echoing up through the chapel as they together recited the hymns customary of the hour. She could even pick out Philip's gorgeous voice, a sound quite unique and familiar to her. Brontë crept as lightly on her feet as she could, toward a familiar leather bench set beside the banister. Sitting down sideways, she folded her arms upon the stone, and rested her head upon them. From her perch, she could peer through the iron down toward the altar. She could listen to the call and response, piece together those parts that were in her own tongue, and wonder at the words that were not.

She could see Cyril through the swirling smoke and flickering candles. He was dressed this time in a white cassock, and had white vestments draped over his shoulders and about his head. He too wore a gold mask, akin to that of the Cardinal attending him. She recognized his trappings from the many effigies and portraits of long-dead founding members. Those saints who, by sheer faith, had their black garments washed white and were granted power unimaginable.

Of course, Cyril's current trappings were no spell, no modification to his usual cassock. They were merely a symbol, an homage, a representation of the lineage he carried on by his station. One of many, one and the same; a vessel for the fire that burned in him and in every lazy candle flame. The same fire that could burn her.

His voice was deep and comforting. Why wouldn't it be? It was the voice she had heard the most, over all these years. Though, perhaps it was the prayer itself, too. The confession of a day of little failures – goodness knows she had experienced her share! – followed by forgiveness, the promise of mercy upon the next morning, and a blessing of protection for the coming night. It soothed her, as did the gesture Cyril made over the clergy upon the recitation's completion. The usual blessing, one that she certainly did not deserve, but it still made her feel warm and satisfied nonetheless. She stole a piece of it for herself, by trespassing this way. Something only the clergy earned, she swiped like a thief in the night. She knew it was wrong.

She sat up there quite a while, even after most of the Brothers had filed out of the chapel. Her cheek was resting against her sleeve, eyes unfocused as she sat, simply content to be in the presence of it all, when she noticed Cyril looking up in her direction. Her heart leaped into her mouth. Surely, he couldn't see her way up here? Through that mask, too? She didn't dare move. He ceased his inspection of the gallery and turned, descending the steps from the altar and opening the gilt gate in the wall that led to the sacristy. She took her chance to flee, creeping along the stone floor back toward her little corridor.

Brontë had only just eased the door shut and begun wiping dust away from her dress when she heard Philip's familiar voice. He practically skipped up the steps to meet her.

"I have a good feeling about tomorrow morning!" He grinned. "Will you come with me for a morning prayer?"

Brontë groaned inwardly at his trying to entice her to pray, again. *It's not such a simple thing*, she thought. But she could hardly blame him; he didn't know that.

"Maybe another morning, I don't feel well," she fibbed.

He knew well her excuses and didn't buy them for an instant.

"Oh, come on." He put his hands on his hips and pretended to scold her. "What's your excuse? *You* room right next to the little chapel! *I* have to walk all the way from the barracks. In the cold, mind you!"

"Maybe another morning."

"You always say that."

"And one day I'll mean it. Good night."

Philip sighed and shrugged, but let her walk past him toward her room. As she walked, he called to her, "I'm going to keep asking until you say 'yes'!"

Once alone inside her room, she pulled her nightgown from the trunk at the foot of her bed and changed into it. Mostly. Brontë then sat quietly in front of her dresser. Her nightgown hung loose over her shoulders only half buttoned as she rubbed her tired eyes. Her feet were ice-cold, curled up in her stockings and resting on the bar that ran between the legs of the stool she sat on, thereby spared the cruelty of the freezing floor. She was no longer a student, and so no longer slept in the novice dormitory. But she, too, was no Sister – and therefore would not be placed in one of the larger, better-appointed rooms reserved for clergy in their dormitory. Instead, she inhabited a small, rather forgotten room, probably once used by one of many lay people. Perhaps a scullery maid, at one point, considering her room wasn't far from the bakery itself. *How fitting.* But still, it was a small blessing on cold mornings, as most were in Windermere. Indeed, she wouldn't have to trundle from the barracks, across courtyards and open air, to reach the southern auxiliary chapel, if she wished it. Which she never did.

Her box of medicine was on the dresser, along with her journal. The little chest hummed quietly, a soft note only she was likely to notice. The medicine within moderated her hunger, or at least that was the simplest way to word it. It was less a true hunger in her belly and more a pull in her chest, like a cry stuck in her throat. When it grew overwhelming, this concoction would soothe it away. It concealed her monstrosity, masked that addictive aroma present in her blood. It weakened her, too, in truth. She knew this. It took away some of the quiet strength she shamefully rather enjoyed – a sort of dexterity and lightness she wished she could indulge in more often. But giving that up was the price to pay for safety, for a pretense of belonging within these storied halls. So, her little taste of power was bartered away, and in exchange her fangs were, thus far, halted from growing in fully. Thus, did she slip beneath the perception of even the Hunters. A bleeding minnow adrift in this sea of sharks, untouched and unnoticed.

On a night when her sense of self was more intact, she might have reasoned that the sinsick reputation it gave her was a blessing. The lie assuaged suspicion, gave her space to breathe. *It was a good thing.* But tonight, she only found it an unjust humiliation, to be considered an invalid, an embarrassment, a burden. *I didn't ask to be born like this.* She pulled hard on a knot in her hair with her fingers until it gave. *It isn't fair.* Another knot.

Her journal was now doctored with notes, with a different handwriting bleeding overtop hers in red ink, correcting her mistakes. A wax-sealed envelope containing further instructions from Cyril was tucked between the pages. She glared at it as she ripped another knot out of her hair. She didn't need to read it to know what it said. Do this, do that ... *do it on time and with not a single hair out of place.* She could practically hear his voice, fresh in her mind from the liturgy, all deep and soothing. She could practically feel his one eye creeping over her, like it had when he'd arrived home, all judgmental and humiliating. She huffed indignantly at the thought and opened the top drawer of her dresser. She stuffed her box in its usual place, along with the journal and notes, and shut the drawer. The matter would trouble her tomorrow morning. Those conflicting emotions were too complicated for her at this time of night.

Brontë combed with her messy, tangled braids between her fingers. She could really only do so much with them. She had not the luxury of a soft hairbrush or someone to help her, not now. Cyril had probably managed better braids with her hair when she was little than she did now. At least he could see what he was doing. She reached over and slid the candles burning on her dresser closer to the mirror. She hardly needed their light to see in the dark, but they offered a different service here.

The silhouette of her hair, wavy from the braids, was the closest she could get to discerning her own figure in the mirror. Her reflection was ordinarily a hazy fog in the glass. But she had learned, with a little effort and a few tricks of candlelight, she could coax the slightest of silhouettes from that fog. Just enough to make the vaguest outline of herself. It of course did no good to help her with those wild, unruly baby hairs that liked to shake free of her veil and fall into her face. It certainly didn't help when she needed to wipe away soot, as she had been so pointedly reminded lately.

Like a visitor on the other side of frosted glass, her reflection taunted her. Her trick of playing with her hair and making it just wavy enough to be discernible was a small comfort. Brontë leaned forward, huffing breath onto the mirror and using one finger to scribble in a silly-looking face where her own would be. Of course, anyone else – or, any human, at least – would see her reflection just fine. She was the only one it refused to answer to. But it was an injustice she had learned to live with. And, despite her braids, candles, and her scribbles, she'd have no answer to the mystery of her own face and features tonight. She blew out her candles and turned around on her chair, preparing to brave the frigid floor for the few steps it'd take to scamper over to her bed.

There were no tapestries adorning the walls here, no ornate, thick rugs, no hearth and crackling, supernatural fire. There was no way to keep the wind from whistling through the gaps in the old wooden window frame. Her bed was a stiff mattress, more a glorified cot, in her mind, with a scratchy woolen blanket and equally scratchy sheets. But it was hers. As she scritch-scratched her way under the sheets, she retrieved her current book from under her pillow, curling up and reading approximately ten words before dozing off.

26

$\mathcal{I}$T HAD BEEN SOME TIME SINCE BENJAMIN last visited Coldwater Keep. Now a Bishop, his growing list of responsibilities made him less and less available to the public. It was common enough for a Cleric of lesser rank to visit: to inspect and maintain the consecrated chapel built into the Keep, to hear the confessions of knights and criminals both, and to give last rites to those due to be executed. But a clergyman of Benjamin's rank drew attention as out of the ordinary. He handled the curiosity of the knights and servants with his usual, effortless grace.

Benjamin was then escorted inside and up precarious stone steps – with many warnings from the butler to prevent him from losing his footing on the deliberately uneven stairs – and through a long corridor lined with antique armor and draped with banners. Banners that, despite the conquering empire's effort to overtake most of the city's emblems, still wore their proud pine and silver colors, still wore the twin stags.

Domingo welcomed his company into the Keep's parlor. A surprisingly cozy room; stone walls were kept warm by the large hearth on one side, and tapestries blanketing the others. Fantastical woven scenes of battling ships and hunting wild game. Narrow, crystal clear windows were half-hidden by thick curtains, to keep precious heat inside, but offered little glimpses of a handsome view over the city. It was a room clearly meant to receive nobility, that shirked the rest of the building's cold, no-nonsense utilitarianism in favor of comfort and class.

Before the hearth, two plush chairs and a comfortably low table had been prepared. On the table was a tray, set with two demitasse cups and saucers, and a brass pot filled with steaming hot coffee. Both were accompanied by a small helping of fresh cream to spoon atop it, and an open box of cigars. Not the sort of fare Benjamin was accustomed to, nor inherently to his tastes – but he recognized them as the polite, thoughtful offerings from a gentleman of a different culture. It was a gesture he appreciated, as he accepted his seat in the chair opposite his host.

"Brother Benjamin, thank you for coming."

Benjamin bowed his head and accepted the prepared beverage that Domingo offered him. "It is a pleasure, Captain. How may I be of assistance?"

Domingo had been examining the Brother from the moment he arrived. Benjamin had an entirely different aura about him, now that he had the time to dwell on it. Oh, he was still authoritative enough, as one would expect from a gentleman of his rank, but he was far gentler. His magic, too, was gentler. It didn't seem to crackle or spark around him the way the Archbishop's did, it didn't seem to be fighting to free itself from his rosary. Instead, it was a content, calming hum.

Benjamin, too, was inspecting Domingo and his accompaniments. Free of his armor, but not without his regalia – including medals of military honor and those gold tags all officers of the crown wore pinned to his chest.

Benjamin was also very well aware of the scrutiny Domingo was subjecting him to. He had read the papers, after all. He knew the good captain was in possession of a rare skill. Few were born with this innate sense, and fewer still could tolerate being taught to hone it without irreparably damaging their sight: this ability to visually discern magic. In some ways, Benjamin envied him for it. But he was quick to rebuke that feeling, believing it an improper emotion for a priest to dwell upon.

"You are looking for something in me, Captain," Benjamin finally said. "Magic, perhaps?"

Domingo shrugged nonchalantly. "Simply making an observation. A newcomer to your fair city, I have much to learn – as you very pointedly reminded me."

"So I did." Benjamin took a sip of the spiced coffee he'd been given and found it strong, but surprisingly pleasant. "And what do you think of Windermere, sir?"

"She is well known beyond her province for her superstitions, for her ... undead affliction." Domingo hid his half-smile behind his own cup of coffee, but Benjamin could hear the smirk in his voice all the same. But as a Bishop, he had bartered beliefs with many a doubter before, and thus trusted himself to handle this nonbeliever, too ... with enough tact and time.

"A cursed, yet holy city," Domingo continued. "How ironic. Some come here to pray the affliction away, while others come to seek it out with morbid fascination. And yet, *I* can find nothing of these so-called vampires. Not a whisper, not a one, of your heretics."

"I am afraid you, sir, will have little luck in tracking down a vampire. While neither their existence nor their blood business are considered criminal in the eyes of your law, they *are* often involved in ... unscrupulous activity. A vampire is likely to condemn themselves to your gallows if they veer too near you, or your knights."

Domingo sneered, and Benjamin realized he must have said something that Domingo had been hoping for.

"Ah, but what threat would my knights pose to such creatures?" he said smugly. "If we trust to your church's teachings, only Hunters can fell these *heretics*. What fear of the gallows do you speak of, then?"

"Vampires," Benjamin corrected, "fear the gallows as any living man would. What Our Lady says is true, only Hunters can kill vampires. But to subdue or disable is not to kill. You may have your executioner strangle a vampire until what you perceive as death, but you have only temporarily incapacitated it."

"You clergy folk really do insist on calling them vampires."

"We call them what they are, sir."

"Myth and superstition." He scowled. "No magic can raise the dead."

"You are misinformed," Benjamin replied. "I understand you and yours place great stock in what the capital alchemists tell you is possible. I, too, respect their work. But this is not the capital."

"The laws of heaven and earth do not bend for one church order."

"Apparently, they do, sir. Here, vampires are real, and so too is their blood. Even if you wish to deny vampires, you cannot deny sinsickness."

Domingo sighed, but could not deny that he'd seen the consequences of this peculiar addiction already. The papers printed off story after story. The coffeehouses and taverns bubbled with talk of the topic. The religious folk flitted about with such paranoia it made even their daily errands a challenge. Even if it was not real, the fear of it was – and fear could make anything erupt into trouble.

"If I may ask ... this sickness. Why would your faithful choose to consume something they believe damns them?"

"When it comes to the faithful, many do not choose at all, sir."

"Enlighten me."

"Vampires are sly creatures. Very little blood is required to encourage addiction. I spoke to you before – of how even the scent of it can cloud the senses. This is true. It is also true that a small amount ingested can engender addiction, if left untreated. A small amount, be it administered by trickery or by force, can and will inevitably create an addict."

"What sort of trickery?"

Benjamin shrugged and held up his small cup of coffee. "A small amount added to one's drink, perhaps. In food, in medicine, in liquor. It can loiter anywhere."

"But if the scent of it alone is enough to cloud the senses, wouldn't it be noticed?"

"Ah. It doesn't have a flavor or aroma of its own, necessarily. When asked, the sinsick often describe it to me in a manner more akin to emotion or memory. A man I examined recently explained that he could smell his wife's perfume, though she has been dead two years now. He was particularly observant, most are not. In such a small amount as what I suspect he was exposed to; it will not inflict any mental bliss or bolster the body. Therefore, a drugged individual is likely not to notice they have been given blood until they begin showing symptoms of withdrawal."

"These symptoms being?"

"It is a most horrid thing, sir." Benjamin spoke with a tone that betrayed his familiarity with the condition. "Most immediate symptoms are mundane enough. It starts with aches and pains, memory troubles, a clouded mind. But at length, I often see a severe degradation of condition, both mental and physical. Hallucinations are common, as is the inclination to damage oneself. The limbs lose function, wounds stop healing, the skin begins to blister and decay. Even food and drink do not satisfy, only blood. It becomes not a matter of achieving bliss, but of merely being."

"And your so-called vampires would inflict such a sickness because ...?"

Benjamin laughed softly. "Because of the coin, what else? To amass wealth."

That wasn't the reply Domingo had expected. He had assumed he'd hear the typical philosophical rhetoric, the silly mythology of unspoken contracts and death-defying puppets. Addiction-inducing drug traffickers made far more sense to him. Perhaps Benjamin presented it this way deliberately.

"But, as I said, sir." Benjamin smiled. "That is only the case among our faithful. There are still the bold, the foolish, and the naive. Those who are not of our faith. There will always be these people."

"And your church equally condemns them for not aligning with your beliefs," Domingo said. "Even if they are not of the church."

"Though we call it sinsickness, the question of this addiction is not simply one of theology, sir. It has very real societal consequences, no matter what one believes. These people are suffering." Benjamin paused, thinking for a moment. "As I'm sure a man of your station will have noticed, the people, too, have strong opinions. Most see succumbing to the addiction as a moral failure, not a physical one."

"Yes, I have seen how intense the reactions of the townsfolk can be already."

"While, to our displeasure, no longer illegal to carry or consume, vampire blood on one's person would earn the ire of the faithful. It is a sort of social unrest that few are keen to invite upon themselves. Many keep it secret, as most would with any other addiction. In that way, it is not so different from alcohol ..." Benjamin paused as Domingo lit a cigar. "... Or tobacco."

"I see." Domingo glared. "I am well acquainted with your church and her tribunals. What will it be, then? Confessions condemning one's neighbor? Anonymous accusations that send Hunters after the sinsick? I know how that sort of poison spreads quick through a people."

"Certainly not, sir." Benjamin remained relaxed, even as Domingo's words grew accusatory. "As one who hears confessions, I can personally assure you no such accusations are used in our Hunters' work."

Domingo let out a puff of smoke from his nose and rolled his eyes. Benjamin continued.

"We Clerics, upon reaching the requisite station, take an additional vow not to disclose the confessions rendered up to us. You may find this unbelievable, sir, but we treat our vows with reverence. They are unbreakable."

Domingo leaned forward, one elbow propped up on his knee. "So, even if a so-called sinsick soul confesses their addiction to you, you will not alert your Hunters?"

"No, sir, I will not," Benjamin replied without hesitation. "I have never broken my oath, and have no intention to do otherwise. If an addict wishes to surrender themselves, they have other avenues to do so. We may encourage this surrender in confession, yes – but we do not condemn. We Clerics only offer mercy; the Hunters handle judgment."

"Judgment." Domingo scoffed. Benjamin spoke of that infernal fire the Father wielded, surely. That pesky flame that was hailed as a blessing, as divine. Yet another piece of religious superstition he had to decipher ... but that could wait. Domingo diverted the conversation back to the more readily addressable concern.

"And how would your church propose to tackle the scourge of this sinsickness, might I ask?"

"We of the Order have only ever been concerned with destroying the source of the malady. It was easier to limit the harm done by addiction when it was a criminal offense." Benjamin paused to adjust his spectacles. "You come to us at a time when we have no answer, sir, not yet – and not one that aligns with your southern sensibilities. The ... explosion in the number of people consuming vampire blood is a relatively recent development in our province's history. A new problem. We can thank your conquering *empire* for that."

"Pardon me?"

"A city-state conquered for her strategic placement along a busy trade route." Benjamin set his empty coffee cup down. "And we are to simply believe that the legality of vampire blood escaped all notice during the drafting of documents?" He laughed softly. "No, I think the coin of the business was seen as too lucrative to criminalize, and so mention of it was forfeit." He smiled and folded his hands in his lap. "But that is only my opinion."

Behind one of the tapestries, in a recess built into the stone wall, Levi was diligently writing down every word of the conversation.

27

THOUGH HE WENT ALONE TO PRAY, Philip was bright-eyed and chipper as always, this morning. Birds warbled in the courtyard and the sky shone a dusty purple as the night began to fade. He had bathed and dressed, and now knelt quietly in one of the smaller auxiliary chapels. He had brought two of the customary slim, tall beeswax candles, and was now carefully lighting each of them. He paused when a familiar voice addressed him.

"May I join you?"

Philip looked up in surprise to see Cyril approaching, his own candle in hand.

"Of course, Father," Philip stammered. "Good morning."

"Good morning."

Cyril smiled and leaned over, lighting and setting his own candle beside Philip's. He then knelt next to the younger Hunter. "Two candles? Did Brother Serge come with you?"

Philip grinned and shook his head. "Oh, no. I keep trying to convince Miss Brontë to come pray with me, but she's always sleeping in late. I bring a candle for her anyway, just in case she surprises me."

How naïve, Cyril thought. *That girl would never go to the trouble.* Outwardly, he only chuckled quietly and nodded, closing his good eye. "I see. And how is your wound?"

Philip reached for the bandage over his eye instinctively. "Healing very well, or so my uncle says. Thank you, Father."

"Good, good. I do hope you'll be careful." Cyril gestured to the white leather eyepatch he wore on his right side. In a way, Philip's bandage mimicked it, heavy and white and making that eyebrow droop a little. "We wouldn't want you to lose an eye."

Cyril and Philip then both resumed the reverent silence that more befitted prayer. Though, Philip couldn't help but open one eye and peek up at Cyril beside him. As nervous as he was, realizing he was alone with the Archbishop, Cyril had a way of putting him at ease. A sort of gentleness and warmth. But maybe that was just the way the Heart revealed itself through him. When Philip blinked, he could see a thin ring around Cyril's head burned into the back of his eyelids.

28

THE FOLLOWING EVENING WAS HEAVY WITH FOG. It bathed the valley, so that only the treetops poked out above. Across the hills, far beyond the thick walls of Windermere, and even beyond the farmland she claimed, the fog obscured a sad sight. The stench of burning flesh was intense, but smothered by the thick ash and smoke as it billowed skyward. It mingled with the fog, until it was difficult to tell the difference. Wailing, hymns, and the sound of snapping whips filled the space between each crack from the fire.

The Flagellants were always the first to know of vampire attacks in this gloomy countryside. Sinsick souls who wandered the wilds, who shunned all comforts – food, shelter, medicine – as penance for their failures. One flogging from the church was not enough. To be excommunicated was not enough. For such a grave offense against Our Lady, the penance must be grave in kind.

These sinsick folk gave up their names, abandoned their belongings, and instead joined a new flock. Penitent souls with bowed heads and bloodied backs whipped themselves raw with rope floggers. Their robes left their backs uncovered for this reason, not even the blessing of a layer of fabric was permitted. They wore long drooping hoods over their heads, held at the throat by knotted thorns that, once applied, would not be easily removed. Only as the fabric rotted away with time did it reveal gnarled teeth, cracked lips, and desiccated flesh.

They walked with staves to support their weight, crosses atop them, and lanterns in hand. The one blessing given by the Lamplighter's Guild – a long-forgotten remnant of some tradition, some binding charity. They must keep some light, something half-holy, near, lest the vampires come for them and cut their penance too short.

The Flagellants brought forth their lanterns and limited oil. All that the huntsman's family had once owned was now consigned to the fire. Not even the orchard was spared, apple and lemon trees crackled and their branches curled in the flames. Fear forbade any salvaging of their belongings. Ripe fruit was left to burn and the house itself was set alight, with the linen-wrapped body of Lucia lying within.

Sybil stood quietly, watching as the neighbors and Flagellants worked together to control the flame, to keep it within the drystone walls that once marked where the homestead began. Many brought flowers, to be thrown into the burning house. Still others brought old gifts, heirlooms; some even brought garments or pelts. Anything, absolutely anything with a tie to the family. Even the tiniest thread of connection was thrown into the flame. A combination of grief and rage boiled in Sybil's chest as she watched, arms crossed beside her horse. That the community must lose not only a beloved family, but any objects that they might remember them by. It was unfair. But vampires were crafty, evil things – and the hunter had never returned to his wife. Indeed, one must not let him return, a cursed, hungry monster, confused by his own undeath and longing to see his wife and child. And so it was that the place he would seek out was destroyed.

And the girl? Well, she'd be taken to the safest place there was. Somewhere not even her father, if he remembered her or thought to look, would be able to get to her. She was sound asleep, cheek smushed to Florence's shoulder as the Sister held her. Her little blue ribbon flapped in the breeze. Both Florence and Sybil stood a fair distance away, so that the smoke and smell did not disturb the poor child.

Sybil was kind enough to speak to the neighbors, to offer what little comfort she could. But her priority was to get the child back to the cathedral. Out of the cold, ideally with a hot bath and hot food. She and Florence had to negotiate her carefully as they mounted their horses, but managed to hand her between themselves without waking her. Only once they were walking along on the path did Florence mumble under her breath to Sybil.

"The orphanage has no spare beds right now."

"I know," Sybil whispered. "We'll figure something out for her."

"You won't be able to sneak a child past Father."

"I'll do what I have to."

⚜

THERE WOULD, INDEED, BE NO SNEAKING PAST the Archbishop – Florence and Sybil bit their tongues at their bad luck of running into him the moment they entered the warming room. The heat of the great hearth seemed to make the girl come to, and she fidgeted in Sybil's arms. Cyril tilted his head curiously and approached the pair.

"Who is this?"

"Another foundling, as of what we yet know. She is injured."

Sybil paused as Cyril leaned in a bit closer to inspect her injured leg. She had fallen and skinned the palms of her hands and both of her knees. The combination of blood and rainwater running down her ankles had ruined her socks and shoes. Blair looked up at him in awe, mystified that the comforting warmth she felt wasn't from the hearth, but seemed to radiate from him.

She blinked rapidly and tried to figure out why she saw a ring around his head. Did the Sisters see it, too?

"Do we have room, Father?" Sybil's eyes glistened already with the prospect of turning the girl away, or surrendering her elsewhere.

Cyril glanced at Florence who, from behind Sybil, mouthed an urgent plea to him. He nodded. "We will make room. Take her to the infirmary, please." He then turned to the girl, who looked away in embarrassment for a moment, until he addressed her. "Be brave a little while longer. After the doctor fixes you up, we'll get you a treat."

She wiped her eyes and nodded her head rapidly. Sybil resituated Blair on her hip and departed in the direction of the infirmary. Florence turned to follow, but Cyril clearing his throat made her wince and halt.

"Sister Sybil does not typically take a shine to children her age."

"No ..." Florence turned back around, chewing her lip. "No, she doesn't."

"Is there something I should know?"

"I think ... that is something better shared at her discretion, in confession, Father."

Cyril nodded. "Very well. Go with her, won't you? I will see about finding the child a treat."

They both departed to their tasks: Florence to catch up with Sybil, and Cyril to stride off in the direction of the bakery. As he passed the auxiliary chapel, he thought he saw a familiar silhouette. Hugo was placing the last in a series of lit candles and was bundled up in his cardigan, as usual.

"Brother Hugo, I am sorry to disturb you."

Hugo turned in surprise, kneeling and bowing his head as Cyril approached through the small aisle between the pews. "Yes, Father? What do you need?"

Cyril bid him stand. "Do you have anything sweet? Biscuits or the like?"

Hugo tilted his head curiously. "A midnight snack?" He grinned. "Since when do you have a sweet tooth?"

Cyril rolled his good eye. "Not for *me*. Sister Sybil found an injured child. She is frightened. I think a little treat will do well to calm her."

"Come, come. Let's see what I have."

The two departed the chapel, back down the corridor toward the bakery. Luckily, they had done so in relative silence, as Brontë was asleep at the worktable. Her head rested upon an open book and she still wore her apron. The nuts she had been obsessively sorting were all neatly compiled in glass jars before her.

Hugo clicked his tongue. "And tomorrow she'll be whining about her back aching, eh? I'll slip past her, best not to wake her."

Cyril didn't reply as Hugo disappeared down the stairs into the pantry. He thought quite the opposite – that he ought to wake her, so she could sleep in a bed, at least. He shuffled up behind her with this in mind, catching a glimpse of the book-come-pillow. A history tome, and a rather advanced edition at that. Even ignoring the fact her arms were folded over it, the book was obviously well loved. He almost smiled at the idea he may have misjudged her affinity for reading as merely an entertainment. Cyril shuffled past her, retrieving one of the folded-up blankets on the window alcove she so often lounged in. He had a brief thought that he ought to carry her there, to a padded bench and real pillows. She was a deep enough sleeper not to be roused by the movement, after all. But that would be far more contact between them than was proper, so he settled for draping the soft blanket over her at the table.

Hugo returned with a small selection of sugared tea biscuits and a bag of Brontë's candied almonds. Cyril thanked him and the two departed. As he bid Hugo a good night, he marched off toward the infirmary with the sweets in hand, a little gift for this newest addition to his flock.

29

AMBROSE CAME HOME TO HIS APARTMENT TO FIND Zemirah slumped on the couch near the hearth, helping herself to the whiskey he kept on the table. She raised her half-empty glass in acknowledgment when he entered. He shut the door behind him and hurried to her side.

"My lady? Is something wrong? Are you in pain?"

Zemirah had changed into fresher clothes, now that she was not traveling and had access to her own wardrobe again. She'd donned a much softer, much better-fitting linen shirt and vest. She'd unbuckled her sword belt and flung it over the back of the sofa, along with her long coat. She grimaced and finished off the last swig of whiskey, holding out the glass to him. He confiscated it and set it aside.

"How is your wound? Let me see." Ambrose knelt down and began unbuttoning her vest. He managed to peel enough fabric back to inspect her bandages.

"That grocer fumbled the shipment." She flopped her head back on the arm of the sofa, eyes closed. "The blood is missing."

"What?" Ambrose hissed through his teeth. "All four vials?"

"All eight," she corrected.

"All eight! How many misdeliveries can one buffoon make?"

Zemirah shook her head weakly, covering her eyes with one hand in frustration. Ambrose bit his tongue and chastised

166

himself inwardly for making the situation worse with his words. He busied himself with inspecting her wounds, carefully feeling the bandages he'd applied.

"Mother will be furious," Zemirah said after a pause. She laughed a sort of stressed, terrified chuckle. "She'll beat me black and blue for stealing that bottle. And now this."

"She *should* be overjoyed," Ambrose snapped. He held her free hand and gave it a reassuring, gentle squeeze. "And thank goodness you had the foresight to drink it when you did. It's the only reason you survived."

Zemirah smiled and stroked Ambrose's cheek affectionately. She knew he was right, at least about her survival. To have regenerated so staggeringly fast – and from a wound inflicted by a Huntress, no less – was a feat even a pureblood like herself could only dream of under the best of circumstances. That little vial had been her salvation. But did it really matter? She'd stolen it! She might as well have ripped her mother's little finger off! Oh, she would be furious indeed, if she knew. So angry that Zemirah might even wish she'd been felled by that Huntress instead of facing her rage.

AH, MOTHERS. ALWAYS SO DIFFICULT TO PLEASE, THEY WERE. West of Ambrose's modest little apartment, in a wealthy, well-to-do merchant's estate, a young woman was doing her best to please her own mother. Another pointless dinner, another table full of boring guests and uninteresting suitors. Candles burned bright over a crisp, flawlessly pressed linen tablecloth. Dishes were being carried by an ensemble of smartly dressed staff, offering this or that to each member seated at the table. Aoife's rosy hair was tied up neatly off her neck, wild ringlets tamed by a careful combination of combing and pinning. She had her mother's tall, slender build and often accentuated it with well-fitting waistcoats, save when her mother demanded dresses and gems. She paused, a glittering glass of white wine in her hand as she bowed her head slightly to hear the comment whispered from her butler. The apparent surprise on her face made her mother curious.

"Is something the matter, darling?"

Aoife shook her head and smiled, setting down her glass and rising from her seat. "Someone at the door, apparently. Please, excuse me."

"At this hour? How odd."

"Indeed. I won't be long."

The butler opened the door for her, and the moment it clicked shut behind her, she let drop all her decorum, picked up her skirt, and raced down the stairs.

"Erwin!"

Sure enough, there was Erwin – dripping with rainwater and boasting a healing bruise or three – as he sogged up the entryway rug. Aoife rushed over to him, reaching out to turn his face toward her to better inspect the bruise, which she realized coincided with a slightly swollen lip.

The two were obviously siblings. Nearly identical in hair color and texture, and the generous helping of freckles. He, however, had a much shorter, stockier build: one that gave away the difference between their parentages. He looked every inch the runt of the litter compared to Aoife, and he knew it.

"Where have you been?" she said. "I've been worried sick."

"Why?" He pulled away from her hand, allowing Finlay to help him remove his cloak. "I was at the Wren, same as last week."

Erwin caught the disapproving glare from Aoife's butler, Darcie, and cleared his throat. She was even taller than his sister and had a harsher face. Aoife only sighed at him. "Were you gambling again? Don't tell me you've blown this week's allowance already ... Father will be furious –"

"I got lucky."

"So I see," Aoife said, tugging at the seafoam-teal cravat around his neck. She pulled it away enough to reveal the smattering of red marks all over his neck. He swatted her hand away and readjusted his scarf.

"I'll earn it back in the arena. I always do," he said confidently.

"Oh, don't even *mention* that wretched place to me. I swear, you'll lose an eye, or worse. Get upstairs, before mother sees you like this."

Erwin shrugged, but Aoife had already turned to Finlay and Darcie. She greeted Finlay, and he of course bowed and addressed her with a formality more befitting his rank as valet. She squinted at him, seeing very clearly that he also had a generous helping of red marks peeking out from beneath his collar. She rolled her eyes, speaking in a slightly lower tone, in hopes Erwin wouldn't hear her as he ascended the stairs to his room.

"Miss Darcie, please have dinner delivered to his room. Something hot and easy to eat. Soup, perhaps? Finlay, please, do make sure he eats. Not a word to mother, as usual."

Aoife then collected herself and rejoined her mother and the rest of the family at dinner, saying precisely nothing about her half brother's return home.

30

At Doubury Lane, to the east of the cathedral, the early evening was descending into dark chaos. Many had seen the clergy arrive. And many more saw the righted cross – the mark that proved they had visited.

"Damn you to the depths of the Rotherdare!" a voice rang out above the disgruntled mob that had gathered. "You'll doom us all with your stench!"

The house was already defaced with rust-colored paint, smeared crosses, and marks of the saints. Soot and rotten vegetables had been pelted at the front window, boarded over with shutters to prevent further damage to the glass. Several folk had brought shoes purchased from the family's business and piled them up. They burned them on the cobblestones before the house, in an attempt to cut any connection to the unfortunate cobblers. As more gathered in the lane, as more shoes were piled and more torches lit, the murmur of simmering anger and resentment boiled and bubbled.

"Burn them out!" one woman shouted. "Purge them like the sickness they are!"

A chorus of agreement rose from the mob, now so large it struggled to fit in the space between the houses. A smash sounded and a cheer, as a boy drove a rock through one of the lampposts. Torches were passed to him, their holders keen to taste the half-holy oil that would ensure a cleaner burn.

"Aye! Out, out!" another man yelled. "Join your kind in the wilds where ye belong! A bloody back and bowed head await you!"

"Leave or burn!"

The bubble burst when an audible gasp rippled through the crowd. Two mounted knights could be seen approaching down the narrow lane. A few of the crowd panicked and fled immediately – only to find the alleys harbored more mounted knights armed with blunt staves. An unsettled whisper overtook the voices still bickering about the matter of the dead man. The knights approached at a steady pace, but upon drawing close enough it became clear that *these* knights were locals. The crowd relaxed some to know they were in the presence of their fellows, of those more understanding of the serious nature of this dead addict.

That reassurance was shattered by the appearance of the two commanding officers. Neatly pressed, borrowed uniforms and berets of green and silver clashed with the white-gold regalia of the sergeant and captain.

The knights were calm and steady, but pushed straight through the crowd on horseback, dividing them. Each duet of knights directed people away with firm, but not aggressive, instructions. They cut the crowd up and dispersed them to different slip roads. The less enthusiastic of the crowd, and indeed those not inclined toward any real trouble, were quick to follow the orders. Those with more heartfelt beliefs took more convincing.

One loud-mouthed, particularly zealous fellow, with a lit torch and a metal cross in his hand, pointed at Domingo with his torch. "A southerner comes to defend what he does not understand! Empirical scum – you drag us down with your nonbelief!"

He stood too close for comfort. A loud snort and Domingo's horse reared up, slamming two steel-shod hooves down hard into the cobbles. The stones rippled unnaturally at the contact and sent up a splash of opalescent light.

"Stand back from the Royal Guard!"

The ripples knocked the zealot back a pace in fright and surprise. Domingo's shout was strangely controlled. Loud and authoritative, but not angry. *There was no need for fetters, not yet.* The gold medals that hung from his shoulder flickered as he muttered an equation under his breath, his eyes tracing a path over the cobblestones. The lines of magic drawn about the captain were cold and sharp. Nothing like the warm, organic gold so familiar to the populace in the clergy's magic.

Domingo then eyed the pile of burning leather shoes. His lips moved as more ripples seemed to appear from beneath the fire. A nod of his head, more oddly geometric light splashed up from between the flagstones. The pile hissed as the flame died, smothered.

"I do not question your beliefs. Burn the shoes if you wish, but not here."

With the mob thus dispersed, save for the one particularly vocal and blabbering man that had to be escorted with more force, the family inside the house could breathe a touch easier. In the living room, the coffin lay open. Their father looked far more peaceful now. Comfortably oblivious to the distress and disgrace he'd brought upon his loved ones. And they, in turn, comfortably oblivious to the flesh and blood torn from his back.

"Thank you, Captain," Georgiana said sadly. The Guard's intervention was, of course, deeply appreciated ... but it did little good. No one would do business with an addict's family. The fall from respectable to pariah was instant and irreversible.

31

SYBIL HAD TAKEN TO LOOKING OUT THE WINDOW of her office. A once pleasant view, she could now see nothing but the distant blackened smudge in a particular clearing of forest. Her throat had been sore for so many days now, her eyes red, her heart heavy.

"Staring at it isn't going to undo anything," Florence said beside her.

"I know. I know that."

Sybil was clinging with all the strength her little finger could muster to Florence's own little finger. They disentangled their hands when the door latch clicked. Florence turned to see Cyril let himself inside the office, his stole already around his neck. She gave a half-hearted, sad smile and leaned over to whisper to Sybil, who hadn't even turned to face her company.

"I'll leave you to it."

Florence pushed herself off the wall she'd been leaning against. She gave Sybil a reassuring nudge and a wink for good measure as she took her leave. She bowed to Cyril and he closed the door behind her. There was some silence, where Cyril gave the distraught Sister a chance to speak first. When she didn't speak, he prodded her.

"Is there anything you'd like to tell me, Sister? Something to do with the girl you brought back, perhaps?"

"I know it was her," Sybil muttered. "I know it was the witch on the train. A child as young as Blair would have no reason to lie about what she remembered." She turned around to glare at

173

Cyril, preemptively defensive. "You will not be able to convince me otherwise. Brother Maddoc tried already. He tried to soothe me by saying it could be a coincidence. I'm not that naive."

"I know you're not."

Sybil took to pacing back and forth behind her desk, arms crossed over her chest, robes and veil fluttering about every time she changed direction. Her fingers curled so hard into her arms they hurt. "I ... I come home and think nothing of it! Idling away and chattering about the bloody weather!"

"None of us could have predicted the future –"

"I should have done more! I should have –"

"Should have what?" Cyril cut her off sharply. "Thrown yourself off a moving train? Did you not pester me all the way back about how dangerous that is?"

Sybil took a deep, frustrated breath and set her jaw.

Cyril eyed her sternly. "Tell me, when have you seen a vampire stand right back up after a blow from your lance?"

"I ..."

"How many times has that happened, Sister?"

"It's never happened," she mumbled.

"Exactly." Cyril's expression softened. "You acted in good faith, to the best of your ability, with all knowledge available to you at the time. We can do no more than this."

She sighed. There was still a hint of frustration in that sigh, but a tinge of relief, too. She felt a tiny fraction of weight lifted. "Then what of that thing I saw her drink? Do you think it's what caused her to regenerate so rapidly? Mother above, what concoction would allow for that? Surely not just a vial of human blood. Not unless –"

"I am not sure," Cyril interrupted her gently, trying to stop her before she scurried off with all her thoughts. "But I am investigating the matter personally. I do not wish to pull you away from your work, I know it is important to you."

Sybil let out a deeper sigh of relief this time. "Thank you." She rubbed her arm to soothe the pain she'd inflicted by pinching it so hard. "And thank you for not treating me like I'm made of glass."

He nodded, half turning to leave. "Spring will come, and another visit to your new convent along with it. You still have much to do, but you will earn your stole, yet."

"Not too soon, I hope." She smiled sadly. "It looks heavy."

"It is, sometimes."

⌖

LATE SUMMER MEANT STRAWBERRIES. It was understood that, thanks to the Clerics' constant keeping of them, those that grew in the infirmary gardens were of the highest quality. Much sweeter and fuller than the often trampled or bird-pecked samples out on the slopes, where the lay people only sporadically attended their produce. Brontë provided Philip one of her woven baskets and requested he gather as many as he could bring back to her. It was a task he was plenty happy to perform, as Brontë expected. She of course knew very well a good portion of those berries would be gobbled up on his walk from the infirmary back to the bakery. When he did finally return, with berry juice in the corner of his mouth and exceptionally sticky fingers, he greeted Brontë with a typical flourish and completely unnecessary bow.

"Here you are, my most lovely baker. A fresh, and might I add, *very* timely delivery."

"Why thank you, kind sir." She pulled the basket from his extended arm, slapping his hand away as he reached to pluck one more from the top of the pile. "Now, go wash your hands before they stick together."

Hugo had a thick leather-bound book open upon a lectern. It was propped up on the far side of his workstation, resting in the corner of the windowsill. There, it was out of the way of both himself and the heaps of flour he dusted the work surface before him with. Brontë and Philip each sat at stools before the great worktable in the center of the bakery. With the basket of freshly washed strawberries between them, they removed the stems and sliced them into halves, one by one.

Brontë had an excellently organized system – setting aside some portions of berries for candying, some for syrup-making, and some for a tea cake she intended to bake. Philip, of course, was ruining it by swiping the best berries out of the dishes and popping them into his mouth, or divvying out the wrong number and throwing off her count.

As Hugo kneaded a batch of dough and shaped it into loaves, he and Brontë indulged in their typical pastime: guessing games. A game wherein Hugo, armed with a great volume of history, would provide the name of a person, place, or event in Our Lady's long timeline – and Brontë was responsible for calling upon only her own recollection and knowledge to slowly piece it together. Philip strived adamantly to keep up with her stellar memory, swift deductions, and needle-sharp wit – but he was embarrassingly less studied than she, even on matters pertaining to the Hunters.

"Let's see ... the first Hunter to summon a weapon was – "

"Methuselah!" Philip blurted out.

"What?" Brontë laughed and shook her head. "He was *centuries* before. Josefa was the first to summon."

"Correct once again, Miss Brontë. Sister Josefa wrote the spell to summon armaments," said Hugo as he leaned over and blew some stray flour from the book, only managing to puff it right back into his face. "She's making you look bad, Brother Philip!"

Philip snorted and turned up his nose. "I'll catch up!"

"Very well – how about this: what metal are the summoned arms composed of?"

"Gold," Philip replied hurriedly, trying to beat Brontë to the answer.

"No, no. It's vermeil."

"Correct again, lass!"

Brontë swayed back and forth where she sat, a cocky look on her face, even as Philip stuck his tongue out at her. She couldn't resist leaning over and beaming a grin at him, taking perhaps a little too much pleasure in her victory.

"Vermeil ... because vampires are innately weak to silver, but it tarnishes."

"And gold is sacred, so it holds blessings longer, right?" Philip asked, directing his addition to Hugo.

"Correct and correct."

Even Brontë looked impressed and Philip had a chance to puff his chest, before Hugo knocked that air right out of his sails.

"I'm afraid *one* point hardly puts you equal with my apprentice, Brother Philip –"

"It sounds like you are all having a pleasant time."

Every stool in the room scraped back against the marble floor as all three of them evacuated their seats, standing upon hearing Cyril's voice. His one eye wandered from Brontë, to Philip, over to Hugo and back again.

"Father, good afternoon." Hugo wiped his hands on his apron as he bowed. "Are you here for the prosphora?"

"I am. Is it ready?"

"Ready and waiting, Father. One moment."

Hugo shuffled away, thumbing through his key ring to unlock the brass gate that protected a cupboard tucked into the rear of the pantry. As he waited, Cyril's gaze slid back to Brontë and Philip, who were still giggling and arguing under their breath about the points they'd earned in their little game. Really, were those two *always* together?

"Brother Philip."

Philip immediately straightened up and shut his mouth, blushing from his button nose to the tips of his tawny ears. "Yes, Father?"

Cyril made him wait, drowning in nerves, while he lazily pulled his pocket watch from his sash to check the time. "Where is your partner? It is not yet suppertime. Have you both finished your chores early?"

"Ah – Sister Jael was polishing tack, I believe."

"And you have left her to do this task alone?"

"I'll go check if she needs another pair of hands right away!"

"Better."

Philip bowed and undid the apron about his waist, setting it over the stool beside Brontë as he nearly sprinted out of the bakery via the rear courtyard. Brontë stepped aside to let him go, glancing back up at Cyril to find him staring rather intently at her. She withered under his gaze and awkwardly busied herself with folding up the discarded apron. Luckily, she was spared any critique of her own time management by Hugo bustling back through the door with a linen-wrapped loaf of round bread. He unwrapped it and set it down in front of Cyril – giving him an opportunity to inspect it. Brontë, too, even though she backed away a pace out of respect, couldn't resist standing up on her tiptoes to get a peek for herself.

Bread of the quality Hugo prepared for the Sacrament was something Brontë could never even hope to achieve. It was made from the finest flour, baked to a perfect pale gold, and stamped with the sacred seal and lettering of the Order. All of this was done with absolute precision, even the loaf itself was a perfect round shape – something she'd never achieved with her own hands.

"You have done masterful work, as always. Thank you, Brother Hugo."

The baker beamed, proud to have Cyril's approval, and wrapped the loaf back up, tying it with twine and handing it off to Cyril.

32

THE COMPETITIVE, CHILDISH PRIDE WITH WHICH a great many young folk indulged in vampire blood was a pitiable thing. The novelty of the newest vice was a contest with no winner. Yet many an adrenaline-rush-seeking adventurer, many a far-too-sheltered rebellious spirit, many a pariah child volunteered themselves. Eager to spend their pocket money on whatever they could afford, believing themselves the outlier. That *they* would not become addicted, that the church was far too conservative, that the old timers of Windermere were just a little *too* superstitious – and really, who cared about their opinions anyway?

Such was the attitude of two young men. Both scrappy, with short hair and dirty faces as they huddled over a tiny bottle. It was no longer than their little finger. A skinny, carefully corked bottle of liquid money. It had cost them both a good amount, after all. One of them rather fearlessly held it up to the lantern light as they sat on a bench. The boys were so busy giggling between themselves that they didn't take any notice of the horse approaching behind them. A hand suddenly swiped the vial right out of their fingers.

"Oi!" one boy said.

They both leaped angrily off their bench, turning around to face the thief. One of them even put his hand on the hilt of his sword. It was half drawn from his belt when he stopped, stammering out in disbelief. The Archbishop sat astride a mean-looking ebony destrier covered with scars. Cyril glared down at him, eyeing his sword – which he quietly put away.

The other boy, however, was not quite as stunned. He was irreverent, maybe out of a need to overcompensate for his embarrassment. Or perhaps that was the alcohol on his breath. One or the other. He laughed and shoved his friend's shoulder, making a lousy show of bowing to Cyril. He almost tumbled over in the process.

"If it isn't His Excellency! Come down from on high to grace us commoners with his presence!"

"Come down to judge us, more like," the other boy said sheepishly.

"Come on, old man, let us have a little fun!"

Cyril heard very little of what they said to him. He was turning the vial of blood over in his hand, and held it up to the lamplight between his fingers, before he smirked. They watched as he shook his head, sighing at the two of them.

"Oh, I'll not interrupt your fun." He tossed the vial back to the boys, who fought to catch it and nearly cracked their heads together in the process. "What you have there is pig's blood. Good evening."

With that, Cyril tipped the brim of his hat and clicked his tongue, urging Adra – his warhorse – off down the road.

Ambrose was so focused on reading the note and request from a patient of his that he almost didn't hear the horseshoes echoing through the alley. Only when he stopped to get his bearings did he realize the noise was rather close. Not the horseshoes – that was normal enough – but a sort of soft, jingling noise: rosary beads. He instinctively pressed himself against the wall. Tucked beneath an archway in a nondescript alley, he peeked down to the intersecting roads a level below him.

Empty, save for a single lamplighter going about their work. They used that long instrument of theirs to close the glass shell about the flame. Ambrose called himself a fool and smiled. But then, a shadow loomed large over the far wall. The silhouette of a horse and rider slowed to a stop. The rider resituated a familiar pointed hat upon his head. Ambrose swallowed hard and stared at the shadow. To his relief, Cyril turned away, and the shadow slipped around a corner as the rider went in the opposite direction.

Ambrose was sure he'd spend the rest of his walk toward his patient's home trying to stop his hands from trembling. He was on much higher alert, now. It grew darker quickly. As he climbed further and further into the eastern borough, he noticed everything. The subtle scuffling and scratching on the other side of the walls, the sound of roof tiles being disturbed, the clink of rosary beads. His steps slowed as he heard the footsteps behind him grow louder, bolder.

Then, up ahead a gold weapon glowed in the dark: a sword. A Hunter emerged from the shade of the arched pathway above. Ambrose huffed in exasperation, turning to look behind himself at the other: a Huntress. She approached from the opposite direction, with a similarly brilliant weapon. Bright, unblemished gold in cautious but confident hands. He groaned.

"You two look young. Eager to earn your scars, your stories, hm?"

Neither Philip nor Jael answered him. He frowned, but stood his ground. Beneath his composure, his legs were tense – ready to run at a moment, should he have to. His hand gripped his briefcase so tightly he thought it might cramp up.

"Give me no trouble," he said calmly. "I am a doctor. Like your Clerics, I do no harm."

"You won't find honor for old laws here, monster," Jael said behind him.

"I do no harm," he repeated. "Let me pass."

They stood close now. Far too close for comfort. He could feel the heat of their weapons. Ambrose slowly reached for the hilt of his rapier.

"Let me –"

He didn't have a chance to finish his sentence. Jael saw Ambrose reach for his sword and let fly an arrow to stop him. He hissed in surprise and twisted to avoid the gold line that came arcing for him. Philip leaped at him right after. Ambrose yelled despite himself and hopped back. He awkwardly parried that awful, red-hot weapon with his briefcase. He kept trying to tumble out of the way, trying to dive between Philip's legs, but these Hunters chose their partners well, and even the young duet were a force to be reckoned with. He smashed his briefcase into Philip's head; a backhanded slap that made the contents rattle, made the young elf stagger.

They were trying to back him up against the wall. Every time those weapons hit the stone; they threw up horrible sparks that clung to him like hot ash. Jael shattered an arrow off the wall and sprayed gold into his eyes. He tried to dart closer to her, so that she was unable to use her bow effectively, but she merely let it fall away and relied instead upon her quiver of arrows. Jael was nimbler than Philip, lighter of foot and smaller in stature. She made for a much harder target. Quick as Ambrose was, and as hard as he pushed her back, it was all he could do to deflect her arrows. They flitted about her like wasps, answering Jael's whispered incantations as she sent them after Ambrose's eyes, his belly, his legs.

Philip landed a hard slice to his shoulders and Ambrose shouted a curse in defeat. He bit hard into his hand. A quick motion, and a red thread of blood spilled to life as he finally tore his rapier from his belt. His blood slithered about the air and wound around his wrist, weaving a path down his hand to his rapier, threading through it like a needle. It made the blade whine, almost as if in dismay, in disapproval.

"He seeks to bewitch us," Philip shouted. "Have care!"

Ambrose whipped around hard and fast, piercing for the closest black blur he saw. Philip yelled as he saw Jael's head snap back and her feet leave the ground. She thudded to the road and her arrows shattered into nothing as Ambrose scrambled out of Philip's way. The Hunter came slashing for him – trying to reach Jael.

His was a shoddy incantation; Ambrose did not have much practice with the magic. But it served as his only defense, here. And it was enough to induce fright. One nick from that bloodied blade could render a human subservient. Well, it could, in the hands of a different vampire. Ambrose didn't have such an inclination, and neither did his blood. But the Hunters didn't know that. It worked in his favor, now. The smell of his blood, even with their protective charms, was smothering. Like a haze, it threatened to distract them, to calm them, make them easy prey.

Philip reached Jael. Her eyes were open, though nonresponsive. Blood bubbled from beneath her chin, spoiling the brilliant white of her coif. Philip squinted and realized in horror that he could see, through her open mouth, the bloody needle that had pierced her chin. He stood protectively over her, held his fist over his heart and whispered into it.

"I seek a reunion!"

The spell sent a flare up, an imitation star that hovered above the rooftops and dripped liquid light. A call for help that never went unanswered. Ambrose saw it and knew it was only a matter of time.

"I am a doctor!" Ambrose repeated again, chest heaving. "I do not wish to fight!" He kept the tip of his bloodied rapier up and tried to back away.

Philip saw him set his feet, as if to flee, and burned with indignation. "Oh, no you don't!"

He leaped at Ambrose again. It took more effort now to protect himself from the piercing needle of this vampire's rapier. The haze was heavy, smothering. But a fire burned in his breast – a spark of defiant life that kept him focused and alert, at no risk of succumbing to Ambrose's spell. He resisted the twisted magic that, to him, smelled of cornflowers, ripe wheat, and clover honey. He had no time for daydreams or idealistic summers – he had to protect his partner. Gold sparks flashed against red droplets when the blades met. Every parry from Philip sent glass-like shards of blood clattering to the cobblestones at their feet, more needles that could pierce if he wasn't careful.

Ambrose tried to swipe at Philip's head again with his briefcase, but Philip saw it coming this time. He snaked his saber between his wrist and the briefcase. The hard twist he made almost snapped Ambrose's wrist. He howled in pain and his briefcase flew out of his hand. It thudded to the ground of the alleyway some feet away. He was about to dive to retrieve it when that soft jingle sounded.

Ambrose's throat went tight. A puff of white-hot breath from the black destrier was the only way to see the horse and rider in the dark. A Hunter's call for help never went unanswered.

Ambrose did not wait. He made a broken sound and the thread snapped, reverting back to ordinary, liquid blood that splattered to the ground. He turned and ran. He left his briefcase. It was not worth his life. He could make another poultice for the patient.

Horseshoes thundered behind him, loud as his heartbeat in his ears. He skidded around corners and leaped over iron railings. He cut as many paths as he could, trying to go where a horse could not follow.

He was swift and lithe, and thank goodness he was. Ambrose slid beneath a gap in a stack of empty fruit crates that cluttered up an alleyway. He thanked his luck, but a metallic crack and the sound of splintering wood told him the obstacle hadn't provided the cover he'd hoped for. Adra leaped over the debris nimbly enough, smashing through whatever was left after Cyril destroyed it with his chain whip.

Ambrose scrambled toward the embankment. There was no second-guessing. He hurled himself over the banister and fell, plunging into the ice-cold river below. Down, down he went. The water was crushing. Pitch black in the night and so very cold. But he swam down, as deep as he could. His lungs burned, crying out at the discomfort – but he could endure that burn. He could not endure the Father's. He fought what remained of his human instinct to gasp for breath, knowing it'd only fill his lungs with water. He'd survive either way. Ambrose reached the riverbed and grabbed onto a boulder, his body drifting with the current as he clung to it, to keep himself from floating up.

Horse and rider were poised on the embankment above. Adra huffed with exertion as Cyril glared into the water. But staring at the black waters would avail him little, and he had a wounded young Huntress to tend to. And so, he turned around and went back up the road.

33

$\mathcal{I}$NSTEAD OF THE MAIN INFIRMARY – the hall lined with beds segregated by curtains – Jael had been taken to the upper floor, where private rooms were available. She had a soft, damp rag over her eyes. It had been doused in a cooling bath of herbal water and similarly saturated with magic, serving now to numb pain and memory both as Benjamin worked.

His hands were steady as he withdrew the needle, lethally barbed and harder than diamond, from her chin. With no way to pry open her mouth, he would have to treat the damage done by removing the barbs after. He was limited by his protective mask, but proved deft enough to withdraw it. He held the crystalline dart in a pair of bloodied medical forceps, dropping it into a tray placed beside Jael on the bed. He had only just set it down when Cyril came into the room, having washed and donned his stole.

"How much blood has she lost?"

"I'm not sure. I sent for her brother already. Sister Nadine can give blood as well, if need be."

"It would be better if her brother shows in time."

Cyril took the tray with the awful dart aside. Setting his palm over it, he mumbled an admonishment under his breath. The needle vibrated, then released – splattering over the dish as a liquid once again. A snap from Cyril's hand, and it was burned away. Completely unmade. He set the tray aside, to be properly cleaned later.

With the source of the magic gone, Benjamin was free to remove his mask. Cyril approached Jael's opposite side. It was unclear how far the bolt had gone up into the roof of her mouth, unclear how much blood had been lost. But flesh could be mended. A different threat still loomed large: her blood had been touched by a vampire's. It'd eat her alive like a rabid infection if left to fester. There was but one way to purge it. Like any other vampiric impurity, it could be burned out by the flame. But how much of her own damaged blood would be lost? The longer he waited, the more she would lose.

"Please hold her still while I work."

Cyril hovered his hand over Jael's head. Even Benjamin could feel the incredible heat. Jael coughed and strained, and Benjamin had to expend more energy than he expected to hold her down. Black, oily blood began to drip from her nose and the roof of her open mouth. Tiny beads oozed out of the pores around her lips. All of it flowed against gravity, drawn up toward Cyril's other hand. But it also resisted, clinging in long beaded lines to Jael's face like tendrils. An infection that did not want to give up its hard-won host.

"It's infected more of her than I expected." Cyril straightened up and called toward the Clerics near the door. "Where is her brother?"

"We sent Hunters to fetch him, but no word yet."

A beneficial transfusion of blood relied heavily on familial connection. Any compatible donor could give, in an emergency such as this, but to artificially muddy the bloodline was less than ideal. Sister Nadine would likely be only one of several donors required, as so much of what she gave would be rejected first. Far better to have family provide to their own, when possible. It made for a gentler procedure, less stress upon the recipient's body. Such was the simple science of blood transfusion that the church, in all her regions, claimed such mastery over.

Leaning forward, Cyril put his hand over Jael's mouth, and flames erupted from that hand. Brilliant gold and blindingly bright, it engulfed her head and the pillow beneath her. A faint voice seemed to screech at the injustice, as the black sludge that had leaked out of her was burned away. Her veins flickered under her gray skin, glowing lines like lightning striking up and down her body as the poison was burned out. She arched and her voice caught in her throat, less a word from her and more a forced reaction of her muscles constricting in shock. It was hot, and intense, but that whine of injustice finally crackled and faded. The blood staining her nose ran pure and red, and no longer answered to the flame. The heat dissipated, and Cyril and Benjamin gently lowered her back down to the bed as her body went limp again.

Sister Nadine had already removed her sleeves and was preparing to proffer her arm. But before Benjamin could fit the needle, the door opened once more. A young Hunter let Jael's twin brother, Emre, into the room. His face was contorted with something between anger and distress. Sticky with sweat from running, and still half-dressed in his lamplighter attire, he had already rolled up his sleeve as he raced over to his sister's bedside.

Cyril took Nadine aside to thank her, and to hand off the tray in need of cleaning. Benjamin handled the blood transfusion, ordering a chair set next to Jael's bed so Emre had somewhere comfortable to sit for the duration of the procedure. Thanks to the enchanted rag over Jael's eyes, and the swiftness with which the clergy worked, she slowly came to with no recollection of the grisly affair; of the fire in her veins, or the barbed bolt in her head.

Jael was confused at first. Disoriented, but comforted enough by her brother's presence. Benjamin could manage pain and stem bleeding, the latter of which he did with more of those white threads, employing them as sutures to close both internal and external wounds. She would be sore, and bedridden, and barely able to move her mouth ... but she would be alright. Emre, too, would eventually overcome his fright. To be suddenly accosted by a pair of Hunters in the lamplighters' stable yard and informed of such dire news still had his heart racing.

With Jael stitched and bandaged properly, Florence was Jael's first official visitor. She ruffled Emre's hair, pleased to see him – though wishing it'd been better circumstances that finally coerced him to visit.

"The pain is something terrible, I know," said Florence to Jael as she sat down on the edge of the bed. "But the tongue heals quick! Trust me, I'd know. Look – why, you and I could be twins now, too."

Florence stuck her tongue out playfully, revealing the piercing that she wore through her tongue and making it catch on her front teeth. Jael smiled weakly, a bit of laughter twinkling in her eyes. She squeezed Emre's hand where he sat next to her, still with the needle pierced into the crook of his elbow and the line of life attaching them.

Thinking the room now quite crowded, and their work done, Benjamin and Cyril excused themselves, walking together downstairs and into the eastern chapel.

"An unlucky blow," Benjamin said as they walked. "To pierce in such a place and not be blocked by her coif."

"She was lucky the blood was weak. The vampire must have been young."

They were both so engrossed in their conversation, muttering this or that about the injury, the confiscated briefcase, and the escaped vampire that they did not notice a rather ostentatious fellow wandering between the pews at first.

He was looking this way and that, leaning back a bit to peek around pillars, in that sort of textbook fashion of naughty ne'er-do-wells. Cyril's voice trailed off as he noticed the man, and he nudged Benjamin to walk with him, across the nave and toward the bloke – who was lurking suspiciously close to the reliquary gate.

"You won't be able to pass those," Cyril said, and made the man jump out of his skin.

He turned around and went beet red, rubbing the back of his head awkwardly. When he moved, he made a jingling noise – the sound of loose coins, rattling about somewhere on him they shouldn't be. Benjamin shook his head and adjusted his glasses.

"Ah, Excellency! I was just ... looking ..."

"Of course you were." Cyril didn't bother playing that game. He raised his cane and delivered a hard whack on the back of the man's hand at his side.

"Father!" Benjamin grabbed Cyril's arm.

A surprised squeal came from the man, followed thereafter by a hollow clunk. His gloved hand popped right off and fell to the floor. It rolled around, trailing in a circle the loose bit of string that had been holding it to the man's arm. A handful of copper coins clattered over the floor, having been hidden inside the glove.

Cyril completely ignored Benjamin and stared pointedly at the man, who held his stump of a right arm to his chest. A telling sign, and one that he'd deliberately tried to hide. Thieves lost their hands in Windermere, both as a lesson and a warning to others. Attempting to hide it was considered another crime in and of itself.

"I am a forgiving man, but forgiveness does not equate to naivety. Now shake it out."

The man winced under his words and bent over awkwardly to fetch his wooden hand. He held up his good hand in surrender, dutifully shaking the false one until the last coin fell out from between the leather and the wood. Cyril looked down and mentally counted the coins now scattered over the floor before him.

"Disgraceful. You could earn double this in a day, if you were but willing to do honest work."
Cyril shook Benjamin's hand away, stepping closer to the stuttering man. "Shall I call for the Guard, then? Have them make an example of your other hand? Or drag you to Coldwater to be whipped out, hm?"
The man backed away.

"No need, Excellency, sir!" he stammered hastily. "I have heard your wisdom! Why, I'll make a right change, I will. I've seen the error of my –"

"Spare me your blathering," Cyril interrupted him. "If you are still in my church by the time I count to ten, I shall cut off your other hand myself, and beg both my Lady and the Guard's pardon after. One –"

Cyril shook his cane. With a click, the threaded blades dropped into a ready position. The thief fell backward over himself, scrambling down the aisle of pews and bolting for the door. Though, not before tripping once more at the little step he missed, that sent him sprawling out over the granite floor in a puddle.

"Was threatening to sever his hand really necessary?" Benjamin approached Cyril's side and murmured to him as the thief fled.

"Strictly speaking, no –" Cyril chuckled and Benjamin winced a bit at the hollow sound of the wooden hand hitting the floor, again. "But more amusing. Besides." Cyril clicked his cane back into form. "A bit of fear makes for a more memorable lesson. Better an empty threat from me than a beating at Coldwater."

Benjamin tucked his hands into his sleeves and side-eyed Cyril behind his glasses. Empty threat indeed.

34

ESPITE BROTHER HUGO'S ROUND, CHUBBY CHEEKS and equally chubby belly, he had a solid frame of muscle lurking beneath his huggable appearance. He selected and hoisted a generous sack of flour on one of his shoulders, nudging the door to the pantry shut with one foot as he carried it into the bakery proper.

"Right, new flour. See to it the jars are topped up tonight, aye?"

He thunked it down beside Brontë, who puffed hair out of her face and nodded. He then rolled his sleeves up and sat down at his workstation, thumbing through a big cookbook. Brontë had barely wiggled the flour closer to her on the floor when her nose wrinkled.

"Are you sure? This one smells off."

"Eh? Nonsense. That's brand new."

"If you say so. Maybe something on the bag."

Brontë took the pair of kitchen shears and snipped through the seal crimped onto the bag of milled flour. As soon as she opened the sack, she frowned again.

"I'm not sure ... It looks fine. But I think this one's all moldy, Hugo. It smells awful." Brontë reached over and pulled a brass ladle from the counter, sifting through the suspiciously dry, visually spotless flour.

"Really?" Hugo huffed and hoisted himself off his stool. "Let me see."

As he reached her side, the ladle clinked against something. Both of them looked at one another. Hugo reached in and spread the flour out to either side, revealing four small, oddly shaped glass bottles tied together with twine. They were all heavily sealed with wax and contained a thick dark-red liquid.

"Mother above – that's vampire blood."

Brontë flinched and sucked in air through her teeth. She was suddenly afraid of the ladle and dropped it in the sack. Hugo maintained his composure a little better, grabbing the ladle and fishing around deeper. The ladle made a sound that suggested at least another bundle of bottles was present.

"You have a sensitive nose on you, lassie. With all that wax, I couldn't even smell it at all, and this rubbish gives me a nasty headache." He took the group of bottles from the top, tossing the ladle aside. "Close that sack right up."

Brontë wiped her hands on her apron and grimaced at the thought of touching the bag again. Hugo went over to the far side of the room, bundling up the bottles in a thick blanket of burlap.

"I'll let the Deacon know. Wait here. Not a word of this to anyone, not yet, not until we figure out what in the world's going on. Pah! That grimy grocer, no wonder he was giving me such trouble about the last delivery. When I see him again I ought to wring his scrawny neck –"

Hugo ranted and muttered as he tucked the burlap under his arm and hastened out of the bakery. Brontë pulled the cord about the top of the sack taut and tied a simple knot. All the while her stomach did flip-flops as that foul yet floral scent flooded her senses. How had he not noticed at all? It felt like it smothered the whole room, to her. She muttered her disapproval, telling herself she'd be better off focusing on her work. She took a single step away and froze.

Something called for her. A voice? Many voices. They all seemed to whisper from the sack, speaking her name. A desperate plea, a kind-hearted invitation to come closer and drink deep. The chorus of whispers practically demanded it. A prickling sensation crawled up her spine. She was too terrified to look behind her, trembling something fierce. She took a deep breath and, summoning all of her courage, marched swiftly toward the rear door. She slammed it shut as she rushed outside. In the safety of the courtyard, she sucked in a grateful breath of fresh air. Vampire blood was known well for its deep, dark magic, and she knew better than to tempt fate in such a way.

By the time she had collected herself and returned to the doorway, the bakery had filled with worried-looking clergy. Benjamin was standing quietly against the far wall, hands tucked into his sleeves as always. At least, she assumed it was Benjamin. He had donned that awful mask as a precaution. He observed as Florence ripped open the sack and fished around inside for the other bundle. A quick search revealed only one other heretical bundle of contraband spoiling otherwise perfect flour. There was a low rumble of deliberation. Concern over who might have tried to smuggle it in, followed by Hugo's insistence that the good-for-nothing grocer had clearly made a mistake, as evidenced by his earlier behavior.

All deliberation ceased and a hush fell over the room as Cyril entered, followed by Maddoc, who had gone to fetch him. Cyril took the proffered bundle from Florence, lip curling slightly as he hefted it in his hand. He and Benjamin exchanged a look. If Cyril had any particular suspicion, he didn't reveal it – and, well, no one knew what Benjamin was thinking. Cyril spoke with an ease that helped settle the sky-high nerves in the room.

"I suggest we stop cluttering up our baker's workspace and carry on this conversation elsewhere." He raised his voice slightly. "That includes you lot, listening from the corridor."

A shuffle and scuttling of feet sounded as a few nosy Clerics and Hunters scattered in the hallway. Benjamin and Cyril spoke as Florence dusted flour from her blouse's sleeves, creating a miniature blizzard that Brontë knew she'd get stuck cleaning up. She was frowning at the idea when she realized Cyril was looking at her.

"Come here."

She wordlessly did as she was bid, thankful that Cyril passed off the vials to Benjamin, who wrapped them up in the burlap from before and bore them swiftly away, and their stench with them. He meanwhile tongued his cheek as she drew nearer, as she tricked his mind into thinking he could taste something pleasant and sweet and far too similar to the blood he'd sent away with Benjamin.

"Brother Hugo says you found the vials. Is this true?"

She nodded, pointing at the sack and gesturing as she spoke. "I thought it smelled off. I didn't realize that's what was causing it."

"Your senses are sharp. Well done."

Brontë stood up a bit straighter despite herself. His praise hit her like a bolt from the blue. He saw her straighten up a touch, a little hint of pride seeming to swell in her chest at being of service to him, and to her peers. She didn't wither under his gaze this time. *How endearing.* He scanned the bakery and pushed his mind back to the matter at hand. "Have you noticed it anywhere else?"

Brontë shook her head. "No. Though, there may be more in the pantry? I don't recall what all was delivered in the last order and what wasn't –"

"It was just this one," Hugo interjected, sucking in a deep breath after he chugged a glass of water and some tablets Benjamin had given him to keep his headache away. "Ol' Greer was kicking up a fuss just after delivering it, blaming a heavy thumb, that mangy, sorry excuse for a –"

"Thank you, Brother," Cyril cut off his insults.

"Is it particularly potent, then?" Brontë asked.

"I am not sure. We'll keep it under lock until we know how dangerous it is to handle, and how to best dispose of it."

"Well ..." Brontë's voice trailed off as she debated mentioning how it tried to speak to her, but thought it better not to incriminate herself in such a way. At least not now, with Hugo present to hear.

"Well?"

She shook her head.

Cyril realized he wasn't going to get an answer. "Come to me immediately if you notice it again. Even if you're unsure, come find me at once."

"Yes, Father."

"Good. Thank you." Cyril straightened up and spoke to Florence, who was still shaking flour out of her shirt. "Sister Florence, please search the rest of the flour for any other contraband. Brother Hugo and Miss Brontë will assist you. Report your findings to Brother Maddoc."

Florence bowed her head and began rolling up her sleeves. "Aye, aye."

With that, Cyril departed, walking just a bit faster than usual to catch up with Benjamin and the awful parcel they needed to inspect. Benjamin was waiting for Cyril in his office. There was a quiet sense of urgency as they descended together into the library, retracing a path back to the workroom – where the first empty vial was kept under such aforementioned lock and key.

The comparison was hardly needed, but the confirmation was provided nonetheless. The same strange shape and design to the glass. One spent bottle, from a dead cobbler. Two clean bottles, brand new and plucked from a confiscated briefcase. And now four full bottles, smuggled into his own church.

Cyril carefully scraped away some of the wax that flooded the stopper, partially undoing whatever magic seal was woven into the wax to suffocate and stifle the contents. The full vial nearly rambled on in conversation with itself, a chorus of curses and curiosity that took even the two priests some effort to ignore. Less a true noise and more a nasty prickle on the skin, an itch inside one's mind. Nothing like the typical vampire blood they so often confiscated. Cyril shut the scraped vial inside a lockbox.

Benjamin kept his mask on as a precaution through it all, speaking quietly from behind it. "Sending it directly to us? That's a catastrophic mistake."

Cyril glared at the lockbox as he moved to pull a cord that would summon one of the Cardinals. "Someone has overplayed their hand."

35

OMINGO ALREADY HAD HIS EYES SET ON THE CATHEDRAL, his teeth already gritted in preemptive annoyance at dealing with the Archbishop, when summons of a different nature reached him. He sighed and, knowing he had no choice, he departed southwest, toward Dunrior.

Upon reaching the palace, he was not, as he had expected to be, shown into the drawing room. Instead, the butler led him on a long and frankly absurdly windy path through the gardens. Said path let out onto the flat, meticulously well-groomed garden. A modest pavilion was placed in the center, at the intersection of two gravel paths. It was quite a distance from the palace, he noticed. A clear line of sight, but no opportunity for prying ears to lurk.

Lady Isabel was sitting at a small table laden with all manner of afternoon tea treats. She was garbed in a flowing pale sunset gown, a well-fitted jacket with puffed sleeves, and a woven hat adorned with flowers. At her feet lay two slim athletic dogs – one white and one red – contentedly panting away as they surveyed their mistress's domain. As usual, she seemed somewhat out of place amongst the dreary backdrop of this cold city.

"Captain, how kind of you to oblige me." She held out her hand expectantly, forcing him not only to come close enough to kiss it, but also to bow his head low before her to do so. It was just as underwhelming to her as the first time.

"It is a pleasure, my lady."

She rolled her eyes and smiled. "Oh, relax, segnor. You are here as my guest. Please, sit." She dropped down into their shared language as he begrudgingly took a seat opposite her. "I would better understand your mind."

"And practice your Azusan, *segnora*," he said. "You're surprisingly fluent for not having lived there in over a decade."

"You truly are quite the avid researcher."

"You are easy to learn about, my lady."

"I suppose that is true. But *I* have done research of my own." She smiled and made an obvious show of inspecting him. "I would never think it by looking at you, a powerful battlemage."

"I am of passing skill."

"And humble," she sneered. "Or a liar."

He frowned and she straightened up, quite happy to have a reaction. "Even the papers spoke of your prowess for detecting and deflecting magic. I cannot help but wonder, then, what you make of the church's magic."

"I lament that my lady is unlikely to find my opinion agreeable to her own."

"All the more reason for me to know it." She poured him a cup of tea. "Though, as I said before, I wish to know your mind. I suspect I have a strong grasp of your opinion already. I wish to know what engenders such a strong opinion." She held out his cup of tea for him in a bejeweled hand, watching expectantly as he took it and set it down before him.

"Frankly, I am somewhat suspicious of the Archbishop and his heavily militarized, magic-wielding guard."

Isabel at once rolled her eyes and gave a dismissive toss of her head. "The Hunters are hardly a military."

Domingo's lip twitched, but he realized quickly that arguing that point with the lady would be futile. He shifted the topic elsewhere. "Lady Sinclair – do you not find the situation odd?"

"Find what odd?"

"Have you ever *seen* a vampire, my lady?"

"Not knowingly, I don't suppose."

"And therein arises my suspicion."

"I'm afraid I do not understand what you mean."

"The only people who can claim to have seen these so-called *vampires* are the Hunters, and the dead."

"What are you insinuating, Captain?"

"I insinuate nothing." He picked a stray flower petal off his hat in his lap. "I only make an observation. In a city-state so isolated from the world, so deep in her own superstitions, it would be easy for a cult ... for an *institution,* to capitalize on such fear."

"A cult." Isabel couldn't resist a chuckle. "You have such a negative opinion of the church."

"I am not a religious man," he stated bluntly.

Isabel eyed the medals worn at his breast. Those gilt tags with inscriptions engraved on either side. They were a mark of rank and a conduit for magic, both. Each unique to the carrier, and worthless as a magical tool in anyone else's hands. In that sense, they weren't dissimilar from the church's belt rosaries.

"Oh? But you knights employ faith, don't you?" She smiled slyly.

Domingo saw her staring and put a protective hand over his medals. "Ours is a science. There is no unknowable god, and no blind faith involved. With your years spent in the capital, I would have assumed you might know this."

"Oh, I've heard my fair share." She snickered. Her tone was mocking. "The capital's alchemists would always say the same thing. A 'precise calculus', they call it. All your rigid rules and your equations."

"Yes." He sipped his tea, mostly to calm himself down lest he snap anything else at her.

"My Lord Vidal never had much talent for Monocerian magic. But you, I am told, have mastered even the fetters."

"I have some ability."

More humility, she thought. But it appeared to be enough, and Domingo regretted saying it.

"I should very much like to see a display of your ability."

His scowl made her almost beam with delight, but she restrained herself.

"My fetters are not to be used for *entertainment* –"

"Entertainment?" She smiled. "Why, I only wish to know that I can trust my Captain of the Guard with my safety." She didn't wait for an answer, gesturing out from the shade of the pavilion to a tree some twenty paces away on the green. "I instructed my gardener not to prune that sickly branch for just this reason. Do you see it, Captain?"

Domingo followed her hand, and indeed saw the wilting branch. One twig with drooping yellowed leaves amidst all the green.

"Do indulge me, segnor," she said. "And do good for the tree besides."

Before she'd finished, Domingo pointed at the tree. All it took was a flick of that hand and a murmured equation to set the path to the tree and back, and cool magic leaped obediently to do as he bid. Pale blue lines, sharp and angular, raced from point to point until they wrapped about the branch and snapped it off at the base. He shifted in his chair and huffed into his teacup after having done so, and the magic fizzled into nothing.

"Brilliantly done, segnor. You are no liar at all, only humble."

He did not seem to value her flattery, by the discontent on his face.

"And so, *this* magic is acceptable to you," she continued, moderating her tone a touch, perhaps out of a newfound respect for him – but probably not. "But the church's magic is not?"

"Their magic is not typical," he whispered out from behind his teacup.

"Enlighten me, Captain. For I am no great scholar of these arts."

Though her words were spoken with her usual haughty air – there was something genuine behind them; an intelligent curiosity Domingo might have found charming if it had been present in any other woman.

"They carry those rosaries, yes. They're a conduit, like any other, a link back to their source – I understand this much of their workings. But the church's source is ... nebulous. No other magic I have encountered behaves this way."

Isabel couldn't resist a smile as she listened to him, restraining a giggle at this methodical, logical man trying to make sense of something so contrary to his own perception of the world.

"And what 'way' is that, segnor?"

It's more than the rosaries, Domingo thought. *The Archbishop doesn't carry magic, he's infected by it like a fever.* He flexed his hand at the thought, remembering how uncomfortable Cyril's hand had been: almost painfully hot. *It wasn't natural.*

"They wear their magic differently," he settled on saying. "As if it is internal to them."

"Your observation makes sense. They eat their magic, after all."

"Pardon?"

Her mouth fell open in surprise. "Surely you knew that much already? Of the blessed bread and wine?"

Domingo tilted his head at this new information. He wasn't sure how he liked it. Of course, he knew of their ritual. The Sacrament, as they called it. But that was symbolic, wasn't it? Even the layfolk partook of that ritual. *Were they, too, infected with magic?* He'd observed no such infection. The very idea that it could be lurking alarmed him, and yet almost made him smile. An explanation for the civilians' exceptional piety. His mind was mulling over this information so intently that Isabel could do nothing but smile.

"My, my. You pick and choose what you research, don't you? I'm far more flattered you spent your time thinking of me."

He glared at her, but she simply shook her head.

"Perhaps you should go to her, learn about Our Beloved Lady. That is, assuming you have not already made yourself unwelcome on her grounds. That would be terrible for diplomacy, wouldn't it?"

A KNOCK SOUNDED ON CYRIL'S OFFICE DOOR, and he looked up.

Brontë poked her head into the room. "Father, may I speak to you about the blood that was found?"

Cyril nodded, but held up his hand before letting her speak. He stood and brushed past her, writing that usual seal upon the door to prevent unwanted listeners. When he approached her to speak, he stood rather close. He loomed over her, so much so she instinctively took a step back.

"Did you notice anything else?"

Brontë hand one of her hands pressed to her stomach, but shook her head. "No, no. Florence searched everything with us. Perhaps it's only my nerves. but ever since I was near it, my head has been ringing, and I feel quite ill." She grimaced slightly. "It ... tried to speak to me?"

"Did you listen?"

"Did I –? No, of course not!" she breathed. "I fled."

"Good. You must never listen." Cyril nodded, circling his desk and fishing a key from his sash.

"Is that ... typical?" she asked. "That it speaks in such a way?"

"Not typical, but plenty possible. It stands to reason that you would be particularly sensitive to hearing it."

Brontë frowned, but inwardly mulled over a newfound respect for the blood she thought she knew. The Hunters often wore the remnants of it on their clothes and skin. Father, Philip, Jael ... they all would have that smell on them. But it never *spoke*, not like that.

Cyril opened a drawer, and a compartment hidden within, to pull a small vial of a familiar gold liquid from it.

Brontë tilted her head curiously. "Oh ... would my normal medicine help? I have more still, and I know you have said it's difficult for you to make –"

"This is slightly different."

How wonderfully vague, she thought. He held it up to a candle and turned it over. It looked entirely the same, to her.

"It will not help with your hunger," he said. "But it should soothe any minor aches or pains. At worst, it will have no effect at all, and we will try something else."

Another knock sounded and one of the Hunters stationed on the opposite side of the door spoke just loud enough to be heard. "Father, the Captain of the Guard is here to see you."

Cyril gestured for Brontë to stand beside his desk. She quietly obeyed, her hands folded neatly in front of her, as he bid his unexpected guest be allowed inside. Domingo brushed leisurely past the Hunter, arm resting on his broadsword at his hip. He hid his surprise well enough, but surprised he was all the same. Just who was *this* young lady?

Never mind the light that seemed to bleed from the reliquaries lining the office wall. Never mind the near-angry pulse of magic that radiated from Cyril's rosary at his hip. Domingo trusted his senses; they'd not steered him wrong yet – this young woman had more magic in her little finger than Cyril did in his whole body.

Violent, but timid – her magic swirled about in her breast, swam through her veins, jumped between her fingertips as she wrung them together, even fluttered about on her cheeks in a flush of color when she noticed the way Domingo was studying her.

And this young lady stood so very *close* to the Archbishop! A privilege he had only ever seen reserved for that bastard of a Deacon, or for clingy school babes. Domingo fought to keep his curiosity concealed as he stared at her.

"Oh?" he finally said. "I didn't know the Father had a little protégé."

Brontë's cheeks erupted into a deeper pink and she averted her eyes from this visitor. She shuffled a step closer to Cyril, practically hiding behind him. Cyril didn't bother acknowledging Domingo yet. He finished penning a small note, then held both it and the little vial of gold liquor out to Brontë. Domingo, of course, eyed that little bottle with suspicion – but the wax stopper and seal kept even his keen eyes blind to the contents. Whatever it was, it was something worth hiding.

"Take half of it now with something to eat, the other tomorrow morning with breakfast," Cyril said. "Come back after breakfast, and we'll see how you feel. Should you start to feel worse, come see me immediately."

"Yes, Father."

"Off you go."

Brontë took the items and excused herself with a small curtsy, moving past the visitor and giving him a small bow of her head. Mostly so as not to be rude, but also to avoid letting this man see the furious flush of color over her face.

Domingo had to fight his own features to betray nothing as she drew closer. She carried something crushing, overwhelming. He very nearly bowed his head to *her*, against all reason. And then she had gone from the room, and taken that presence with her. At least, most of it. He could swear that she lingered, now that he recognized her. Perhaps what he had mistaken for judgmental relics or echoing music was just ... her. She even seemed to loiter on the Archbishop, as he finally deigned to address him. Cyril rested his fingertips on his desk, seeming quite annoyed at the interruption, but forcing courtesy.

"An unexpected pleasure to receive you, Captain. What can I do for you?"

"An apprentice of yours?" Domingo couldn't help but ask.

"A patient," he corrected. "Now, what can I do for you?"

Domingo's mind was still reeling at the information he'd learned, and was now weighed down doubly by curiosity, but he knew better than to voice his thoughts and questions prematurely. He eyed the towering bookshelves and ornate reliquaries lining the wall, the gold chalices and carved angels that caught the light. They still dripped beaded threads of light, in his eyes. His skin crawled as he finally spoke.

"One of your priests confiscated the body of a dead man on Doubury Lane, as I understand."

"Our undertakers did their work at the request of a family in mourning," Cyril corrected him again. "Yes."

"And you did this because the deceased was presumed to be an addict, yes? An unforgivable act, in your law, is it not?"

"Our autopsy confirmed he was sinsick. Consuming vampire blood is a sin, as far as church law is concerned, yes. The townsfolk, too, have strong opinions on the matter."

"So I've gathered. The Royal Guard had to put down a riot on Doubury. The mob were moments away from burning the man's home down."

Cyril had half a mind to remind the good captain that this near riot had only escalated due to his knights preventing the Hunters from guarding the house. He decided to keep that opinion to himself.

"Yes, I was informed."

"They seem to take after you in your zealousness."

"I will take that as a compliment, and not the thinly veiled accusation of inciting arson that it is."

"I must have worded it wrong."

Cyril's good eye narrowed at Domingo, and he met the intensity of his look in kind.

"Have care where you start your fires, Excellency. Lest they burn you, too."

36

PUDDLES SLOSHED IN THE STREET WHERE WATER DRIZZLED lazily from rooftops. A gentle storm was showering the city, the thunder confined to far in the distance. Ambrose drew his collar and coat tight about him as he hopped out of the way of a carriage that trundled by. Having crossed the road, he wove nimbly down into the alleyways, taking sharp, memorized turns and even squeezing his slender frame through a gap in a wrought-iron fence. He had kept to these poorly lit and makeshift desire paths ever since his close encounter with the Hunters and their accursed leader. It'd been days, but the tremor still hadn't entirely left his hands.

He shoved open the door to the lower floor of his shop with his shoulder, closing it swiftly and rubbing his hands together, as if that would do any good to warm them. Crates of empty bottles and overflowing cabinets in need of organization would have to wait. He was tired, cold, and wet from the rain, and so he shuffled upstairs to start a fire and change clothes.

He shed his coat and hat, untying his cravat when a strange sound caught his attention. Jingling bells, maybe? Fear pounded in his chest. He listened for the sound of a horse and carriage, perhaps one of the cabs going down the road out front, but heard nothing. Again, the sound came. Somehow much heavier, as if dragging its feet. His neck craned back and forth, trying to discern the direction of the noise. He looked down at his hand. That horrible tremor had worsened. He chastised himself for his paranoia. It was only after looking down at his hand he noticed the oily-black cane leaning nonchalantly against the dining cabinet.

The bells clinked clearly this time. Alas, he realized belatedly his paranoia would have served him well, if only he'd listened to it. The sound had come from above. A black figure was crouching up in the rafters, and the sound was no bell at all. Gold chains tangled up through the beams, and were rattling as Cyril toyed with the blade at the end of his whip, as he spun it around his finger.

Ambrose was too slow to even yell in surprise. A gold blade flashed and a flutter of robes dove for him. Heat like nothing he'd known enveloped him. No ordinary Hunter had this burn. Chains snapped around him, writhing about as if they had a mind of their own. *Was this a live serpent or a weapon?* It seemed to crawl to life. He shouted in pain as the blade dug into his side, just below his ribs. Caught like a fly in a web, Cyril held him as he jabbed the blade deeper and deeper. Ambrose writhed and tasted his own blood, tossing his head the further the metal went. Ambrose felt tears, hot as the blessed metal, burning lines down his cheeks. A deft motion, and Cyril yanked the chain back out of him, tearing a new wound in his flesh. The chain was looped through his ribs.

When Cyril let him go, Ambrose was only halted from falling to the floor by the chain strung through his ribs. His bones creaked at supporting his weight. Awkwardly hung sideways from the rafters of his apartment, arms ensnared tight to his body, Ambrose's feet frantically tried to reach the floor below. He spluttered and screamed, overwhelmed by pain, by the burn. He tried to right himself, to no avail. Wherever those damn chains touched bare flesh, they burned. His side hissed and bubbled beneath what was left of his shirt.

He blubbered, coughing out broken sobs. Teary eyes could barely see Cyril walking over to retrieve his cane. He drew rather close, and Ambrose instinctively snapped at him, needle-sharp fangs clashing together. He was rewarded with a hard backhand, a stinging blow and a few scrapes from his rings as an added insult. Cyril grabbed his face and pulled him back, directing Ambrose's attention away from his own blood beginning to puddle on the floor, back up to himself. He spoke slowly, with a strangely quiet voice. It wasn't what Ambrose had expected.

"Pull yourself together. I would have words with you." Cyril looked around a moment before deciding to fetch one of the simple wooden dining-room chairs from the adjacent room of his apartment. He dragged it back toward Ambrose, setting it before him. "I am told this method of hanging is common for criminals in the south. An execution used for pirates and smugglers."

It was hard to see any other emotion on Ambrose's face other than anguish, but confusion seemed to wash over him. Cyril straddled the chair backward. He held up a familiar, oddly shaped bottle of blood to Ambrose. One of several bottles retrieved from the bakery – identical to those found in Ambrose's recovered briefcase.

"Fitting for you, don't you agree?"

It didn't take long for Ambrose to make out the object. He inhaled sharply and fidgeted in his binds, forcing words out through a bloodied bottom lip and a heavy tongue. "I'm not involved in that!"

"You're lying." Cyril sighed and reached into his breast pocket. "Prisoners are said to last some three days or more, when hanged by the ribs."

Ambrose visibly flinched, unsure of what he'd produce from his pocket – only to feel rather foolish when he harmlessly revealed a slim cigarette case.

"Now." Cyril clicked the case open. "While I do not have quite that much time to waste on you" – he tapped his cigarette against the back of his hand and smiled innocently – "you will find me to be a remarkably patient man."

"I only procure the bottles!"

Cyril clicked his lighter shut. "Keep talking."

"And enchant the wax … to seal them, that's it!" He coughed at the cigarette smoke, as if he needed the extra discomfort on top of the immeasurable pain. "That's all I do! She does the bleeding, not me!"

"She," Cyril repeated in annoyance. "Your mistress?"

Ambrose shut his mouth.

"Ah, I see. Your sire, perhaps? Poor lad. She's bewitched you, hasn't she?"

Ambrose fought to retain his composure.

Cyril took a long drag from his cigarette. "Thomas Greer is your mule, yes? Where is he taking …" – he turned the bottle over in his hand – "this filth?"

"I don't know!"

"You're lying again."

Ambrose began to cry in earnest. "I gain nothing by lying to you, Father!"

"Hm." He paused to think, glaring at the blood in the vial. "This isn't for humans, is it? This is for your own consumption."

Ambrose didn't answer. Cyril stood up from the chair. A quick scrape peeled back the wax and uncorked the vial. The smell of it, now freed from the wax, flooded the room – as did the cacophony of indistinct whispers that trickled from it.

"Curious. Just how potent is it, I wonder? Shall we test it?"

Too weak to snap at the Hunter now, and knowing better than to do so, Ambrose accepted Cyril's touch. He cupped Ambrose's face and tilted his chin up. Chains rattled as he weakly shook his head.

"I don't want it!" he whispered.

Cyril dug his thumb into the corner of Ambrose's mouth. "Don't fight me. Open."

Ambrose had to give to the pressure as his mouth was pried open.

Cyril smiled. "I have a pet with teeth like yours. You are young."

The second the first drop hit Ambrose's tongue, his eyes snapped open and his pupils constricted. His burnt flesh and open wounds bubbled and swelled, swallowing up his frayed clothes and even eating its way up the chain in an effort to stop blood flow. The new flesh burned itself on the blessed chains, which only made it overcompensate, climbing higher and swelling thicker. Anything, anything to regenerate and close the wound. Cyril pulled the vial away and put his thumb over the opening, containing the remaining blood. Foam and spittle pooled in the corners of Ambrose's mouth and his eyes glowed a sickly, hungry red in the dark.

"I see. It speeds your regeneration. How horribly useful." Cyril chuckled as, with his newfound strength and supposed numbness to pain, Ambrose thrashed about again in his binds. He seized violently, hands curling too hard and muscles cramping.

"And even you monsters can overindulge, it would appear. Fascinating."

There was no doubt in his mind. This explained why that fiend on the train had managed to come to within a day. He put a strangely soft hand on Ambrose's head, petting his hair. "You can put right some of the wrongs you've done. Here, with me. No one else will hear you. So, tell me: who is this mistress? Where is she sending the blood?"

Tears streamed down Ambrose's cheeks and he shuddered. He shook his head as he forced a reply, as if he didn't want to say, as if he would rather answer Cyril's questions, if only he could. "I will not betray my lady."

Cyril sighed and his hand fell from Ambrose's hair. He took up his cane in that hand. "I'm tired. I would prefer not to go to the trouble or effort of motivating you."

Cyril circled behind him. The cane whistled and struck Ambrose's thigh. He screamed and gouged himself deeper on the chain through his ribs. A second blow fell in the same place, and the cracked bone buckled, misshaping his leg. Ambrose yelled and tossed his head. His body flexing in his binds tore through the mangled flesh intertwined with the chains. More blood rushed to the wound piercing his ribs. It flowed fast down his hips and pooled on the floor.

"Nine is traditional. How many strikes will it take to motivate you?"

"Please, no more!"

"Then talk. I am only as cruel as you make me be. You need only do what is right."

"Greer is the mule!" he stammered out. "He takes the bottles ... the blood ... takes it east."

"Where?"

"I don't know."

Crack. Ambrose screeched as his shin was shattered. His foot flopped down at an unnatural angle. He sobbed and sucked in pained breath after breath, wailing.

"Tell me." Cyril tapped Ambrose's limp foot with his cane. "Where is he taking it?"

"If I knew, I would tell you!"

Crack. Both of Ambrose's arms were held tight to his body. He felt the force ripple through his whole chest when Cyril broke one of them. It made him sway in the chains, and they seemed to tighten to compensate. Blessed metal dug into him like a thorned vine and he bellowed a curse at the new pain. Cyril put his index finger over the bottle in his hand, flipping it upside down to wet the tip of his finger. He smeared that drop over Ambrose's lips. He at once hastily lapped up the blood, sighing with relief as it immediately sent numbing pleasure through his system.

"Your mistress, then," Cyril said as Ambrose's cries quieted. "Which one is she?"

Ambrose only shook his head. He had no time to repeat his loyalty before another hard blow was struck to his bones. The pain returned all at once. He began to laugh, his mind breaking from the incredible pain, the injustice of it all, the questions he had no answers to.

Crack.

"I won't!" He screamed more broken laughter as another blow followed. "I can't, I can't –"

Crack. Ambrose's head hung limp. Blood in his hair, limbs shattered and blood soaking into and ruining the floor. Cyril held up the bottle, still half-full of that awful miracle tonic inside. He swirled it around, holding it out toward Ambrose.

"Tell me."

Ambrose looked at the bottle, eyes wide with desperation. Relief, so close he could smell it. His voice was hoarse from screaming as he relented.

"Zemirah," he finally said. He hung his head, half in exhaustion and half in shame. "Zemirah, my dear ... forgive me."

Cyril's good eye narrowed at the name, but he put that awful softness back in his voice. "Good lad."

He snapped his gloved fingers and the chains vanished. Ambrose plummeted to the floor, landing in the pool of his own blood and crying out as he cracked his head. A snap and a broken cry sounded as his teeth and nose were jammed down into the floor. Instinct took over and he attempted valiantly to scramble away from his hunter. A bold but wasted effort.

Cyril rested his cane against the chair, leaning over to take hold of Ambrose by the hair. He hoisted him up to his knees. Ambrose writhed, barely managing to turn his head and spit out shards of a broken, bleeding tooth. The rest of that bottle was upended into his mouth – spilling over his chin and shirt. His rapidly healing hands corrected themselves. He grabbed desperately for the bottle, clutching it and Cyril's hand as he drank. As Ambrose relaxed, Cyril flung the bottle aside and took up his cane again. Ambrose saw the weapon raise up like a serpent about to strike. He wept and clung to Cyril's cassock. He tugged at it, no matter how it stung him.

"Please! I don't want to die!"

Cyril hushed him with that uncomfortably soft voice. "Shh. Take comfort in knowing you were of use to me."

"But I'm innocent!"

"None of you are innocent." He shook his cane and the lethally sharp linked barbs snapped into position. "You are damned by design."

Ambrose wailed and his legs, only half-healed, tried to push him away. His heart thudded hard in his chest. He couldn't tell what was blood and what was sweat on his skin.

"Please, pray for me!"

"I would pray for any penitent's soul." Cyril set the barbed blades of the cane against Ambrose's exposed neck. "But even my prayers would be wasted on you."

BOOK II
The Thief

37

GREER WAS DOING VERY WELL NOT TO SOIL HIMSELF on the floor in front of Zemirah. The sisters' office beneath the Cannoneer felt more like a prison cell to him, in this moment.

"You blundering fool, can't you do *anything* right?"

Greer's head thudded into the floor, his cheek stinging from the smack Zemirah had delivered. He scrambled backward and laughed awkwardly. He spoke his words through his hand on his cheek.

"I'm terribly sorry, my lady!"

"You think your *apologies* will remedy this?"

Esther sat on the desk, knees crossed and curly hair flipped over one shoulder. She pursed her lips and watched her sister pace back and forth. She had pricked her finger in boredom and was now paying more attention to the cat's cradle between her fingers. Her blood obeyed her readily, a glistening thread woven about her fingers that allowed her to cheat in her quest to tangle it into geometric patterns. She commanded it with such a lazy grace it put her sister to shame. This little bit of magic was the only thing keeping Greer from losing his mind with fear, whether he knew it or not. In all her little knots, Esther weaved a calming pattern – one that slowed the human's restless heart and soothed the panicked mind. It was done out of consideration for her sister, of course, not him. Zemirah would get further with him if he remained *somewhat* in control of his faculties.

"Eight vials. Gone. All eight, gone! Have you any idea the damage you have done?" She picked him up by the shirt and shook him. "We labeled everything, can you not *read!* I ought to take your head here and now to make up the difference, as you are not bothering to use it!"

"Wait, please! I know a sneak thief!"

"Keep talking."

"Simple and quiet as they come! Cares for nothing but money, he does! He can get in and out of that church for you, I'm sure of it!"

She shoved him back to the floor and put her hands on her hips, resuming her pacing as she chewed on her lip. She glanced up at Esther, who shrugged and gave her a sad, half-joking smile.

"Well," Esther said, "neither you nor I could waltz in and fetch it."

Zemirah crossed her arms and rolled her eyes, huffing a deep breath. Greer glanced awkwardly from sister to sister, waiting for a verdict and holding on to his own neck.

"Fine. Show me your thief. You had best hope he is as sly as you say, or I'm selling your head to the college to dissect."

"I understand!"

Philip's curiosity was getting him into trouble ... again. With Jael injured, he had just a little too much free time on his hands, so instead of doing something productive, he was snooping on the Royal Guard's activities around the Warbling Wren alone. *Heavens*, he thought, *there were so many of them!* He leaped across the alleyway from the nearest building, landing as lightly as he could upon the roof of the inn. The Royal Guard had barred Hunters from entering the lane, so he endeavored to keep himself somewhat concealed.

With his body low, his black cassock made him difficult to see. Timber creaked beneath his weight, but didn't reveal him.

He crept along toward the edge of the roof: where below, a shuttered window with gaps in the wood let a few odd whispers escape. Philip could tell both by their words and by their brogues that these knights were Windermere folk, not imported crown fare.

"Did you see Greer leave today? Bundle of nerves, he was."

"Fellow looked sick as a dog; I hope he didn't have something catching."

"Maybe Mother Superior finally severed his contract. That'll put a shake in his boots."

"I doubt it. For all the blood he peddles, he's been decent about keepin' the church's goods separate."

"For now. One too many bottles of Wren brew could change that quick."

Greer was smuggling blood! Philip now dearly wished he'd brought something to write with. He was so entangled in this gossip, he didn't notice the guard patrolling the roof's perimeter until they were nearly on top of him.

"Halt there, Brother."

"Oh, shit!" Philip hissed under his breath. He would have leaped back to the other building if the guard wasn't barring the path. The guard snapped at him, but he hurried over the roof's edge and scrambled down the balcony, surprising idle knights and civilians alike. He'd only just reached the road when a muscled knight twice his size hauled him up by the collar.

Philip was agile and well trained, and it wasn't hard for him to wriggle right out of the unsuspecting knight's grasp. Alas for his pride, he only freed himself in time to dart into a disgruntled horse, and equally disgruntled rider. Levi rolled his eyes and stroked his horse's neck as the Hunter stumbled backward, right into the waiting grasp of the bulky knight. Philip was already snapping at both of them.

"I've committed no crime! Your good-for-nothing captain can't detain me!"

Levi was surprised, if a little impressed, that even this snappy Hunter knew the law. It was worrying, in a way, that even the lower ranks of the clergy be so well versed. Nevertheless, Levi kept his face indifferent and signaled to his knights.

"We will escort you back to your church, sir."

"Brother," Philip spat at him. "You ought to use our proper titles if you want to last long here."

Philip fell in step behind Levi's horse, flanked by four knights. He shook off the hand of one who attempted to guide him by the shoulder.

The gate they arrived by proved crowded. One of the cathedral's ambulances had arrived with two wounded Hunters, quickly borne inside upon stretchers. Serge was overseeing the affair, assigning Clerics to patients and tasks as best befit their skill. He himself was only half out of the ambulance when he saw his nephew being escorted by the Royal Guard. He hurried toward the entourage, meeting them several paces away from the open gates, so as not to disturb the healers and their patients.

"What is the meaning of this?"

Philip was equally ashamed and relieved that his uncle should see him in such a predicament. One glance from Levi, back and forth between the two, was enough to see Philip's ears had gone red with embarrassment. Serge did look very much like Philip. From the distinct shape of his ears to his goldenrod complexion, they were obviously related. Levi might very well have thought him Philip's father, if not for the clergy's well-known vow of abstinence from marriage and intercourse both.

Serge wore an even deeper scowl than usual, but bowed his head politely to Levi. At least this elder could mind his manners, Levi thought as he returned the gesture.

"Sergeant Levi Sterling, sir."

"Brother Serge, Head of Infirmary." Serge was already leaning around Levi's horse and fellow knights to glare his disapproval at Philip. "Might I have an explanation?" His tone was one that would be taken with a bratty child, directed at Philip – but Levi answered it all the same.

"This Hunter was apprehended disrupting the quiet of Gutteridge Lane."

"Disrupting the quiet, my arse –" Philip mumbled under his breath as he shoved his way out from behind the knights. This time, the knight's hand on his shoulder was firm and stopped him.

"Please be advised that my captain has barred any entry to Gutteridge Lane by Hunters," Levi continued. "Per his notice posted and acknowledged by your Deacon. Any further trespasses may incur the involvement of Coldwater. Am I being understood?"

"Yes, Sergeant." Serge closed the gap between himself and his nephew, pulling Philip away from the knights by the shoulders. "He understands. It will *not* happen again."

Serge's last words, much like his tone, were intended for Philip, but the young elf only huffed, muttered an uncharacteristically cold 'good day', and marched off.

"Please excuse my nephew his manners, Sergeant. His eyes are bigger than his ears, oftentimes."

Levi scoffed. "Impressive. I hope for his sake your words land better than mine."

"Likewise." Serge glanced at Levi from head to toe and back again. Levi couldn't have been much older than Philip, but he carried himself with a poise that put even his polished knights to shame. Levi had already signaled to retreat across the bridge, and turned his horse to follow, when Serge spoke.

"You're young to be a sergeant. Quite accomplished, are we?"

"Only blessed to be in the command of an excellent man, Brother."

Serge nodded. "Indeed. A good man begets more good men." As the old Cleric spoke, he turned back toward the ambulance and the gathering crowd beyond, and frowned. Cyril could be seen in the courtyard, his attention wholly on the Hunter upon the stretcher – with a burial shroud already laid over half his body. Serge spoke with an almost callous ease at the sight. "Alas, my nephew's venerated icon, the Archbishop, is but a manifestation of pettiness and vengeance." He spat the words in disgust.

Levi at once was paying full attention. "Is it ... proper to speak of your Archbishop like that?"

"Perhaps not, but my Lady will forgive me a slip of the tongue."

38

SUGO FROWNED AT THE INSTRUCTIONS WRITTEN on a small slip of parchment. He drummed his fingers atop the parcel left for him and clicked his tongue in thought. An unpleasant task – and frankly a dishonest one, which did not please him at all. But his distaste was outweighed by complete trust in Cyril's words. A personal request, given over to him with similar trust. And so he took the parcel into the pantry, locked it away, and waddled off to retrieve a mask. One could never be too careful when handling vampire blood.

DOMINGO COULD WEATHER THE BATTLEFIELD without as much as a whimper. Not a word of complaint from him, even if pain should be his constant companion. The howls of knights as they lay wounded and dying, the echoed screams from the interrogation chambers of the dungeons, the mourning of women and children whose husbands and fathers never returned – all these horrors and more did not stumble him.

But there was one burden he could not shoulder. A guilt and a grief so heavy it stung his heart even now. It hurt deeper than betrayal, deeper than heartbreak, and it would not let him sleep.

The odd attempt at courage reminded him of his weakness. How quickly he groped about for his medals when the sensation came! Catapulted wide awake, cold and shivering with sweat, a knot so tight in his throat it became hard to breathe – and a gentle voice in the back of his mind. He rushed to silence it.

Domingo fought for air and rolled over in a hurry in his bed, kicked the sheets away. The longer it whispered, the harder it was to breathe, the more his heart pounded, the deeper the pain pierced. The more he could swear he felt hands on him, clinging to him, begging him. His own hand fumbled over the bedside table in the dark. He flung open the velvet-lined box that held his medals. Never far away, especially not at night. He grasped them so hard he might have bent them, if they were composed of a softer metal. He rapped out the words he needed, disappointment and defeat thick on his tongue.

The voice in the back of his head grew quieter, as if apologizing for disturbing him. Back down, down it went, slinking beneath a manufactured inky-black sea of forgetfulness. He muttered an apology of his own, for banishing it there. Those clinging hands went with it. In his panic he had flung back the sheets half expecting to find them there, but was relieved to see nothing. A few awful moments to slow his heart and the pain crept away in defeat, too.

There were many things a hardened man could bear. So many things. But that was not one. Whether it was a weakness, or evidence of tenderness, none could say. Domingo only resolved to sleep with his medals in one hand, clinging to them – that they keep the wretched pain away.

Clinging to the wall and keeping watch over him was Noel, a smudge of black against the darkened stone of Coldwater. She was braced in the niche of a window, legs burning with the effort, but her breath still even. Moonlight eyes were barred by the curtains of the window, but she was equipped with a keen enough sight to see through them – a sight not dissimilar to his, though not as honed. This captain wore death, this she knew; she only needed to find out where he was keeping it. It wasn't in those medals, those fanciful talismans that gave him his fetters, his ferocity. It wasn't in any of his rings; his sign of station and seal were ordinary, his mourning rings on his little fingers plain as could be. And really, who was it that could unmake a man like him, and why did he bring them with him?

39

OEL WAS ENGULFED IN A MASK, HAT AND CLOAK. Her moonlit green eyes and collection of fangs were hidden behind a faceless mask. Her layered cloak fluttered about her shoulders as she escorted Esther – who had looped her own hand through Noel's arm and squeezed the muscle of her bicep appreciatively.

Esther had the look of a lady about her – she wore fine-fitting clothes kept clean and fresh. It was unusual to see a lady with her hair down, though, especially in public. It perhaps spoke to that certain level of bratty, rebellious spirit she possessed. Curly, pastel-green hair bounced softly with each step, ringlets floating about her billowy shirt and framing her face in a manner quite adorable.

One of the many stone pavilions stood on the outskirts of this hamlet. Countless others dotted the province, each sheltering some saint or martyr beneath their domed roof. Esther glared at the statue beneath one as she and Noel passed by. It was the most well-kept structure in this miserable little hamlet.

The local inn here was a dingy place, even compared to the Cannoneer. Instead of sailors and dockworkers, farmers and shopkeepers drank away their days' wages. Instead of cold fog and ever-present moisture, everything was coated in a fine layer of dust: a combination of wheat, flour, and dirt – as was inevitable.

Esther wasn't fond of her role in this scheme, there was no glamour in it, but it relied on her charms – and others' perceptions of her as a young, flirty, wealthy heiress – to succeed.

The innkeeper behind the bar, a balding man with a thick beard, was always happy to see her, and she for her part always pretended to be so in kind. She reminded him of his own adult daughter, from the way she covered her mouth when she laughed to the perfume she wore. It must be a popular aroma among young ladies, he reasoned.

She made her regular inquiries into his health, his family's well-being, his children's success or difficulty in school. Then, she would request two hearty meals – one for herself and one for her loyal bodyguard – be delivered to the private table she had begun to reserve for herself some time ago.

Said reservation was nothing special or particularly comfortable; only a private room with a small table and barely enough space for the chairs around it. A ratty rug, moth-eaten curtains, and a crooked chandelier were hardly impressive accents, but it was a reasonable accommodation for a lesser lady and her escort only passing through on business.

With the doors shut, Noel slid a short wooden stave from her belt between the iron handles, barring any entry from outside. Behind her, Esther had pulled a small bottle of a clear liquid from her satchel and doctored the two generous helpings of grilled vegetables, thickly sliced bread, and roast fowl. The odorless, tasteless tincture was absorbed readily into the foodstuffs.

"If I hear him complain one more time about that worthless son of his," Esther whined as she spread the bread with drugged butter, "I'm going to find and skin him myself."

"His skin wouldn't be worth the trouble, my lady."

Once Esther had finished, she wrapped the dishes in napkins and removed them from the table. Noel was quick to stack the chairs and scoot them into the little room's corner. The table went next, upended onto its side. Noel then flipped the filthy rug back and drew her sword. It took a few seconds of jostling and coaxing to free the cut section of floor. With it nudged out of place, Noel revealed the cavernous pitch black below. She helped Esther sit on the floor, slip her legs into the hole, and scoot forward until she could drop down. Noel followed suit the next moment, and the two departed underground with the bundle of haphazardly packaged food in hand.

⁜

IT WAS ALREADY BLACK OUTSIDE when Cyril rapped his knuckles on the doorframe of the bakery. Hugo looked up and, upon seeing Cyril, took the key ring from his belt. He slid it across the table without a word. Cyril retrieved it, locking and sealing the bakery door against curious ears.

He then descended the remaining steps into the bakery, looking about as he made his way to the rear door, to lock and seal it in the same manner. The courtyard was empty and the ovens outside abandoned – Hugo would use the smaller indoor oven built into the wall near his workstation. He scraped coals into a bucket and wiped ash out with a stiff brush.

"Your apprentice has retired for the night?" Cyril asked.

"Aye, Father. I sent her away early."

Hugo caught his keys as they were tossed back, then unlocked a small, inconspicuous cupboard in the corner as Cyril shuttered the windows. The batch of bread dough Hugo took from the cupboard was a deep, dark brown. Doctored with sugar and edible flowers, it smelled pleasantly sweet. A deliberate effect, and one the skilled baker had invested great effort into perfecting. He set the bowl atop his workstation, floured the board, and turned the dough out upon it.

"Oh, now where in the ...? Fetch me that honey, would you?"

231

Cyril looked around blindly for a moment, and Hugo realized he'd slipped back into habit, a little embarrassed for it.

"Oh, ah, oh dear. Excuse me, Father. The glass jar with the wood cap, behind you. Next to the knife block, there."

With a little guidance, Cyril found the jar and delivered it to him.

"Thank you," Hugo said. "Apologies, Father. I must confess, I'm quite used to another pair of hands."

"Miss Brontë is helpful to you, then?"

"Oh, very. Quick as a whip, she is. Does all I ask, and does it well."

"Good, good."

Hugo worked with the skill and ease of a professional, shaping the small batch of dough, brushing each roll with honey, and sliding a tray with several into the oven. As Hugo hoisted the big kitchen timer and gave it a firm wind to set the proper time, Cyril pulled out one of the stools and took a seat at the worktable. Hugo wiped his hands and, rather than sitting down, fetched a small wooden case from beneath the table. The contents rattled slightly, and he slid the box over to Cyril.

"Set that up, aye? I'll be right back."

He disappeared into the pantry, leaving Cyril to set up the chess set within. As he did so, he heard the clunk and scrape of the icebox as Hugo rummaged through it. He returned with a bottle of amber whiskey, oranges, two small glasses, and a bucket of ice. As Cyril finished setting the pieces in place, Hugo mixed each of them a drink – topping Cyril's with orange and his own with nutmeg.

Only when the tubby Brother had seated himself comfortably – and had taken the liberty of spinning the board around so he could go first – did Cyril venture a question.

"Did the blood bother you, Brother Hugo?"

Hugo took on a more serious tone than usual as the board game commenced. "No, no trouble. I wore a mask when preparing it, as a precaution."

"Very good. Thank you. I am sorry to ask this of you."

Hugo shook his head as he thumbed his glass. "Do you … think it will work? I can hide medicine from a babe, but even with my work, she's sure to smell the blood. You know how sensitive the sinsick are."

"I suppose I will find out." Cyril slid a bishop across the board. "I am reasonably confident she won't notice." He chuckled. "With any luck, she'll gobble it up before she has a chance."

Hugo scoffed, but the idea of tricking Lady Mara into consuming blood still made him feel a smothering sense of shame. He knew Cyril would not employ such an underhanded method, not without good reason.

Cyril saw the contemplative look on his face. "Do you doubt my decision?"

"Ah, it's …" Hugo hurried to play a piece. "It's not my place to say, Father –"

"No, please." Cyril reached behind his neck and removed his stole. He folded the garment and set it aside, making it clear he was speaking personally – not as Father, merely a friend. A wordless indication Hugo had come to recognize, over the years.

Hugo smiled sadly and shrugged in surrender. "I just … There is really nothing else you can do?"

Cyril shook his head. "I have tried everything. I know the archives like the back of my hand. Every concoction, every elixir, every enchantment."

A few helpless pawns were lost as control over the board was established. By the time he replied, Hugo was nursing a felled rook, and Cyril had lost a bishop.

"What about that tincture you give Miss Brontë?" Hugo asked. "She's always got a little bottle in her pocket. She sips at it whenever her affliction requires, or so she says."

Hugo spoke of the gold liquor that kept Brontë ... contained. Of course, Cyril's predecessor had settled upon a blatant lie – that Brontë was born an addict; that she was a strange exception the church had been forced to make. Hugo would assume the same medicine for Brontë would work for Mara, and none could fault him for thinking it.

"That medicine, I am afraid, is ill-suited to Mara's needs. Their respective afflictions are too different." Cyril took a drink and set his glass down.

"I see." Hugo sat back on the stool and crossed his arms in earnest thought. He'd never had an inclination toward magic, nor was he schooled in such things. He was no Bishop, no mage – but still he racked his brain all the same. "And the usual remedy does no good? Those tablets? I know they're no cure, but –"

"I'm afraid not. Sister Beatrice was very thorough in her letter to me, urging me to hurry back. She followed every instruction I left, made every adjustment to her dose, to the administration, everything. It made no difference. I suspect her withdrawal is advancing beyond what my remedy can alleviate."

He leaned forward and nudged one of Hugo's knights aside, replacing the piece with a bishop of his own.

"And so ... blood it is, then." Hugo lowered his voice and grew quite serious. "If the wrong ears hear of your doing this, Father, I dread to think –"

"I know." He rubbed the back of his neck. "But I would rather risk a scandal coming down on my head."

Cyril had a bishop and queen cornering Hugo, now, but Hugo wasn't paying very much attention to the game.

"Is that a risk Lady Mara would want you to take?" *She ought to know, she's the one you do this for, after all. Shouldn't her wants matter, too?*

Cyril huffed a bitter laugh and Hugo nearly reeled back in surprise. "I had to bribe her with a new gown each month," Cyril said, "*just* to coerce her into taking the tablets at all. She'd happily refuse treatment if she had such a noble reason to do so."

"Hah!" Hugo scoffed in amused disbelief, patting his knee. "Come now, you're her son! Sinsick guilt or no, as if she'd treat your work with disdain. She's nothing but proud."

"Hah." Cyril swirled his glass and downed the rest of his drink.

The joy drained from Hugo's face. "You're her son," he repeated quietly. "She –"

The timer chimed behind him before he could speak. He rose to his feet and retrieved the blood-infused bread from the oven.

It took only a few minutes to pull the dark-brown buttery rolls out and set them aside. Doctored with honey, stamped with a protective seal underneath – and a blessing from Cyril about the bag for good measure – they made for an unassuming medicine indeed. Hugo bundled up the bread carefully and handed it over to Cyril.

"Please ... let me know how she takes it. I can make adjustments to the recipe; you need only tell me."

"Thank you, Brother Hugo."

"At your service, Father."

40

NOEL WAITED PATIENTLY, LEANING AGAINST THE WALL with her arms crossed in the dark of the tunnel. A shaft of warm candlelight flooded in from the grate above her, only just illuminating a rickety ladder leading up. Quiet voices babbled overhead, idle chatter between mouthfuls of food. Esther could be heard between the others, offering praise and comfort and generally employing more of her charm, as was necessary.

When the grate opened, Noel moved to offer Esther her hand and help her descend the ladder. She had to sidestep the two empty pewter plates and soiled napkins that were thrown down first. Upon reaching the dirt floor of the tunnel Esther sighed in relief. Her clothes were wrinkled and her palms stained from accepting the many touches of needy hands.

"They've eaten," she said, wiping her hands on Noel's cloak. "Scarfed it down without a second thought."

"And the tincture has taken hold?"

"It has. They'll not resist you."

"Debauve is good for something after all."

Esther rolled her eyes. *My sister and her favorites.* "Hurry now, harvest a limb and let us away from this place. I can't abide the stench." She shook dust from her hair. "Or the dust."

"Yes, my lady."

Noel ascended the ladder and drew her knife. There was a weak chorus of fearful and timid pleas at the sight of the cloaked bodyguard – but it was true the drugged food had taken hold. There was no resistance. It was now Esther's turn to wait in the tunnel. She tapped her foot impatiently as Noel selected and severed a suitable limb for her lady's needs.

IVY HAIR WHIPPED ABOUT AND STUCK TO ZEMIRAH'S face as she marched through the drizzly streets. She had the route memorized, so the pitch black of the rain and guttering streetlamps was of little concern to her. She stepped over beggars and snarled at a barking dog as she went on her way. Finally crossing over one of the smaller canals, she pulled her collar higher against her neck and held her hat to her head. The little courtyard behind Ambrose's shop had one of the brighter lampposts in the center, though she did not need its help to navigate her key ring. She lifted the appropriate key to the lock and grumbled about how bloody bright that lamp was.

She paused. There, just above the lock, was a familiar symbol. A small cross had been carved into the mahogany door.

Zemirah turned the key as quietly as she could. She then drew her rapier and slowly slipped inside. The smell of blood was potent, overwhelming. Not human blood, her blood. Her heart raced as she looked around the shop's backroom. Nothing was out of place. Not so much as a bottle overturned. No evidence of forced entry, of looting, or of a struggle. She crept toward the stairs to Ambrose's apartment, careful only to set her feet on the narrow carpet, to dampen the noise as much as possible. She kept the point of her rapier up. The smell of blood grew heavier, as did the lump in her throat. She felt fluid in the carpet under her feet.

She stood before the door to his apartment. Her feet sunk too deeply into the sticky, saturated rug. She felt sick. She pricked her palm with her sword and called to life thin threads. She very nearly turned to flee – to leave this awful, marked place with herself intact. *He's just a doctor, I can get another doctor,* she thought.

The wood beneath her groaned at her hesitation. She threw open the door and dove into the room. Her threads snapped to obey and made a protective web about her – but there was no need. No Hunter waited for her, only Ambrose, all alone.

A cry was stifled in her throat and she stumbled forward, buckling as if punched in the gut. Ambrose's body was hanging from the rafters. His arms and legs were broken and deformed, just like his ribs – which she could see through the gash in his clothing and flesh both. Blood had stained his clothes red and dried a ruddy brown. It had dripped down his boots and seeped into the carpet, making the floorboards beneath warp and swell.

He hung there like a criminal broken upon the wheel and left out for carrion to devour. But not all of him. His head was missing. A trophy, taken by a sadistic Hunter. It was not a clean cut. His head hadn't been severed so much as twisted off; torn away like a young twig that had refused to snap. Every wound inflicted had tried and failed to heal, his neck had tried to find his head, and even now the growing flesh writhed like a vine searching for something to climb. Overindulgence.

Silently, gently, she took the body down. Her throat hurt with the effort of containing her grief, her anger. *This one was mine!* With the corpse free, she sunk to the floor with it, and her composure finally cracked. She screamed into his broken chest, a curse against the clergy and that damned Archbishop. Alone in the apartment, she cradled what remained of Ambrose's broken body – rocking it back and forth in her lap, blubbering apologies and curses with every alternating sob.

41

THE STARS HAD ALREADY BEGUN TO RISE LIKE SPARKS from a fire as night closed in. Levi finished filling his lantern with oil and secured it to his hip, freshly lit. It burned with a glow almost blindingly white by comparison to the church's many lamps and braziers. Her gold fire required no fuel. No oil, no wick – even the petrified logs in the hearths were but glorified decoration. Those flames were merely set upon empty dishes or in empty lanterns. It felt wrong to him.

One of the stable hands – a loyal member of the liturgical layfolk who was none too happy to service a royal guardsman – had both tended and watered his horse, and now stood with the animal awaiting him. Levi thanked her, though she barely acknowledged him, and mounted his horse.

When Levi approached the southeast gate, he was surprised to find it already open. Not just the smaller door built into the gate, which he and his horse usually passed comfortably, but both of the massive, thickly timbered doors. A gap wide enough for a carriage to pass through, or a hearse.

Several Hunters stood guard; more than usual, with the gates thus ajar. Still more were swarming the hearse. A few of the older, possibly more experienced or higher-ranking Hunters, held tongues of flame ahigh like torches in their palms, allowing their fellows to inspect the vehicle. The horses huffed and steamed with sweat, indicating an unusually hurried trip. Brother Benjamin appeared from the rear of the hearse. He held a smoldering censer on a chain, and was giving instructions to the

Hunters. He still donned his hat and mask. Levi saw the protective, beaked mask and became aware of the sweet, almost floral smell emanating from the hearse. It was mingled with the incense from Benjamin's censer, but now that Levi paused to focus, he realized the latter barely overpowered the former. He realized, too, it was beginning to give him a headache.

The lenses of Benjamin's mask caught the fire the Hunters held in their hands, and when he turned to look at Levi, they flashed bright white from his own lantern. Benjamin hung the censer off the side of the hearse and approached Levi.

"Sergeant Sterling, yes? You are come from Our Lady?"

"I am, Brother."

Skulking about again, Benjamin thought. "I see."

"And what manner of magic is this ... ritual? You do this with all your dead?"

"No, no," Benjamin said. As he replied, a murmur arose from the Hunters, who leaped back as blood and flesh bubbled up from inside the coffin and dripped down the side of the hearse.

"An addict, particularly advanced in consumption and beginning to mutate," Benjamin said in a bored tone. "Sometimes such simple coffins are insufficient, and so they leak. And filth is drawn to filth, so it brings others looking."

One of the Hunters was carefully using their summoned weapon to pry off a mangled hand and arm from one of the wheels. The remnants of a vampire that had attempted to grab the hearse as it passed, and instead had their arm torn off and braided through the spokes in a grisly mess.

"Why not ... take it inside, then? If it draws attention."

"If we pass the threshold with the body in this state, it may be irreparably damaged. It would be of no use to Father in such a state." Benjamin chuckled softly. "Though I take pride in my skills, some things my wax cannot repair. And someone expects her back looking something like herself."

"I don't know how much luck you'll have with that ..." Levi mused. The coffin was dripping black sludge, and the lid was slightly askew, as if pushed out of place from inside, as if the dead woman was trying to escape the clergy.

"One can only hope. But, please, do not let me detain you, Sergeant. I'm afraid I have kept you overlong, and night is upon us. A pair of Hunters can escort you." Benjamin turned, intending to call out some pair of Hunters, but Levi was quick to interrupt him.

"No, no. Thank you, Brother, but that is not necessary."

"Very well." Benjamin allowed Levi's horse to sniff inquisitively at his hand as he spoke. "A word of caution to you, then, young man."

Levi fidgeted with his feet in the stirrups, eager for the conversation to be over. "Yes, Brother?"

"It is already quite dark, and you have that look about you. If you hear your name, do not answer."

With that, Benjamin folded his hands into his habit and pointed with his beak behind Levi. "Behind the brazier, just there, are steps that will return you to the avenue faster than the longer route over the bridge. They are well lit, and wide enough for your mount, but watch your step, as they are old and thus uneven. Good evening."

Levi bowed his head and turned to take the Brother's prescribed path. He found it, a carefully hewn flight of stairs, carved into the rock and protected on the cliff side by a banister of chiseled granite. Though the steps were worn down, they remained well lit by brilliant lanterns. He and his horse had no trouble navigating them down to the road below.

42

THE NIGHTS IN WINDERMERE WERE PURE BLACK and thick as pitch. Her tall architecture did not help. There were the lamps, yes – candelabras of wrought iron that burned with a pale yellow fire. Their flame was something between the clean white of the lantern at Levi's hip and the raging gold of the Lady. Oil imbued with a blessing from the church rendered it so, or so Levi had heard. A flame half-holy, if that was even possible. Even still, the lamps struggled to cut through the unnatural dark here. But Levi was unafraid of the dark – not even cryptic warnings from masked priests could disquiet him. He and his horse trotted through the eerily empty road toward the Warbling Wren.

When Levi heard someone talking, he thought his ears were playing tricks on him. Not someone, several someones. Voices deep enough to be men, he assumed, all mumbling in angry tones under their breath. The clop of his horse's shoes on the cobblestones seemed to silence them, as the sound of an approaching knight often did ne'er-do-wells. Probably just drunkards playing cards the next alley over. He continued on his way.

The second time, the sounds he heard were running water, a feminine voice, and the jingle of coins.

Saint Lilian's fountain had once been a simple pavilion, like so many others. Just another octagonal, colonnaded arbor that sheltered the statue inside from sun, rain, and snow. Hers, though, was now surrounded by a wider basin of ever-flowing fresh water. It tumbled out from the stone beneath her feet, hiding the copper she hoarded in her fountain – little prayers and pleas in the form of offerings.

She, and her surrounding square, were abandoned this time of night. Empty, save for a young woman kneeling at the edge of the fountain's pool. Georgiana was hunched over, her head buried in her arms as she sobbed. Beside her was a small coin purse, barely bigger than her hand. She only came out of her grief at the sound of Levi's approaching horse. She was started right back to her senses, and almost looked as if she might flee.

"I apologize, ma'am," Levi said as he slowed his horse. "I did not mean to startle you."

Her mouth fell open in surprise that one of these glittering officers be speaking to her. Her eyes roved over his uniform, his armor, his horse's tack and barding. Not a speck of dirt or a wrinkle in sight. Levi meanwhile observed her in kind. She was near in age to him. A little scrappy, a little unkempt in body and garment both – though her shoes were polished and lovingly maintained. She wiped her eyes and bowed her head, finally replying.

"Hail to you, sir knight. Please, excuse me my condition."

"Is there trouble, ma'am?"

"No, sir!" she said, almost a little too hastily. "No, I … I just came for my father, to pray … he was sinsick, you see. And now he's dead."

Levi realized the potential to glean precious information from this young woman. He dismounted his horse, that they might speak on more equal footing.

"My condolences for your loss, ma'am." He softened his tone. "Were you close?"

"Very." She stared blankly ahead, thumbing the last few copper coins she had. "He worked his poor fingers to the bone for us. It's no surprise they began to pain him so. He'd come into the kitchen at night with them all red and swollen ..."

Levi eyed her work clothes, noting that the sleeves were too short, that he could see panels of a different fabric sewn into her bodice, added on as it had grown too small for her. Her rosary was wooden, simple, and worn down with time. Poorer folk, this family. An apothecary could be devastating to their coffers. He ventured a question with this in mind.

"Could the Clerics not help him?"

"They tried, I suppose. It would take him hours ... to trek all the way up to Our Lady and home again on foot." She looked up at the cathedral, looming on the plateau above. "Or spend precious coin to hire a cab. And even then, well ... the Clerics are so very protective of their medicine. They gave it freely to him, yes, but only in small doses. Those tinctures they give could numb the pain for ten, maybe eleven days." She laughed bitterly. "But a bottle of blood? Oh, it could last him months for the price of the cab and back."

Levi's hand flexed behind his back and he had to withhold a smile at his good fortune. *Finally*, some information on that concoction the church condemned. Georgiana did not know it, but her value was increasing by the second.

"It did him good, then?"

"In body? Of course. It always does. In soul, though? Mother above, I fear for his spirit. What horror awaits him, that he had not time to confess ..." She clutched her coin purse to her bosom as she spoke.

"Is that what these coins are?" Levi asked. "Confessions?"

"Confessions, prayers, wishes. As Archbishop, she heard them all."

Levi looked up in surprise at the statue sheltered beneath the pavilion. A knight, at first glance, though upon closer inspection she wore a coif and veil. Similar to what the current Huntresses wore, but of a more archaic style. Though armored, she held no weapon, only a staff topped with a cross leaning against her body. She held up two fingers on her right hand, in the gesture Levi recognized as the church's blessing.

"She was an Archbishop?"

"Yes." Georgiana was near breathless with admiration. "An exceptional mage and a merciful woman. She was one of the first to wear white, after all."

"To wear white?"

She only nodded, smiling at the statue. Levi wasn't sure she knew he was even there anymore, so enraptured she was by the gentle face of the saint. It was incredibly lifelike. When she spoke, it sounded more as if she was repeating scripture she had heard.

"White ... soaks up all the blood it encounters, all the sorrow." She sighed. "I like to think that Mother Lilian would have forgiven Papa. He talks ... he used to talk about her so fondly, about her voice in the belfry, how it was the sweetest thing he'd heard in his life. He had hoped we'd hear it together, but now ..."

She leaned over the basin's edge and released another coin in the fountain. Levi blinked as he watched it sink ... and sink. That fountain was deeper than he'd realized. He could have dived into it, submerged himself head to toe, all without reaching the coins. Yet, from up here the water looked shallow as any ordinary fountain. It made the back of his neck prickle. He wished to be away from the fountain at once, and his words came out quicker for it.

"It is not safe after dark." *Or so I am told*, he thought. "It would be better to be indoors. The fountain will be here tomorrow."

"Oh, I dare not come during the day, you see."

"And why is that?"

"How dare you sully Mother Lilian's well with your presence."

Levi turned around, instinctively placing himself between the young woman and the voice.

Three men emerged from the haze of the alleyway. They were better dressed than this girl; neat and tidy hair, groomed beards, polished shoes. They had pricier, metal rosaries in their hands and about their necks, peeking out from beneath coat collars. One held a lit lantern, while another had a burlap sack tucked under his arm. All three had swords at their hips – the sort of simple, lightly ornamented tool of middle-class men – and one looked a little too keen to use it. The man with the lantern spoke again, though he completely ignored Levi's presence.

"Come, answer for what your bloodline has done!"

He was sinsick, you see, Levi heard her words in his head again. *And now he's dead.* A crime, in the mind of these folk – an infectious, damning one. And with him safe in his grave, who else could hear their anger but his daughter? What a miserable state of affairs, this city.

"A man's crimes are his own," Levi ventured cautiously.

"Don't you try to speak of old Hackett, southerner! You didn't know him. Sleazy little man, all he cared for was coin."

"How dare you speak of Papa that way! You –"

Levi held out his hand to silence Georgiana.

"The man only prayed when he needed it! Crawling back to Our Lady, thick in sin, when he fell ill –"

"Aye!" Another broke his silence. "And to take his life when his guilt overtook him? Words do not convey my disgust. Cowardly filth!"

"She was his favorite." The last man pointed an accusatory finger behind Levi. "She knew what he was doing, his sins, all of it! He infected her, no doubt. I reckon she drank it herself, too."

"This is not a trial," Levi said. "And you are not her judge. Depart at once."

"You southerners. So much love for law, but no respect for ours."

One of the men drew his sword. Levi's eyes snapped over to him, as he contemplated his options. His horse could trample them easily, but these were civilians. Three of them, all armed, and he with a valuable witness he wanted to keep. Levi inhaled and set his feet before drawing his sword, twirling it in an arc so swift it whistled. He kept the point of the blade down, for now.

"Stand back from the Royal Guard," he said, with a voice surprisingly loud and authoritative.

"You're no guard of ours," one of the men replied. "She deserves a pyre, and we are come to provide. It is what Mother Lilian would want. So stand aside."

Their leader raised his lantern, burning with the same oil as the lamps, and this time Levi saw the sheen of moisture over the burlap. It was drenched in oil. They meant to bag and burn the girl. What was this city and its obsession with fire?

Levi shook his head and raised the point of his sword. "Depart, or cross blades with the Guard."

Levi wasn't a large bloke; in fact, he was rather petite. Narrow shoulders and a short stature limited his reach, but he had learned to both compensate for this and use his smaller size to his advantage. He was nimble and swift, especially compared to three thick-boned men.

The one with two free hands rushed him, and he had to parry the blade away from himself. Levi had no fetters, no grand Monocerian magic to muster; he had only his sword and skill. But three grown men with swords of their own were far from a fair fight, and he could only parry so much.

A second, smaller blade seemed to leap from Levi's belt and into his hand. Not a moment too soon, as he parried an incoming strike with it and guarded against another with his sword. Clanging notes of metal hitting metal sounded as Levi was forced to shuffle away from the two men. He pivoted to draw them away from the girl – but the third man saw the opportunity and seized it, hurrying toward her.

He hadn't closed even half the gap when Levi slid past the other two and dashed for the third. A hard kick and a good wallop with the flat of his blade threw the man off course. As he staggered, his flailing hand caught on Levi's head, ripping his beret off and snagging hard on some of his curly hair. Levi shouted and had no choice but to fumble after him, lest his scalp split apart. He tumbled with him, swords clattering to the road as they rolled into the gutter set in the center of the boulevard.

The glass of the man's lantern had smashed in the fall, and oil leached out over the road, carrying fresh fire with it. The man grabbed a glass shard and raised his hand, keen to gouge out Levi's eyes and destroy his face. The heel of Levi's hand jammed straight up into the man's chin. The shard of glass fell. A jab to the gut and a knee to the groin were enough to daze the man. Levi rolled out from underneath him, snatched up both his blades, and shook stars from his eyes. The other two were closing in on the petrified girl.

The two men had to scramble backward out of the way of Levi's dagger. He was still being careful, still minding that they were civilians – but this needed to end. Levi saw one of the men stumble on an uneven cobblestone and at once capitalized on it. He charged him, bashing his elbow into his belly before headbutting him straight in the nose. He yelled and fell backward, holding the bleeding appendage.

The last was the bloke with both his hands free. He was no great sword fighter, but he had a strong arm and a fist that could put Levi to sleep if it landed. He pushed hard into Levi, anger and size working to his advantage. One handful of knuckles crossed Levi's cheekbone and made him gasp. He tasted blood and was worried it'd loosened teeth. The man was smiling with delight at the landed blow, and had brought up his sword to cleave down a nasty blow. Untrained in war as he was, this left him entirely open.

Levi whipped his dagger around and put all his strength behind a hard push, catching the man in the stomach with the dull back of the blade. He still howled as if he'd been cut – or the breath that left him at the impact sounded as such. He skidded backward on braced feet before dropping to one knee, wheezing for air.

"I'll not ask again!" Levi turned his dagger over in his hand. "Depart at once. I will not use the back of the blade a second time."

The man with the lantern had to be hoisted off his feet by his comrade, hauled up with his arm about the other's shoulder. The smashed lantern burned at their feet, illuminating angry faces. The one with the broken nose snarled as if he wished to speak, but Levi didn't wait to hear it.

"Coldwater beckons you," Levi said. "But depart now, and I will spare you the whipping post. Go."

It was enough. Soundly beaten and bruised, the men muttered their curses and limped off into the dark to lick their wounds – and plot their next attempt, surely. But Levi had already resolved his next step before he'd drawn his sword. He turned around and, with a slight apology for his forwardness, pulled the young lady to her feet.

"I will take you to the Warbling Wren. You will board there for the time being."

"Sir?" she stuttered out, still in a daze from the commotion.

"No arguments." He whistled his horse closer. "I'll escort you."

Levi laced his fingers together and, with a bit of pressure, convinced her to set one foot in his hands and let him lift her onto his horse. She sat sidesaddle upon the animal and – after fixing her skirts and setting her foot in the stirrup, and picking up his hat – Levi took the reins and led his horse toward the Wren.

43

ℬRONTË HOISTED A BASKET OF LINENS she had taken down from the line. True, she could hang the bakery linens down in the washroom, but she preferred drawing a line out here, behind the small conservatory. It allowed her peace and quiet, and she could meander through the orchards on her way back to the bakery, which she did so love to do.

The orchards in the west garden were lovingly tended. The older trees closer to the wall, with their gnarled roots and cold soil, were her favorites. She felt they had more character, were a bit more familiar. She looked up, shielding her eyes from the sun coming through the leaves, to see fruit oh so slowly beginning to flush red as autumn approached. Soon, they'd be bright, brilliant red and in the perfect state for all manner of delicious applications. Fresh cider, pies, and candies would, for a brief time, become acceptable. The yearly apple feast, an event held for the orphans housed at Our Beloved Lady, was her absolute favorite time of year – even now, as an adult.

She remembered her own years attending the feast with such fondness. Bobbing for apples in icy cold water, staying up late enough to hear the bells toll hours beyond what her fingers could count, getting second helpings – second! – of apple pie, dolloped with fresh cream and cinnamon. It was a rare treat, to indulge in such sugary, sweet foods – and to have an evening for play and mischief. The clergy were always nearby, of course, to ensure nothing *too* rambunctious was taking place. Brontë recalled the way she'd made poor Cyril worriedly chase her about as she climbed trees and nearly fell several times. He had coaxed her down with an offer of hot, spiced cider. That recipe still eluded her, somehow. She had tried many times, but never could recreate the flavor.

She was so lost in thought she didn't notice Philip on a stone bench just beyond the orchard. He was seated next to one of the small, bubbling fountains that provided fresh water for cups or canteens – having opened the spigot with hands too full to make use of the flowing water as it tumbled to the drain. Brontë came back to reality when he exclaimed in surprise as his hands fumbled a little metal tin.

"Ah, drat!"

She readjusted her basket and emerged from the shade of the orchard. "Oh? What's that?"

"Huh? Oh, Brontë. It's some salve my uncle gave me for my head." He awkwardly clutched it to his chest, just below his chin, as he attempted to hold a mirror and remove the bandage above his eye. Brontë laughed and set her basket of linens on the bench, pulling the tin from under his chin.

"If *only* there was someone less than ten steps away who would be more than happy to help, if you but asked."

Philip grinned up at her, then put his hand over his eyes as if to shield them from the sun and scanned the otherwise empty courtyard and sprawling orchards. "Is there? Could you introduce me?"

"Oh, shut up and turn to face me."

He laughed at his own joke, but did as she asked. "Are you sure? I think it's still a bit bloody. I don't want it to make you woozy."

Brontë picked up one of his hands, positioning it so he held his palm flat. She put the tin back in his grasp while she leaned in to remove the bandage adhered to his face. "It won't bother me, don't worry."

She carefully peeled the bandage away and he flinched as some crunchy scabs inevitably came off with it. A few beads of blood bloomed from between the lines of the wound, but nothing severe. Brontë clicked her tongue and rolled her eyes. "Oh, tch, it's not bad at all. It looks like it's healing very well. Open the tin for me while I wash my hands."

He obliged her, holding up the open tin so she could dip her clean fingertips into the ointment and dab it onto the stitches. It had been a relatively long gash, stretching about the length of his brow and only just missing the hairs. Before she could finish, however, a voice interjected and made her hop in surprise.

"You! What do you think you're doing?"

Brontë stood to attention, turning to face Serge who was marching over from across the courtyard. She bowed her head politely, her voice barely a whisper. "Brother Serge, I was just helping Philip to dress his wound –"

"You are in no state to do that. Look at you, all covered in dirt and flour and goodness knows what else." He practically shoved her aside, standing between her and his deeply apologetic-looking nephew. "And it's *Brother* Philip. Learn to use proper titles, you weren't raised in a barn. Now shoo, away with you! Go do something useful!"

Brontë snatched up her basket and practically fled back to the bakery. Serge meanwhile grumbled and turned to face Philip, tilting his nephew's face and looking at the exposed, half-healed wound.

Philip frowned. "I asked her to help."

"And you should know better. She's a baker's apprentice, not a Cleric. Do you want this to get infected? It could cost you an eye."

"She washed her hands."

Serge waved his hand in dismissal and rolled his eyes. "Come along, I'll redress it properly."

Brother Serge was the only member of the clergy, aside from Cyril, who knew what Brontë was. He despised her, and made no real attempt to hide it. He had an easy excuse, of course. If ever pressed, he could fall back on the decided upon story: that Brontë was born addicted to vampire blood. He hated that story, that *lie*, just as much. He hated that he was compelled to keep this ugly, unbecoming, heretical secret. Curse that he should live in an age where the church kept such filth tucked between her robes. He believed Our Lady better than this. If there was one blessing in the midst of this mess, it was that these lies let him vent his rage on the girl whenever she was nearby, and arouse no suspicion for doing so.

After all, Serge's contempt for addicts was well known. He refused to treat addicts in the infirmary, refused to ease their pain in any way – even if they were penitent and humble. Even if they had confessed and surrendered themselves. It was not enough, in his mind, that they be flogged. It was not enough that they be excommunicated. They, too, should be denied the care of the Clerics. They should be left to suffer the consequences of their actions, of their sins. Some admired him for this mindset – admired him for his steadfast commitment to the church's most ancient of doctrines. But just as many disapproved of his refusal to change, to adapt, to forgive. The younger, more forward-thinking clergy would often debate this amongst themselves. *Brother Serge was too old-fashioned, too stuck in his ways*, they would say, *that was why he hadn't been chosen to be Archbishop.*

The moment Serge parted ways with Philip – after a lecture about wound cleanliness, a new tin of salve, and a fresh bandage – he marched swiftly off in the direction of Cyril's office. He threatened to extinguish the many candles in tall candelabras as he swished past. He was spry for his age, a testament to his good health – both physical and spiritual. His eyes were the clear, honey-dipped gold that most clergy could only ever aspire to. A mark of faith, maturity, and fulfillment. He was, after all, well versed in the liturgy, and just as much a learned theologian as a skilled medic. Hunters bowed to their senior as Serge marched past, though he barely acknowledged them in return. To think he'd been the one everyone expected to become Archbishop.

"Father, a word, if I may?"

Cyril looked over from scanning one of the bookshelves behind his desk to see Brother Serge in the doorway of his office. Serge closed the door behind him, locking it and sketching a line in the air that sealed the room against unwanted listeners.

Cyril gestured to the pair of armchairs closer to the hearth. "Of course, Brother. May I offer you anything?"

"No, no, no. I will not take up that much of your time." Serge approached his desk, disregarding the comfortable armchairs and crackling fire. He looked at the many documents and notes, and eyed with suspicion the little vials of gold liquid Cyril had in a small box. He wore an unimpressed look. "Your little test subject is hanging all over my nephew, again."

"Hm." Despite his frown, Cyril resumed his survey of the bookcase, apparently disinterested. He traced his fingers along the spines of a few books, retrieving one of them. "And? They are often together, those two. Unless you mean to insinuate you have noticed something out of the ordinary. I have made no such observation since my return."

"Philip is wounded. Recovering from an injury that still, on occasion, seeps blood."

"He has been injured before, and will be again," Cyril said matter-of-factly. "So, I will repeat that, unless you have noticed behavior out of the ordinary –"

"She was attempting to dress the wound!" Serge snapped, cutting him off. "A bleeding, open wound!" He pointed an accusatory finger at Cyril. "You may be perfectly comfortable gambling with lives, *Hunter*, but I am not."

"Do not insult me, Brother. I understand your worries and will speak with the girl. However, do know that, in spite of your reservations, she is not dangerous. I ask none of us to gamble."

"You have always been so confident in your" – Serge curled his lip and gestured at the collection of bottles and boxes littering his desk – "philters, and your charms."

"Yes," Cyril replied without hesitation, turning a page in his book. "And I still am. If you doubt me, I can call a Cardinal to give you their opinion on the matter."

Serge frowned at the idea, but didn't relent. "She was trying to treat an open, bleeding wound."

"I have her well under control," Cyril repeated. "She has never tasted human blood. She has no craving for it."

"She is cursed with it. She craves it whether she admits it to you in confession or not."

"I have her under control, Brother."

"I was *lucky* to stumble across them and intervene!" Serge shouted and slammed his fist on Cyril's desk. The potions rattled. This was far less about making his point known and far more an opportunity to vent his frustration. Cyril set his book down.

"If Philip knew what she was, he would never spend so much time near her." As Serge spat out his disagreements, Cyril pulled a key from his sash. He unlocked a drawer in his desk.

Serge's ramblings slowed and ceased as Cyril retrieved a sealed letter, tapping it against his other hand.

"We have a formal agreement not to speak of this matter, do we not?"

Serge frowned and eyed the letter in Cyril's hand. That damn envelope practically sneered at him. He didn't need the reminder. That pesky letter could be mailed tomorrow if he dared speak his mind.

"Brother?"

"Yes." Serge straightened and folded his hands into his sleeves. "Yes, we do." He turned on his heel to leave, defeated, but not before hissing through his teeth. "You are playing with fire, Father. Burn yourself, if it pleases you, but do not burn my nephew. He is not kindling for your experiments."

44

THE MAP LAID OUT UPON THE TABLE WAS HORRIFICALLY out of date and unreliable. Domingo already had his cartographers compiling and creating a new one. To temporarily atone for errors, Domingo had penned notes and set them atop places of interest. The Warbling Wren was one such place: where he'd stationed Allermane to watch that sleazy, good-for-nothing grocer. He thumbed through her notes: a detailed report of his routine, who she understood to be his clientele, and the questionable routes he was taking.

He set aside these notes and shifted his attention to Levi as he was shown into the room. He had a stack of parchments with him, the coveted paper that Domingo recognized immediately as being enchanted – a necessary conduit for the sort of espionage Levi was employed in performing. The sergeant saluted and Domingo motioned him toward the table.

"Well?"

"I have compiled a report on the Hunters as asked, sir."

"As you were."

"Your suspicion about documentation was correct. The Deacon is contracted to the church, and not a vowed member of the clergy."

"As we suspected, then, but what is the rest of this?"

"The Deacon," Levi said as he set out his stolen information on the table, "is but one of many such conscripts, and is in fact the only one not to formally enter the church. In the last fifteen or some years, almost all of the Hunters have been recruited by the Archbishop personally."

"He's not been the Archbishop for a full decade yet ... How did he wield that sort of authority?"

"Prior to becoming Archbishop, he was what I believe is considered the Captain of the Hunters, the position the Deacon now holds."

"He had power there first, I see. What else?"

"In comparing the records of those individuals who join the Hunters and those who join the Clerics, there is a great disparity in their upbringings."

"Upbringings?"

"In their class, sir. Those of middling or upper class tend to become Clerics. But those from poverty become Hunters." Levi scoffed. "The highest-ranking Hunters were all sellswords, fighters, slaves, sailors. All of them."

Domingo sighed and rolled his head back on his shoulders. "So, a band of street dogs and orphans are being given free roam over the city. I should check my pockets going in and out of that church." Domingo sat down and stroked his beard. "He has gathered a gang of guttersnipes and dressed them in priestly robes. No wonder they are so fiercely loyal to him."

"The Hunters are, indeed. The Clerics, however, are more divided in their approval."

"Oh?"

"There is a Brother named Serge. Tall, skinny, long ears. Introduced himself to me as the Head of Infirmary, a Cleric. I had a brief interaction with him, and he was quick to speak a lesser opinion of the Archbishop."

"I see. I need to speak with him, he may be useful." Domingo sat back and crossed his arms. "Under what pretense, I wonder ... You said he was Head of Infirmary?"

"Correct. To get him talking, I might suggest that you inquire about the church's handling of their so-called 'sinsick'."

"Did he speak of the matter to you?"

"He did not. However, I do know there is some internal debate over the Archbishop's methods. That Brother is bound to have an opinion. Specifically, the Archbishop's initiatives both to administer medicine to the 'sinsick' and to collect their dead are rather controversial, within and without the church."

"Controversial how?"

"According to church law, consuming vampire blood is a grave sin. It's unforgivable, and if someone consumes, they are to be expelled, and most certainly are not to be embalmed by the church. I'm sure you start to see the conflict."

"I do. Isn't the church offering to embalm the bodies as a form of payment for their surrender?"

Levi nodded, and Domingo had a dawning realization.

"And those who are most for want of coin ... will be the ones to utilize that service, I'm sure."

"Exactly. And the slums in the eastern district boast the highest amount of blood trade and alleged vampire-related deaths, be it from consumption or attack."

Domingo nodded and clicked his tongue. "He's recruiting Hunters from poverty, and he is raising the poor dead to a standard never before attainable."

"And I should note," Levi added, "that the populace believes embalming done by the church prevents vampirism."

"He's no fool. He is cultivating an army of loyal followers. No wonder they flock to the church, or scramble to get close enough to touch his robes. Clever bastard." Though Domingo was clearly annoyed, there was a tinge of admiration in his voice. He drummed his fingers on the table before he seemed to remember something. "I will go speak to that Cleric. You will go with me."

"Sir?"

"While I speak to this Brother, I need you to look for someone: a young woman. A novice, if I am not mistaken. She did not wear the garb of a Sister. I believe her to be the Archbishop's apprentice."

"The Archbishop has an apprentice?"

"He denied it. He called her a patient, but I have my doubts." *She wasn't sick at all.*

"I see. And what does this young woman look like?"

"I suspect she is close in age to yourself. Short, plump, pale with dark eyes. I want her name, if nothing else."

She sounds plain, Levi thought, but nodded nonetheless. "I understand. I'll see what I can find."

NOEL, WHEN UNMASKED, WAS MORE CHARMING than intimidating at a glance – when her rapier was not drawn. Her green eyes squinted and strained at the light bleeding forth from the Warbling Wren. She endured the sting of it as she let herself inside.

Noel walked straight over to Greer's table, and earned the attention of Sergeant Allermane upstairs in the gallery by doing so. She had not worn her cloak and mask, and it took Greer a moment to realize who this newcomer was. Tucked back in the corner, out of direct eyesight from most parties, Noel sat down and tossed her braided blonde hair over her shoulder. She swiped one of the expensive cigars he had in a box before him. He sat upright, taking his foot off the table in surprise, until he caught a sharp look and a bared fang from Noel.

"Dame Noel?" he spluttered. "What in hell's bells do you mean by coming here, ser – I, my lady?"

"Ambrose is dead," she said simply.

"What!" hissed Greer. He scooted in closer and dropped to a whisper. "Immolated?"

"No." Noel accepted the proffered light from one of Greer's men sitting next to her. "He joined the Archbishop's collection. This is your doing."

Greer stammered and rubbed his neck, biting his tongue until his face contorted with the effort. With every second he could feel his head being loosened from his shoulders. "Damn the Father to the depths of the Rotherdare!" he hissed. "He's only *just* come back and –"

"Save your curses, Greer, for someone who wants to hear them," said Noel. "We need a new doctor."

"Eh? And what am I supposed to do about it?"

"You can read, can't you?"

Greer curled his lip in both disgust and insult. "It ain't that simple."

45

CYRIL KNEW HE'D HAVE TIME TO ENJOY A MID-MORNING coffee and a few pages from his book; Brontë was always running late. He'd finished his drink by the time she let herself in, as he'd instructed when he sent for her.

"You wanted to see me, Father?"

Brontë stood in the doorway of his study and waited for him to acknowledge her. He bid her enter with a gesture, and she approached him, kneeling on the hassock by his chair. She couldn't help but gnaw her lip nervously as Cyril took far too long to close his book and set it aside.

"Is it true you were attempting to tend to Philip's injury?"

Brontë swallowed and twisted her fingers together in her lap. "He happened to be fixing the bandage, I only –"

"That is not what I asked."

"I was only trying to help."

"That is not what I asked either. Do I need to put you over my knee to pull the truth from you? Look at me."

Brontë winced under his words and bit her tongue, but did as he asked. His good eye pierced right through her and made her feel stripped bare. He quite liked the look of her nerves, all a mess on the floor before him – though he'd enjoy it much more if she wasn't causing him genuine trouble.

"Did you attempt to dress Philip's injury?"

"Yes, Father. I did."

"Then you've disobeyed me."

"N-no!"

Brontë panicked, hopping in fright and awkwardly sliding off the hassock. She was of a mind to scramble backward, to put distance between them, lest his patience run out when she was within arm's reach. Where an impulsive, snap decision could snuff her life out. Her mouth opened, instinctively spitting out more denials followed by empty apologies. He wasn't interested in hearing any of them, pinching the bridge of his nose before sitting back in his chair. He was remarkably calm, considering her offense toward him. She wasn't sure if she should be relieved or terrified. Worse, she could swear she saw him chuckle at her, swore she heard a deep noise and saw his shoulders move. When he spoke, his voice sure didn't *sound* like it hid a chuckle.

"Stop making a fool of yourself in front of me. Come here."

Brontë shut her mouth before she said something stupid or upset him further, crawling to sit on her knees on the hassock. She folded her hands in her lap and eyed Cyril's cane where it rested, leaning against the inside of his knee as he sat back in his chair. She realized her eyes were lingering on his legs in an unflattering way and stared directly at his boot instead. He repeated to her what she had heard many times in a disappointed tone.

"You are forbidden to place yourself near open wounds, forbidden to go near or in the infirmary, forbidden from entering the Hunter barracks. I sincerely hope I do not need to reiterate why."

"No," she whispered in a hurry. "You do not need to." *Please, no reminders, this was humiliation enough already.*

"Speak up, lass," he said, "and *look* at me when you speak."

"No, Father," she repeated, immediately sitting up and looking at him. "I understand."

"Then I should hope not to hear reports of you disobeying again." His manner indicated the conversation was over, as he looked away from her and back toward his book on the table.

Brontë's lip curled and she mumbled under her breath. "Serge must have told you, that nasty, crabby old man –"

"*Brother* Serge," he cut her off in a forceful tone that made her wither. "Mind your tongue, and have respect for your betters."

Her voice trembled just like her hands. "Yes, Father."

"Serge knows what you are. It is within his right to be concerned over his nephew's safety."

Brontë leaned forward where she sat, standing up on her knees and grabbing Cyril's hand. "But he wouldn't tell Philip, would he? You've forbidden it, haven't you?" *Haven't you?*

Cyril sighed. "Brother Serge and I have made an agreement not to speak of the matter, yes. But even the best men and women can fail, if pushed too far. Do you really wish to test his temper?"

Brontë sat back down on the hassock, hanging her head and realizing, as usual, Cyril was right. "No, Father."

"Good. Then you will do as I have bid, for the sake of young Philip's safety, if nothing else."

"I ... As I am, I am not a danger to Philip, am I?"

"No, I do not believe so."

"Then why isn't that good enough for Brother Serge?"

"You needn't fret over his opinion of you." He withdrew his hand from hers and put it atop her head. "Mine is the only one that matters." Brontë was about to sigh in relief, but as he spoke his fingers curled into claws on her head. "My good opinion is not freely given. You must earn it by obedience. Do you understand?"

"Yes, Father!" she squeaked out in a hurry.

He released the pressure on her head. "Good. That is all. Off with you."

It took a few tries to pull herself to her feet in front of him. He almost smiled, watching her. All it took was a few words to render her unable to walk. She fumbled her way out of his chambers and back toward the bakery.

Hugo saw her walk in, wearing a look laden with self-pity. In the time it took to wander to her destination, her humiliation had morphed to frustration, and she was feeling very sorry for herself indeed. She grumbled and griped as she marched over to her workstation.

"It's not *my* fault," she mumbled bitterly, and not nearly as quiet as she should have. She vented her frustration on her palm with a wooden spoon. "Do this, do that. Take your medicine and don't say a word. All Father ever does is scold me."

Maybe it was his conversation with Cyril that had him feeling so conflicted, maybe it was that he'd caught his cardigan on the door handle this morning, or maybe it was that he hadn't had a letter from his friend south of Meli in two weeks. Whatever it was, Hugo was in a poor mood and his normally brimming vessel of patience was bone dry. *As if she'd treat your work with disdain*, he remembered himself saying. In his naivety, he'd struck a bad nerve. Here was another patient: similarly blessed by Father's work, yet wholly ungrateful. It made his blood boil. Brontë was still grumbling when Hugo spun around and pointed a stern finger at her.

"Don't you complain about Father to me, young lady!" Brontë was so stunned by his severity her hands halted in what they were doing. The strength of his own voice seemed to startle even him, and he had the good sense to moderate his volume. "Do you realize how lucky you are, lass? To be *here*, of all places – at the same time as Father?"

"Lucky?" She scoffed in disbelief. "I think it a curse. Hugo, he despises me."

"Then you are a fool as well as ungrateful."

"I –"

"In another era, you would have been raised up a Torch. If Our Lady had not found you, you may have found your way into the Flagellants' abysmal cult." He set his knuckles on the worktable opposite her and leaned in. "But here you are: being kept, fed, and dressed. Being taught a *trade!* How lucky you are, lass. *Enough.* I'll hear no more of your whining, pull yourself together! I *know* you're a proper lady. Father knows it, too. Act like one."

Hugo then stomped back to his workstation and yanked his towel from over his shoulder.

"And," he added without looking at her. "You ought to *thank* Father for his good work. That you be in the personal care of one of the greatest men of our age is a blessing. I shudder to think how many children are born without."

"But, I –" Brontë prickled at his words and snapped defensively back at him. "I do thank him!" *I do, I do! I take a candle every morning.* Her attitude began to cool in shame as she thought of it. Worthless gestures Cyril didn't even know about could hardly be counted as thanks.

All Hugo heard was *more of her excuses!* "Gratitude" – Hugo whirled back around and pointed at her again – "is in one's *actions,* in one's heart. You think your confessor can't tell when you pay him lip service? You think him a fool? You ought to be grateful he is merciful enough not to answer your insults in kind! If it were up to me, I wouldn't coddle you so. Be grateful Father is a better man than I, with more patience to spare for you."

<h1 style="text-align:center">46</h1>

OUTSIDE THE WESTERN GATE, THE SUN WAS BEGINNING TO set. The rolling hills and dusty roads had grown quiet as workers wandered their way home, as windows began to glow with firelight. Philip and Jael rode through the twilight at a leisurely pace upon the backs of two hardy horses.

Philip was enjoying the sound of his own voice too much. He talked about the shifting of the fields from fallow to fertile, the way the wheat would paint the hills gold come autumn. Even as a Hunter, he couldn't quite escape his miller's roots. He had quite the opinion on the Sunderman mills and their operations for having never once operated a mill, or business, in his life. Jael smiled at his commentary nonetheless, only motioning for him to stop talking when she spied a familiar silhouette on horseback on the road leading back toward the city wall. The silhouette, in turn, recognized her, and moved to close the gap.

Emre and Jael were identical twins in every possible way. Their dusky gray skin and petite builds, their pointed ears and moonlight eyes. Those eyes had occasionally given the pair trouble, looking a little too close to the clouded, reflective eyes of vampires for the local's tastes, especially in the dark.

"Why are you out here?" Emre frowned at his sister as he turned his horse about to walk alongside her. "I thought your patrols were keeping you close to the church while you recover."

Emre sat only slightly taller than his sister upon his horse, with his lamplighter's cloak and scarf wrapped about him, and his rod resting in the designed slot of his stirrup. He held it as proudly as a knight might hold a lance, and none could fault him for it. The guild took great pride in their most essential work.

"We just were speaking with a family out by the hamlets," Jael said, replying with much the same disapproval in her tone. "What brought *you* this far? A new route?"

"Just a delivery. Come on, let's hurry and get you back to your church. It'll be dark soon."

"Philip wanted to stop by –"

"He can stop, then," Emre cut her off. "He won't get lost without you, will he? He's a big boy."

Philip inhaled and had to force his usual smile. "Go on ahead." He patted the leather satchel attached to his saddle. "More for me."

Jael gave him an apologetic smile, and then she and her brother urged their horses on faster. Philip was content to continue up the hill toward the city gate at a much more relaxed pace.

He was not born with eyes that warranted suspicion. And while Jael had the blessing of being clergy, Emre had not quite the same reception in the public eye. Not even being a lamplighter could entirely assuage the locals' superstitions. Therefore, Philip attempted to find it in himself to forgive Emre's ever-abrasive demeanor. At least, that was the sort of thing his uncle had always encouraged him to do. Whether Serge set a good example of that practice ... Well, *that* was debatable. Serge was a judgmental old goat; one need only to look at his opinion toward the sinsick to see that.

The sun was setting, and in doing so painted the valley in splendid colors. The shade of Philip's favorite tree provided a perfect vantage point to survey the rolling fields of cereal crops. He'd been happy to accept the assignment to visit the hamlets, as he knew it would take him through this gate, and right past the tree. Philip had the last mushroom-and-leek pasty he'd been saving for himself still in his satchel. He'd stolen it from the windowsill Brontë had left it on to cool, along with several other delectable morsels, so he and Jael could stop for a picnic at their leisure.

Imagine his surprise as he reached the crest of the hill and found his would-be picnicking spot occupied.

It was rare to see a Flagellant alone. They often drifted through in packs, wailing their warnings and trailing bloodied whips over the roads. A brief inspection of her revealed why this one was alone: her legs no longer worked. Her bare feet and atrophied legs poked out from the worn hem of her tattered robes. She could not keep pace with her ostracized kin, and so she had been left behind. Such was their way – Philip knew this – yet he couldn't help but feel a twinge of pity.

She clung desperately to her staff to stay somewhat upright. After all, with her back bare by design and her wounds still raw, she could not lean back against the tree without putting herself in more pain. Tattered robes were filthy with dirt from the road and stained muddy-green from the grass. Her head was bowed low, or perhaps she had not the strength to hold it higher, her hood drooping and entirely obscuring her face.

Any citizen of Windermere would pretend not to see her. Philip knew his uncle certainly would ignore her, if he were to see such a sight. At first, Philip bid his horse walk past the towering tree, lamenting that his picnic would need to be somewhere quiet on the grounds. But the feeling of pity nagged at him, and so he turned around. He dismounted his horse and secured the reins to a fence post before meandering over to the base of the tree.

He did not take his picnic foodstuffs with him. Those who consumed enough blood were often cursed with a strange sort of survival: they could not waste away by refusing to eat or drink. So powerful and corruptive was vampire blood that it did not take a great amount to render one's body undying. So, denying themselves food or drink, deep in the throes of pain and hunger, the Flagellants endured unending starvation as part of their self-inflicted penance. As if bloodying their own backs was not enough. It would be unreasonably cruel to offer her food.

"May I sit with you?" he asked.

He must have surprised the Flagellant by approaching her, much less speaking to her. She hissed like a frightened feral cat, though one would be forgiven for thinking she hissed at the pain of her own movements. Her raw back was still bleeding, and the whip at her side glistened with the proof. She flinched in such surprise that she had to correct her hood. Philip caught a glance of her haggard appearance, her balding head and patchy, straw-like hair. Her skin, once probably quite human in tone, had dulled to an ashy gray, and was flaking off. Her nails were cracked and brittle, black and blue beneath from bruising.

"What mockery do you make of me?" she said with some effort.

"Nothing of the sort. I'm Brother Philip." He sat down beside her at what he hoped was a respectful distance, and conversed with her as easily as he would an old friend. "I come here to watch the sunset when I have time. You must come by in autumn, though. This old girl above us turns the most beautiful colors. Far more red in her leaves than all the birch that goes yellow."

All his words earned was a bitter chuckle from the woman. "My eyes do not see such things as yours, Brother. But you are quite the orator."

"You should hear me sing! My mother used to say I had the voice of an angel."

"Heh. You are ... young. You will grow to make your mother proud."

"I do hope so."

"Aye, hope young one. It is a precious thing. You should not squander it here, on me. I have no need of it."

"What do you need, then?"

She rested her head against her staff, against the wood to which a homemade cross of rushes and twigs was tied. "Courage," she whispered. "I have need of courage ... to go on."

"I am no confessor, no Cleric. Just another sinner, like yourself. But I know the struggle to find courage. I know it very well."

He couldn't see her smile from beneath her hood, but he could hear it when she spoke. "I am sure you do, young man. You Hunters are a brave sort."

Though outside the city, the toll of the bells carried far. Beneath the tree, both of them perked up to listen.

"Ah, hear that?" the woman said. "Your Lady calls for you. Answer her."

"Aye, but before I go." Philip shuffled in the grass to stand on his knees. He then turned to face her, and offered his hand. Her rosary wound about her skeletal wrist jingled as she set her shriveled hand in his. He beamed a grin, and said a small, quick prayer with her. One of those old, traditional verses that begged for sight in the dark, for safety, for a spark of courage to keep the path lit. When he'd finished, he released her hand.

"May you find the courage you seek," he said.

"Thank you, Brother." She drew her hand back to once again clutch her staff tight. "Godspeed and good hunting to you."

He stood and dusted his cassock off. With the last of the sun's fire disappearing over the mountains beyond the farmland, and the stars beginning to make themselves known, Philip mounted his horse and departed. Beneath her robes, the Flagellant gripped tight the flask of liquid courage the lamplighter had brought her.

47

SERGE HEARD THE FOOTSTEPS IN THE CORRIDOR BEYOND his office, coming to disturb his perfectly pleasant morning, and sighed. He had only just set aside his monocle, and a nearly finished carving, when the door opened. To his surprise, a Huntress announced a visitor for him – and Domingo strolled in after with his beret tucked under his arm.

"I apologize for the intrusion, Cleric."

Serge didn't bother forcing a smile, though he stood from his desk to greet his company. "Captain." He dipped his head. "How may I be of assistance?"

"I am told you treat addicts in your infirmary. I am unfamiliar with this affliction, and had hoped you might be able to enlighten me."

Serge frowned. "You will want to speak with another Bishop: Brother Benjamin. He stomachs that ugly work, I do not."

"Your negative opinion of these addicts seems to be the more popular one," Domingo said. "I am given to understand that your doctrine condemns these folk."

"Your understanding is correct, Captain." Serge narrowed his eyes. "But a southerner like yourself would not come here to speak of doctrine. What is it you actually want?"

Domingo smiled. "Only to understand. A church that simultaneously condemns and cures an affliction is an odd thing indeed." *As if this place needed to be any more odd than it is.*

"We do condemn. And we do *not* cure. I suspect what you call a 'cure' are the pills Father has devised; the tablets dispensed to the penitent fools, the liars –" Serge cleared his throat to keep from fuming his lesser opinion in an unbecoming way. "The addicts who humble themselves and admit their sins of consumption. They are treated in the auxiliary infirmary *outside* our walls, to the east. Never here. Not in my infirmary." He tilted his head up some. "The medicament they peddle there only moderates pain. It is a sort of half-mercy, given to forfeit souls. Well, some call it a mercy, others call it heresy." *And it is!* he thought. *The sort of heresy that would, in another era, have resulted in a hot poker driven through the tongue.* Serge almost smiled at the idea.

"The Bishops at this hospital, then – they are still from among your clergy?" *Or are they more contracted criminals?*

"There are *some* Bishops among us who are content to blindly obey Father. Those content to do so participate in the Archbishop's ... endeavors. I am not among their number." He puffed his chest a touch, evidently quite proud of his convictions. "It is *my* fear that by offering this sort of ... half-pardon, Father facilitates more addiction than he intends. After all, if there is a remedy for the consequences, more will be inclined to take the risk, and come crawling back to his hospital, souls forfeit." Serge set his fist against the desk in frustration. "He cares too much for the body, and too little for the spirit."

All this talk of blood and spirit – but Domingo had caught quick the word he was looking for: heresy! And Serge was delightfully talkative, as those with negative opinions often were. All Domingo needed to do was encourage him in the right way, to give this seminarian at heart an opportunity to preach.

"Therein arises my confusion, sir. How is it that your Archbishop can challenge such a strongly held belief? Would such a heresy not risk removal from his position?"

Serge shook his head. "There is no risk to him. The Heart abides, and so must we all."

"The ... Heart?"

"For such a learned man, sir, you are naive to the workings of our fair city."

"I delight in the opportunity to learn them now, sir. From what you say, your Archbishop's rule is absolute."

"In many ways, it is."

"And how in the world is such power earned?"

"There is no earning it." Serge snorted a laugh. "If there was, he wouldn't be Archbishop."

"Oh?"

Serge puffed and knocked his knuckles on his desk. "If you had told me that a scrappy, skinned-knees street rat ..." He broke off his words with a callous laugh. "A rat *I* stitched back together more times than I could count ... If you told me he would become *my* Archbishop, I'd have laughed aloud. I'd have called you a fool. And yet, here we are." Serge's face drooped. "My Lady ... seems to have a sense of humor, I suppose."

"Your Lady, the church?"

"My Lady, my god," Serge corrected. "Here in Windermere, sir, fire chooses its kindling. We cast no votes, we make no decision – the torch passes as it pleases, whether we agree or not."

"One more question, if you would indulge me."

"Do I have a choice, Captain?"

Domingo smiled. "There is a young lady belonging to your church, she seems to be in the personal care of your Archbishop –"

"Hah!" Serge's outburst was bitter enough to taste. "That *girl* is a curse, and a stain on our church. She was ... born sinsick." He clicked his tongue, muttering under his breath as he shook his head. "Damn Cyril for demanding that we keep such a filthy child."

"Born ..." Domingo thought aloud. "But she's a grown young lady? Your Archbishop has not yet held his position a full decade."

"My apologies, I spoke too simply. The Cyril *I* speak of was the first of his name, dead and gone. The Cyril *you* speak of, our current Archbishop, is the second."

Of course Cyril wasn't his real name. The clergy took on false names as part of their faith. Of course there was no record of him existing before. A street rat – perhaps a criminal himself – hiding behind a predecessor's name was now the unquestioned, almost infallible Archbishop. He needed to know who the man really was. The only outward indication of Domingo's thoughts was a low hum.

"I see. Thank you, Brother. This has been very informative."

48

OMINGO WAS NOT THE ONLY KNIGHT OUR LADY welcomed this morning. Music swam through the air and echoed down the halls as Levi meandered between the columns. It wasn't quite a song, it was more a sustained murmur, fragments of voices and chimes that should have stopped echoing some time ago. If Levi focused, if he tilted his head and leaned his ear, he could make out voices, just barely piece together lyrics. Sometimes, the music seemed echo down from the high ceilings, as if the painted saints and angels were carrying on their praises between the hours of the liturgy. Sometimes, the notes and chimes seemed to crackle from between the candles that lined every wall, every walkway, every niche. The chandeliers hummed along, and Levi felt both a great comfort and a great dread. Something deep in his heart told him to stop listening, to stop lending an ear to magic he did not understand. Hah, if *he* heard this much noise, he could only imagine the ungodly din it must sound like to Domingo.

As Levi wordlessly wandered the nave, he looked up at the row of colored windows lighting the corridor. All together, they formed a storybook scene of knights defending the city from monsters. The first faithful of this order rose up from a fire and brandished weapons of every kind: hoisting spears and crosses, swords and shackles. They wore armor more akin to knights than the cassocks of their modern counterparts. They marched under a gold sky, across a field of blue flowers, and bore their arms against a churning cloud of many monsters: a mass of entangled

278

sinners. *Of vampires, surely,* Levi thought. Wailing vampires tumbled from the belly of a winged creature, a representation of that monstrous old brood – with too many limbs, too many joints, too many eyes and teeth. Its children carried rapiers, those horrid needles through which they strung their threads of blood.

The further away from their source the vampires fell, the closer to the clergy they drew, the more human they became, until the only thing monstrous about them was their teeth. It was difficult to render such detail in glass, but it was there, crystal clear. But then Levi reasoned the church would have good incentive to portray them that way. That the hunt, their so-called mercy killings, were a matter of purification.

So engrossed was Levi in his curiosity, he bumped into a cold shape. He spat out an instinctive apology when he looked down to see a figure kneeling. He then shut his mouth and felt rather stupid when he realized the figure was just a statue: a part of the gravesite. The wall beneath these windows was lined with several stone sarcophagi – each with a carved effigy of the entombed inside lying atop, hands folded in eternal prayer. On the wall behind them, beneath the windows, were weapons mounted to the wall. Hunters from another era.

The marble statue he'd bumped into was a veiled woman on her knees. The statue's head rested atop the burial place of a Huntress, and her hands clung to the sculpted legs of the burial effigy. Perhaps the statue represented a mourning mother or sister, likely long-dead herself, now. Still, it tugged at Levi's heart in an uncomfortable way. The church loved to render sorrow in such ... detail.

Levi looked up at the sword mounted on the wall behind the sarcophagus. It was a simple, utilitarian thing, as most of the Hunter's weapons were. Gold, or rather what he understood to be vermeil – a potent base of vampire-repellent silver covered in blessed gold. It was long enough, in both hilt and blade, to be wielded in two hands, and had a flat nose at the end of the blade, like the ones in the stained glass above. Oddly, he associated the design more with executioners than knights. But then again, that's what the Hunters were, weren't they? Executioners.

He looked back down at the effigy carved of the Huntress. He swallowed a confused noise and leaped back a pace. The statue was gone: the statue kneeling at this knight's feet was gone. He felt his heart speed up in his chest and hissed at it to calm down. Up, down, and back again his eyes scanned the nave. There was not a single statue at any of the graves, not a one. *But he'd touched it*, his lantern had rattled when he'd bumped into it, he'd felt it. His heart wasn't listening to him. Each thud in his chest began to sound like a crash, a bang, like something – someone – banging on a door, demanding to be let in.

Out, he thought, *I need to get out*. He fumbled and hurried backward, almost tripping over his own feet as he went fast around a corner, and thudded straight into *another* cold shape. Cold, but soft, that gasped in surprise as much as he did.

"Seven shoals!" he whispered in his start.

Brontë regained her composure faster than he, and in fact had to hold back a smile at his unfamiliar exclamation.

"Is that what you southerners say?" she asked, fixing her habit from the impact. "When you are surprised?"

Levi backed away and corrected himself, bowing his head to – who was this? She wasn't a sister. "Please excuse me." He eyed her. *Pale, plump, dressed like a novice, close to his age.* Surely this wasn't the right girl? "Miss ...?"

"Brontë."

"Sergeant Levi Sterling. Honored to meet you."

Brontë vaguely recognized this knight: his jaw-length, curly hair and lithe build made him stand out from his fellows. So did his adherence to the church's demand that all weapons be surrendered at the gatehouse; his scabbard hung empty from his belt. A gesture of goodwill, from a southerner, as the crown officers were not required to disarm themselves as civilians were. She'd seen him meandering about the grounds these past weeks.

But he looked unsettled. Though he hid it in his features well enough – Brontë found his eyes easy to read, and the speckles on his cheeks even easier.

"Oh, I see," she said, tapping her own cheek with a finger. "You have the look of a listener." She pointed with her nose to the nave behind him, which he'd just tumbled so clumsily out of. "All these effigies, all the glass, it may be overwhelming to stand shoulder to shoulder with the choir."

You have that look about you. Levi remembered vaguely what that Cleric had said to him. What did she just say? *Listener.* She almost sounded envious. "Is that common?" he asked. "To be overwhelmed in ... here?"

Brontë watched him look up and about at the cavernous interior of the cathedral. It was indeed common, though outsiders always struggled the most, when beset by the overwhelming magnitude of Our Lady and her choir.

"To those with keen enough ears, it can be quite intense." Though she spoke of the church, of local customs and beliefs, she didn't sound in the least bit patronizing or haughty to him. "I might suggest the gardens, sir," she offered. "They are quieter. I am walking there, if you would care to join me."

Levi nodded, more out of curiosity than true belief – but entertaining her invitation catered to both his curiosity and his orders. She led him, then, through the nave and out a small door, into a sheltered cloister. At once it was quieter; he could hear himself breathe again. The rattle and echo of an unseen choir was silenced, and instead the rustle of leaves, trickling of water, and chit-chat of birdsong replaced it.

This garden was empty, save the two of them, and indeed rather small: only a square lined with pristine shrubs, a bubbling fountain in the center, and a niche overflowing with candles against the wall. There were no bodies here, no burials, and no crackling echoes of long-dead voices. *And not a single marble statue knelt at a deathbed.* He watched as his newfound guide went over to a small chest in the corner of the cloister. He debated asking this girl, this Brontë, about the vanishing statue, but resolved to tackle a different question.

"You know much of this ... listener phenomenon?" he whispered.

Brontë gave him an inquisitive look over her shoulder as she retrieved a beeswax candle from the chest. She both envied and pitied him something horrible. What she'd give to hear just a *whisper* from Our Lady, while he hears a whole ensemble against his will. It wasn't fair, not at all.

"Oh, no. I am afraid I am no scholar, sir. No student of the seminary."

He caught another note of envy in her voice. *But wasn't she an apprentice?* Perhaps she was the wrong girl after all.

"One of the Bishops would be better suited to speak more on the matter," she continued. "I only know as much as anyone else here would. Though, if it troubles you, you might consider piercing that ear. Wearing silver earrings, one or many, is known to help moderate the noise." She shut the chest and strolled toward the niche. Levi watched her all the while, hands clasped behind his back.

"Sister Cecilia is a Bishop," Brontë offered as she passed him. "She oversees the public library in the western wing. You might consult her, if you wish to know more."

"I ... may do that, Miss Brontë. Thank you." He looked about at the comparatively humble garden, toward the niche she apparently intended to add a candle to. "Though, you are right. It is quieter here."

She smiled and nodded as she then excused herself a few paces from Levi, kneeling down to set about lighting her candle. A knight was set inside this niche. A comparably small statue to the many the church boasted, a woman Levi thought looked vaguely familiar. The flame Brontë lit sparkled brightly before settling into color among the rest, and she set it in a vacant candlestick at the foot of the niche. Levi had expected her to then pray, to perhaps say some enchantment ... grasp at her rosary, *something*. Surely there was *some* magic to be worked by this ritual. Otherwise, why bother? But she did nothing other than sigh quietly and lean back on her knees, looking at her candle amidst all the others.

"You are quite pious, Miss Brontë?" he whispered behind her.

"Hah." Her callous laughter surprised him. "Not at all. Not compared to most, I don't think."

"Yet you come to pray?"

She shrugged and shook her head, just a silhouette of black against the glow of the candles. "It's not a real prayer. If it was real, I would go to one of the chapels," she said bitterly, before correcting her tone. "I am not much good at prayer. I only come to light a candle." *It's not really praying, it's a worthless gesture.* "Though, not for me."

Levi wasn't sure if it was improper to approach the niche without kneeling, but he did so anyway, walking up beside Brontë as he addressed her. "Who then? If I may be so bold as to ask."

"It's for the Archbishop."

"Oh?" Levi tilted his head and couldn't resist a smile. *So, she is his apprentice after all?* "I was under the impression *he* would be the one to pray on behalf of others, according to your church's beliefs."

Brontë chuckled and nodded. "Oh, yes. His prayers are worth more than mine ever could hope to be." *Not that he'd waste them on me.* She laced her fingers together. "I know mine hold little value. I suppose it's more a habit than anything else, silly as it may sound."

"I don't find it silly at all, Miss Brontë," Levi was quick to say.

She glanced at him and scoffed a bit, but her expression was one of gratitude. She turned back to look at the candles. "I don't always know when he leaves, or where he goes, but I always try to keep a candle lit here."

"Here?" Levi looked at the knight.

"Mother Lilian is the Saint of Reunions," she explained. "Many pray to her, to ensure loved ones come home safely, to ensure Hunters return safely."

Every candle here, a Hunter away? He felt dizzy trying to count them all. *How many bloody executioners did one church need?*

"My prayers, I'm sure, are filthy as rags to her. I can only offer a candle and hope it's enough."

"Enough?"

"I ... used to leave a candle each morning. All the children are encouraged to. For family, for friends. I have no family, so I often left it for Father. Though he was a Brother, at the time." She smiled at the reminiscence, before her joy morphed into a frown. "But there was one morning, when I was young, where I overslept ... and I didn't light a candle."

"And?" Levi coaxed.

"And he lost his right eye to the hunt, that day." She curled her fingers into her dress. "I know it's a silly thing, and a worthless gesture, coming from a ... coming from someone like me. But I have never missed a day since, and I do not intend to."

How nonsensical! was Levi's first thought. But the moment after he'd had it, his heart softened. What a horrible guilt to carry. Surely, she didn't believe that? She seemed clever enough, *real* enough, to know better. But Levi had seen enough grief to recognize the patterns with which people moved through it. They must have been quite close for it to have such an impact on her, even all these years later. *How close?* he wondered. Perhaps she wasn't an apprentice at all, but *what* then?

"I cannot speak for your Father, or your Lady," Levi said. "But I imagine such a heartfelt gesture to be far from worthless."

Another good-natured scoff, another one of her smiles. "Thank you, sir. That is very kind of you to say."

The bells were distant, gentler, when in the garden – but they made their demands known well enough. Levi took his hand from behind his back and offered it to Brontë to help her stand. She accepted it, bowed her head as she bid him a good day, and departed to resume her work. Levi looked at the candle she'd placed – he was now alone, save for Cyril.

The Archbishop had been listening, watching, from the second floor of the cloister, hidden in the shade and half behind a column of stone. The cigarette he'd stepped outside to smoke had been forgotten. He glared as Levi flexed his right hand, the one he'd offered to Brontë. Cyril looked, too, at the candle she'd left behind ... for him. It burned a little brighter than the others, in his eye.

49

THE NIGHT WAS CLEAR. THE USUAL PATTERN OF WINDS had driven the cloud cover out beyond the walls, to churn about above the farmland. The steeple at the heart of Our Lady rose to dizzying heights from one's perspective on the ground. The glittering yellow stars that formed her constellation seemed to reach down to touch the cross at the top, aligning with it as the sky turned and the hours tolled.

The lone Flagellant could hardly see Our Lady, now. Her eyes were failing rapidly, growing foggier and heavier. Her legs had failed her weeks ago. Even if they still answered her, they would doubtless have been worthless now. Every inch of her shuddered with fear, with weakness so consuming she felt herself faltering with every bit of ground she covered. Her feet were bruised from banging on curbs and corners as she crawled, but it hardly mattered – they would not be serving her again.

Her hands were raw and stung something horrible. She'd torn back nails trying to drag herself forward. Tears cut lines through the grime on her face as she struggled onward. The base of her staff dug into the grout between cobblestones, seeking desperately for purchase – for any leverage that could be used to continue this pilgrimage. The lantern tied to it was fading rapidly. The wood had splintered and broken off nasty needles in her hand, but she continued. She knew the path.

On a rope about her neck, rattling and sloshing with every lunge forward, was a sealed flask of oil and the tools with which to light it.

The first pyre stones were close. They were waiting. If only she had dispelled her cowardice sooner, they might not be so unhappy to see her. The wooden steps up to each pyre had long since been dismantled. Bloodied fingertips grasped at the edge of the blackened stone, but she could not pull herself up. She tried to use her staff to push herself up, but it snapped under the weight and clattered to the road. She fell and cried out in both pain and frustration, and her lantern smashed and hissed as it went out.

A knight blessed – or cursed – with good hearing caught the sound from some alleyways over. She adjusted her lantern at her hip and began in the direction of the noise.

The Flagellant slumped against the pyre, hands too weak even to cling to it. Then, with her ear to the stone, she swore she could hear the choir. She heard the prayer chant, in her head and in her heart. The judgment of a thousand and one voices pronouncing her sentence, her salvation, so close at hand. Saints and fellow sinners crashed through her head, words she knew well and still more of a tongue she did not know.

At the foot of the pyre would do.

She hurriedly opened and upended the vessel of oil over herself. She and her robes were doused, the fabric saturated until it clung to her skin. Her fingers fumbled with the flint and steel as her own words tumbled out, echoing the choir she heard. What began as a whisper swelled to a near shout with each failed spark from the steel.

"Hear me, hear me, hear me, my Lady! I give what remains of my flesh. Bear me from this place of sorrow and suffering. Such is the path to the stars." More sparks, not enough. "Such is my path to the stars."

The royal guardswoman heard no choir. Only the ramblings of a lunatic, the frantic scratch of flint, and the fizzling of sparks. She began to run.

"Wait! Halt, there!"

The last of her prayers morphed into pained screams as the fire took hold.

50

Masked Clerics formed a flock upon the bridge. Benjamin had taken up his censer again, and two more Clerics with him. Together with the Hunters, the clergy enforced a boundary around the still-smoldering corpse of the Flagellant. Even the Coldwater undertakers ordered to intervene were reluctant to handle it.

The fire provided was not holy, it could not purify. Half-holy oil was a poor substitute – a crude and failed attempt. It, too, could not purge the sinsick filth. The body was a leaking mess, so much so that the cheap, simple coffin provided by the church was not enough to contain it. Never mind that the corpse had settled into a horrible posture, so the lid could not close. A blackened hand and open mouth pushed up the coffin lid, and so a burial shroud was draped overtop of it – doomed to be soaked with spluttering filth as the natural progression of death happened on an irregular schedule.

The chaos on the bridge was not helped by the appearance of the Archbishop. Maddoc and several other Hunters had to stand between him and the crowd, many of whom scrambled to touch his robes as he walked by, or reached for his hand to kiss it. Just as many who clamored for his affection shouted their disapproval. Would the church, too, embalm this Flagellant? Unthinkable! He had to fight to ignore the deafening din of conflicting beliefs.

A peek under the burial shroud was more than enough. The Flagellant's oiled garb and her skin were so intertwined, it was impossible to tell which was which.

"The arsonist finally arrives." Cyril straightened as Domingo spoke to him. The two men moved away from the body, and away from the crowd.

"You are a learned man," Cyril said. "Surely you knew of the Flagellants before you came here."

"Your Lady's rejected faithful who have wandered the wilds for centuries; aye, I know them. And I know that they never enter the city proper."

"Well, apparently, they do."

"They do *now* – drawn to you. Are you satisfied, Excellency? Have you made your point? How many will you burn to satisfy the appetite of your god?"

"This suicide is not my doing, sir."

"The zealot mimicked *your* magic, Excellency," Domingo said. "She sought to imitate *your* spell, believing it would save her. It is very much your doing."

"Do not insult me. My spell is a mercy. It is not comparable," he pointed at the body under the sheet. "To this. My interpretation of the Torch would have been kinder to her."

Domingo tilted his head, unsure of what on earth *the Torch* might mean. Cyril noticed, and pointed with his head to the body beside the stone. "I believe it high time you learned Windermere's history, sir. I might recommend you start with that accursed treatise, and you will see it was your god that damned her, not mine. Good morning."

Cyril had turned his back already, but Domingo snapped at him. "We have no god, priest. Do not attribute Monocerian magic to something so flimsy as faith."

✠

TO SAY THAT THE PRINTING PRESS was owned by folk with a bias against the sinsick would be a grotesque understatement. A most horrific etching had been rendered across the front page, showing the charred remains of a body blackened by flame, along with bold titles of the scriptures and songs that praised the death as wholly deserved, the inevitable will of Our Lady.

Hugo frowned to see Brontë with a copy of the day's paper. He knew full well what was splattered over the front page. With his outburst about her situation, and the graphic etching of the burnt remains, the paper would make for a heavy read indeed. As he walked by the table, he pulled it out from under her hands.

"No reason for you to be reading this, lass."

Brontë was too quick for Hugo, and snatched the newspaper right back. "There is reason aplenty. I don't need you to coddle me."

Hugo immediately tasted regret in his mouth for his outburst at her. "It ain't coddling."

"Yes, it is." She picked up the paper and pushed herself away from the table. "I'll be outside if you need me."

Hugo put a hand on his hip and watched her march herself outside. As he sat down at his workstation, he could see her through the window – going about her tasks and tending to the ovens, but always going back to read the paper. Perhaps he'd been too ungentle with his words; perhaps they'd been ill-timed. The doubt lingered in his mind, but as he watched her, it began to dissipate. She went about her work this morning with a little more ... purpose than usual. She was being more careful, more precise, maybe a touch more thoughtful.

I don't need you to coddle me, she'd said.

Aye, he thought, *perhaps she is through being sheltered. Or perhaps the fire has grown too hot to ignore, now that it burns at our doorstep in such an ugly way.* He drummed his fingers on his workstation, shaking his head. The dead Flagellant was horrible, and wholly out of his control. It meant change. Still, he felt a certain sense of pride, of comfort, that Brontë would endure the encroaching change.

Outside, Brontë was oblivious to Hugo watching her. Her mind was fully occupied in the environment of her many tasks. The smell of fresh bread and smoked butter, the honeysuckle and cornflowers, the climbing ivy and trickle of fountains. A sanctuary, a haven, a shelter.

As she scraped ashes from one of the ovens, she reached out with one hand and splayed her fingers to feel the heat. It didn't take long for it to become uncomfortable, to become painful. She withdrew her hand and looked down at it – already pink from the agitation of the heat. *It could have been me.* Her hand grew blurry as her eyes strained. *Why not me?* She blinked, trying to fight back the sting in her eyes. Her hand hurt from the heat. She could swear she saw tongues of flame reaching for her hand, melting through flesh. *Why not me? Why not –*

She blinked again. The vision of her hand consumed by fire faded. *Why not me?* A tightness in her chest, and a familiar sensation in her throat that rose to soothe it, answered her question. *Why not? Because I'm here. And aren't I lucky?* Brontë shook her head at herself and puffed through her nose. She had a confession to make. No, not a confession, an apology.

"Brontë?"

A voice she vaguely recognized as Philip's sounded somewhere behind her. He'd already called her name three times, reaching for her shoulder when she hadn't acknowledged him. She pulled away from his hand.

"Not now, please." She put her hand down and took up her tongs. "I have work to do."

In a rare display of empathy, Philip listened to her this time. After all he, too, was feeling a strong ... guilt? He was unsure. He had sought Brontë out to moan to her, as he often did. He'd only realized how cruel it would be to speak of this to her – another sinsick soul, likely far more impacted by the news than he was – when he'd seen her staring at the oven, holding her hand out toward it. Who, then, could share the burden? Not his uncle, not this time. Oh, his uncle would praise him for pushing the sinsick to her death, for unknowingly goading the Flagellant on.

Perhaps Father, in his mercy, would be better equipped to hear his confession about the Flagellant. Philip resolved to seek him out, and left Brontë to her work in the bakery.

51

CRUMBLING RUINS WERE EVERYWHERE AROUND Windermere. Some were great, colossal things: shattered remnants of once-grand keeps and bridges. Others were humble affairs: a few arches and walls jutting from the foliage of the thick forests. Many were churches; forgotten sanctuaries deconsecrated and abandoned as the pilgrim's path diverted, as the march of time demanded it.

It was customary of the Flagellants to never disturb such sanctuaries, and so they held their mass in the remains of a watchtower. Now no more than a few toppled rooftop battlements and walls, it was poor shelter from the drizzling rain, but provided some buffer from the wind. Every night was the same, reciting that familiar old hymn to the Lady with raspy, pained voices – and crying out at the sting of the whip on their own shoulders.

It was their miserable music that made them easy to find, however unsettling it was to hear. The sound of horse hooves in the grass and the jingle of armor made the Flagellants fall silent. The lanterns worn at the hips of the two royal guardsmen burned their cloudy eyes, approaching from between the trees that sheltered the site from the road. Domingo's gilt armor and Monocerian medals at his breast earned him a displeased mumble from several of those present.

Levi and Domingo both dismounted their horses and approached the addicts at a cautious pace.

"I am Captain Castillejo, I come from Coldwater. Who is your leader?"

No answer.

"One of your ... kind." He glanced around at the congregation. "She self-immolated upon the bridge."

Still no answer.

A twig snapped under Domingo's foot as he walked further into the group.

"We" – Domingo spun around to face the speaker – "have no words for *you*, southerner."

The speaker was a man garbed like the rest; in a ragged robe and low-hanging hooded cowl. He held his staff upright, as they all did, never daring to let the cross waver or dip too far, and always keeping his head bowed below it. He was seated on an exposed block of stone.

"Our ways are not known to you," he said.

"This is true." Domingo took a step forward. "I wish to learn."

"Liar!" He stood and pointed a bony finger at Domingo. "You do not want to learn." He stomped his staff defensively into the grass at his feet. "You people of the sea never wanted to learn. You want to conquer, to fetter. You want to make sense of and subdue." He shook his head beneath his cowl. "Even this is too much breath wasted on you. Begone! Quit you from this place. We have no words for you."

"Nothing to be gained here," Domingo mumbled to Levi. "Let us away."

As Levi turned to follow, a Flagellant leaned in a little too close for comfort. The lantern at Levi's hip illuminated a horrible sight beneath her cowl – a desiccated, leathery face, sunken eyes and rotting teeth. She drew cracked lips back and smiled, pointing up at him.

"You ... you have the look of a listener about you, young man." There it was again, that term. *Listener*. Her finger traced a line down to his hip, and she pointed to his lantern. "Have care in the dark. That little lantern will avail you naught, when they come calling."

52

GINGER CAP PATRONS WERE LOUD AND EAGER to be entertained. Erwin's name was written in chalk upon a board, like the other competitors, for patrons to try their luck and place their bets. Zemirah was unimpressed by the rowdy, unkempt atmosphere of the place. She and Esther followed behind Greer, and Hezekiah behind all of them. Greer may as well have a dagger to his back for how tense he was. Esther was more preoccupied with smiling and waving at patrons, though Hezekiah swatted away hands that made untoward passes at her.

Erwin's bloody chest heaved as the ring arbiter held his hand aloft and declared him the winner. An equally split chorus of cheers and boos filled the room as coin was, in that moment, both won and lost. Blood from his nose still flowed over his freckled chest, already glistening with sweat. His opponent was being hauled off the ground, leaving a tooth behind and in a far sorrier state than Erwin. Zemirah was watching with her arms crossed beside Greer.

"That's your thief?"

"Aye, my lady."

"He's a stubby little fellow," Esther mumbled from where her head rested on her sister's shoulder.

"Holds his own in a fight, despite that."

"I like the tall one beside him much more."

Esther was clearly referring to Finlay, who was indeed taller and lankier than Erwin. He handed him water as he sat down and gave him a towel to help stem the bleeding. Zemirah shrugged Esther off her shoulder.

"We're not choosing a new toy for you; we're choosing a candidate for a delicate task."

"No reason he can't be both?" she pouted.

Greer sent Hezekiah to fetch both Erwin and Finlay. Both wore evident confusion on their faces as they were invited into a private room. Erwin was still pulling his shirt on. Both immediately noticed the way Greer was acting. Nervous, terrified, even. They couldn't help but be a bit intimidated by the older, taller woman. Zemirah was a cruel-looking thing, with sharp, angular features, a strong jaw, and dark eyes. She explained her task in straightforward, no-nonsense terms, though some of her archaic language took him a bit longer to parse.

"You want to rob the church?" Erwin finally replied.

"No," she snapped. "We want what the church robbed us of to be returned. There's a difference."

Finlay didn't seem convinced, leaning against the table behind him with his arms crossed. But Zemirah's words were more than enough for Erwin.

"I can get in," Erwin said. "But finding whatever it is they've taken is going to be much harder."

"Yes, they're usually horribly efficient about these things. We fear they may have already taken every parcel from the flour and stashed them. But we would still like to make an effort to salvage anything they might have missed."

"And you believe this misplaced item was delivered to the bakery?"

"Aye, they've a great shared pantry there, part of the cellars and the bakery," Greer offered helpfully, or tried to.

"Do you have a map?"

"I'm surprised you don't have that church mapped out already," sneered Greer. One glance from Zemirah shut him up.

Erwin shrugged. "Never had much of a reason to. Anything valuable they bolt down or lock up. And it's not like they carry anything of value on their person. Vows of poverty and all that. Unless you get their robes or rosaries off them, I suppose."

"You probably wouldn't have much trouble with that."

Erwin scoffed. "If I have time, maybe."

"Greer has a rough map he will provide to you," Zemirah changed the subject. "But you'll need to get past the second gate, where only the clergy and students can go."

Erwin genuinely paused to ponder the dilemma.

"They have that charity event coming up. Lots of nobles visiting the children. It will be busy. We might be able to slip in during that."

"When is this event?"

"It's usually early autumn?" Erwin looked at Finlay, who confirmed it with a nod of his head.

"The papers are already advertising it," Finlay contributed his own knowledge. "I agree, that would be the best bet, to get in and out without the Hunters flogging you raw the moment they see you."

Esther smiled at Finlay's words, her chin propped up on her hands and her legs kicking back and forth in delight beneath the table.

"So soon! How lucky we are."

"What's in it for us?" Erwin wasn't interested in Esther's flowery smile or Zemirah's urgency. True to Greer's original words, he cared only for the coin. Zemirah smiled. She tossed Erwin a coin purse.

"Twenty now, for taking the job. One hundred silver if you get in and out. An extra one hundred per full vial that you recover. You'll bring it back to Greer by whatever means you wish, but do not let the Hunters follow you."

Erwin peeked into the coin purse, satisfied. "Done."

The two were shooed out of the room, then Esther gave Finlay a flirty wave. The two were out in the stables, fetching their horses, when they spoke more on the matter.

"Old Greer sounds beside himself," Finlay said. "It's just a few vials of blood. He could pay them back for the loss."

"If they're sending us to look for it, it must be something special. He'd never go to the trouble if he could bribe his way out."

"How special could it be? So what if the church has it? They confiscate blood all the time."

"Honestly," Erwin pulled down the stirrups on his saddle. "I suspect it's less that the church has it, and more that he wants to keep his customer. He's a businessman, first and last."

"I don't see the point." Finlay stroked his horse's head. "It'll probably have congealed by the time we get to it anyway."

"Well then." Erwin mounted his horse. "Let's be as quick as we can about it then, aye? You heard her, that's liquid silver being wasted."

Finlay mounted his horse. "How do you intend to get in?"

"The carriages can go to the southwest gate, that puts us behind the second gate of the grounds."

"They only do that for the nobles. Where do you intend to get that kind of invitation?"

He smiled. "With a bit of luck, I may already have one."

The two took off south through the winding streets. A quiet choir of thunder rumbled as a storm approached. The two boys urged their horses faster, hoping to escape the torrential rain the late summer brought like clockwork to Windermere.

<h1 style="text-align:center">53</h1>

A RATHER SLENDER FIGURE MEANDERED THROUGH the church, clad in layers of dark linen and leather, wearing a hood and scarf high over their nose and mouth. Like a shadow to the unobservant eye, they blended into the mass of faithful who shuffled into the chapel. But the Hunters could rarely be called unobservant.

Two Hunters noted the hood, glancing at one another and nodding quietly in unspoken suspicion. Their concerns faded when the figure fell in step with the other churchgoers. The hooded unknown knelt before taking a seat of their own, following all of the church's unspoken rules and customs flawlessly - and so sank back into anonymity among the pews.

They were no fool. They had seen the Hunters watching them. Mahogany eyes were bright and alert, shifting beneath their hood as they watched the guards. The service was a long one – full of sitting and standing, of hymns and recitations – but as it ended, and the parishioners began to depart, the evening was only just beginning for the figure in black. The courtyard just beyond the chapel would naturally fill with people. The churchgoers tended to congregate here, making use of the safety and quiet of the grounds for idle chatter or even debate.

It was here, the figure knew, they could meander and slip past the guards. The cloister that surrounded the courtyard, with its many pillars and meticulously trimmed trees, thronged with people. Even with the church's brilliant lampposts, the nights were dark and deep. The black served the figure well as they wove

302

a path like a needle through fabric, winding and twisting their way through people, keeping their head down near the Hunters, and finally slipping nonchalantly behind a tall shrub that grew close to the wall.

The branches they had cut before to make an easier path for themselves had miraculously already sprouted new buds, and they swatted them aside with annoyance. Really, did everything in this bloody church boast magic? Tight up against the wall, they counted every second, every footstep, moving quietly from the shelter of one towering shrub to the next in the dark. They counted where they were, and looked up. The leaves above glittered gold from the light shed by a window. A quick stretch, and up they went, fingers digging hard into the divots in the old stones and feet doing the same.

Shielded by the tall shrub from outside viewers, the old window latch was simple to undo, even from the outside. A thin blade did the trick. It swung open silently and the figure hopped nimbly indoors, dropping to a crouch and shuffling to the cover of a nearby curtained alcove. Not a moment too soon, as a breeze rippled through the shrubs outside and made the window clatter back against the wall. A nun jumped in surprise and hurried over, looking down outside the window to see nothing, and closed it.

The figure waited and waited, not daring to poke out from their hiding place until they were absolutely certain the nun was gone. It was then a careful circle around where they had infiltrated: the library. They zig-zagged between bookshelves until they reached a ladder intended for accessing taller shelves. A quick check showed that the library seemed uninhabited – that nun must be long gone – and they raced up the ladder, scaling it nimbly and leaping to the banister of the floor above. A quick pull and they rolled over it, crouching yet again to get their bearings.

The library was a great beast of a room. It bewildered the mind to think this was only one of several, and that supposedly the largest chamber went deep, deep underground. Luckily, at this time of night, very few had reason to be in the library that housed boring documents such as public records, builders' blueprints, or tariff codes. Very few, but not zero. The figure in black knew they had to go higher to get what they wanted. Already they had ventured beyond what the average citizen could walk in and find. The higher floors held higher sensitivity documents, things that one would typically need a Brother or Sister to fetch, if one were considered worthy in the church's eyes to read it at all. The figure in black didn't need to worry about the church's good graces as they clambered higher, curling fingers into wrought-iron banisters and decorative filigree to pull themselves up and over another level of bookshelves.

They halted on the fourth floor, circling the walkway that let out into the atrium of the library at large, until they arrived at a pair of double doors. This was where their venture would prove challenging. A lockpicking set made only the smallest clicks, but a racing heart and nerves made it sound like thunderclaps. It was not a giving lock, but they were skilled, and with some bent tools, whispered magic to coax it along, and a final desperate shove, the doors unlatched and swung silently inward.

The library inside was certainly not unloved ... but it was largely unused. A thin coating of dust was visible on the sheets thrown over furniture and shelves. A few books were out of place, copies pulled down for review and now sat on bookstands or the long tables between shelves. But even these tomes had a thin layer of dust. As the figure shut the doors behind them, they crept forward on the floor and felt a slight give beneath. This room was internal, with walls of bare flagstones and sagging, ancient timbers holding up the floor, a small vein of the ancient structure visible just beneath her newer, polished exteriors. They crept forward carefully, low to the ground, attempting to minimize any squeaking or whining in the old floorboards.

They came around a bookshelf to find one workstation, surprisingly clean. It had one of those ever-burning lanterns set upon it – the only light burning in this abandoned room. Upon this workstation was the very tome our figure in black needed ... and they were not oblivious to this. They circled the small writing desk and the stool that sat before it. They waved their hands, expecting to encounter some shield – brushed their foot over the floor, expecting some threadwire trap to dissuade them. They encountered no resistance. Still unconvinced, they poked the book with their dagger, flipping a page over and hopping back a pace to see if this earned the ire of some protective entity. It did not.

Satisfied, the figure set to work, whipping out spare pieces of parchment and unfolding them from their pocket. They flipped meticulously through the pages, looking for names they knew to be of interest, and pausing on some that piqued their curiosity. Upon finding the information they hoped for, they set their own parchment down atop the records, mumbling a spell of their own and lifting copies of the ink up into their own brand-new parchment, duplicating the lines they needed and nothing more.

A bronze voice yelled out and the figure jumped. It was a strange sound, a new sound – something they'd never heard before. This was no call to worship or prayer, no chime for hope, nor peal for the dead. It screamed out like a warning. Angry and obstinate and loud. The alarm bell. Voices and scratching could be heard in the distance, and the figure in black cursed under their breath. They quickly ran their eyes over the remaining pages, trying to memorize all they could, before spinning around and dashing for the double doors and leaving that dusty, dead-end room behind.

The doors closed softly, and thank goodness. On the floor below, Hunters were pouring into the room. The Deacon was barking out orders to comb each floor and check each room, as well as the exits. The figure in black smiled as they realized one such exit was on the same floor, just opposite them. They hugged the wall, practically crawling on their belly, careful that no Hunter see them out of the corner of their eye. But the Hunters were quick and efficient, and had already begun to climb the stairs to the upper floors of the library. Though the thief's heart pounded, they kept their pace steady, silent, until they finally reached the door they needed. They reached up to find it unlocked, and thanked their luck – but cursed it the next moment. A Hunter with sharp hearing hollered and pointed, and the Deacon's voice boomed out as they threw themselves through the door.

"There! Fourth floor, after them!"

As they found themselves racing down a columned corridor, with true parchments tucked tight inside their chest pocket, the decoys they carried flapped at their belt, billowing like a pale brown banner against their all-black ensemble. The slick marble floors made for difficult maneuvering, and twice already they had slipped and had to correct with a haphazard turn down a different hallway. This was bad. Disoriented and off course, they had no way of knowing their whereabouts in the maze-like structure of the cathedral. How many bloody hallways did one church need? Dodging locked doors and tumbling down spiral staircases, they tried eagerly to make their way down – down, down, to somewhere they could hope to flee, even if it meant tumbling down a small drop onto a courtyard or roof.

The bell screamed and voices could be heard, panicking. The thief came around a corner and smashed into a Sister. She screamed in fright, but they only shoved her aside, bolting for the door at the far end of the hallway. It opened! They spun themselves around and locked it. Wheezing for breath, they put their hands up on the door as sweat dripped from their brow and nose. They knew they had precious little time. The Deacon, at least, would have a key. But they could reorient themselves, if for but a moment. So, they gathered themselves and turned to survey the room for escape routes.

They stopped, dumbfounded to be standing in front of the writing desk again. The ever-burning lantern seemed to laugh at them. Fear and confusion gripped them. Had they been knocked out? Perhaps a Hunter struck them when they ran. Did they fall and hit their head? The desk they could see, clear as day – but the rest of the room seemed ... fuzzy. Indistinct. Smoky, almost. The overwhelming aroma of frankincense smothered the room. They stumbled back a pace, whipping their head around, eager to leave, even if it meant meeting the Hunters head on. They cursed aloud in surprise and fear to see someone standing there, barring the way back.

Maddoc burst through the door, and two Hunters spilled into the room after him with blindingly bright flames in their hands that illuminated everything. But the room was empty. The only disturbance was the three Hunters and their lamps. One of the Hunters lifted their hand, trying to cast light over to the far corner.

"Hiding somewhere?"

"No."

Maddoc had already seen what he needed to know. He'd smelled the incense the second he entered the room, and now tapped with one foot at the ashy, smoldering red mark of a small cross on the floor: a rare token from the Cardinals, demonstrating their intervention.

"It looks like our guest earned himself an audience with the Cardinals. Come on, back we go. Inspect every lock, follow every path. I want to know everything."

Not a Hunter, not a Cleric. This figure wore red, from head to toe. They were perfectly still. Two hands pressed palm to palm. They wore a mask cast in brilliant gold that matched the chains hanging from their wide-brimmed hat. Not even the fabric of their robes moved. The thief in black backed away.

The Cardinal dashed toward them. They yelled in surprise, reaching for their dagger, but it was swatted out of their hand before they'd even had time to brandish it. The strange, gliding movements of the Cardinal were off-putting. The very air around them thrummed with magic. They seemed almost to float, rather than walk or run. And they moved impossibly, terrifyingly fast. A spindly, ice-cold hand grabbed the trespasser's arm, gripping it so hard they gave a surprised yell at the pain. And they were *strong*. The figure in black thought their arm might be simply crushed. They were then unceremoniously twirled about, arm jammed up behind their back, between their shoulder blades. It strained their muscles in such a way that they cried out against their will.

Another cold hand wrapped about their head, half cradling and half clawing into their cheek. Then a second gold face was in front of them. Closed eyes and a soft smile, looming closer. Through the pain in their arm, the black-clad thief realized there were two of these people, these *things*.

A red hand took hold of the captive thief's free wrist, forcing them to hold it out. In the dark, there was a faint glimmer between the clergy's fingers. A gold needle, lethally barbed and looking more like an adder's fang, materialized in the Cardinal's raised hand. The thief voiced what they could of their disapproval, as if it mattered. The hand that cradled their face clapped over their eyes. Pain seared hot down the thief's outstretched palm, and they felt blood dripping from their fingers.

Several voices spoke then, in an old language. Too many voices for the two that were present, some that sounded almost familiar, familial? And still some like nothing they'd ever heard before. Then, nothing.

Levi gasped and his eyes snapped open as he lay in his bed at Coldwater. His heart pounded hard inside his chest as panic trembled through his body, and his bed was damp from sweat. He nervously sat up, clutching his heart, flexing his fingers, trying to ground himself. He felt a deep, deep unease, and a nagging sense of forgetfulness. Fragments of what must have been an anxiety-induced nightmare fluttered from his mind. He rubbed his eyes and groaned. A disconcerting flash of red and unblinking pair of eyes were vanishing from his memory with haste.

It must have been a nightmare, then. Yes, surely, a nightmare born of anxiety. The sort of nerves he knew himself to suffer from the night before any attempt at infiltration. *Yes, that's right*, he thought. Tomorrow would come, and he'd go to the church, as his captain had ordered. He'd take the path he prepared, up into the library at night, to learn more of the Father's connections and work – to learn his real name. He repeated it over and over to himself: the path, the steps, the count he'd memorized for the changes of the Hunter's guard.

As his heart slowed and his tremors subsided, he sleepily shook his head at himself for his foolishness. He slumped back down and rolled over. It was just a nightmare, born of nerves.

Come morning, he would roll up his sleeve and find a gnarly, blue-black bruise telling him otherwise.

54

THE PIPING HOT CUP OF COFFEE BRONTË HELD in her hands would go cold if she did not hurry and make up her mind! She held it gingerly upon a saucer, though it practically rattled with how she trembled now. Her eyes burned with the effort of being up so early. It was still horribly dark outside, and the orangery had precious few lamps to speak of. Still, she could see Cyril, sitting in a wicker chair beneath a flowering orange tree, with a small table and lantern beside him.

He was already dressed for the day, with his stole about his neck and his cassock neatly pressed. Oh, she should have ironed her dress, too, before coming to see him. She argued with herself whether to leave now, before he noticed and demanded she come over, or swallow her pride and nerves both, to stay and approach him on her own. Never before had any confession required such courage from her.

Cyril sat silent with his head bowed, facing one of the orangery's pools, a wide basin of water filled with lily pads. He was known to frequent the orangery early in the morning for a precious few moments of solitude and his usual prayer, and Brontë felt an incredible guilt at intruding upon such an intimate part of his day. But this could not wait – if for no other reason than her courage would wane.

She watched, sheltering the cup of steaming coffee from a falling leaf, for Cyril to lift his head up and set his prayer book aside. She saw him do so and then, with considerable effort, she forced herself to step out from between the trees. Her voice was hardly a whisper, as she approached him.

"Good morning, Father."

There she was again, smelling sweetly of vanilla and myrrh, tricking his mind into thinking he could taste brown sugar on his tongue. He lifted his head from where it'd been perched on his hand to see her already wearing her work apron and carrying a small cup of coffee upon a saucer. It was early for her to be up, even earlier than she'd be up to leave a candle for him.

"Good morning."

"I wasn't sure if you'd already had coffee this morning."

Brontë smiled sheepishly as she set the coffee down on the table beside him, pushing an empty cup aside to make room. His lips parted in surprise at the gesture.

"How thoughtful. Another is always welcome, thank you."

No hassock accompanied his chair here, not like in his office or in his study. But Brontë felt that a just penance as she sank to her knees beside his chair. She sat back on her legs and fumbled with her apron. He was warm, and it kept the chill of the morning away. Or maybe it was the butterflies that still hadn't settled in her belly that warmed her. *Courage, courage!* she tried to tell herself. *And don't you dare mumble! You know how Father hates that ...*

"Do you wish to confess?"

"No. Well, yes, but –" Brontë put a hand over her eyes and shook her head, taking a moment to compose herself. He graciously allowed it. And when she'd taken a deep breath, she straightened her posture, folded her hands in her lap, and looked up at him. Though her voice trembled, she forced it forward. "I wanted to apologize. Not ... not to Our Lady, but to you."

"Is that so?"

His unimpressed tone threatened to sap her courage dry. Still, she swallowed the dryness in her mouth and did her best to speak clearly.

"I realize you ... have been very kind to me. And I have not demonstrated the appropriate gratitude to you, for all that you do. I'm sorry. I hope you can forgive me." *Please don't think poorly of me.*

Cyril was taken rather aback by this. Gratitude? And not empty, either. Here she was, up early, bathed and dressed, with even a little gift in tow. This wasn't her typical confession, muttered with bitterness and drenched in self-pity. She spoke clearly, as he always told her to, with conviction. Who was this strange lady, and what happened to the entitled, insecure girl he'd been tolerating all these years? What force conspired to shake her so soundly? She must have been nose-deep in the newspapers, he reasoned. He could imagine it, imagine her, reading that article over and over, perhaps picturing herself in that Flagellant's place. And learning of her little ritual recently had him feeling an odd sense of endearment besides.

"You are already forgiven," he said.

She smiled, but shook her head. "You are giving me a priest's forgiveness."

He paused, tilting his head in a manner indicating his confusion. "Yes?"

"But I am not ... this is not a confession." She scooted closer, standing on her knees as she reached with both of her hands for his. He let her take it from the arm of his chair. Goodness, she held it so gently, so close to her chest. "My apology is to *you*. Not as a priest, just ..."

"Just?"

"Just you." She clasped his hand in a manner so devout, and here she was proclaiming such reverence to be for *him*? And heavens, did she really need to look up at him like that? Since when did she wear a pout like that on her lips? Since when did her eyes catch the light in such a way?

"And how, may I ask, do you envision *my* forgiveness to be different?"

She shrugged, a sad smile on her face. "I suppose ... I assumed I would need to do more."

"Forgiveness is not earned."

"Our Lady's forgiveness is not earned. Hers is unconditional. You dispense it on her behalf." She stroked his hand, fingertips sliding over the leather of his glove, over the veins beneath it. It made his arm prickle beneath his sleeve. "And you do it so well. But what I seek is human, not divine. I want *your* forgiveness, human and earned, with any terms or conditions you require." She tilted her head and looked up at him, heart pounding wildly at her own bravery. "Can you forgive me for this ask, too?"

He could see the rise and fall of her chest beneath her apron, the quiver in her lip, he could even feel her heartbeat rapidly in her fingertips. She was so very nervous, more nervous than she had been for any confession he recalled. And he recalled many of them. Was it wrong of him, he wondered, to prefer her like this? Flustered and clinging so tightly to his hand, begging for penance. Oh, there were many things a mind like his could conceive to coerce her into. He could tell her to do anything. *Look at her*, he thought, *she wants to obey.*

"Of course, little one," he replied. "I will forgive you."

Brontë perked up despite herself at this ... endearment? No, surely not. And more forgiveness promised, but no cost? Was he coddling her, *still?* Humiliation burned hot in her breast. She tugged his hand closer and leaned in further still, her body brushing up against his leg.

"But what would you have me *do?* Please, I want – I need to do right by you. Anything. Anything at all?"

Don't you dare say that. Not anything. Never anything. Cyril watched as she studied his face intently. She still held on to him so tightly, still stroked the back of his hand with her fingertips, still had her body so perilously close to his leg. He took a deep breath and regretted it, it only filled his head with her scent, with all her vanilla and sweetness.

"I have told you to obey me," he finally said. "To faithfully take and record your medication, to have respect for your betters, to serve Brother Hugo as his apprentice and learn well from him. I would see your continued obedience in these matters."

"Is that all?"

Don't look so disappointed. "I think it is suitable." He eyed her sternly. "Or is earning my good opinion through obedience not enough for you?"

She pressed up against his leg and shook her head with haste. She even dipped her head to kiss his hand and apologize. "No, no – forgive me, of course it's enough, I just ..."

"You just?"

"I just think you are being rather gentle with me."

"Would you prefer I be rough?"

"I ..."

A long pause. "Would you?"

He flexed his hand in her grip, and she became at once very aware of the discrepancy in their size and strength. Her eyes wandered down to his lap, tracing the shape of his legs beneath the pleats of his cassock. Why, she was right up against him! When had they grown so close? Why hadn't he corrected her? Heavens, he wouldn't really make good on his threat to put her over his knee, would he? She was half there already. The more she thought about it, the more she convinced herself he absolutely would bend her over, and without hesitation, if he saw fit to do so. Her cheeks reddened as she imagined it.

Cyril was very well aware of her inspection of him, and even took a little guilty pleasure in being subjected to it. Her eyes traveling all over his thighs like that, what was she thinking, the little fiend? Her face had erupted into red so swiftly, too. What an active imagination she must have. My, my, how she surprised him this morning! It wasn't even light out.

"Well?" he said. "Answer me."

"I … suppose I feel something rough is … deserved."

No, absolutely not. Do not encourage this. "And I feel it would be unnecessarily harsh."

Oh, how she trembled against his leg. Would she do the same bent over his knee, he wondered? Ah, what was he thinking? A man of his age, his station, his *faith* had no reason to be entertaining this. It had gone too far already. He needed her off his leg, away from his hand, away from *him*. Heavens, why was she so *close?* She spoke before he could act on his thoughts.

"Do you think that poorly of me, Father?"

"Pardon?" He couldn't help but look down at her. Her face had fallen. It was plastered with shame, embarrassment – she really was so expressive, so easy to read.

"You think that I would be unable to endure even the smallest discomfort, the slightest pain." *And perhaps you are right,* she said. A bitter puff of laughter from her nose, and Cyril caught a glimpse of the brat he knew better. He almost smiled. "And so you shelter me. You coddle me."

She has something to prove. And how vile to take advantage of it, a man like him? *But who else?* What sort of example was this?

"I want your honesty," he said. She at once straightened up and looked right at him, nodding obediently in understanding. "Is to endure a harsh penance what you want, little one?"

"Yes, Father. It is."

Cyril nodded. *Bastard! Don't you dare.* "Come see me tonight, nine o'clock. You need bring nothing with you."

55

BRONTË FELT AS IF SHE MIGHT KEEL OVER as she approached the door to Cyril's study.

He motioned her inside with two fingers from where he sat in his chair, and bid her close the door behind her. She approached him, then, but he tucked the hassock she would usually claim underneath his chair with a nudge from his ankle. Brontë saw him pull his rings from his right hand and set them in a dish on the table beside him. Her stomach felt like it had flipped over and back again. He was going to hit her.

"And still you ... conspire to be gentle with me?" she breathed.

"I do."

She wrung her fingers together.

"Take my kindness for what it is, little one," he said. "I would not ask you to endure more than you are due."

"But who decides that –"

"I do. Now come here."

She shuffled closer, and he guided her to his right side, where he then instructed her on how he'd like her to bend over his lap. What was she thinking, asking for this? What humiliating mess had she put herself in? She went along readily, too, with his instruction. Her toes fidgeted on the floor behind her as she was prostrated over his knees.

"Pull your skirt up for me," he said.

"But –"

"Obey."

She reached back and gathered up her skirts in her hands. She tugged them up, her dress and her petticoat, until they revealed the end of her stockings above her knees, revealed the tail end of her corset and the chemise beneath it that fell slightly shorter than the rest.

"All of it," he said.

She hung her head and had to grasp a few times to take a firm hold of her chemise. But that, too, she pulled up and over her hips, revealing her backside to him, though she instinctively tried to cover herself with a splayed out hand, as if that'd do any good to conceal her in this position.

Cyril's hand was so very warm, though it frightened more than comforted her when it took hold of her wrist.

"Don't try to hide."

She squeaked a vague acknowledgment, and he smiled as her hand flailed a bit nervously in his hold. It felt good to hold her like that. He pulled her arm back just a bit, just enough to make her back arch and a confused note sound from her throat.

He could hold her hands behind her back ... but, oh, she was already shaking something horrible. Perhaps that would be a touch too frightening for her, for this first time over his knee. *First and only*, he told himself; despite already daydreaming otherwise. He guided her arm forward, setting it upon his leg before he wrapped his left hand about her hips and held both her and the accumulation of her skirts firmly.

The first hit from his right hand made her catch her breath. *It hurt!* One foot came up to rub the back of her calf and she gasped in quiet surprise. Still, a little smile formed in the corners of her mouth. *It hurt!* He wasn't being gentle, he wasn't coddling her, and she felt rather a sense of pride in knowing it. She bowed her head, then, in a sort of wordless submission. Her backside shook from the impact of the flat of his hand, and the snapping sound of his glove against her skin made her blush something furious. A blessing, then, that she be bent before him in this way, where he could not see her flush with color, or her lips dare to curl into a satisfied smile.

He was a Hunter, a man whose body was experience-hardened to impact. Such dainty blows as what he administered to Brontë were nothing compared to what his body was accustomed to, she knew this. But she, well – she in contrast was a tender thing, soft and supple and delicate. Cyril was biting back the urge to grope her backside. Refraining from such a thing was a means of hiding behind the excuse this was penance, and nothing more, and therefore it was not a vile abuse of his authority to coax a girl half his age into his lap.

Every blow his hand struck felt harder, hotter than the last, the pain increasing far more rapidly than she'd expected. All the while, as her legs shook and her arms trembled, Father repeatedly struck his blows, hitting harder until he finally won a desperate, ungainly yell from his charge.

With that noise escaping her lips, Brontë's slender fingers curled against his leg, and she instinctively tried to pull away from the source of the overwhelming pain. Her wriggling achieved nothing, her toes simply slid back a few inches across the rug, leaving more of her weight to fall forward over his knee. She trembled so pleasantly in his lap, just as he knew she would, just as she had this morning, wooing him into this arrangement.

This wasn't for pleasure, it was for penance: a lie both were trying and failing to sell themselves. Brontë, bargaining with herself that it was only a just humiliation, a lesson and her comeuppance – and Cyril hiding behind the excuse that he was her confessor, and therefore had the right to impose whatever penance he deemed appropriate to better her. But the sound of her cries and the sting in his own hand had him imagining things far beyond a simple spanking over his knee.

It's not for pleasure, she thought. *So why does it –*

She made the most delightful squeal as he struck a sensitive nerve. She wriggled, too, and he moved to hold her still. When she opened her mouth to speak, a long, sweet moan prefaced any serviceable words.

"It hurts ..."

"It hurts as it should."

Her hips rocked over his knee and her thighs rubbed together. She hummed a questioning note as she felt the skin of her legs becoming slick. She began to cry in earnest. Embarrassment at her tears made them spill faster down her cheeks. Cyril's hand hovered over her backside, and he leaned in a touch closer.

"Shall I stop?"

"No, I ..." She sucked air in through her teeth and rubbed her thighs together. *Why were they wet?* "I ..." *Focus! I can handle this.* "I can continue."

Of course she'd say that, he thought. *She wants to prove herself.* It was up to him to set the limit. What a terrifying thought. He could color her black and blue and still not be satisfied.

"Five more," he decided. "Count them."

"Nnh? What –"

He hit her again and she cried out. Her back arched up and her legs shook.

"One," he said.

"One," she repeated.

"Good. Now the rest."

Such simple praise smothered her senses so much that she almost forgot to count for him when the next strike came. The third was slurred out between wet lips as his hand somehow grew even heavier. *Would this bruise her?* she wondered. The fourth hit answered that question with a resounding 'yes'. She had to pant and practice the word several times to get it out.

"F-four ..."

"Say it properly, or I will start the count over from one."

"Four!" she hurried to say, and earned herself a smile she couldn't see.

The final hit found her and she yelled despite herself. Before she could be embarrassed by it, she corrected herself and counted it. "Five!"

"Very good."

His praise drenched her nerves again and made her shiver something horrible. She even moaned out a broken syllable, a vague sound of satisfaction. Cyril could practically hear her heart racing as he slid his left hand forward. He reached underneath her and cradled her head. She settled her cheek into his palm without a hint of shame or hesitation. Her head swam and she felt warmer than she ever had before, both from pain and very confused arousal.

"Take deep breaths," she heard him say.

There was no answer, could be no answer, between sobs and gasps for air. Look what he'd reduced her to with just his hand! Cyril found himself looking at her bare ass in his lap, red and glistening with sweat, purple bruises beginning to form. He took pleasure in seeing his good work – but that pleasure was a reminder, a bell in the back of his mind, and he moved to cover her up, unfolding and pulling her chemise, petticoat, and skirt back down.

"I could ..." she panted. "I could –"

"Breathe." He stroked her head and she felt something pleasant travel through her body. "Slower."

She obeyed without thinking, taking in a long, shaky breath.

"I could ... have handled your rings."

The low laugh she earned made her cheeks light up cherry red.

"I know you could have," he said. "But you must learn, too, not to mistake my kindness for coddling."

She moaned in frustration and tried to push herself up, but her arms struggled too much to hold her weight, and she sank back down.

"How," she whined, "am I supposed to tell which it is?" She nosed into the palm of his hand, which he opened further for her, allowed her to put her lips to it and blink her way through a few tears and further shudders. Another chuckle made her cheeks burn hotter still.

"You will learn, with enough time," he said. The adorable disagreement she gave, shaking her head and pouting into his hand, made him smile. "And until then, you will simply need to believe me. Have I earned your confidence enough to make this agreeable?"

"Yes," she breathed, only half thinking. "Yes, of course ..."

Imagine her – *her!* – bartering confidence with the Archbishop himself! As if he needed to earn anything from her. *Do not mistake my kindness for coddling,* he had said. Kindness, for her? How many years had it been since she'd felt a drop of kindness from him? She ... she'd missed it. She'd missed it dearly! She soaked in both his praise and his kindness; rare delicacies she was afforded, no, that she had earned, and was lavished with in reward. Both in his words, in the soft, strangely affectionate strokes of her head, the comfortable quiet between them where she needed to do nothing but breathe and just be.

A slight shuffle was enough to convey she was ready to leave his lap. Though, as she sunk down onto the hassock he had waiting between his legs for her, she almost regretted removing herself from him. Would she ever be that close to him again? The thought distracted her from noticing the way he tugged his sash between his legs to cover himself. Brontë winced a little as her sore backside touched her legs, and shuffled so that she might sit upon the hassock in a way that caused her the least pain. Even as she did so, she felt a strange satisfaction from feeling the ache. Almost reassuring, in its own way, that it was real, that it remained, even after her time being held by him was over.

Cyril watched her collect herself in front of him. Between his legs on the floor before him was right where she belonged, he thought. She wiped her eyes on the soft heel of her hand, shuffled her hips on the hassock, fixed her skirt and petticoat. When she managed to look up at him again, he had a look of subtle satisfaction that made her feel an immense sense of pride.

"You have endured your harsh penance, little one. Well done."

More praise, more of it! "Thank you, Father." She reached for his hand, and again he provided. She pressed her mouth to his knuckles, soft and gentle against the tingle that still swam through it. She opened her eyes to look up at him as she did so, and he was grateful for his sash obscuring the consequences of such a look. "And do you ... forgive me?"

"I do."

56

JUST AS DUNRIOR WAS SURROUNDED BY ACRES of parkland within the city wall, so too was the Folville Estate edged by parklands. Far less private, the big house was close to the main boulevard, with a long gravel drive that allowed for carriages to loop through and deliver guests both personal and professional. Behind the house, in the sprawling lawn, Erwin was entertaining himself on a makeshift archery range. Hedges lined the gravel yard, and he was making a decent display of fiddling with a new trinket he'd taken a liking to: an incredibly small and lightweight handheld crossbow.

"I'm glad to see you home, rather than out causing trouble."

"You sound like Nanny Wallace." The string twanged and he let fly a bolt. "Next you'll send me to bed with no supper."

"If anything, I'd rather you ate more."

Erwin rolled his eyes as he loaded another bolt. "Loose."

The servant obeyed, tossing a clay pigeon out in front of Erwin. It exploded in a puff of orange powder as he hit it midair.

"Good shot."

The little grin that flickered at the corner of Erwin's mouth betrayed how much he enjoyed his sister's praise. She smiled earnestly at him, but he was quick to wipe the expression off his face. He fidgeted with the crossbow, inspecting it and loading a new bolt.

"The reload should be faster."

"Maybe you're just slow."

"Oh, really?"

"I bet you I can reload faster."

Erwin sneered and bowed to his sister. "May the best Folville win."

Erwin knew well his sister's weakness for trinkets and gadgets – as well as her love of friendly competition. Indeed, he'd been counting on it, as he needed to distract her while Finlay snuck into her office.

Finlay slunk into the house and quickly ascended the servant's stairs; under the pretense he'd been sent indoors to fetch an item for Erwin. As he strode down the carpeted hallway, Finlay pulled another pair of letters from his breast pocket. The first one told him how to access Aoife's office, and gave further instruction after. The other was a blank recreation of her already written reply to the church's charity event.

It didn't take Finlay long to sift through her desk and find the letter he was looking for. His sharp eyes and her excellent organization of her documents made it fairly easy. He switched the sealed, blank letter with her already signed, sealed, and stamped reply to the church. He held it up to the window to be certain. The light passed through and illuminated the invitation inside, as well as her inked note containing both her gratitude and her refusal to attend.

Finlay tucked her letter into his breast pocket, ensured her desk was exactly the way he found it, and scrambled out of her office and down the hall toward Erwin's room in opposite wing.

When Erwin came into his room, after being *soundly* beaten by his sister, he found Finlay sitting at his secretary desk. He was squinting through a pair of crystal spectacles and working diligently.

"Well?"

Erwin tossed the set of servant's livery he'd swiped onto his bed and came up behind Finlay. His skill with ink and quill were excellent under normal circumstances. Finlay employed them for a less than honorable purpose here, masterfully forging a reply to the church's invitation in Aoife's handwriting.

"You were right," Finlay said as he dipped his quill in the inkpot. "Lucky for us, Aoife was a touch late to reply. I wrote up a new copy that says she's sending you instead, with a charitable donation in tow."

"Perfect. We can have that lamplighter deliver it. He's good for a few coppers. When you're done, try these on."

Finlay straightened up and turned around to eye the livery Erwin was holding up. The Folville family's grooms all wore long, double-breasted coats with a dropped waist and slim silhouette. The ensemble was completed with a deerskin tricorne hat and boot covers. Both were studded with silver, matching the coat buttons.

"You'll be both my driver and valet. That'll let you accompany me instead of waiting with the carriage or in the servant's hall."

Finlay tried on the overcoat and found it fit well enough – well enough to pass for a single evening, at least, if not under intense scrutiny.

"And we'll both need to conceal our weapons entirely," Erwin added as he perused his own wardrobe. "Nothing those old priests hate more than carrying weapons on their oh-so-hallowed grounds."

57

CYRIL COULDN'T HELP BUT KEEP HIS RIGHT HAND up to his face as he lounged at his desk. He had the backs of his first two fingers to his lips, and in them, swore he could still feel the sting, the sensation of striking her. It was horrid and pleasant and wholly unacceptable. He was angry with himself, but that anger tasted an awful lot like indulgence if he let it linger long enough. Some of the ever-present pain in his head was gone, and his jaw didn't feel so tight. He couldn't help but laugh at himself, some, to realize how good it felt to vent his stress on her.

But it was more than that, worse than that. He was busy imagining a chance to seize her alone. To pull her aside and tell her to lift her skirts up for him, that he might see how her bruises were healing. She'd obey him; he knew she would, if he but conspired to make it happen.

But his mind went too far too quick. The idea of pushing her up against the wall with her backside bare, of unfastening his trousers and sliding between her thighs for pleasure's sake. Imagining the noises she'd make as his hips made contact with the bruises on her ass. *Would she cry?* Surely, she would; she was so sensitive.

Perverted old man, remember your virtues! That cross isn't for decoration! He felt for his cross where it rested against his chest on the end of its chain. Every morning, he repeated the virtues as he dressed himself, as all clergy did, saying the prayer that corresponded to each part of their dress. He groped about for the fourth button, the one to which he pinned his cross. Temperance, moderation, restraint … everything he was failing in, in this moment. Bartering with himself, making excuses, as if he didn't want to corner the girl and lay claim to her, hold her down and –

Enough, he told himself. A flutter in his chest and a familiar ache of desire between his legs practically shouted their disapproval as he silenced his daydreams. Daydreams, though, were already too much – never mind the very real danger of him acting upon them, the danger of how easily she'd give in. A failure on his part, giving in to her charms, to entertaining the masochistic whims of a naive young lady. Penance, they'd both called it, but he knew better. Surely, she did, too.

A knock interrupted further thoughts, which brought a visitor with them. Cyril wasn't sure whether he was glad for the distraction or not.

Levi was stiff as he was shown into Cyril's office. Whether from the cold weather, the rising tension, or some other reason was difficult to discern. Cyril was polite, as usual, though clearly none too happy to see him. He offered Levi a seat by the hearth and a hot drink to dispel the cold, but he refused. Cyril stood behind his desk, reading the letter Domingo had penned. His face betrayed no reaction, not yet.

"So," he said upon finishing reading. "A formal notice from Captain Castillejo that he will have knights guarding the pyre stones." *What a logical approach.*

Levi stood resolute with his hands at rest behind his back, not giving any reply.

"Tell me, young man. Does the captain's upset at these developments justify your attempted burglary?"

Levi swallowed hard but quickly regained his composure. He donned a confused look. "I beg your pardon, Excellency?"

"Don't play coy with me." Levi didn't think, even in all the interactions watched between Domingo and Cyril, that he'd ever heard the Archbishop raise his voice. But there was a slight shift in volume that Levi read, alarmingly, as anger. "My Cardinals tell me everything. I know better than you what you did that night, how you earned that bruise on your arm." *I healed the prick to your little finger.*

It was as if the bruise heard Father address it, and dutifully sent a throb of pain up Levi's arm in acknowledgment. Cyril set the letter down and walked around his desk. Levi had to restrain himself from instinctively shrinking away as he drew closer. His cane swung lazily by his side where he carried it, gripping it beneath the handle in a manner more akin to how one would hold a sword. He walked by Levi, skirting around behind him, and closed the door. Levi somehow felt very uncomfortable with the idea of Cyril not being in his direct line of sight.

Cyril tapped the door in four places, and Levi nervously glanced over his shoulder to see what he was doing. A shimmering mark flickered on the door – some seal.

"No one can hear you, now," Cyril said as he turned to face Levi. "So, let us speak candidly to one another. You can drop that bumbling act of yours."

Levi glared at Cyril and stepped back a pace, of a mind to draw his sword at what felt like a thinly veiled threat, but resisted doing so.

"Your offenses against me are many, young man. You pretend to be of our faith. You trespass into one of our libraries." *You touch the young woman in my charge.* He stopped in front of Levi, facing him as he glared down at the younger man. "You come into my church bearing weapons."

"Carrying a weapon offends you?"

"On holy ground, yes. We make a formalized exception for you guards because we must. But you weren't in uniform, were you?"

"You and yours carry weapons on the grounds," Levi retorted. "Why should I surrender mine? To be easy prey?"

"We carry no weapons beyond what our rosaries allow us." As if to prove his point, Cyril flicked his wrist and a length of gold chain flashed from it, winding about his forearm until he caught the end of it in his hand. "And these, well ..." He stood worryingly close to Levi, looming over him and glaring down at the knight. "These will not harm the likes of you."

Levi yelled and jumped back as Cyril effortlessly let fly a rattling crack from the chain whip he wielded. It cut a blurred line straight through him, and he felt it like a punch to the gut. It sent sparks flying where it made contact with the stone floor behind him, carving a bright red-hot arc behind Levi's heels.

Levi stumbled back and clutched his chest, his lungs and stomach stinging with unnatural heat. He patted himself, expecting blood, a break in the fabric, a breach of his breastplate ... but found nothing. He looked back in confusion at the scarred floor behind him. The line in the stone floor was already fading. His head whipped back to look at the length of chain still wound about Cyril's arm, dangling from his hand. The priest sneered and laughed callously, releasing the chain and letting it flicker away into nothing.

"Were you not paying attention? Aren't you knights trained to listen to your betters?"

Levi glared at him, chest still heaving and sweat beading on his brow as he straightened up. A dull ache remained in his body, but even that was rapidly dissipating. Indeed, the chain, though he was certain it had passed straight through him, had done no harm.

"Our weapons are a defense against the undead, nothing more," Cyril stated nonchalantly as he rested his hands atop the handle of his cane while Levi composed himself. "Against you, it is no weapon at all. So, if you wish to skulk about, you need not do so armed to the teeth." He leaned in and snarled. "Nor do you need to insult me by feigning faith."

He meandered back over to his desk. "I cannot stop you, nor your captain, from your scheming. But, if you *truly* have your heart set on being a thorn in my side, might I be so bold as to request that you do it in a manner that will *not* risk physical harm to my faithful, hm? Poor Sister Vivian was a bundle of nerves all night. And after all, I doubt the good captain would be glad of the publicity surrounding such an incident."

Levi watched Cyril pick up a set of parchments from his desk and felt his heart drop into his stomach. *His decoys had failed? He always carried decoys.* No matter, the Father had the real documents. Levi recognized them right away, having been marked with a small – to the untrained eye, inconsequential – blotch of ink on the corners.

"Now then, what were you after? What was so valuable you would trespass onto church grounds and draw steel against my Cardinals?"

Levi stayed silent, lest he incriminate himself against what he knew were, thus far, accusations and nothing else.

"You and your captain are very keen to learn about me, it would seem? How flattering. But I'm afraid I'm nowhere near as interesting as you may think, young Master Sterling."

Levi's lips parted just a touch and he squinted.

Cyril looked up from his parchments and eyed him. "Your uncle, Simeon, used to call you that, didn't he?"

"What –"

"He was disappointed in you," Cyril cut off whatever Levi was going to say. "Wasn't he? For forfeiting your inheritance and disowning your family? On account of ... what was it, your own moral code? How ironic."

Levi marched over to Cyril's desk, only slowing when he grew too close and realized what he was doing. "I don't know where you've learned such things, Excellency, but my family matters are none of your concern –"

"Slavery, wasn't it?" Cyril continued. "Something about a jewelry enterprise you were set to inherit ... it would seem it's gone to your sister, now. What was her name ... Sophia?"

Levi instinctively moved his hand to his sword, and this seemed to be the reaction Cyril was looking for – because he met the movement with a hard swipe from his cane. It cracked hard against Levi's sword hand, and he recoiled. He yelled aloud in pain as an awful snap sounded from beneath his skin. He tried to draw the blade with his other hand, but Cyril didn't give him the chance. He leaped nimbly over his own desk. A flutter of black robes and blurred swipe of his leg, and Levi was knocked right off his feet, tumbling hard and hitting his head on the floor. He landed on his injured hand, which made him genuinely cry out in pain. Before he could roll over, Cyril stood over him, the sole of his boot soiling Levi's curly hair.

"A wound to the hand befits a *thief*, does it not? So, we see where you draw your moral lines, don't we?"

Levi inhaled sharply through his teeth, gritting them and refusing to acknowledge or reply to Cyril. It didn't matter; the Archbishop had more to say all the same.

"Let this be a lesson to you, my boy. Do not play games with me you cannot stand to lose. I can know all this and more with a prick of your little finger." Cyril held up the parchments, flinging them down at his unlucky guest. They fluttered to the floor next to Levi's head. "You forgot these."

Cyril withdrew his foot and rang for a doorman as Levi collected his documents and painfully pulled himself to his feet.

"Yes, Father?" came the Hunter's voice.

"Would you please fetch Brother Benjamin at once? I'm afraid our guest has a small injury, and I would like to see him tended to properly before he departs."

Levi glared at Cyril.

As the Hunter left to fetch the Cleric, Cyril returned to his desk. "Remember this, too, boy. My chains can only punish the undead, but my cane is far less picky. Disrespect my Lady again, and you will not receive such a gentle warning from me."

Benjamin was quick to arrive, padding quietly into the room with his hands folded into his sleeves. "Father Stacy, good morning." He bowed politely, straightening up and giving a small nod of his head to Levi. "And to you, sir."

"I suspect his right hand is broken, Brother. Please see to it."

Benjamin approached Levi and looked down at his hand where it hung, limp by his side. Though Levi bore the pain well, the sweat on his brow made it obvious he was in pain. Benjamin looked up in confusion at Cyril, who was preoccupied shuffling papers about on his desk.

With a quiet but frustrated sigh, Benjamin moved to obey. "Of course, Father, right away. Come with me, please."

Levi reluctantly fell in step behind Benjamin, not bothering to do the polite thing of bowing to Cyril before he left.

58

UCH TO LEVI'S RELIEF, BENJAMIN SPARED HIM the ignominy and publicity of the infirmary, and instead brought him to his own office. More of a greenhouse, what with the sheer amount of herbs and flowers growing everywhere. Instead of glass reliquaries and towering bookshelves guarded by carvings, the walls here were lined with apothecary cabinets, each drawer stuffed to overflowing with all manner of herbs, and each shelf filled with organized bottles of every shape and color. Benjamin wasted no time creating a comfortable place for Levi to sit, and a padded place to rest his arm upon.

"Can you move the hand at all? I'm afraid I may need to cut the glove off."

Levi attempted to straighten his fingers, but only winced and sucked air in through his teeth. "Gentle warning, my arse," he mumbled.

Benjamin chuckled quietly, retrieving a pair of sharp scissors and starting to cut at the loose cuff of his leather glove. His hands were remarkably steady and gentle, which gave Levi some confidence as the scissors made such easy work of sturdy leather.

"I see Father Stacy treated you to one of his ... lectures."

"He does this often?"

"To those that deserve it." Benjamin smiled and ripped off the now ruined glove, doing it so quickly Levi didn't have time to react or fear pain, in much the same manner one might distract a child from an injection. Levi's mouth opened in offended shock, but even his quick reaction was too slow, and he shut it again – feeling a bit silly.

"I would ... expect better conduct from a priest."

"And we would expect better conduct from our Royal Guard."

Benjamin's hands were pleasantly warm and oddly refreshing, a symptom of the soothing spell he mumbled as he hovered his hands over Levi to survey the damage.

"Father is a good man. Nothing matters more to him than his church, so of course he will protect it. Insulting Our Lady is even worse than insulting his mother." Benjamin chuckled. "And he is *very* protective of her."

"What about his apprentice?"

"Pardon?"

"Is he this violently protective of his apprentice, as well?"

"I'm afraid I don't understand. Father has no apprentice. Perhaps you saw one of the seminary students with him?"

"Perhaps." Levi decided to leave the matter there.

Something about the gold chains dangling from either side of Benjamin's spectacles reminded Levi of the Cardinals. The more he thought about them, the harder they were to recall; fuzzy and distant. *He wasn't a Cardinal, was he?* Benjamin rolled up Levi's sleeve, getting a good look at the bruise on Levi's arm.

"I see you even riled the Cardinals. My, my."

Levi glanced down and was startled to see the bruise looking even worse.

"Now, now. Do not be alarmed," Benjamin said. "Though it looks severe, I assure you that your arm is in no way permanently damaged."

Benjamin finished his inspection and pulled a corked bottle of small deep-green leaves from the assortment of objects he'd set aside. He also took up a small bottle, fitted with a dropper at the throat and filled with an oily cloudy-green liquid.

Levi shuffled in his chair. "I won't take any of your potions, priest."

"Nonsense. You already do." Benjamin smiled and popped the cork off the bottle of leaves in his hands. "Or did you think your Guard's medicaments were provided by the main street pharmacy?"

Levi could do nothing but sit quiet and feel rather embarrassed as Benjamin fished a portion of leaves from the glass jar. He pinched them between a strip of linen, crushing them briefly before dragging the leaves over Levi's arm, and down his palm. They smelled faintly medicinal and highly floral, and left a cool, tingling sensation over his skin. Levi only realized his hand had been thoroughly numbed when he felt the Brother uncurl his fingers without experiencing any pain. He sat a bit upright at the realization, and Benjamin released his hand.

"Still in pain?"

"No?"

"Then hold still. Please."

Benjamin pulled Levi's hand back to rest on the cushion, straightening out his fingers and resuming his curious work. Numbing in such a fashion was a perfectly mundane procedure, but for it to achieve such strength was indicative of additive magic. To smother the body's senses so well as to convince it to ignore fractured bones was quite a feat – and this priest had done it so effortlessly. Levi watched intently as Benjamin gently prodded his swollen hand. Upon finding the fractures, he whispered in a language Levi did not know, but immediately recognized. A slender, wispy thread sprouted from his fingers, floating about beside him. He twirled his fingers through it, spinning it about his hand like yarn about a spindle.

"Are you a Cardinal, too?"

Benjamin looked up at Levi a moment before laughing softly and shaking his head.

"No, no – not I. Perhaps one day. But Cardinals are beyond the distinctions of Cleric or Hunter."

Levi watched as, with careful movements and a few murmured words, the white threads in the Brother's hand wove themselves into strips and wound about his hand. He could feel the warmth from the magic, but nothing else. With each pass of Benjamin's hand, the strips grew tighter and tighter.

The incantation ended, and Levi was left with a meticulously bandaged hand. The bandages had a faint, irregular shimmer to them, wrapped about his wrist, palm, and up to the first knuckle of each finger.

"Now, try moving the hand."

Levi reluctantly moved his hand. There was an uncomfortable grind in his hand, something that felt wrong and unnatural – but the movement could be made, carefully, and without pain.

Benjamin nodded, evidently satisfied. "The threads do nothing but provide structure, to keep the bones aligned while they heal. I can encourage fast healing, and manage pain, but you will still need to be gentle with that hand for several weeks."

He slid the potion bottle over his desk toward Levi. "One or two drops a day, to numb the pain, as needed. You can apply it overtop my bandages. Write or simply come inquire if you need more."

A knock on Benjamin's office door interrupted any questions Levi might have asked. Upon bidding the visitor enter, Philip let himself in. He had a pencil tucked behind his ear and a small stack of parchments. He was so engrossed in his tallying up of items that, as he nudged the door shut with his hip, he didn't even notice Levi.

"Good morning, Brother Benjamin. I'm helping my uncle with his inventory and –" Philip stopped short halfway across the room and failed to hide a disgusted look. He corrected himself and bowed. "Please excuse me, I didn't realize you had a …" Philip's eye flicked back and forth from Levi's injured hand to Benjamin, unsure of whether he should refer to Levi as a visitor or a patient. "A guest."

"Not at all, Brother." Benjamin held out his arm in a gesture for Philip to approach. "Sergeant, may I introduce Brother Philip Gaboury."

"Yes," Levi said, giving him a look up and down. "We've met."

Levi caught a glimpse of the metal rosary hanging from Philip's belt. It was identical to the one Benjamin wore, though Levi made a subtle observation in the medallion dwelling in the middle of the length. A different seal, or perhaps the opposite side of a coin, he couldn't tell.

"I believe it was Brother Philip's idea to have a member of the Royal Guard chaperone our Hunters." Levi was suddenly paying close attention. "It's a shame that Captain Castillejo wasn't interested in the proposal."

"Maybe in some time," Philip offered, feeling rather obliged to present himself amiably in the presence of Brother Benjamin. "Sister Jael and I would be glad of your company, sir."

"Oh, yes, I recall now. You Hunters operate in pairs, don't you?"

There was a pause in conversation as one of the bells fastened to the wall of Benjamin's office began to ring. One of the many interconnected calling bells that alerted Clerics they were needed. The label for this bell was the infirmary, and so Benjamin took up his briefcase.

"Excuse me. Brother Philip, may I ask you to please escort the sergeant to the gates. That is, if he intends to leave us right away. You, of course, are welcome for as long as you wish, sir. Good morning."

With that, he bowed and departed his office, to be of help to the next patient that needed him.

"Well, where shall I escort you, sir?" Philip's tone betrayed a bit of smug delight. "Our Lady is quite the maze, if one is unfamiliar with her. I think she likes it that way."

Levi gave a half-hearted smirk and a puff of air from his nose. If only this bright-eyed brother knew. He stood and took up his belongings before falling in step with Philip as the elf led him from the office and back toward the atrium.

As boots crunched over gravel, the quiet sound of hymns began to echo through the church. Philip half hummed along as they walked, but Levi was still side-eyeing him. When he wasn't butting heads or snorting his distaste, he seemed an affable enough young man. Though, he seemed far too chipper, far too cheerful, to be a bloodthirsty Hunter. Levi eyed his rosary swaying at his hip and couldn't resist a question.

"So, do you summon a weapon from your rosary, too?"

"Hm?" Philip blinked and took a moment to process Levi's question, caught up as he was by the music floating through the air. "Oh, yes. Every Hunter does."

Philip clapped his hands together in front of him, palm to palm as if in prayer, before exhaling and letting his hands lay flat in front of him. A saber flashed into existence and dropped down into his waiting palms. He held it lightly, but in his hands, it seemed to have considerable weight – just as a real physical weapon would.

"Fascinating." The gold light from the weapon illuminated Levi's curious face. "And it only works against vampires?"

Philip gave the blade a quick flourish, sheathing it into his hand held at his hip and letting it disappear into sparks when the hilt met his knuckles. "Just so. We are only ever a defense against the undead. We never harm civilians." He pursed his lips. "Or knights."

Levi had to bite his cheek to keep from laughing. Luckily, the embarrassment of having been so easily bested by an old priest was more than enough to keep his silence.

"Your Archbishop said the same. Though, I am more inclined to believe you over him."

"Please do not speak ill of Father." Philip's voice grew surprisingly serious – an immediate shift from his cheerful countenance. "I am not oblivious to the troubles. But the Archbishop is a good man, and whether you agree with him or not, he does not do anything without reason."

"You have a great deal of blind faith in your leader."

"It's not blind. Father leads us by example. I should be lucky to live in the same era as he."

Philip jogged on ahead to fetch Levi's horse from the church stables, leading her out by the bridle. Levi thanked him and, with some effort due to his hand, mounted her and adjusted his beret.

"I did mean what I said earlier," Philip said as Levi adjusted his stirrups. "That Sister Jael and I would be glad to have you accompany us. Even if just for your own sake, not on behalf of the Guard." He gave Levi a surprisingly earnest smile and bowed his head. "Good morning."

59

DOVES FLUTTERED ABOUT THE COURTYARD, keen to pick up discarded seeds of every shape and size. The gentle, mournful coo of that particular bird was a staple sound of late summer at Our Lady. They scuttled and waddled about on the ground, until driven to flight by the priest that marched through the yard, keen to reach whatever his destination was. Cyril had been up several hours already. His breath puffed about him in the cold as he walked. He had intended to speak with his mother, to ascertain her condition, only to find her apartment empty. Now on the prowl to track down his brattiest patient, he looked to and fro as he patrolled his domain, until finally spying a familiar shape in the apple orchard.

Sitting under the apple boughs with a woven basket in her lap, Mara was gazing upwards. She was well this morning – the crisp, fresh air certainly doing much for her. She, too, had bathed and was properly dressed in another one of her expensive, expertly-tailored tea gowns.

Cyril bid her good morning, leaning over to kiss her forehead and set his cheek against it, feeling for her temperature. She returned his greeting with a great many kisses of her own to his cheek. As she did so, Cyril squinted at a familiar pair of discarded shoes, set side by side at the base of one of the trees. His one eye roved up the trunk and between the leaves as he straightened up.

Brontë had crawled and clambered her way up the tangled boughs of a healthy tree, and was now half hidden by boughs and branches. Her cheeks were rosy and her tongue poking through her lips as she very happily went about her task. She plucked plump apples from the branches, reaching and twisting to get between the stubby thorns this particular tree wore.

"What in the world are you doing?"

Her body froze like a naughty child caught with their hand in a cookie jar at his voice – and from where he stood beneath her, he could just barely see that she was trying to withhold a smile.

"What a silly question!" Mara puffed through her nose. "She is fetching me fresh apples, is that not obvious?"

Cyril shot a glance down over at Mara, who in turn shrugged innocently and looked away, pursing her lips.

"Come down," he said. "If the children see you, they'll start clamoring up the trees and may hurt themselves doing so."

Brontë hopped nimbly – a little too nimbly – down to the ground. She held in her apron a small collection of freshly-picked, ruby red apples. Her eyes twinkled with a mix of pride and delight, though the sheepish tilt of her head betrayed her underlying embarrassment.

Cyril did as he always did, glancing at her from head to toe and back again. The resulting warmth in her face felt different this morning. She was unsure if that was proper or not, to feel such an inexplicable way at being subject to his inspection. It made her feel exposed in a way it hadn't before, in a pleasant way. And then, if her eyes weren't deceiving her, she could swear she saw the tiniest flicker of a smile in the corner of his mouth. Brontë managed a shaky curtsy.

"Good morning, Father-"

"Come, come, girl!" Mara interjected impatiently and twisted the basket in her lap.

"I see she has roped you into performing favors." Cyril said as he watched Brontë load the harvest into the waiting basket. As she did so, he noticed something familiar, and leaned over to inspect her.

"You're bleeding."

"Hm?" Brontë looked down, twisting each of her legs a touch until she saw the offending evidence. She gasped in guilty surprise and pulled up her skirt a touch to look closer. True to his words, a long gash had been torn through her stocking, and a superficial prick on the back of her calf was bleeding.

"Oh, no ... I'm so sorry, I didn't notice."

Cyril knelt down, pulling a clean cotton kerchief from his breast pocket and taking hold of her leg. She squeaked out at the sensation of his extremely warm hand wrapping about the back of her knee, but he ignored it. He dragged the kerchief up her leg and pressed it to the wound itself to soak up the blood. A bit of firm but gentle pressure would be enough to stem the immediate bleeding, it always was.

"Be more careful." He said quietly.

Mara, who found the whole ordeal quite entertaining, tried and failed to contain a snicker, pretending to take great interest in brushing leaves from the apples in her basket. Brontë was keenly aware of how serious the matter of her shedding blood was. She could only be grateful that this happened in front of Lady Mara – where Cyril naturally softened his normally lethally sharp tongue. Goodness, if it had been anywhere else, he might take his hand to her backside again, and keep his rings on as he did so. *Heavens, not right away, she was bruised badly enough already!* Or perhaps he would have conceived some other punishment for her. His hand tightening around her leg pulled her out of her wandering thoughts.

"Do you hear me? Be more careful."

"Ah! Yes, Father!" She replied in a hurry, awkwardly hopping on her free leg as his grip sent an awful heat traveling up her thigh. "I'm terribly sorry."

He folded the now bloodied kerchief in on itself and shook his head, standing.

"And you," He addressed his mother. "I remind you that we have gardeners who are happy to fetch produce for you."

"Yes, yes, I know. But I wanted Miss Brontë to assist me with testing this recipe, and she is quite capable of fetching the fruit herself."

Cyril pinched his brow, his jaw tense as he prepared to lecture both of them, then and there. Before he had the chance, Mara spoke in a sing-song, playful voice.

"Surely our kind Archbishop will honor us with a taste of our work when it is finished?"

"I-"

"It *is* for the feast, after all." Mara added, puffing her chest. "If it pleases you, I intend for it to be my contribution to the table for the children."

Brontë and Mara both looked up at him expectantly. After a few agonizing seconds and muttering something in his native language about their being his two most difficult patients, he folded. He held his arms out to his side in defeat.

"Very well."

Brontë and Mara made their way back towards Mara's apartment, to the comfort and convenience of the indoors, to negotiate the challenges of Mara's memory and a nebulous recipe. Mara especially was quite happy to have bested her son in this little battle. Cyril stood quietly after they'd gone, one hand resting on his cane. He kneaded the square of white cotton between his gloved fingers, squinting down at the blood that had so easily soaked through the thin layers of the kerchief and stained it brilliant, ruby red. A rose petal of a stain. *How careless*, he thought. And yet he smiled. Mara had been so near Brontë's blood, but not shown any negative reaction. It was unexpected proof that his last resort had succeeded, that the blood bread had done its task.

He glanced at the nearby brazier beside the orchard path. It burned with the familiar gold that would gobble up the cursed blood in his hand. Cyril instinctively approached it and made to drop the cotton kerchief into the fire. When it came time to let it go, he hesitated. A quick glance about to ensure no gardeners or clergy were near enough, or taking any interest in him, and he instead tucked the bloodied kerchief back into his breast pocket.

DOMINGO FELT THAT HE SAW THE LADY'S BUTLER more often than he saw his own reflection. Once again, he was not steered toward the drawing room. Instead, he was led far back through the palace's many marble hallways, to arrive at a lush conservatory overflowing with plant life. The panes of glass allowed one to look out over the grounds. Out over the deep, dark grass and the trees, melting into yellow and orange. A herd of deer were crossing the meadow, meandering across the long gravel road to cross from one portion of the park to the other.

Lady Isabel didn't greet Domingo at first. Not properly. She merely opened one eye, met his gaze, and resumed her music. Domingo stood with his hands at rest behind his back as Lady Isabel plucked at her harp, waiting for her to address him. It was an elegant, classical instrument – ultimately simple in construction and a bit out of place amongst all the ostentatious finery. A bit like the lady herself. She had a pale peach tea gown on, with a burgundy robe over it, drooping off her shoulders and collecting about her elbows.

"Ah, Captain. How good of you to answer my call."

"Do you have a task for me, my lady?"

"I only desire your conversation." She played a few more notes before continuing. "I understand that you have written a rather demanding letter to the Archbishop. With my husband's approval, no less."

"You hear of my actions quickly."

She smiled. "Like you, I have eyes and ears in many places."

"So I gather."

"Alas, despite my counsel, you seem to have coerced my husband into complacency regarding your … schemes."

"Hardly schemes, my lady."

"Of course." She played one note a little sharper and glared at him a moment, before fixing her features and returning to the original, gentler medley.

"Do you have any children, Captain?"

"No, my lady."

"I cannot say I'm surprised." She earned herself one of Domingo's frustrated squints and a small twitch of his upper lip. She gave him another one of her coy smiles. "Oh? I pray you do not take offense. I only mean it in the sense that you hardly seem the sort to settle down."

"No offense is taken, my lady."

"I thought as much." The haughty toss of her head as she lifted her hands back to her harp made his blood boil. "I understand it may be difficult for someone like you to understand how dear certain matters are to me."

"By 'matters', you refer to your charity event."

"I do, Captain."

"And you perceive me as endangering this event."

"Your conduct, yes. And it saddens me, sir, that you would let your ideals endanger the futures of our city's children."

"A harsh accusation. I think I endanger your ability to buy your way into the hearts of the locals."

Isabel splayed her hand out flat over her harp, silencing the vibrations. She began to play again a moment after.

"You do so love to research."

"It is a skill I take pride in, my lady. But surely you didn't call me here to lecture me on your dedication to the city's children."

"No, I did not. I intend to have you as my escort during the event."

Domingo nearly spat out a curse in disbelief.

"I beg your pardon, my lady?"

"Was I unclear?" She set her hands in her lap and looked at him. "I didn't stutter, did I?"

"I ... do not believe this to be a wise course of action."

"Because you have already made yourself unwelcome on the grounds, yes."

"With all due respect, my lady –"

"This is my direct order, Captain," she cut him off sharply. Her eyes were fierce, almost angry. "Will you defy me?"

"No, my lady."

Her expression softened and she gifted him an almost genuine smile. "Wonderful." Her smile shifted into her more typical coy sneer. "I shall feel much *safer* with you there, I am sure, Captain."

60

HE APPLE ORCHARDS WOULD, ORDINARILY, BE SWEPT clean of any fallen leaves in the autumn. However, on this particular night, the leaves were left. Some of the most colorful were even raked up into piles, so the children could take turns jumping into them, under the very close supervision of overly fretful keepers. Lanterns were being carefully set alight with that usual golden flame. They covered the orchard – set at the foot of trees, draped between the branches, lining the long wooden tables beneath.

Domingo was sure he'd never seen quite so much money moving around in one night. Each noble brought a donation of some kind, and most also chose a specific child to sponsor. There were letters the children had written – showcasing their penmanship, level of education, and personality all in one little package – combined with documents of how the children came to be at the orphanage. Pitiful stories of abandonment and vampire attacks were used, in his opinion, to garner sympathy and money. And these nobles gobbled the stories up like the children gobbled down their sweets.

The clergy were excellent hosts. Brothers and Sisters milled about with all the poise and manners of aristocrats in their own right, ensuring their guests had everything they might need. Especially the Clerics. In fact, the Hunters mostly lurked in the background. They did far less of the socializing compared to their fellows. Except Philip, of course. He was ever the social butterfly, taking far more easily to conversation, and to being the center of attention. Brontë rolled her eyes as he very proudly sang a part of one of the hymns he'd written for an enamored audience of young noblewomen, probably in an effort to earn himself a few innocent kisses by the end of the evening.

Isabel was at the height of her charm and control, here. Many of the nobles attending were couples – and she charmed the ladies just as easily as she did the men. Even the oldest families greeted her with, if not fondness, a respectful appreciation. Levi, too, who had been roped into attending by his superior, was quite astonished at his first real glimpse of aristocracy. He'd not seen anywhere near as much of it in his time as Domingo had, and suddenly his captain's jaded, bitter demeanor made a great deal more sense.

But that was far from the only thing Levi was grappling with. He struggled to reconcile the Archbishop he saw with the Archbishop he knew. That same man had shattered his sword hand to prove a point. Thrown him to the floor and stomped on him like a rabid animal. Yet here he was, shambling forward with a giggling schoolgirl on his toes. And then, there was Brontë.

"There she is," Domingo murmured from the side of his mouth. "See how close she keeps to the Archbishop's side?"

Levi didn't feel he had reason to be surprised, yet he was. *She was the apprentice after all?* Did she really boast the sort of magic Domingo had claimed? She must, he'd never lied once, and had no reason to now.

"Her? She hardly has the look of a mage, even a neophyte one."

"No," Domingo whispered. "There's something there."

Levi now struggled to reconcile *both* the Archbishop and Brontë in his mind. She had spoken so fondly, so thoughtfully of him, with her little ritual. With what Levi now knew of Cyril, the gesture felt less like a kindness and more like a penance, a demand she adhered to. And though Brontë seemed quite pleased this evening, smiling and socializing, was Cyril as unforgiving with her as he had been to himself? *Surely not*, he reasoned. But the idea made an unease eat away at his stomach.

Cyril was being pulled in twenty different directions, as was to be expected. He had to greet the nobles, had to pray the usual blessing over the children's meal, and had to perform a myriad of other duties. The children all flocked to him, eager to see more sleight-of-hand magic tricks or be waltzed around on the tiptoes of his boots.

Miriam, a member of the layfolk herself, operated the kitchen with rigorous and sometimes foul-mouthed efficiency, though she was possessed of the good sense to confine her language to inside the kitchen walls. The task of catering to such noble crowds as these fell to her, and she had arranged for Hugo and Brontë's prepared stock to be brought to the much larger kitchen preemptively. Pies, tarts, sweetbreads – and a couple of Mara's cakes – were one by one put into the ovens, baked, and borne piping hot to the courtyard. The layfolk, servants in truth, went about this task with their usual silent professionalism, virtually invisible. It allowed the baker and his apprentice to enjoy the evening without scurrying about, stressed. Brontë was enjoying it immensely, while Hugo was playfully lamenting that the strongest drink available was spiced apple cider.

Hot cider was poured by the cupful, served from great copper pots, in which slices of orange and sticks of cinnamon floated on top. The children took great delight in seeing Father render a fire poker red-hot with just a brush of his hand. The bubble and hiss of the poker into the cider, as was the typical way of heating it on special occasions, was always met with cheers and amazement from the orphans. It contributed to the hearty amount of already delicious smells – clove and nutmeg, cinnamon and apples – floating through the cold evening air. But it still wasn't quite the same recipe Brontë remembered.

Domingo knew Isabel had intended, by having him here, to mend some of the tension. But she would not see much success in this venture. Occupied as she was, it was all Domingo and Levi could do to politely ignore the Hunters – who largely attempted to do the same. The exception was Cyril, who of course had been forced to greet Domingo again, to shake his hand. After this formality had been fulfilled, Domingo and Levi had a moment to stand beside one another as they observed the event. Domingo flexed his hand, looking down at it and grumbling.

"What?" Levi chuckled. "Strong grip?"

"No, no. He was plenty polite … but his hand is painfully hot."

"Come to think of it, he did seem rather warm."

"Perhaps he had a fever." Domingo scoffed. "Let's hope I've not contracted it."

With all the warmth and laughter surrounding them, it would be distressingly easy to fall into the illusion. But all Domingo needed to do was glance upward to be reminded of where he was. For as pleasant as the orchard was, the stone walls rising beyond felt cold and imposing. Gold-capped steeples and domes sheltered angry-looking saints. Carvings of the faithful seemed to glare at him, to stare at him, no matter where he was. He was sure that, despite the Archbishop's politeness, this Lady still despised him. It made him shiver, despite the warmth of the braziers.

Domingo's eyes were alert, flicking about the courtyard and apple orchard. In the relative dark, he could better see the sustained shimmer – the glittering trail left by magic as it lingered in the air. Barely there, metallic petals that wafted through a nonexistent breeze. The flecks followed each clergy member as they moved about. Every time Domingo blinked, he saw them a touch clearer, just for a moment. Little fragments of faith that fell from their rosaries and fluttered about.

It was an observation only someone markedly attuned to magic would be able to make. A phenomenon likely lost on the aristocrats and children, but far more obvious to the clergy, Domingo reasoned. Perhaps it was even *more* obvious to them than it was to him, what with their magic being fueled by their fervor. What they saw through faith, he saw through logic. Fragments of light bobbing around on the evening breeze, getting caught like dust on robes, or nestling on low-hanging leaves like frost.

It was easy for Domingo to tell where that accursed Archbishop was, at least. His rosary and robes both dripped a much heavier gold. Nearly like a trail of coins being scattered, out of the corner of his eye.

And then ... there she was again, that young woman. The supposed invalid, suffering some unnamed affliction. *Nonsense,* he thought, *that girl's not sick.* But there was something else. Something that made it difficult for even his keen eye to observe her. Something ... around her, maybe? Domingo blinked and let his eyes unfocus.

There it was: a charm of some kind. It wound about her like a venomous serpent would a dormouse. Coiled around her possessively – protectively? Was it containing her, perhaps? It seemed to smother her, to calm all that energy inside her. How strange – was every novice thus afflicted? Come to think of it, she was the only novice present this evening ... why? Were *all* novitiates throttled until they learned to control their magic? Perhaps it was the lack of rosary she carried. She had a wooden one strung through the cord at her belt, yes, but it was a mundane, powerless thing – clearly only for prayer and not for magic.

Maybe this was the church's way of containing magic until it coalesced into their rosaries. Domingo shook his head to stop his thoughts from trotting off any further.

With Cyril preoccupied, Hugo trundling off in search of stronger drink, and Philip busy pointlessly wooing young ladies with his voice – Brontë was left to wander a bit deeper into the orchard, just beyond the last little garland of lanterns. Few would converse with a mere novice. Most mistook her for kitchen staff, and kept handing her things or making requests. She decided to slip away, deeper into the orchards, where she wouldn't be troubled. As she did, she caught a glimpse of one of the Clerics pulling a young nobleman behind a column.

She smiled and shook her head. Kisses stolen by opportunistic clergy or less-than-pious churchgoers never much captivated Brontë's imagination. The excitement with which she heard the other girls gossip – giving their scathing opinions on appearance and character – didn't pique her interest. Not for a lack of butterflies at seeing a handsome fellow, or a lack of delight at seeing elderly couples sneak kisses to hands or cheeks. Her interest in affection was tempered by the simple knowledge that, at best, she was an untouchable invalid; and at worst, she was a monster. What kisses of value could be traded, then? None, she reasoned, and so she did firmly put the idea from her mind.

But a kiss from Father? Oh, the idea had her near woozy! What she wouldn't trade for just one kiss of her own. On the hand, on the forehead, even on the cheek – just one! One to hoard and hold, even if it could never compare to the wealth of kisses the ladies her age collected from doting men and women. Just one, she wished, and it would be hers – from the only person that would ever think to give her one. *Would he, though?* she thought. *Surely not.* Her imagination had simply run wild with the idea ever since he'd bent her over his knee.

Why? She hadn't the slightest idea. But she harbored a strange regret for not loitering in his lap longer, for not being bold enough to request a kiss as a sign of his forgiveness. Instead, she imagined it, knowing her opportunity had come and gone. But to endure her loneliness, was it so wrong to imagine an innocent kiss? If such chaste daydreams as this were the reason the saints refused to speak to her, she preferred their silence. At least her imagined affection could not leave her lonely, too.

Brontë was so lost in her thoughts that she didn't hear footsteps behind her. When Erwin spoke, she turned around in surprise. It took her a few seconds to come out of her daydreaming. A part of her hoped it might be Cyril, with a cup of cider in hand for her. She was disappointed to instead see a vaguely familiar young man about her age, with orange-auburn ringlets and a teal cravat.

"Are you a novice?"

He smiled innocently, leaning against a tree, but Brontë wasn't fond of the way he wore his smile. She looked back toward the lanterns and the bustling of the feast, unsure why he would have wandered off into the orchard the way she did.

"Can I help you, sir?"

Before he'd even answered, Brontë regretted her manners. He seemed to like being called 'sir' a little too much, judging by the way his already off-putting smile curled.

"I apologize if I startled you," he said playfully.

He was dressed like a noble, albeit a lesser one, with a doublet and overcoat that fit him well. But still, something about the way he carried himself, his lack of propriety, his sunset hair – it stirred a memory in Brontë's mind. She tilted her head and swore she recognized him. It was the hair, she thought, and his shorter build. He stood out among the group of men she knew she had seen, somewhere. She realized the connection with a bit of discomfort. She'd seen him with the grocer before, in the courtyard during one of their deliveries – she was sure of it.

She limited her reaction to narrowing her eyes. And though her cheeks betrayed her, flushing pink as they often did, she commanded her voice well enough to sound perfectly nonchalant.

"Oh, you work for the grocer, don't you?"

Erwin nearly spat a curse, unnerved that she should recognize him. He didn't think he'd ever seen her before, but then with those veils all the women looked the same to him anyway. She didn't seem immediately alarmed, so he played it off with equal nonchalance.

"Old Greer wishes he could afford me regularly." Erwin flashed what he believed to be a charming smile and offered an eccentric, ultimately patronizing bow. "No, no." He chuckled. "I am just paid protection. Surely you and yours have heard of the recent dangers? At least four robberies-"

"I am lucky to be spared the details of such unpleasantries."

"But you haven't answered me!" He was more than happy to change the subject. "Are you a real nun? Your skirt is awfully short. Isn't that a bit promiscuous for a Sister?"

His eyes dipped down to her legs in a way Brontë disliked. She'd never felt self-conscious about her legs being visible, but her cheeks flushed in indignation at his brashness. He seemed to like that, too.

"I'm a novice," she corrected him bluntly. "Not a nun."

"A novice? I've seen Sisters that look younger than you. How old are you?"

"I'm ... not obliged to answer you."

"Oh, I see ..." Erwin sauntered toward her, sneering as he looked her up and down.

"Are you a failed Sister? Maybe you refuse to take certain vows, give up certain things?"

"You should keep your suppositions to yourself." Brontë didn't back away from him, frowning and making it very clear by her tone she was not appreciative of his insinuations.

"It's a genuine question." He shrugged and smiled, still encroaching on her space. "Anyone could understand. A pretty girl like you, with those legs and hips." He paused in front of her and tilted his head. "And those lips."

Brontë rolled her eyes. "Are you trying to compliment me, or take an inventory?"

"Why shouldn't I offer a lady an inventory of compliments?"

He reached as if to put his arm around her, or rest his hand on her hip. She slapped his hand away with a surprising amount of strength. Perhaps enough to leave him a welt, so he could look at it later and think about his behavior. She didn't dignify him with any other reply, instead marching off in the direction of the light and laughter, cursing him under her breath for ruining her pleasant moment of reminiscence.

Finlay chuckled as he slid over to Erwin's side, where he was flexing his walloped hand. "She's not a whore," he said. "She's not paid to find you charming."

Erwin shrugged. "It was worth a shot. She's too chubby for my tastes anyway."

His failed attempts at flirting had created a different opportunity than his intentions: with Brontë gone from the orchard, no one else was nearby. With no one paying them any attention, they slunk into the unlit sections of the orchard, in the direction of the bakery.

✣

HUGO WAS BUSY DIGGING THROUGH HIS STASH of liquor for a favorite whiskey of his. That, a bottle of bitters, and a few cubes of high-quality sugar would make for an excellent end to the night, in his mind. Hugo thought he heard a shuffle, and turned around, expecting to see Brontë.

"Ah, did you need something, lass –"

Hugo saw a brown blur as Erwin let fly the hilt of his sword, smashing it against the baker's temple. Brother Hugo's head snapped to one side from the blow. He went down hard, thudding to the ground.

As Erwin returned his sword to his belt, Finlay prodded the baker with a foot. "Is he dead?"

Erwin shook his head, but the shrug he made with his shoulders clearly indicated he wouldn't have cared if he was. He knelt down and shoved the knit fiber of the Brother's orange cardigan aside. Finding his belt, he followed it until he found the key ring, wrenching it away. It took some time to find the right key to the pantry door, but with the correct key inserted, it swung silently inward and revealed several sacks of flour, well-stocked cupboards, and the gated cabinet that held the more precious items.

"Alright, help me with the fat bastard first."

Each of them took one of Hugo's arms, dragging him down into the pantry and leaning him against the wall. Hugo groaned and blood trickled from his now rather scrunched nose and bottom lip, where he'd crashed into the stone floor. The two then took steel to the sacks, slicing them open and letting the milled flour spill out. They stomped about and kicked and prodded, coating the pantry in a blizzard of powder – but found nothing.

"No luck," Finlay said, holding up an empty sack and flicking the broken tag. "The church checked all of these already. The seals are broken."

Erwin clicked his tongue in frustration and reached into his breast pocket. Finlay was still shaking out a destroyed sack of flour when Erwin read from the note. "If it's still here, it'll be either in the flour or barley," he said. "Look for barley, I don't see any here."

It took some more digging through the pantry to find what they were looking for. Finlay pulled a sack of barley from underneath a step stool, upending the contents in a hurry. Glass clinked as one bundle of the offending vials – oddly shaped and sealed with a generous amount of wax – tumbled out.

"All that trouble for this?"

Erwin sounded unimpressed as he picked it up and weighed the bundle in his hand. Finlay meanwhile curled his lip. He could feel the tingle at his fingertips, see the faint ripple in the air around the vials, hear a quiet, sustained noise.

"I don't like it; it's making my skin crawl," Finlay said. "Let's get out of here."

After a quick sift through the flour and spilled grain with their swords to ensure nothing was left behind, the boys shut the door, hiding their vandalism and the injured Brother both.

Back in the courtyard, Philip had finally been shooed away from his harmless flirting with the noblewomen, and was now enjoying a freshly poured cup of hot cider. He plopped down on a bench next to Brontë, who was cupping her own beverage in her lap, one ankle behind the other. The two chatted quietly as the evening wore on. A comment from Philip about how he preferred Hugo's blend of spiced wine over apple cider made Brontë look around.

"Where is Brother Hugo? I haven't seen him in a while. I'm sure if you asked him, he'd get you some spiced wine. The children will go to bed soon anyway."

"Oh, you know him. He goes to sleep even earlier than my uncle."

"Not on feast days ..." she said quietly, her voice trailing off. She looked around again, with purpose this time. She didn't see that redheaded boy, either. Something nervous and uncomfortable bubbled in her belly. Philip could see by her eyes that she was thinking intensely. She stood abruptly and set her drink down.

"Come with me."

Philip blinked at her curiously, but her tone alone was enough to make him stand up. "What? Is something wrong?"

"I hope not."

Cyril paused as he caught a glimpse of Brontë leading Philip by the hand off into the orchards. Against his will, he heard himself humming low note of disapproval. *What was this? Envy? Surely not.* Philip was always flirting, but Brontë had always seemed too clever to be drawn in by his hollow flattery.

The children tugging at Cyril's hands and the expectant noblewoman approaching to speak to him meant he could not follow. And really, why would he? He had no reason to care what two young people did when they snuck off into the dark; no reason beyond scolding them after the fact for their impropriety, maybe twisting Philip's ear if the boy indeed tried to kiss her.

"Hugo?" Brontë called into the bakery as the pair approached the steps. "Brother Hugo, are you down here?"

"See, I told you, he's already gone to bed –"

Brontë grabbed Philip's arm and nearly crushed it in her hand. Goodness, she was stronger than he thought! How tight she held him was of no concern to her. She smelled blood. Human blood. Not like that supernaturally floral aroma – this was metallic and heavy. She didn't provide an answer to Philip's curious noises, and similarly ignored how he was trying to uncurl her hand from his arm. She let him go and rushed down into the bakery.

"What is it?" Philip fumbled in after her.

Brontë looked around frantically. Her eyes combed the dark space, from her bay window to the worktable, to the … floury footprints on the floor behind it. She darted around the table, following the flour to the closed pantry door. She threw it open and leaped back at the sight. Flour and grain were everywhere, sacks slashed through and trampled over the floor. Hugo was slumped over, a puddle of blood under his nose.

"Ring for a Cleric! Now, now!"

Philip came up behind her in worry, but she shoved him away, pointing back up toward the bell.

"I said ring, *now!*"

He caught a glimpse of Hugo and rushed instead to do as she said, pulling the cord in the corridor that rang for help from the infirmary. He rushed back to Brontë, who had grabbed her apron, holding it to Hugo's split lip. Through the chaos, she could make a quick count of the pilfered pantry's contents. Nothing was missing, only the sacks of flour and barley had been spilled.

"There must have been more blood." Brontë chastised herself for not trusting her instincts when she saw that redheaded boy. "Go sound the alarm! The thief has curly red hair. Go, now! He might still be on the grounds!"

Philip flew past the poor unsuspecting Sisters that had answered the call, yelling at the top of his lungs. "Thief! Ring the Joshua bell, somebody!"

Finlay and Erwin had split up. Finlay had circled his way back to the stables, to prepare the carriage and two horses. Meanwhile Erwin had slunk back through the orchard. He only needed to get close enough to the merrymaking to make it look like he was coming from that direction when he approached the stables. Plus, the trees allowed for some precious cover that made him harder to spot.

Erwin had not closed half the distance when the Joshua bell began to scream.

This was, perhaps, not the view of the church Lady Isabel had wanted to show Domingo – but he would see the clockwork efficiency with which the Hunters worked nonetheless. Every shadow seemed to come alive as the Hunters moved. There were far more of them than he realized. Had they been there the whole time? They leaped out from the shade of the walls, poured out from behind gates and doors, raced up to ramparts. Philip was among them, and frantically trying to find someone who matched Brontë's description.

Domingo knew an alarm bell when he heard one. He closed the gap between himself and Lady Isabel, instinctively drawing his sword – though that would be far from necessary with this many Hunters about. The Clerics were corralling the orphans, counting heads and trying to keep them under control as some cried, some laughed, and some brandished sticks as swords, intent on following the Hunters. Cyril gently set one child down with a keeper and turned to join his Hunters. From the corner of his eye, he saw Brontë come tumbling out of one of the buildings. She had no trouble spying Erwin in the trees. She was frazzled, teary-eyed, but shouted with conviction and clarity to be heard above the din.

"Thief! There, the red hair!"

Erwin heard her, shouting the dreaded word – *thief!* He immediately began sprinting toward the carriage, abandoning his plan. He yelled for Finlay to get the horses moving.

Finlay leaped up into the driving seat. As he did, he saw a young Hunter bolting for Erwin. Philip had a longer stride than the ginger boy, and would easily overtake him. But without a weapon to avail him against such an opponent, it was all he could do to try and tackle the thief. Still, Erwin would rather not risk this.

The massive gates took time to close. But even half-closed would be enough to bar the horses and carriage. Finlay ran the horses straight for it. Erwin was fast enough to grab the rear of the carriage and pull himself up. Unfortunately for him, so was Philip. Erwin attempted to scramble over the roof of the carriage, but Philip grabbed his leg and yanked him back. He kicked the elf hard, but it did not have the desired effect. Erwin shouted and drew his sword. He slashed it hard up across the elf's face and sent him tumbling from the back of the carriage. Erwin attempted to blink the streak of red from his vision, but as the wind whipped his hair in front of his eyes, he could swear he saw a figure in a red robe standing over Philip in the dirt. Brontë felt her heart stop when she saw Philip fall back, a cloud of red around his head.

Children giggled, unafraid of the chaos, oblivious to the danger and rather delighted to see the Hunters moved to action. What adventure! The black monster of a mare came thundering to Cyril's whistle, slowing just enough for him to leap astride her back and take control of her reins.

Finlay would not slow the carriage. The Hunters at the gate had to dive out of the way or be trampled to death. They knew this. And then they were through the gate. Erwin clambered up to the front seat with Finlay, sheathing his bloodied sword and shouting over the wind, the rattle of the carriage, and the pealing of the bells.

"Head east, toward the embankment."

"All according to plan, aye?"

"Shut up and turn off this road before they can come after us."

Back inside the church walls, Domingo whistled a signal to Levi. With an angry gesture, Levi nodded his understanding. He darted for the stables and leaped astride his own horse. He did so at the same time as Jael, who eyed him up and down before the two took off side by side in pursuit.

A shrill whistle and hoofbeats against cobblestones told the pair of criminals that the Hunters had given chase. Erwin stood up in the seat and looked back at the bridge. He saw what must have been two Hunters on massive horses barreling toward them. If his mind wasn't playing tricks, two more followed behind – one with Royal Guard colors.

A streak of gold light shot over the carriage, shattering into a flash of gold dust. Erwin ducked instinctively, but the shards startled Finlay and temporarily blinded him.

"Shit!"

"Ignore it!" Erwin shouted. "They're all bark, it'll not hurt us!"

The sudden addition of more weight to the carriage made the vehicle swerve and the already panicked horses whinny in fright. Erwin turned to see a dark silhouette looming over the rear of the carriage. Florence growled out like an angry animal as she crawled onto the roof.

"Stop this damn thing before you kill someone."

Florence knelt atop the carriage, snarling at Erwin as he returned the expression in kind. His sword flashed bright as he drew it, and the Sister – having only seen Philip's bloodied head in a blur as she'd flown out the gate – knew very well he had no reservations about using it. Florence gripped one hand tight to the carriage's frame, the other arm up to protect her face. Erwin's sword could only glance off the blessed fabric of her habit. The sparks that flew from the contact briefly illuminated her scowling, scarred face and made him swallow nervously.

Finlay could only glance back to see if Erwin was still in one piece for split seconds at a time. This time, when he turned his attention back to the road, a blur of brilliant red clouded the center of his vision. He blinked furiously. He squinted. He waved his hand in front of his face. But it didn't disappear. It lingered on his eyes when he blinked, gradually coming into focus, yet not getting closer – not even as the horses sped onward. In fact, the road itself seemed to be ... stretching on forever. His eyes strained and the shape became clear. A clergyman garbed in red stood in the center of the road.

The noise and speed at which they were moving suddenly came back to Finlay and he yelled in surprise. Steel shoes slamming against the cobblestones, Erwin's yelling, Florence's angry orders to stop the damn carriage, the townsfolk in panic, the whistle and scream of those darting golden arrows. Now the road flew past beneath his feet, and the clergyman drew closer with every heartbeat. Unmoving, unyielding – glaring, almost. Finlay gave a defeated cry and yanked the reins, attempting to swerve hard and miss the Cardinal.

The carriage slid, metal wheels throwing up sparks as it slammed into the wall and the glass windows shattered. One of the oil lanterns smashed in the collision. Oil spewed forth and instantly carried the flame. Florence went tumbling off the side of the carriage, and so did Erwin. Erwin only caught himself on the still-moving carriage's frame at the sacrifice of his sword, flung from his hand.

"What the hell was that!" Erwin snapped at Finlay angrily as he tried to pull himself up. As he did, he caught a glimpse of Cyril on a black horse beside the carriage. Adra's snorts were almost as loud as her hooves against the stone as Cyril pushed her onward. He was trying to pass the carriage – to take the lead horse's reins and stop the carriage by force.

Jael was easily one of the best riders within the clergy. And she knew the city far better than most, especially Levi. She watched the carriage hang a sharp corner as Finlay panicked. She said nothing, but reached over and grabbed Levi's horse by the bridle. He exclaimed in surprise as she turned both their horses onto a different path that led upward. A path she knew would intersect with the road the carriage had turned onto. Levi had no decision but to trust her judgment and follow her lead.

Cyril yelled to the unsuspecting civilians on the road. A man grabbed his daughter and had to dive aside to keep her from being struck by the careening vehicle. The Archbishop was almost close enough now. He reached out to take hold of the driving horse's bridle.

"Crush him against the wall!" shouted Erwin as he fought to right himself.

Finlay heard him, but instead let fly a hard crack of the whip. It caught Cyril in the side of the head. He grunted and lost his balance, slipping alarmingly low. It sent Adra out of stride and made her bump into the wall. Cyril's hat went flying off, revealing his seafoam hair and making Finlay curse aloud as he realized who he'd just wounded.

Blood splattered from Cyril's cheek at the line cut down his face. He pulled himself up, reaching once more for the lead horse's harness. He was able to grab it, but between the crack of the whip, the string of curses from Erwin, and the chaos of the chase – the horses were too frenzied to obey his attempts to slow them down.

Jael and Levi both came thundering down a gently sloping road close behind the carriage. Jael's bow flashed back to life in her hands, and she fired another shattering cloud of gold at the thieves. Erwin had only just managed to get back up on the carriage when he had to contort out of the way of an arrow. They were too close. He made eye contact with the guardsman and cursed this unlucky heist.

Cyril leaped from Adra onto the back of the driving horse. He grabbed its partner and grasped the reins to each. Overriding the commands from Finlay, he tried to slow the two panicked beasts, all while his cheek and lip bled from the stinging blow of the whip.

The river flowed alongside the carriage as they whipped along the embankment. An ordinarily peaceful walkway, lined with lampposts and a stone banister overlooking the river. Erwin scrambled forward, clapping his hand over Finlay's nose and mouth.

"Let go!"

Finlay instinctively let go to clap his own hands over Erwin's in confusion. A crack sounded, followed by a loud hiss as Erwin smashed a strange smoke bomb into the roof of the carriage. It clung like tar, enveloping it in a sickly, silver-blue cloud and leaving an acrid fog behind that filled the alley up to the roof tiles. Jael and Levi were both caught in it and began coughing uncontrollably. They swerved their horses away, running back up the embankment to spare themselves and their horses the chokehold.

Hidden from view, Erwin grabbed Finlay by the shirt and yanked him up, throwing them both off the side of the carriage and into the river. They were lucky to clear the rocks. Shocked by the freezing water, they both had to surface and gasp for air. The cover of the reeds allowed them this, but the shouting voices on the road above told them this cover wouldn't be enough. As Levi and Jael halted their horses on the embankment, they couldn't see Finlay or Erwin in the dark, dipping beneath the water and swimming east.

Philip lay on the ground, winded from landing on his back and yelling in pain as blood rushed from his head. His right ear had been shorn off. Even now as he clutched where it used to be, the wound bled profusely, rendering him lightheaded and even more disoriented.

"Get me bandages!"

Serge was only half-awake and half-dressed. He'd been woken by the alarm bell first. Then by hearing Philip as he'd barreled past in the corridor. He shouted at the Hunters in the yard, trying to hold Philip still enough to press a kerchief to his head. Brontë could do nothing but watch, heart pounding against her ribs, as Philip writhed on the ground. She dare not go near when Serge was present. She dare not go near an open wound, as Father forbade. Still, her eyes stung as she looked on, not knowing what damage had been done in the dark.

An awkward hush settled over the courtyard as one of the Cardinals moved toward Philip. Strangely enough, as they walked across the gravel, their shoes made no sound. They clutched a small blood-soaked kerchief in their hands. Kneeling down, they opened it before Serge. It was Philip's severed ear, dusty from the gravel it had landed in.

The Cardinal then put the ear beside Philip, back where it should have been. Their other hand cupped his face, gently holding him still. There was no murmur, no sound at all. Philip's pained wailing stopped and he seemed confused. Serge looked on in wonder as the Cardinal withdrew their hands, revealing the ear now perfectly reattached. Glistening red threads thinner than a hair seemed to be holding it in place, though only visible if the light caught them.

Philip fondled his ear nervously, relieved to find that, when he touched it, he could feel the sensation. The Cardinal tilted their masked head, perhaps the closest they could make to a smile and booped Philip on the nose with one finger. With that, they stood, placed their hands together, and nonchalantly strolled back towards the cathedral doors – but not before pausing to look at Domingo, who had his sword drawn, and was standing between the Cardinal and Lady Sinclair.

Domingo could see many things. The fact that he saw absolutely nothing unsettled him deeply. The Cardinal bowed their head to him, and disappeared inside.

BOOK III
The Addict

WINDERMERE WOULD SPEAK OF NOTHING ELSE FOR the coming weeks. So much excitement! So much *curiosity*. Something about this incident had the church on edge, and the whole city noticed. Brother Maddoc had doubled the guard on the wall and at the gates. Oh, the odd criminal sneaking into the church wasn't uncommon ... petty thieves keen on stealing candlesticks or pickpocketing the faithful. But the guard was not doubled for a petty thief. A Cardinal did not step outside, did not intervene, for a mere petty thief. And then there was the miraculous nature of the Cardinal's healing – a feat not even the most esteemed and studied Cleric could achieve. Gossip babbled between lips and bubbled like foam atop glasses of ale, in both posh and poor establishments.

Brontë, for her part, eagerly wished for the whole ordeal to be done and over. To first find poor Hugo, bloody and deliberately hidden behind the door – and *then* to see Philip fall after a flash from that awful thief's sword. Though she dearly wished otherwise, her memory was far too vivid, far too clear, to do anything other than recount the whole affair with awful clarity. Her heart would still speed up in a panic, even when she knew there was no danger, as she tried to work. As she tried diligently to stay atop the extra chores she'd taken on in Hugo's absence.

Brother Hugo had been borne to the infirmary. He remained there now, some days later – with stitches in his lip and reparations to a chipped tooth needed. Brontë could not visit him, and so only heard of his injuries secondhand. He had, however, been of a clear enough mind to write instructions for her, to guide her through as much of the work as she was able while he was incapacitated.

Of course, a proper Cleric had separate instructions on how to make the prosphora. Brother James was a nice enough fellow. Polite and mild-mannered, if a bit awkward. But he had many duties of his own, and so his time in the bakery was limited. He also, frankly, did not want to be long in the company of a controversial, corrupt invalid. Brontë had forgotten how lucky she was for the company of people who were not quite so judgmental. It sure didn't help her heart to feel any lighter when she caught the Brother's skeptical glance from the far side of the bakery.

Philip, for a blessing, had offered to help Brontë in the bakery. To help her as much as his own duties, and his uncle, would permit. His flamboyant retellings of his ultimately quite small role in the story didn't make it any easier for her to forget the whole ugly affair.

While Philip puffed his chest and bragged about his healed ear, Florence had not fared so well. She, like Hugo, was in the infirmary. She'd weathered her injuries with the endurance befitting a Huntress, but cracked ribs and bruises were her constant companions. Along with Sisters Sybil and Jael, of whom she was very glad for their company. Philip had brought back the news of her, and Hugo's, condition to Brontë, but that was more a happy coincidence. Even with the Cardinal's exceptional healing, Serge had of course still dragged Philip back to the infirmary for a thorough inspection.

Brontë was listening to Philip tell the story over again as she worked. The recollection of events made her hands tremor and her eyes glisten in a way that frustrated her. Philip beamed a massive, perhaps a bit haughty, smile to Brontë, tugging lightly at his miraculously healed ear.

"See? Still attached!"

Brontë shriveled at the idea of his ear being shorn off, *again*, and grimaced. She puffed out her cheeks to keep from screaming at him to stop mentioning it. He seemed to know this, and giggled.

"Bah, don't look at me like that," he said.

"Do you have any idea" – Brontë angrily stirred the bowl of soon-to-be dough – "how *worried* I was?"

Philip laughed across the worktable and flicked her in the forehead. "You're such a crybaby!"

"Don't tease me –"

"I want to tell mum what happened tonight. Will you come with me?"

"Oh, I … I think I have too much work to do tonight, but I could probably bake her something small, if you'd like to take it to her?"

Philip tried not to look disappointed, but smiled at her offer. "Yes! Oh, she'd like anything with apples in it!"

Brontë smiled and nodded, giving him a little salute. "Apples it is."

PHILIP'S BREATH PUFFED OUT IN A CLOUD AROUND HIM. He rubbed his hands together and regretted not bringing a cloak. He smiled to himself at the irony of it. He pulled a small clean rag from his pouch and set about wiping his mother's headstone down. The granite had aged somewhat, in these sixteen years – it wore some wear and tear from exposure to the elements. But even with this, it was clear someone was tending far more regularly to her grave. Of course, the groundskeepers kept the graveyard clean, seeing to general maintenance and trimming overgrowth where necessary. But Emilia's headstone stood out among the rest. Even the fresher graves with newer headstones somehow paled in comparison to how well kept her resting place was. Philip took some pride in this.

He neatly arranged and lit the small tray of incense he'd prepared, as well as the tall, slim beeswax candle. Kneeling, he recited the more formal prayer for her, gesturing over his chest and pressing a kiss to his fingertips, and then those fingers to her headstone. With this small bit of ceremony completed, he shifted and sat down, legs crisscrossed and elbows resting on his knees. He unwrapped the little pastry Brontë had prepared, setting it down in front of him and sliding it toward the slab of granite. He smiled, though a bit teary-eyed, and spoke as if she could hear him.

"I hope you're not angry. I know you said to be careful. But! You'll never believe what happened ..."

Philip had only recounted the first few chapters of his story when footsteps interrupted. Serge came up beside him, with two steaming cups and a spare cloak over his arm. He leaned over, offering one cup to his nephew. Philip could smell the aroma, and it was just bright enough to see the dollop of whipped cream Serge had added.

"Don't you think I'm a bit too old for hot chocolate, uncle?"

Serge tilted his head and withdrew the offered cup. "Too young for white hairs, too old for chocolate, I see."

Philip quickly took the cup before it was out of his reach. Serge smiled and set his own down, freeing both his hands to wrap the cloak he'd brought about his nephew. Philip meanwhile squinted and sniffed his beverage appreciatively – if a little too close, rendering him with a white mustache of cream.

"Did you add nutmeg?"

"Of course."

Philip licked whipped cream from his upper lip. Now sitting with his uncle, Philip was able to continue retelling the story to his mother. Serge interjected to make corrections and to moderate his ego, that his departed sister have as accurate a story as possible. It was the sort of thing she had appreciated, at one time.

Brontë had been watching all the while from the terrace. Behind her, the rooftop garden was alight with fireflies. The fountain in the center caught every little flicker of gold. Even the leaves, still wet from rainwater, glittered in the dark. Brontë's eyes strained as tears welled up, *again*. She could still feel the heat in her cheeks and the frustration in her heart. She wanted to scream. And yet, she just couldn't get the image of Philip falling – bleeding – out of her head. Couldn't forget the way her throat had tightened when she found Hugo. She felt it, even now, that same crippling, heavy tension. Tears caught on her eyelashes, though she tried to blink them away. *What a crybaby!*

She left the balcony and stood before the fountain, looking down into the rippling water. It reflected everything: the stars far above in the heavens, the parting clouds, the gold steeples, the fireflies as they fluttered about the air. But it did not reflect her. She was, as always, a dim silhouette with vague, indistinguishable features. A constant reminder always waiting for her; be it in water, a pane of glass, or a mirror proper, she could not see herself. Just like she couldn't visit Hugo in the infirmary. Just like how she, too petrified, couldn't attend the graveyard with Philip. Just like she couldn't work in the bakery without Brother James's glare. It all hurt, and yet she chastised herself inwardly for pitying herself at such a time as this.

"Why are you crying, little one?"

A sensation very pleasant dripped down the back of her neck at his words. The poor girl almost swatted Cyril in the arm with her veil by whipping about so fast in surprise. Brontë stammered and hurried to wipe her eyes on her sleeve. Cyril stood quietly, giving her a moment to collect herself, both hands lazily behind his back, holding his cane. Thanks to his own still-healing injury, Cyril favored the right side of his face, and spoke with a soft mumble because of it.

"Look at me. Why do you weep?"

"Please, Father," she said, laughing softly at herself. "You mustn't look at me in this state."

I disagree, he thought. "And what state is that?"

Self-pity would have been her honest answer, but she knew better than to confess *that* of all things to him. Still, it was true she had been afraid for Philip, for Hugo, for Florence, for him. It was the sort of trouble, the sort of trauma, that she was not hardened to.

"I am not sure," she finally said. "Perhaps overwhelmed. But oh, please don't tease me for it. I assure you Philip has quite fulfilled that quota on your behalf."

"I would not tease you." *Not like that.* "Don't be ashamed. You cry because you have compassion."

"Hah." Her eyes stung again and she shook her head. "You will bring more tears on inadvertently, Father, with words like those. Philip would just call me a crybaby again, if he knew."

"Well, it can be our secret. I won't utter a word."

"Do you promise?"

"Of course. Come, know me better."

I would like to, she thought. She noted and appreciated the simple ease at which she felt with him nearby. It was both familiar and new, an old feeling that had taken on a new character. She tapped her lip with a finger in thought, and he would really rather she did not do such a thing in front of him. He didn't need to be paying attention to how soft her lips looked.

"If I confess that I am a crybaby, you are vowed to keep it secret, yes?"

Confessions ... were sacred things, he thought. They were not to be used to *flirt*. That's what this was, wasn't it? A bit of harmless flirting. *Harmless?* Yes, harmless ... Improper, but not damaging. *Not yet*. And then, she had so wooed him with the idea of skulking past the formality of confession. Away from something sacred and into something more personal.

"Instead of a confession," he said, "I will offer you an alternative."

He held out his hand, more precisely, his little finger. She recognized it at once as the little gesture of promise.

"Just as binding, I assure you," he said, as if he needed to assuage her doubts.

She hooked her little finger into his. Somehow his hand felt much warmer this time.

"You have me at my word, little one."

She beamed a gentle grin and quite contentedly held on to his little finger. After a moment of looking up at him, her eyes drifted to the injury on his cheek.

"Oh." She lifted herself up on her tiptoes, her little finger still entwined with his. "How is your injury?"

Cyril leaned down a touch to compensate for their disparity in height, tilting his head enough to let her glimpse the red line raked over his right cheek and down his jaw. It was near impossible to see Benjamin's stitches keeping the wound closed, but Brontë caught the faintest glimmer and put a hand over her heart in relief.

"It already seems to be healing well, oh, thank goodness," she said, "Does it pain you?"

"No, no," Cyril said as he straightened up again. "Mildly uncomfortable, but no pain."

Brontë scoffed a moment. "You know, you may very well match the Deacon, once it heals."

Cyril smiled and shook his head. "Not I. Benjamin's work will prevent a scar. Besides, it would hardly flatter me."

Brontë gave a small laugh, still inspecting that side of his face. The new, still-healing gash on his cheek now fell on the right side, just beneath the eyepatch he wore over that much older wound. She could still remember her unfortunate glimpse of Cyril's harrowing injury.

She'd hardly been about ten years old, then. Naive and not yet of an age to understand. To know to heed her handlers' warnings *not* to peek. To just *stay put*, when the alarm bell rang and the courtyard came to life. She remembered seeing Maddoc haul a lifeless Cyril through the gates. Half carried and half dragged while his head gushed blood and Clerics raced to him. Cyril had been thirty or so, at that time – already a grown man and an experienced Hunter. And yet he, too, was just a human that could be undone by the Hunt. The similarity of that memory to Philip's bloodied head splattering gore as he fell made her frown and her stomach feel sick.

Cyril saw her face fall. He also realized she was still clinging to his little finger. He disentangled his hand and set it atop her head, stroking her veil. Brontë leaned into his hand like a kitten expecting affection.

"Is there anything else troubling you?"

The invitation made far too many thoughts rush through her mind. Her own misplaced pity, the pain of being reminded what she was, the fear that still clung to her, all doused with confusion and guilt. Really, could she even form such things into words? And what was the remedy for that? She opened her mouth to speak, but the bells began to ring. They tolled out the familiar melody, calling the clergy to prayer, calling Cyril away. She closed her mouth and shook her head. She could bear her burdens just fine – he did, after all. What right had she to do any different? She took a respectful step back and curtsied. He tilted his head, but turned to venture back inside, to answer the bells that demanded him.

"Very well. It's a warm night, but don't stay out too late. I will be in my study, if you have need of anything."

"Thank you, Father."

"Unless, of course, you'd rather sneak into the gallery and attend the liturgy in secret again tonight."

Brontë clapped a hand over her mouth, but an embarrassing squeak escaped it nonetheless.

62

ERWIN SQUINTED AT THE WRINKLY SCRAP OF PARCHMENT he'd been carrying. It had been dunked into the river with him, so the ink was smudged, but he believed this was the correct address. A nondescript warehouse that straddled one of the roughhewn channels near the docks. It looked utterly average, but he knocked in the pattern as the note said, and waited. Hezekiah opened the door for them, and they were led deeper inside the warehouse by the scruff like two tardy schoolboys. The warehouse was full of stock of all kinds, and an office was tucked into one corner, up a small flight of stairs. Both boys could see Esther through the slightly ajar door, though she was preoccupied with a tangled mess of red threads and several tiny bottles.

Below that office was a smaller, much less comfortable-looking sitting area. Greer paced back and forth in front of a small brazier, chewing on the stubby remains of a cigar and smelling of cheap liquor, as usual.

"There you are!" Greer sounded both angry and relieved. "What in the hell were you thinking? It's all over the papers, the whole damn city won't shut up about it. Assaulting a Brother, fleeing the Hunters through the streets, the Royal Guard?"

"How should I have known the Captain of the bloody Guard would be there?" Erwin snapped.

"They drew your picture!" Greer flung the newspaper at Erwin.

He squinted down at it. He wondered if that nun at the church who called him out to the Hunters had described him to the papers. It was a reasonable likeness, freckles and all.

"I don't look half bad."

"This isn't a joke, you stupid, unwanted bastard of a child!"

Erwin and Finlay both gave Greer a fierce look that told him he'd overstepped his bounds. He crumbled beneath it, like he always did. He cleared his throat and slicked his frizzy hair back, holding out one hand. "The parcel, then. What did you find?"

Erwin handed Finlay the newspaper and reached into the satchel at his belt. "We went through the whole bakery. Only one. The rest was gone."

Greer tried to hide his disappointment, but reached for the clump of vials anyway.

Erwin withdrew his hand. "Where's the money, Greer?"

"Fine! Fine. Go get the coin."

Hezekiah was sitting nearby. Attie's head rested atop his leg, and he absentmindedly stroked her ears as he stared blankly ahead at the fire.

"Oi, huntsman! I'm talking to you. Go fetch the coin."

Hezekiah couldn't speak beyond a hoarse whisper. His jaw had been sealed shut by an overgrown yellow fang that jutted out from his skin, just below his cheekbone. It grew so long and sharp it had curved to pierce his face below his lip, and was boring a hole into bone. The mess of scar tissue and rotting skin that surrounded the growth was beginning to mangle his face beyond recognition. Such was the fate of nobody's favorite. He rose to do as he was bid.

A limb with too many hands of too many sizes had bubbled and swelled until it was hard to distinguish. It sat on the desk, and Esther was focused entirely on pricking each vein she could find, bleeding the contents into tiny, prepared bottles as if she was threading needles. Some of the hands fidgeted, and a few even tried to grab the desk, as if to pull themselves away from the witch that was bleeding them. The door whined as Hezekiah opened it.

"My sister should have taught you better than to disturb me, when I am doing Mother's work." Esther said absentmindedly as she guided a thread of blood into a pointed bottle. "What do you want?"

Hezekiah only moved aside and gestured with his head behind him. Esther leaned back a touch to get a clear view, and caught sight of the three men down by the brazier. Mostly Finlay, who she still found the more attractive and eye-catching.

"Ah, our thieves. Take the coin purse in the top drawer to Greer."

Hezekiah did as he was bid again, without a word.

There were four vials, all held together, and Greer counted out the appropriate amount of silver. One hundred for getting in and out ... on a technicality. Another hundred per full vial. Thus counted, Hezekiah took the rest of his mistress's money back, and Erwin's portion was handed over in a small leather coin purse. Erwin smiled and tossed Greer the blood.

He panicked, but caught it, shooting him a nasty glare.

"A pleasure doing business with you, old man."

"Yes, yes, now get the hell out of here. And *try* not to draw attention to yourself. Notoriety ain't fame."

Erwin shrugged and smiled, turning to leave with Finlay. He couldn't stop chortling to himself as they walked through the alleyway outside the warehouse.

"What's so funny?"

They were but thirty paces away when the door to the warehouse slammed open. Greer shouted. "Stop that bastard! He's running off with my head!"

Finlay turned and looked at Erwin. "What did you do?"

Erwin was already laughing and dashing away. The two had to dive down a corner as bolts came whizzing for them. Hezekiah was lacking with a sword, but punishing with a crossbow. And while in life his brigadier size might have rendered him slower, in death, animated by magic, he could catch up to even the two young men, and they knew it. He rounded the corner, loading another bolt. Finlay and Erwin had dropped down to the rooftops below, rather than staying on the road. Hezekiah let a bolt fly.

Finlay yelled as it pierced him in the back, just above the hip. A second hit his shoulder. With a pained stutter of disbelief, he lost his footing. He stumbled and fell, rolling off the roof and thudding hard into the alley below. Erwin cursed and dove down into the alleyway after him. Without Finlay between him and Hezekiah, he almost met the same fate. A bolt whistled past his head by an alarmingly small margin. He tucked and rolled, tumbling a few extra yards than he intended thanks to the momentum. He pulled himself to his feet.

"Fin!"

Finlay was gasping for breath, each gasp gradually giving way to a pained wail. The combined pain of the bolts and the fall to the ground rocked through him. He pulled himself up on one elbow, crawling toward Erwin. A bolt thudded into the stone just beside Erwin and he had to scramble backward, throwing his body against a building and ducking behind the stone steps to the door. Finlay was still crawling, leaving a line of blood over the stone. Erwin looked at him, back to Hezekiah, to the perpendicular alleyway that could provide him cover. His hand felt for his satchel, and the coin purse inside. Erwin's panicked breath made his next words hard to hear.

"Sorry, mate!"

He shrugged his shoulders apologetically and dove out of Hezekiah's line of sight, leaving Finlay behind. A thief had no loyalty but to himself, after all.

63

MADDOC GLARED AT LEVI, LOOKING HIM OVER FROM head to toe with a curl in his lip. Levi stood resolute beneath his scrutiny, hands neatly behind his back. Without his armor filling out his silhouette, his form was rather more petite in appearance. Though toned and taller than Jael, he had some of the same softer curves to his body that she did. His garb was only slightly doctored from what he'd worn to infiltrate these very halls. A dusty black ensemble of carefully maintained leather and linen. His hand was still bandaged with Benjamin's magic, though it was healing extraordinarily well.

"You mean to take this one with you?"

"Yes, Deacon," Philip said.

"And you?" Maddoc crossed his arms over his chest. "Your captain was willing to let you off your leash for this?"

Levi didn't acknowledge Maddoc with words, only nodding quietly to prevent from snapping some equally snarky reply that would worsen the tensions.

Maddoc wasn't particularly pleased, and his gaze narrowed even further. "And you will not interfere with our work?"

"No, Deacon."

"Very well. You two first, step up."

Jael and Philip stood before Maddoc's desk as he opened a tome. He held out one hand then and read – or rather recited – a small prayer. Nothing visible happened, aside from the gold beads of their rosaries seeming to flicker.

"Godspeed and good hunting. Alright, now take a hold of the boy."

"I beg your pardon?"

Philip smiled and offered his hand. "Don't worry, it's just a protection charm."

Levi glared suspiciously at Philip's hand, but took it nonetheless. As the two faced Maddoc together, a second, equally short prayer was read, directed at Philip. Levi felt a strange, oddly warm sensation shoot through him.

"What manner of magic is this?"

"Philip already told you," Maddoc groaned. "It's a protection charm. You're not of our church, so you can only borrow it, at the goodwill of your host. So, try not to lose it, eh?" Maddoc shut the tome with a heavy thud. "Don't worry, I'll have them keep to the well-lit streets, for your delicate sensibilities' sake. Off you go."

The summer evening was deep and dark. Levi hadn't realized just how much light the church's lanterns provided, until they passed through the small door built into the southwest gate, and darkness swallowed them. The city's many lampposts really were a poor imitation. He blinked as his eyes adjusted. As the three walked, Levi kept clenching his good hand, feeling strangely warm.

"What does this charm do?"

"It obscures your scent," Jael said, looking both ways before hopping down from the cobblestone curb. "We are human, and liable to attract vampires. The charm wards them off by temporarily rendering our blood holy."

"I'm sorry, holy?"

Philip smiled. "Ever seen a vampire drink holy water? They turn inside out."

Jael made a whooshing noise with her mouth and gestured with her hands, and the pair of Hunters both laughed.

"I ... should say not, no." Levi didn't share in the levity of their macabre humor.

"Blood is mostly water. So, we employ a spell that temporarily blesses it."

"So, if a vampire was to bite one of us ..." Jael trailed off, twirling her hand, waiting for Levi to finish her statement.

"It would turn them inside out?"

"He got there in the end, didn't he?"

"A good effort!" Philip commended him in a singsong tone that sounded more patronizing than he meant for it to. "Yes, with this charm, we're in no danger of being bitten. Well, almost no danger."

"Almost?"

"Sometimes," Jael interjected. "You get the really stupid ones, the stiffs. Just a corpse, and not a true vampire. They'll bite anything."

Levi squinted in thought. "If a vampire knows not to bite us, then how did one drink holy water?"

"Well, to say she 'drank' it would probably be the wrong word," Philip said as he hopped up on the banister of the bridge, neatly keeping his balance as he walked along and swung around lampposts with one arm.

"She?"

"Some vampire a good ... what would it be, Sister? Ten, eleven years ago?"

"Oh, more than that," Jael said from Levi's left side. "Probably closer to thirteen."

"Sometime, then, back when Father was just a Hunter." Philip hopped down from the banister. "A vampire had lunged to bite him, and he threw his bottle of holy water right into her open mouth."

"You could probably still find the stain on Penrose Lane even now, if you knew where to look. The city talked about it for months!"

"I bet Deacon Parnell has the newspaper clipping of it stashed somewhere, hah!"

"I would think he'd have it framed."

Levi seemed horrified by the idea, but Philip and Jael seemed to find it rather hilarious.

"Not quite *drinking*, I admit. but I'm sure some made it down her gullet, between the bits of glass."

"A good thing, too. It was only after that vampire's attack that Father created the warding charm. I wonder if she knows all the good she did."

"It was created that recently?" Levi's shock surprised both Jael and Philip, who looked at each other before giggling.

"Yes? What were you expecting?"

"I just suppose I thought all of your church's spells would be ancient things."

"Some are, some aren't." Jael shrugged.

"True. Unfortunately for you, you probably won't even be able to see the newest spell Father has created, Immolation."

From up high in his chambers, Cyril could vaguely see three shapes rounding the corner – having watched them all the while as they departed the glowing gatehouse, crossed the bridge, and ventured out into the cold city.

The night was, thankfully, uneventful. It was more an opportunity for Philip and Jael to give Levi a tour of some of the borough immediately surrounding the church. Philip and Jael could both point out the location of almost every single saint in the borough, too. There were so very *many* of them. Even the two

Hunters admitted they struggled to memorize *every* single one by name, and so only venerated a handful personally. Levi feigned ignorance as they excitedly introduced him to Saint Lilian, at that disturbingly deep fountain filled with wishes. The way Philip explained it, she was the Saint of Reunions – of families finding lost loved ones, of faithful returning to the church, and such similar happy circumstances. She even had a bell named for her, though neither Philip nor Jael had ever heard it.

The three sat down on the edge of the fountain as Philip pulled out three small loaves of dark brown buttery-looking bread studded with edible flowers, unwrapping them from linen.

"You swiped those from the bakery, didn't you?" Jael rolled her eyes as she accepted the one he handed to her. "Or did you convince Brontë to smuggle them to you?"

He chuckled as he held out one to Levi, who was trying not to perk up at the mention of Brontë's name.

"Oi, credit where it's due, thanks very much!" Philip said as he held up the bread to his mouth. "I can smuggle things out of the bakery myself just fine."

They were each about to take a bite when a strange, animalistic snarl sounded. It was unclear what direction the noise had come from. Something scratched against the cobblestones, somewhere. The web of streets and alleys made it sound like it was coming from all directions. Quiet, but undoubtedly getting closer. Something gnashing, chewing. All three of them put their makeshift picnic down and stood.

Levi looked around, expecting something, anything, to jump out at them. A street dog, a wild animal, a drunkard, maybe? He was looking across the short bridge that breached the nearest canal when something black skittered from the safety of one shadow to another. Something ... far too human to be moving like that. He was so startled by it that he sucked in a quiet breath and hopped.

Philip turned around to look across the bridge in the same direction. "Did you see something?"

"I'm not sure. But it was moving west. From that corner shop to the alley, there." He pointed to where he believed he'd seen the shape.

Philip moved his hands and called up one of his swords. He'd no sooner set a foot on the bridge than another one of those snarls sounded. It was clearly on the side nearer to them. Philip turned around, as did the other two – but saw nothing.

This time, though none of them saw it, Philip heard the skitter behind him, across the canal, where Levi had pointed. He puffed hair out of his face.

"I'll walk the other side; you walk this one."

Philip crossed the short bridge and walked on the opposite side of the waterway, a small gap some twenty paces wide, with a clear line of sight both ways, thanks to the lampposts. Both he and Jael cocked their heads and listened intently, spinning about as they walked and squinting into the dark. No further noises or jumping shadows revealed themselves. Philip even poked his sword into some of the bushes, but found nothing.

"You and Philip have rather morbid senses of humor," Levi mumbled to Jael as they walked.

"Hah, yes, I suppose we do. I think it's necessary, when you see the amount of death we do."

"You kill that many vampires?"

"No ... not these days. They hide from Father. It's their victims we often see. The bitten and dying, the dead, and the sickened with blo –"

"Blood," came that snarl, clearly this time.

Levi's hand leaped to the hilt of his sword, and Jael's rosary glowed.

A woman stumbled from the alleyway. She was dressed like the living, but was unraveling like the dead. Eyes cloudy like the full moon, she swayed, seemingly confused, almost in a trance, blinking at the two of them in the lamplight.

"What's this one doing all the way out here?" Jael murmured aloud in disbelief. "Why is she out in the light?"

The vampire hissed and smiled as she spoke, half her face decayed and her skin beginning to droop.

"Blood. Give it here!"

For the first time, Levi saw fangs. Awful, yellow, crooked things – needle-sharp and hungry. She leaped at the two. Jael shoved Levi away from her, letting fly an arrow that splintered apart into a shower of sparks. The sparks that made contact with the vampire clung to her like tar, melting through clothing until it burned at the skin below. The woman wailed and thrashed, clamoring forward on all fours as flesh bubbled and burned.

Levi watched, petrified, as this tiny brush with what was holy revealed the vampire for what it was: dead flesh reduced to animalistic urges. Philip was sprinting hard to get to the next bridge. The vampire gnashed pointed teeth and brandished dark, rotten fingertips, nails overgrown into claws. Jael dove and rolled, forfeiting her bow and instead relying on her quiver of arrows. But this stiff was still swift. And strong. She left marks in the stone as she clawed into it for traction. Levi realized he'd not even drawn his sword when he heard Philip's voice.

"Don't just stand there, you coward!" he yelled. "Help her!"

An awful shiver traveled through Levi's body, up from his feet to the nape of his neck. *Coward!* He suddenly felt very cold. Was this fear? It felt like nothing he'd felt before. The vampire stopped, whipping her head around and smiling. Levi realized that cold feeling must have been the blessing leaving him. It was only borrowed, at the goodwill of his host – and what Hunter would have goodwill for a coward? His blood no longer blessed, he suddenly had all of that *thing's* attention, and his sensitive ears were no longer guarded from its voice. The screech was enough to deafen and disorient him, and the string of frantic words he heard made him wonder if she had already infected him somehow.

Arrows clipped into the stones as she scrambled toward him like an imp. He finally drew his sword, thanking his training for serving him well. He held it up and braced the flat of the blade against his elbow. It saved him from being slashed through, but he watched in shock as the vampire's claws bounced harmlessly off the steel. It didn't cut her, not even a scratch. She howled in frustration and jumped at him, kicking the sword with both legs. He flew backward, kicking up dust as he slid over the cobblestones. The blow winded him and he gasped.

Philip made it to the bridge. He dashed across and, using his sword jabbed into the stone as an anchor, swung himself around the corner. Levi saw a black-and-gold blur as Philip leaped over him and joined the melee.

Jael and Philip moved with ruthless efficiency together. Philip could deflect and parry her many swipes and kicks, while Jael pierced her with arrows from behind at every opportunity. It made her screech at the injustice of such an unfair fight.

But she was still swift, and had some little fragment of her wily wits yet about her. She saw an opening and rolled out of the way of Philip's saber. Instead of lashing out at him, she leaped up onto the banister. Philip reacted quickly, but not quickly enough. He whipped around and sliced an innocent lamppost through. The hot metal melted straight through the post, and the severed half fell into the water. The vampire dodged the swipe just fine, and leaped from the banister back to Levi, who had only just pulled himself up to one knee, trying to keep from hyperventilating.

The only thing that stopped her from tackling him back to the ground was a well-aimed arrow from Jael. It caught her in the neck and tore a chunk of flesh from her throat. The force of it knocked her past Levi. He scrambled away from her. The injury only made her that much more desperate for blood. He was half up to his feet again when she lunged.

Levi could only see her extra teeth – sharp and curved and coming right for him. Fear clutched him, a completely different ice-cold feeling in his chest. He didn't want to die. Philip kicked the back of Levi's knee. He collapsed just in time. The vampire would have sailed over him if Philip hadn't slid in between them and kicked her back.

A handful of teeth were knocked out as her jaw clicked out of place. She was thrown on her back. Philip was already righting himself and charging for her. She braced her arms behind her head and forced herself upright via momentum, only to be greeted by Philip's blade piercing straight through her belly.

Philip knelt, chest heaving. The vampire twitched and sank lower with him. His blade protruded from her back, bloody and bright – and his empty hand was over her heart.

"Finally," he breathed. "I seek Immolation."

His rosary flickered bright and hummed at his hip. A tongue of flame leaped to life in his hand. That familiar, unnatural gold that illuminated the cathedral grounds. The same fire that burned, unceasing, in the many hearths, keeping her faithful warm. A tiny flicker of godhood, in the palm of his hand.

The sorry mess of flesh impaled on his sword screeched and tossed her head. The flame swept through her brutally fast. It tore through her chest, swallowing up flesh and fabric both, eating through her until it found and devoured her heart. Her shrieks were silenced abruptly as she was consumed. Philip rose to his feet, untouched by the fire and unaffected by the heat, even as his cassock fluttered and the magic swelled. To Levi, some ten paces away, it put out such an incredible heat that he had to squint his eyes and guard his face with his hand.

Then, through his bandaged fingers, he saw ... nothing. Only a moment, and there was nothing left. The stench of burning flesh, the sickly-sweet smell of vampire blood, the ungodly *noise* – it was all, all of it, gone. The last few flickers of the holy fire lingered. The rest was already drifting away in gold sparks. Flickering motes of light carried up and away, like dust on the breeze. It was strangely serene.

Philip gestured and his swords disappeared. He stood over Levi and offered him his hand, to pull himself to his feet. To say Levi was embarrassed would be an understatement, but he took Philip's hand and let the Brother pull him up.

"Is burning them like that really necessary?" he mumbled.

"Yes." Philip's tone had lost all of its cheerfulness again, now gravely serious and somber. "Vampires always regenerate. Some faster than others, aye, but give them enough time –"

"Aye," Jael added, walking past Levi to join Philip. "Be it five months or five years, they always come back."

"I imagine it's difficult for a southerner like you to understand." Once again, in what was likely an earnest attempt to sound understanding, Philip instead sounded patronizing.

"It just seems ... extreme."

"We used to bury them," Philip said quietly. "Rather than burn them."

Levi blinked and had to take a moment to process what Philip said. "But, if they regenerate, then –?"

"Then they're trapped, undying, somewhere inside a coffin, buried who knows how deep in the earth."

Levi's heart sank into his stomach at the thought.

"Father, too, thought that was cruel," Jael added sympathetically. Levi failed to hide his surprise, but she ignored his shocked face. "So, he wrote Immolation, to spare them that fate."

Back down the road, past the severed lamppost, another figure scratched across the ground on all fours. It took the blood bread left at the foot of the saint and slipped off with the prize.

64

THE NIGHT CRAWLED ON. Stars twinkled behind ribbons of clouds, oblivious to the bloodshed far below. To the fulfillment surging in the hearts of the two Hunters, and the questions boiling in the heart of one other. Levi was terrified to walk the streets alone that night. He only took solace in the very well-lit path, thanks to the diligent work of the lamplighters. He had a new and very real appreciation for why so many of the local knights carried so many sources of light. This fear was new to him. He hated it.

Brontë was sitting at the bakery worktable. She had one of the bulky, bronze kitchen timers in her lap and was using her apron to keep the key from oiling up her fingers too much as she wound it. She had only just set it down, looking forward to a cup of tea and some time with her current book, when Philip trotted into the bakery. He pulled up a chair on the opposite side of the table, and she fetched a second cup from the cupboard.

"Oh, are you making tea?"

"Yes?"

"Blegh. What about cocoa?"

"With nutmeg?"

"Always."

"Fine, fine." She rolled her eyes and gathered up the sugar, spices, cocoa, and kettle necessary.

Philip sat with one knee up to his chest on the stool, regaling her with a, to his credit, far less graphic account of the evening's hunt. Brontë was grateful she could hide her face behind her mug of thick, piping-hot chocolate, because enduring his descriptions would have been difficult for her, even if she *wasn't* what she was. But this time was different. In the course of his storytelling, he let slip that Levi – the sergeant from the Royal Guard – had in fact accompanied him. She was all ears, then, asking question after question.

"He's probably damn good with a sword, when he's not scared out of his wits."

"I'm surprised he had the courage to go out at all."

"Eh." Philip made a vague gesture with his free hand. "Less courage and more ... doubt."

"Well, he's hardly a doubter now, I imagine."

"You can never tell with these southerners. They're all logic and bureaucracy, doing things by the law – Oh! And in regard to your flour mystery ..."

He finished off his cocoa and leaned his head very far back to do so. "Well, you didn't hear it from me." He smiled and put a finger up to his lips. "But as it turns out, ol' Greer was already under investigation by the Guard for smuggling. No wonder they didn't want us around the Wren. Why didn't they just tell us in the first place –"

"But the Royal Guard wouldn't care about blood smuggling ..." Brontë repeated the word over to herself in thought. "And the bag was sealed."

"Eh?"

"The flour was still sealed. I had to break it to open it." Brontë turned and rummaged through the cabinet behind her. She pulled out a glass jar filled up with broken tags. "It's a lead tag, see?" She held it out in the palm of her hand. "It gets stamped with the mill. It even has the date on it –"

"We know the flour came from the mill, obviously," Philip interrupted and rolled his eyes. "But Greer snuck the blood parcel into it –"

"Will you just listen to me for once?"

Philip stared blankly at her, a little stunned. Brontë, too, was a little surprised at how forceful her voice had sounded. Her cheeks even wore a little bit of color. He cracked a smile and thought about teasing her, but thought better of it the next second. She felt a bit embarrassed, but shook it off and kept talking.

"Greer would have had to break the seal to get something into the bag after it came from the mill."

"Come on, I'm sure he could replicate a tag like that."

"Doesn't it at least warrant investigation? You're really that certain the miller had nothing to do with it?"

"Of course not! Sunderman? That family has been serving the church for centuries."

"I don't mean Lady Sunderman herself; I mean the mill workers. You honestly don't think some employee could have been bought by –?"

Philip laughed, cutting her off. "Greer would never take the fall himself if he could blame it on someone else. If there was some employee he could blame, the knights would have dragged the name out of him by now."

The kitchen timer chimed out. Brontë tossed the tag down on the table and shrugged, throwing her hands up in defeat. She huffed her annoyance and mumbled something about having work to do, marching outside into the courtyard to both cool her temper and her cheeks. She really hated that she blushed when upset. At least she'd be able to blame it on the heat of the ovens she now had to tend to.

Philip meanwhile had picked up the tag, turning it over in his hand. She was right about the date, at least. It was obvious where the seal had been crimped to the bag, and where Brontë had used her shears to break it. He clicked his tongue and pushed himself away from the worktable.

The map room was empty, save for Maddoc. He stood between the table and the hearth, studying the map as he so often did. It granted him a great knowledge and familiarity, but also made him lament his being cooped up within the cathedral most of the time. He rubbed his forehead, a cigarette between his fingers. When Philip came abruptly into the room, Maddoc snapped at him out of sheer embarrassment for being caught smoking. Reduced to a child with his hand caught in the cookie jar.

"Where are your manners, Brother! How dare you barge in unannounced – what's that?" Maddoc forgot to pretend to be angry when he saw the little trinket in Philip's hand.

The younger Hunter came up on the opposite side of the table, trying not to wrinkle his nose at the cigarette smoke to be polite. "Deacon Parnell, I was speaking with Miss Brontë, and she pointed out to me that the bag we found the blood had been sealed originally."

Maddoc groaned and rolled his head back at the sound of Brontë's name. "You waste your time talking to that girl."

Philip shrugged. "She was the one who found the blood in the first place." He put the tag on the table and slid it across the map to Maddoc. He picked it up, turning a bit toward the hearth to have more light while inspecting it.

"If Greer did smuggle the blood in, as we suspect, he would have had to break the seal on the bag, and reseal it after. But the seal wasn't tampered with at all."

"Sunderman is a good woman," Maddoc mumbled through his cigarette as he turned the tag over.

"Yes, I said as much. But Miss Brontë made a reasonable assumption – that it might have been one of her employees."

Maddoc didn't seem convinced at all, but that may or may not have been entirely because this was Brontë's suggestion.

"The sinsick can lurk anywhere, yes?" Philip continued. "And their affliction makes them that much more susceptible to coercion. Maybe there is some employee –?"

"That girl isn't as bright as she thinks she is." Maddoc snorted. He flicked the tag back over to Philip with his thumb. "That tag is from mill number eighteen – the one they stopped using last winter. Greer must have swiped the stamp so he could reseal bags with it."

Philip looked down at the tag in his hand, feeling rather silly. "Oh. Well, then."

65

ERWIN WAS NECK-DEEP IN ALCOHOL. He'd lost the vampire, and kept his prize money – a good portion of which he'd already spent at the Ginger Cap bar. He told himself it was celebratory, a toast to his good fortune. He'd gone back to the arena to open his locker, to fetch the real blood, which he'd swapped into different bottles for some thick cherry syrup he found behind the bar. Even now, it practically sang against his chest, humming with energy where it was tucked into his pocket. He waited until it was dark – when his bright red hair was harder to identify – to begin the long walk home.

He didn't get far. Stumbling and swerving on the uneven grade of the alley, he immediately felt like sitting down. His low moan turned to surprise as someone grabbed him by the shirt and flung him to the ground.

"Just like I thought, you mangy, sorry excuse for boy." Greer had a tinge of laughter to his voice, a tone that implied he was enjoying this too much. After all, he couldn't normally push Erwin around, being a weak, uncoordinated, and unathletic fellow. Erwin spluttered and rushed to right himself, but overcorrected and tumbled forward.

He made an easy target. Greer punched him straight in the jaw. He balked at it, flailing his own arm out and trying to shoo him away.

"Get lost, old man!" His words were slurred and his voice sad. "Leave me be!"

Greer had both hands on his knees, laughing. He punched Erwin again. He threw in a kick, because he could. Erwin's fighter instincts seemed to surface. But as he brought his fists up to protect his face, he stumbled. The world warped around him and his feet were far too heavy. Greer laughed and jabbed him hard in the gut. He leaned back against the wall, holding his stomach. Greer hit him in the face. Once, twice, thrice – until he spluttered and fell to one knee. Greer kicked him in the head, and he tumbled over. Flat on his back in the alley, he tasted blood between his teeth and dripping from his nose. One eye watered, already struggling to open.

Greer leaned over and yanked Erwin's satchel from his belt. He opened it and took back his coin purse, and Erwin's as recompense. He tucked them into his own pouch on the rear of his belt and kicked Erwin in the ribs.

"Alright, boy – where's the blood?"

Erwin smiled. "I don't have it," he fibbed.

Greer grabbed him by the shirt, shaking him. "Where is it?" He shoved Erwin back down and patted his pockets, trying to find any vials or potions on him – but there were none. "Fine. Worthless boy. Die in the gutter where you belong."

Greer marched off, back toward the warehouse, already thinking of how he'd explain this to Esther. Erwin coughed and couldn't tell if his injuries were the culprit, or if the tears in his eyes were something else. Still, as he lay there, he smiled, applauding his own forethought and slyness. He'd hidden the vials of blood in his boots before he left.

CYRIL WAS ENJOYING A CIGARETTE AND QUIETLY LEAFING through a book in his lap. He almost didn't hear the knock at his chamber door, all the way in the adjacent room of his study. Luckily, Brontë managed to summon her courage and knock again, and he stood to answer it. He was surprised to see her, but bid her inside all the same. They went back into the study together, where he hurried to extinguish his cigarette, almost trying to hide his ashtray behind a stack of books like a child hides a broken vase.

"What do you need? Are you feeling unwell?" he asked.

Brontë had already become distracted by the nearest plant hanging in a basket. She looked back to him and took a moment to process his words.

"Oh, yes. I feel a bit better." She walked over to him and dug the tiny glass bottle he'd given her out of her pocket. She handed it over to him, now empty. "Thank you."

He nodded and took it, setting it on his desk. "Did it help?"

She nodded. "I don't feel as sick, the uneasy feeling has subsided." Her brows furrowed and she fiddled with her veil as if it was her hair. "Though, I am not sure if that's ... the intended effect."

"Unfortunately, it is not an exact science." He sat down at his desk. "As much as I wish it was."

He habitually began writing down what she'd told him on a spare sheet of parchment. One of many more scribblings that'd join his mountain of notes. She meanwhile wandered back over to the plants dotting the little library. He took better care of them than she had. They had survived under her care, yes, but they flourished under his. New buds and leaves had sprouted. She pouted and told herself it was due to her being busy, and away from his chambers. But so was he, oftentimes, so that excuse fell apart, even to her.

Cyril finished writing down his notes and turned to see her leaning over, inspecting one of the plants he had on a small pedestal. She was oblivious to him, until he stood and began rummaging around. He opened a cabinet and pulled down two small copper watering cans.

"I still need to water them tonight. Would you like to help me?"

She was so delighted by the idea she forgot to actually say yes and just rushed over to his side. He handed her one of the two, and led her to the sink in his washroom to fill them up.

66

$\mathcal{I}$T WAS A SAD SIGHT, IN A WAY: such a solid, well-built structure and ingenious engineering left to decay, to crumble into disrepair. Many tiered floors jutted out here and there from the whitewashed timber and stone building. The blades of the mill had since been removed, lying stacked upon one another in the fallow field nearby. On the other side, the lower portion of the building jutted out on stone pillars over the river, accompanied by a quaint little fishing dock. Her stone foundations had long since been overtaken by creeping vines and a generous coating of moss. Roots grew so thick that they threatened to claw their way through the stones, and the occasional roof tile had clattered to the ground as the beams shifted and sagged with age. There was neither hide nor hair to be seen of anyone, not even the littlest scuff in the hard, cracked dirt.

"See?" sighed Jael, crossing her arms at having been dragged all the way across the river on behalf of Philip's curiosity. "It's completely abandoned."

Philip pursed his lips and blew a stray tuft of hair out of his eyes. "Then why are they still using the seal for this numbered mill?"

"Some bloke wasn't paying attention and used the wrong stamp, probably."

"Maybe." He didn't sound convinced.

"Greer already admitted to putting the blood in the flour shipment." She leaned her head back and groaned. "Come on,

Miriam's making shepherd's pie tonight ... I want to get back while it's still hot."

"Fine, fine. Just a quick peek inside. Maybe they're still using it as a warehouse?"

"Curiosity killed the cat." Jael frowned at Philip.

"But satisfaction brought it back!" He beamed. "You can stay out here if you want, should just be a quick peek in, to make sure it's abandoned." He shielded his eyes from the setting sun and looked up. "I think I may even be able to look in from that window up there."

"Not in this light, you won't."

"Well, maybe I can't ... but I know a pair of lovely eyes that would do that very well." He grinned at her.

The pair began to climb, fingers hooking into cracks in the whitewash and testing old beams with their feet. They reached the glass window with relative ease, but even Jael's sharp eyes struggled to make any sense of what was inside. Philip pulled his dagger from his boot and, with a little fidgeting and finesse, forced the window open. An awful, musty smell rushed out as soon as he had done so, and both looked to one another with concern. Vampire blood and decomposing flesh mingled together in a particular smell that would be hard to forget. They both nodded and assumed silence immediately. Philip swung in first and landed carefully, lightly, on his feet and crouched down low. Jael did the same, and they both crept forward into the supposedly abandoned mill, wary to not disturb the aging floor or announce their presence by stepping on creaking beams.

The Sunderman mills all had similar constructions. Staircases and walkways that spiraled around the wall, and an open shaft in the center for the mechanism that powered the mill. It had been dismantled, of course, and now all that really remained were a few leftover chains from the winch and particularly stubborn beams that didn't want to budge, or were needed to ensure the building's integrity. The two shuffled down a staircase and the smell grew heavier. The floor began to grow stickier. Rot filled the air. And voices could be heard. Several of them, all muttering and mumbling in quiet conversation. They whispered unintelligibly, holding a hushed conference, yet oblivious to the two trespassers. It prickled like a bite on the back of the Hunters' necks. The voices stopped all at once.

"What did you bring me?" a single voice from the group whispered. It sounded incredibly young, much too young.

In the dark, Philip and Jael could just barely see a large and ... bumpy figure curled up on the ground. Several people all sitting in a group, maybe? It would explain the whispers. They sat together on what could only be described as a makeshift bed. A mound of discarded grain sacks, rugs, blankets and straw, all heavily stained with blood and bile. A thin, massive series of linen sheets had been stitched together haphazardly and thrown over whoever or whatever it was. Like a shared blanket, thrown over a bed full of children. The one that had spoken stood up slowly. They were ... very tall. Unusually tall, abnormally tall. Or maybe it was being hoisted up on the shoulders of the others, like a leader. Their head then lolled over, limp on their shoulder, jaw slack. But they spoke again. The voice didn't come from that head.

"I'm hungry. What did you bring me?"

A shaft of light revealed a gnarled, filthy face, with incompletely formed lips split up to their nasal cavity and a bulbous, likely infected eye. That incomplete head was cradled in the bony arms of a woman. Long-dead, by the look of her. At least one would hope. A spindly hand reached down to hold their weight as they turned, and Philip squinted at it. In the dim light, it looked as if they had several hands on that arm, some of them still beneath the skin, wriggling about like worms as if trying to escape. It kept turning. The flesh of their bodies had melded together, the head half a part of her belly, and her own head limp off to one side. Another arm, and another. *How many of them were there?* All grown together, like a rat king of corpses.

"What did you bring me?"

Philip was too stunned to speak. It crept closer to the two of them.

"Philip," Jael whispered. "What is it?"

No answer. The mass whined and grew closer, scratching lines in the dust as it crept forward.

"Philip? What do we do?"

"I don't ..." he murmured. "I don't know what ..."

Two hands took hold of Philip. Jael panicked. Her bow flashed bright into her hands and she loosed an arrow. Sparks flew immediately. The thing wailed and two of its many hands released Philip, reaching up to hold the wound. Philip yelled and snapped out of his stupor, scrambling backward and shuddering at the thought this thing had touched him.

If it bled, it could be killed. If a Hunter's weapon could hurt it, it had to die. Different from what they had seen before or not, they were Hunters, oath-bound to slaughter any vampire on sight.

It recovered alarmingly fast and dove for the pair. Philip's blades leaped into his hands and he sliced through one of their flailing arms, severing it off. It screeched, but that screech sounded an awful lot like a child crying, in a way that made Philip choke and stagger at the noise.

"You are going to start cutting me up, also?"

The creature thrashed and writhed about, cradling its severed arm and lashing out a kick at Philip to push him away. Another arrow embedded itself in its back and it howled.

"Stop it! You're hurting me!"

A second arrow. A third. It turned and swiped at Jael, but only awkwardly fumbled and fell over, disoriented from pain. More arrows. Jael and Philip slid back over the sludge of blood covering the floor as the creature moaned and doubled over, blood seeping from its many wounds and golden arrows sticking from its back like a hedgehog. The howl of pain changed in tone. The creature's flesh rippled and the arrows one by one snapped. This time, when it looked up, the face with the split lip didn't seem interested; instead its head kept turning, revealing the other face further along the head, fully formed. When this face spoke, it was louder and older.

"I said stop!"

An awful sound heralded one of those hands that Philip had seen beneath the skin flailing and bursting out from the creature, settling itself in position to replace its severed fellow. Jael shot an arrow straight through its chest. The creature shrieked at the burn it caused. It reared back and clawed at its own chest, tearing itself open to rip out the burning holy item and fling it aside. Philip and Jael watched in shock as the wound quickly bubbled up and closed, scar tissue forming a glistening, bloody mass over it. It swallowed up some of its own spare heads, who cried at the injustice of being suffocated.

"Out!"

It screamed and fell forward, gasping for breath. It twitched and shuddered, coughing blood as each head seemed to argue for dominance, for the right to speak. A consensus was reached, and when it spoke again, all of the voices shrieked out at once.

"You brought me nothing, get out!"

The creature leaped forward. Nimble like a spider and angry. It swiped at the Hunters, forcing them to leap in opposite directions to anywhere that they could. It struck the rotting timbers of the mill with enough force to crack the beams, never mind how it skinned itself apart in the process. Strings of flesh were left behind, rapidly regenerating like some horrible version of spider silk being spun into a web.

"What do we do?" Jael yelled as she leaped out of range. "It just regenerates!"

Philip's chest was heaving and his eyes combed the floor the creature was on. The mill had really been abandoned in haste more than deliberately shut down, it appeared. Everything was still coated in the fine dust of grain. He yelled as one of the creature's hands gripped his ankle and dragged him back. He was swift enough to hack through it and scramble out of the way, but only just.

"I have an idea!" he shouted, shaking gore from his foot. "Get to the winch there, at the bottom!"

Gnarled hands and weak feet scrambled up along the wall, tearing old plaster away in powdery puffs. Philip wove a path upward through the many supporting beams, trying to dodge the bloodied hands that came grabbing for him. The winch had been left unused, and was frozen with rust at this point, but no matter. Philip grabbed a length of chain and flung himself over the railing.

He kicked himself off the wall, swinging from the locked up length of the chain. He sliced a cut across one of the faces, buying himself precious time to loop the chain around them and dive out of the way of the many hands that raked through the air looking for him. He grabbed a hay hook from the floor, scrambling up the stairs and leaping onto the thing's back. He jabbed it into the creature, twisting it and shoving it as deep as he could, before getting grabbed and flung off. The breath was knocked out of his lungs as he hit the wall and sunk to the floor.

Jael took Philip's lead and laced her arrow through a link of chain at the bottom of the winch. She aimed it dead for the beast's center. She let it fly. It worked as intended, carving a line straight through the monster with the arrow tearing out the far side, rusty chain in tow. Philip shook his head, shook the stars out of his eyes and forced himself off the wall. He jumped up and grabbed the chain that protruded from the monster. He swung back around the creature's shoulder to prevent it from pulling it out. A hard yank and a quick dive to safety, and he tripped up the mass. The flesh regenerating around the wound forced the chain to remain in place, and the monster cried out in pain and frustration. This time, all the voices shrieked at once, and a flurry of limbs punched and swiped through the timbers of the mill, trying to get to Jael despite being held back by the tension.

Rust powdered and puffed up in clouds from the winch. The chains whined. This thing was strong. Philip leaped atop it and sliced more rapid, crisscrossing wounds into its back, giving Jael time to dive out of the way. The winch snapped and was pulled from its stone foundation. Philip lost his balance and tumbled to the floor, rolling through the bloody sludge to break his fall. The monster spun around and slithered beneath the stairwell, accidentally looping the chain about a beam as it chased after Jael. The beam whined out in dismay, too old to bear the pressure. The roof creaked and tiles rattled.

"It'll bring the whole thing down!"

"Out! Jump into the river, go!"

"What?"

"Don't ask questions, just get into the water!"

The two sprinted up the stairs back toward the open window. The beam cracked and splintered. Chains rattled and voices wailed as the creature scrambled up in pursuit, pushing beams aside and tripping up the stairs. Grimy nails made the most awful screech over the floor as it clambered after them, kicking up splinters from the dry floor. The rusty links got caught in and snapped the spindles of the banister as the creature raced up the narrow stairs. Mouths open wide, crooked fangs flashing, it bellowed both broken curses and pleas for help. It overtook them too quickly. They reached the open window only to have to dive further up the stairs to dodge snapping mouths and bloodied hands.

Glass shattered as Jael kicked the glass pane out of another window. She had no time to think, as Philip shoved her through it the next moment. She collected herself with a yell and managed to brace and roll to safety on the roof a few floors below. She could only hear Philip's voice faintly from the mill as she stumbled over the roof toward the river.

"Run, run! Into the water, now!"

Confused, but fully trusting his words, she ran along the roof of the building that jutted out over the water. Philip ripped his belt rosary out of his sash where he stood at the top of the mill. Below, the monster was still trying desperately to crawl up to him. Crumbling rubble tumbled down onto it as the very mill seemed to tremble. Philip held his rosary to his chest, praying with every ounce of faith he could conjure.

"Hear me, hear me, hear me, Father! I seek Immolation!"

The medallion at the end of his rosary began to glow fiercely, radiating a heat so intense he struggled to hold it. It flickered and erupted into a flame. Philip prayed his hunch was right – and flung his rosary down into the mill.

The creature paused when it saw the holy beads coming down for it, hissing in confusion. Philip's feet had never moved so fast or pushed so hard in his life. He bolted as hard as he could for the window, diving out and throwing himself into the open air. He'd only made it past the window when the mill exploded behind him.

Jael was flung from the roof by the force and hurtled down into the river some feet below. The same force sent Philip tumbling forward into the air out of control. He slammed into the river.

⌖

METAL CLATTERED AGAINST THE FLOOR and water splashed. Brontë whipped around in time to see Cyril stagger, the little watering tin rolling away from him where he'd dropped it. He swayed precariously, reaching out with one hand to steady himself against the open door to the balcony.

"Cyril!" Brontë's voice was shrill in alarm as she rushed to him, her own watering can also forgotten.

His free hand was pressed to his chest, clawing into his shirt as he gasped. Brontë reached his side, slipping beneath the arm he had propped against the wall and wrapping her own around him. He was terrifyingly warm, even without his cassock.

"What's wrong? Are you in pain? I can call a Cleric –"

He swayed slightly, leaning into her, but steadying himself a moment later. Though his brow twitched and glistened with sweat, he seemed to be rapidly recovering from the sudden onset.

"I'm ... well. It has passed," he mumbled slowly, rubbing his chest as if it was sore or tender.

"What happened? I don't –"

"Someone ... drew a great deal of magic from me."

A shockingly loud clap like thunder rattled the very heavens. Brontë nearly leaped out of her skin. They both wordlessly looked up and out over the city in wonder, trying to find the source of the sound. It revealed itself not a moment after. One of the mills on the hillside burst into a cloud of golden flames. It sent shockwaves rippling through the surrounding fields like an angry ocean.

"Is that ... one of the mills?" Brontë asked, eyes wide in fear and realization.

Cyril straightened, shaking off his exhaustion and gently disentangling himself from Brontë. He rushed to where his cassock hung, pulling it on and tucking it into his sash without much care for how it looked. He paused only long enough to put a reassuring hand on her head. And just like that, he was gone, and Brontë was left standing in his room alone. Water puddled on the floor as she stood in the open doors to his balcony, watching smoke climb high and smudge the sky black.

THE ENTIRE CITY HAD HEARD THE NOISE. Domingo instinctively leaped up, drawing his sword from where it was slung over his chair. He could have sworn he felt the very world beneath his feet shudder with the noise. Chaos in the courtyard made him rush to his window. He looked over to see the soldiers below all rushing out of their barracks, similarly confused and bewildered. He looked westward, toward the setting sun – to see a black cloud of smoke beginning to ink a line into the sky. He grabbed his sword belt from his chair, buckling it about his waist as he yelled down the hall.

"Fetch my horse!"

67

HE GUARD WERE QUICK, BUT THE HUNTERS WERE FASTER. They were too, for a small blessing, closer to the mill. The west gate of Windermere thronged with people, as did the hills just beyond. Horses thundered through the streets, riders bellowing at worried pedestrians to get out of the road.

Confused, alarmed farmers congregated on the opposite riverbank of the smoking, destroyed mill. The little cobblestone pier and warehouses on the other side had been spared serious damage. The entire area was coated with still-warm ash, though. It fluttered about like snow, and many had scarves or shawls over their faces to prevent breathing too much of it in. The buildings had been rattled. But, much like the mill itself, the foundations were too solid to be upset. The crowd all murmured and mumbled, voicing concern of what might be lurking in the waters that the Hunters were very keenly investigating. This was only tempered by a complete trust in the Hunters, of course – as well as a calm that settled over the watchers as the Archbishop and Deacon both came into view on horseback. A strange sort of calm. A sort of relief that he would tend to matters, that they were safe – and a great unease, that whatever caused the blast warranted his attention.

The clergy swarmed over the river. Some paddled around in dinghies, graciously lent to them by the locals. Some were knee-deep in the shallows, swatting reeds aside and sending fluffy cattails up into the wind. Still more waded in up to the waist. Carefully, wherever the current and solid footing allowed. Jael had been found relatively quickly. By the time Cyril had dismounted and rushed over, she'd already been pulled onto the riverbank. Concussed, bruised, likely with broken bones - but alive. The ambulance arrived not soon after, and one of the Sisters who accompanied it ensured Jael was loaded inside with great care.

Cyril was still looking around at the odd scene. The ash floating around, the ruined mill, the nervous crowd. The whitewashed timber of the mill had crumbled and given out, gobbled up by flame and pushed aside by the explosion. What was left of it, sitting atop the stone foundation, crackled and hissed. It still put out a strangely comforting amount of heat, too. A specific heat that betrayed the origins of the spark that had set it alight. Cyril took a few steps toward the mill, frowning as a familiar stench grew a little more noticeable.

"Wait, Father!" A Huntress rushed to him and held up her hand. "There's something inside."

"Something? How vague." Cyril glanced up through the drizzle at the smoldering building.

"We ... don't know what it is."

"But it is of vampiric origin?"

"Most definitely."

"I see." Cyril turned and gave a short whistle that Maddoc recognized and answered to.

"You and I will venture inside, Brother."

The two slowly entered through a destroyed pair of double doors. They had been knocked down, right off their hinges, by the force of the blast. But one foot inside, and their boots were several inches deep in powdery ash. Maddoc's nose scrunched up in disgust. The sickly-sweet stench of burning flesh permeated everything, even his hand clasped tight over his nose and mouth.

Fragments of flesh had been blown apart, torn to shreds by the sheer force of the blast. Gnarled limbs had been pelted to sludge against the stone walls. Skin hung in bubbled, blistered sheets from the spiderweb of chains that had been woven by the two Hunters. A charred mass of sludge gurgled and moved in the rubble.

"What in hellfire?"

Maddoc's rosary hummed as he set his stance and balled his hands into fists, but he was halted by Cyril's extended arm, gesturing silently for him to stand down.

What remained of spindly limbs pushed up the blackened, sorry excuse for a body. Skin slipped down like sheer fabric as it crinkled and fell away. It had burned, but not perished. Even now, as bits of it coated the walls and were caught up in the chains, the largest mass remaining clung to life – or whatever imitation it could make of it. Molten eyes and crooked jaws dripped pus from blisters. Each withered head, or fraction of one, was trying to look at the two men, making it twitch and contort as it fought itself for the best view.

"What is it? What are they?" Maddoc whispered.

Cyril's one eye stung. "They're children," he murmured.

It's a monster, he thought. *Disgusting.* An overgrown mass of unwanted, unloved bastards.

They're children.

Kill it! Burn it and be done with it. Until it smolders, until it stops moving, until it stops crying.

Have mercy.

A chorus of mangled voices whispered through rotting teeth, blackened gums, and charred, conjoined throats. An entire orphanage crying out.

"More of you? To burn me?"

"No." Cyril took a step forward. "I am here to heal you."

"Be *careful,* Cyril. *Cyril!*" Maddoc hissed behind him, his voice panicked as he glanced nervously between Cyril and whatever this thing was.

Cyril spoke in a tongue neither Maddoc nor the throbbing mass of flesh knew. An old incantation. Deep magic that forced his robes to flicker white from head to toe, and his one eye to glow. A flash of gold from behind his head, that familiar, ringed crown the saints wore.

The mass hissed and recoiled at the light instinctively. Even Maddoc staggered back a step. He had to shield his eyes with a hand, squinting through his fingers. But, in contrast to the violent ripping and tearing that the golden flame engendered, this light was something else. It was warm and comforting and ... forgiving. A soft, sustained note seemed to echo – somewhere between a chime and a hum – through the air around him. Cyril spoke with a voice that wasn't entirely his own.

"Come here. I will be gentle with you."

He took another slow step toward the thing, the soles of his boots barely seeming to touch the ground, no longer disturbing the ash, blissful white no longer dirtied by soot or soil. His cassock seemed weightless, floating about as if he was submerged, as he extended his hand in the way one might toward a scared animal, with two fingers poised to pass judgment. The creature dug shattered, raw fingernails into the floor, desperately clawing toward the source of this warmth, this light, that seemed to make all the wretched pain fade away.

One featherlight touch did the deed. Mercy struck swift and true. A painless, instant blow to the mass of grafted souls, relieving them of their turmoil. It was, as Father had promised, a gentle thing. One burnt, misaligned chin rested softly in his hand, and each of the voices united to that mess of flesh sighed in contentment. A little shudder, and it collapsed.

Cyril, too, sighed in exhaustion. The brilliant white fell from his garments like scales as they slithered back into the mundane inky black. The fabric draped over him as it became reacquainted with gravity, and the weight of even this seemed to drag him down, pulling him to earth as he sank to one knee and gasped at the effort, clutching his racing, burning heart. Maddoc rushed over to him, grabbing Cyril's arm to steady his friend, giving it a nervous shake.

"Cyril? Speak to me! Come on, now. Are you here?"

Cyril's one eye was still open. A sort of glassy, blank look that made Maddoc's heart drop in worry. He blinked, then, shaking his head and seeming to come out of the stupor. His one eye slid down to the mass on the floor. He gritted his teeth and snarled at it.

"Filthy thing."

Maddoc smiled in relief at the familiar voice, clapping him on the back and helping him to his feet. Cyril raised his hand, pointing with two fingers. He stumbled, just barely, taking a deep breath and steadying himself.

"It should do no more harm. Good riddance."

The body went up in tongues of gold flame. Not a chaotic, crackling spark this time – fueled by fear and sustained by a masterless rosary. It was controlled, contained, pure. Cyril focused, ensuring that it obeyed. It was limited to only consuming the mangled scraps of flesh, forbidden from touching anything else. The chains rattled as flesh was burned away from them. Rather than a dusting of black ash, the Heart carried the mess away on gold sparks heavenward. Each dark, dreary piece of the creature was lifted from the wall, from the floor, from between each link of metal, into a glittering storm of dust that fluttered up. Up, up into the rays of light that pierced the clouds and ruined roof both – until they flickered into nothingness.

"What a surprise," came a voice from behind the two that made Maddoc groan aloud in annoyance. "That I should find our city's most talented arson upon my arrival."

Maddoc turned and blocked Captain Domingo's path to Cyril. Feet set wide, hands balled into fist, he made himself a shield, protecting Cyril's back as he focused on burning away what remained of the slain vampire. Domingo strolled into the damaged mill, looking about at the carnage. Maddoc didn't ignore the way Domingo still was encroaching upon Cyril's space, and took a hard step toward him, snarling and curling his lip as he spoke.

"Took you bloody long enough. What, did you stop off for a pint on your way here?"

Domingo ignored Maddoc, stopping some few paces away from him. He simply continued to look up at the destroyed mill. The stench of rotting and burnt flesh was rapidly dissipating, seemingly borne away by the motes of light that bled from every corner, from beneath floor beams and between cracks. Timbers were black and glowing red in cracked grains. There was no ongoing incantation from Cyril, no words that motivated it, it just ... answered to his gesture. *How strange,* Domingo thought. Smoke slithered out from deep gashes and crumbling stones, and the floor itself was covered in a layer of damp soot and dust.

"I am addressing you, Excellency. Do not ignore me."

"Mind your tongue!" Maddoc snapped. "Let him work."

"It is finished," Cyril mumbled and lowered his hand. "I sense no more of it here."

Cyril turned around to face Domingo, who stood with his head high and hand perched on his sword at his hip. His one eye glanced at the knight from head to toe, before he spoke to Maddoc.

"Thank you, Brother. Would you please go assist the ambulance with anything they may need."

Maddoc glanced at Cyril, gesturing not-so-subtly with his eyes and head at Domingo. Cyril simply nodded and Maddoc moved to abide, grumbling.

"I'm never far, *Captain*," he whispered as he shoved Domingo aside with his shoulder.

Domingo ignored the petty slight, approaching Cyril where he stood, in the center of the now damp, destroyed mill. Water dripped in through the holes in the roof, and Domingo glanced about at the crisscrossed chains, woven messily through the beams, now clean of any flesh.

He nodded at them. "More of your handiwork, these chains?"

"No, Captain."

He scoffed. "I'm surprised. You seem to have quite the penchant for such things, I'm told."

"You have humorous sources."

"Or honest ones."

Uncomfortable silence settled over the two, only broken by the creak of beams and the splash of water as a roof tile fell into a puddle.

"What happened here, Father?"

"I cannot tell you, Captain. I was not the instigator."

Domingo sighed in frustration, rolling his head back on his shoulders and tonguing his cheek. "One of your minions, then. Doing your bidding. Surely you see how little difference it makes."

Cyril's voice dropped as he grew deathly serious. "I was not the instigator," he repeated. "But I have full faith in my Hunters. Such magic would not be used lightly. Upon my arrival, I could see at once why they took such drastic measures."

"You see" – Domingo glared at him – "what you want to see."

"As do you, Captain."

Cyril slowly approached Domingo, descending some of the pile of rubble he stood on. "What, then, should I tell you, sir? That a vampire of exceptional power was found, unexpectedly, by Hunters who had not the skill, nor the rank in our Order, to subdue it. That they channeled whatever magic they could muster in a desperate attempt to contain it. That despite a shoddy, sloppy incantation – they succeeded in this task. And that, as a result, here you see me: having finished their good work. Would this answer satisfy you, Captain?" He halted his steps as the timbers groaned overhead. "No. I think not." Cyril stood a mere pace away from Domingo, eyeing him fiercely. "Because you do not want an answer, you want an excuse. You long to see a villain in me, sir. And to that end, I cannot help you."

A smile flickered at the corner of Domingo's mouth as he met Cyril's gaze. "Ever the orator. Your faithful may swallow your every word with a smile, Father. But your speeches do not sway me."

Maddoc reappeared behind Domingo, his face crestfallen as he gnawed his lip. As usual, he ignored Domingo.

Cyril saw him and clocked the look on his face immediately. "What is it?"

"Sister Jael has been taken back to the infirmary."

"And Brother Philip?"

"Has not been found."

68

THE AMBULANCE WAS RELUCTANT TO LEAVE with only one patient in tow. Immediately upon arriving back at the cathedral, it would be dispatched again – this time with Serge as the accompanying Cleric. The farmers and shepherds that inhabited that stretch of the riverbank were more than happy to open their homes to the clergy. So it was that the Hunters and Huntresses were kept well fed, warm, and comfortable in the midst of their search. Those lent dinghies meandered further and further up the river in each direction ... but each time returned with no news, good or bad, to speak of. There was nothing to report. No blood in the water, no body on the shore, not even a disturbance in the earth.

Those who did not comb the river took instead to combing the surrounding farmland. Indeed, every single request or plea that normally crossed the Deacon's desk was ignored. Letters went without answers for days as all efforts were invested in locating Philip. Any sign of him – even a dreaded uncovering of his body, drowned or dashed somewhere – anything at all. There were rumors rippling that, just maybe, he had been consumed by the blast. That perhaps he had been in the mill when it erupted into flame. After all, the Lady Sunderman, when she had come to investigate – with an army of laborers to sift through the rubble – had found his rosary in the ashes.

The rosary had, of course, been surrendered to the cathedral. Along with a good letter or three detailing the lady's shock and horror, and her promise to both comply and assist in any way she could. Both now sat on Cyril's desk, in a shallow box to keep them separate from everything else piling up upon it. He stared at it in silent contemplation before being brought out of his thoughts by a knock on his office door. He glanced up to see Brontë peeking through the crack.

"Father, may I come in?"

"It's rather late, little one. Why are you not abed?"

Brontë winced a little at his tone, and debated simply closing the door and going back to her room. Cyril finished reading a line of the letter in his hand and looked up again. He caught the disappointment on Brontë's face and sighed. He chastised himself inwardly for his tone, again, and gestured her into his office with a hand.

"Of course you can, come in." He waited for her to approach his desk before speaking further. "Are you unwell? Trouble sleeping?"

"Has there been any word of Philip yet?"

"Hm." Cyril looked back down at his letter. "I have heard no word yet."

"And you're just going to wait for word?" she mumbled.

His disapproving rumble at her tone made her almost regret her words. Still, though she refused to look at him, her clenched fists and set jaw were evidence of frustration. Frustration bordering on anger. Or perhaps misplaced guilt.

"What would you have me do?" he asked.

"Shouldn't you be out looking for him?"

"Our Hunters comb the city for him. Rest assured that we are doing all we can –"

"You're not doing anything!" she yelled. "You're sitting at your desk reading *letters!*"

The door opening was the only thing that spared Brontë a tongue-lashing, and she knew it. No sooner had her words left her mouth than she shut it, shielding her eyes with her hand in embarrassment.

"Father?" Benjamin eyed her in confusion. "You ... wanted to see me?"

Cyril softened his expression and bid Benjamin come in. Brontë didn't wait to be dismissed. She dipped a small curtsy and rushed out of the room, closing the door behind her. Benjamin set his briefcase down on one of the chairs before Cyril's desk.

"Miss Brontë seems particularly distraught."

"Yes." Cyril didn't look up. "She is very upset. Best to leave her be."

Benjamin tilted his head, folding his hands into his sleeves as he stood before Cyril's desk. "Is that wise?"

Cyril ignored the question, sifting through the letters on his desk and pulling one of his sketchbooks out from underneath them.

Benjamin hummed quietly and prodded the topic again. "Don't you ... think you could be a touch gentler with her?"

"I beg your pardon?"

"Forgive me if I am being too bold, Father. But the girl has lost arguably her best friend. She may need gentleness –"

"Thank you for your opinion, Brother. But that isn't what I called you here for."

"Then I beg your pardon, Father."

Cyril leafed through the sketchbook until finding what he was looking for. He severed the page and held it out to Benjamin. The Brother took it and turned it over toward himself. It was a remarkably accurate portrait of Philip, especially considering it had been done from memory.

"Do you think it's a suitable likeness?" Cyril asked.

"I do, Father."

"Very good. I'd like you to deliver it tomorrow morning. I've arranged to have a missing persons advertisement printed. While unlikely the townsfolk will have seen him, a posted reward may motivate even the likes of body snatchers or vampire lackeys. That lot tend to leap at coin."

"I see. And the Hunters –?"

"Have volunteered in droves," he finished Benjamin's sentence. "Maddoc's hands are overflowing with patrols and assignments. He's sending them down every alley, every gutter known to us. The map is livelier than ever."

"I am sure the Guard must be fond of that."

"Damn the Guard," Cyril snapped through gritted teeth. "I have not the patience for their games, not now. Let the captain come spit his vitriol at me if he wishes."

The tail end of Cyril's sentence was cut off as a sting of pain shot through him. He grimaced and pressed a palm to his good eye, trying to blink the heat away, but failing. Benjamin at once set down the sketch and clicked open his briefcase. He skirted around Cyril's desk to stand beside him, moving his hand out of his way. Though a notoriously poor patient, Cyril allowed Benjamin to tilt his head up and inspect him.

His good eye was bloodshot and irritated. The same gold that had long since stained it with faith was leaking into the veins surrounding his iris. In fact, upon this much closer inspection, the gold seemed to be leaching into every vein of his body. It streaked subtle lines down his neck, disappearing beneath his clerical collar.

✤

STEAM HISSED AND CONSTANCE GRIPPED HER LANTERN tight as two figures approached in the dark, light catching on their eyes.

"I trust you checked the ledger thoroughly this time." Esther said. Though she was several inches shorter than the conductor, she nearly made the woman wilt under her gaze. Noel looming behind her sire surely helped. Constance bowed her head.

"I did, my lady."

Esther demanded the conductor's hand to help her board the train. Constance glanced up and down the abandoned platform as both vampires crept aboard. Noel had the blood Esther had drawn concealed under her cloak. Without Ambrose's wax to contain it, it sounded like a muffled child crying under her robe.

Constance then picked up her skirts, took a big step aboard herself, and gave the familiar wave forward with her lantern. The massive engine several cars ahead lurched, screeching out a warning whistle before crawling leisurely away from the platform, leaving Windermere behind and departing north.

69

ANOTHER COLD DAY WITHOUT A WHISPER OF PHILIP, another quiet dinner among the clergy. Cyril could see Serge, barely picking at his food. He was far more interested in his prayer book, reading the lines therein over and over, as if he'd find comfort there, while his meal went cold before him. Serge was not the only one. Brontë, too, had lost her appetite. She couldn't even bring herself to pick apart the dinner roll she'd made.

Hugo was not oblivious. And while Brontë would rather be kept busy with work, he – in his good nature and with good intent – shooed her away, to not be troubled with chores or work the remainder of the night. She understood the gesture as a kindness, but couldn't help feeling frustrated and restless with nothing else to do. She paced around one of the rooftop gardens, looking out over the city; as if by staring at it and all its streetlamps, she could force it to reveal Philip to her. But the night grew darker, and the bells rang out the hour, and still no great revelation came. No cry of victory from the Hunters, no flickering signal for help, nothing. Brontë slumped down to sit on the steps that led up toward the cloister, rubbing her arms and trying to keep her lip from quivering.

Brontë heard Cyril's footsteps and bowed her head away from the sound. He stopped somewhere behind her. She waited for his usual disappointment or disapproval. Surely, she was about to get an earful for her earlier behavior. Surely, she shouldn't be out in the cold. Surely, she had work she should be doing. Surely, surely …

"Have you eaten today, little one?"

Brontë bit back a groan. "I took my medicine this morning."

"Good. But have you eaten today?"

She shrugged and fiddled awkwardly with her fingers.

"Going hungry will not bring him back to you any sooner."

"Please," she cried. "Not now. I can't bear any more of your disappointment in me. Not now."

There was an uncomfortable silence, during which she waited for his tone to deepen as it often did when he reprimanded her. Instead, his reply came out much softer.

"Is that what you think it is?"

He stepped down, taking a seat beside her. She looked at him, a mixture of confusion and surprise at his not immediately finding fault in her. He didn't say anything, he simply sat quiet, patiently waiting for her to voice what it was that kept her out in the cold, what stopped her from eating. One of many tactics he knew could coax out a confession.

"It's all my fault," she finally whispered. "I did this."

"We often blame ourselves, little one –"

Brontë stood abruptly and let out a shrill, frustrated yell. "That's not what I mean!" she interrupted Cyril. She held back her cries, but her words came out in broken pieces. "I told him about the seal on the bag, me!"

She faced Cyril and gestured emphatically to herself. "Me! Can't you understand the misery I'm in? I can't sleep, I can't possibly eat, knowing *I* am responsible!"

She balled her hands into fists and stomped in anger. Overwhelmed with emotion and with no idea how to release it, she wove a path back and forth in a rage that threatened to descend into tears. Cyril sat silent as she fumed and paced, both his hands resting atop his cane, and his chin atop his hands, letting her vent her rage on the frigid air, the oblivious fireflies, and herself.

"If I hadn't mentioned it, or if I had just told Sister Florence, or Hugo, or *you*." She gestured out toward him. "If I had told *you*, come to you right away, the way you always tell me to …" *Would she have sent him to his death instead, then?* She paused and began to weep in earnest, words disintegrating into blubbered sobs.

"Come here."

Brontë wiped her eyes to see Cyril patting the step she had been sitting on. She sniffled and shuddered, but shuffled back toward him to sit down again. He pulled his kerchief from his sleeve and offered it to her. She took it, though it was only crumpled up in her lap as she felt still more embarrassment and frustration. Cyril waited for her sobs to slow before venturing to speak. His voice was still surprisingly quiet.

"When I was nineteen, I made a very foolish decision."

Brontë looked up from the kerchief in her lap. Cyril kept his gaze straight ahead, and though perhaps it was those pesky fireflies flitting about to blame, she could swear a tear welled in that one eye of his.

"I led myself and my partner into a trap. Of the many deaths I have witnessed, his was the worst." Cyril paused, taking a slow, deep breath to compose himself.

Brontë could do nothing but stare open-mouthed at him. She realized how silly she must sound, shouting about being responsible, as if Cyril – in his station – would have no inkling of such a feeling.

"He had trusted my judgment completely, and I failed him. His name was Leonard."

"I …"

"But I am still here." He looked down at her, a sad smile playing at the corner of his mouth. "And I must carry on, little one. So must we all."

Brontë gave an awkward, stunned half-chuckle and fiddled with the kerchief. Realizing that she was in perhaps very good company, human and flawed company – despite the perfection she had so long attributed to him.

"You make it look much easier than it is. I do not have your fortitude, Father."

"Well, I might have a touch more practice than you."

She smiled weakly and sniffled yet again. There was one more pause, and she sighed to herself. "I apologize, for my conduct earlier, for yelling such awful things at you. I know you are doing all in your power, I just ..." She made a vague gesture with her hand, but hopelessly shrugged, unable to even think of a valid reason or excuse. She let out a long sigh. "I am so sorry. I am sure you think me very childish for it."

"Not at all, little one."

She tilted her head at him. "And yet, you keep calling me 'little one'."

He looked surprised, almost disappointed. "Do you dislike my calling you so?"

"You only ever seem to call me that when you're cross with me."

"Goodness, you must think I am cross with you quite often, then."

"Aren't you? What else could it be?" She laughed sadly. "Always with your questions ... have I eaten, have I done this or that –"

"And you truly think I ask these things only because I am cross with you?"

He sounded saddened by the idea, a little twinge of melancholy in his voice that was different from what she usually read as his disappointment. There was then a rather long span of quiet between them – one where Brontë could see his good eye intently studying her face, as she stared back in a daze.

"Well ... I ..."

"Very well," he said matter-of-factly. "If you dislike it, I will not call you so."

70

OW IN SOME DECENT CONTROL OF HIS FACULTIES, Erwin slunk onto the grounds of his family's estate. He still limped as he slipped through the servant's entrance. He poked his head around corners before taking them, trying to dodge the household staff or, god forbid, any family members up and about. At this time of night.

He had managed it well, until he desperately made a last dash for his own bedroom and nearly collided with Aoife. She dropped the handful of letters she'd been thumbing through and almost squealed, but he put a hand over her mouth before she could. Erwin dipped his head in the clearest show of an apology she'd ever get from him. Aoife ripped his hand away from her mouth, whispering his name in disbelief through her teeth.

"Erwin?"

She held his shoulders, dipping down to try and get him to look at her, but he only tossed his head away and snarled.

"What on earth? Tell me this isn't from that cursed arena! Where is Finlay? Did he not go with you?"

Erwin shook his head and moved to limp past her. She grabbed his arm and wordlessly helped him spare his injured leg the weight. A small gesture, and one he'd ordinarily rebuke, like he did all her other displays of affection. But he allowed it this time. She helped him inside his room, setting him down on the edge of his bed before hurrying to lock the door. She went to his washroom and wet a rag.

When she returned with it, though, he was already resuming his normal behavior of tossing his head away and whispering to be left alone. Aoife gripped his chin firmly and wiped his face anyway.

"The Royal Guard already came looking for you," she said as she rubbed blood from his lips gently. "They've been told you wouldn't be welcomed back here."

"What about Lady –"

"She doesn't have a say in the matter." Aoife looked at him as she folded over the rag. She was holding back her own emotions, a skill she had much practice with. "You have truly made a mess for yourself this time, haven't you?"

He shrugged, apathetic as always. Aoife continued washing away blood and spittle. She cleaned his hands, too. When she'd finished, she set the rag aside and knelt in front of him, holding his hands.

"Please, promise me you will *stay here*. Let this blow over. We'll figure something out ... maybe I can write the capital office, you could move there. I'm sure Mister Bradley could make you a company apprentice."

Erwin shrugged again, gritting his teeth and setting his jaw while he looked in any direction but at her. Despite that, he was clinging onto her hands awfully tight, she thought. His hands had an awful tremor she hadn't noticed. But then, when had he ever let her hold him?

"I'll have food sent up for you. And I'll arrange for a doctor. I think there's an apothecary on Ashgrove that is known to ask no questions. I'll make inquiries."

She stood up, leaning over and giving him a kiss on the forehead. He made some little sound at this, she didn't quite catch it, but she took it as what he meant it to be: a thank you.

71

DOMINGO WATCHED FROM COLDWATER KEEP as the city refused to sleep. For such a large city, the faith surely ran deep. While there was certainly the odd nonbeliever, the odd doubter, their faith was as natural to them here as breathing. In a way, it impressed him. That so many be moved to find one missing clergy member. But behind that touching sentiment was a profound danger. He recognized it for what it was. It was proof of how quickly these people could, would, organize on behalf of their faith, on behalf of their church – their Beloved Lady. Every man, woman, and child was infected with the fervor of a martyr. A hundred and some worried letters had already been penned and shipped south. *How could Sinclair have let it get this bad?*

He thumbed through the stack of documents in his hand. The report given to him by the church. Well, less given, and more demanded. It contained a full record of questions and answers from the surviving Huntress – her recollections of the events. And of the apparent *creature* encountered. She described it as a ghastly, nightmarish thing. Ghoulish and unsettling. More fanciful talk, more ways to excuse their hunt, more ways to cover up whatever it was the church didn't want him to know. *Surely, that's what this was.* Why else had Father rushed to erase the offending heretic before he could see it?

Domingo turned to face Levi, who was standing at ease beside the worktable, as usual. He had read the report as well, and was similarly distraught by the description. But his distress was of a different sort. He'd already seen a vampire, or what the church called one. She'd been a strange, animalistic thing. He still remembered her skittering about on all fours. Moving terrifyingly fast. How she'd only sounded human the moment the flames hit her – as if they purified her. And the ungodly *noise* of it all.

"I'm addressing you, Sergeant."

Levi snapped to attention. "Yes, Captain! I apologize."

Domingo eyed him sharply, flipping over a page in the report. "Have you read it through?"

"I have, sir, yes."

"And what do you make of this nonsense?"

"I do not doubt it entirely."

"Oh, please." Domingo groaned and rolled his eyes. "Not you, too."

"I do not know yet what I make of these so-called 'vampires', sir," Levi hurried to explain himself. "But similar to your observation of the church's magic, and how it appears to engender changes in the body – it would not be unbelievable to me, now, that the magic the church condemns creates similar changes. But I am no scholar –"

"No. You are not. You are a knight, who is trained to follow orders. My orders."

"Yes, sir."

He is no scholar, Domingo thought. *But I know someone who is.* He knew what he needed: a capital alchemist.

HEZEKIAH FELT A CLUMSY HAND trying to snake its way into his pocket. He reached down and grabbed the offending limb, causing the owner – a scrappy little girl dressed in rags – to screech at him. He nearly crushed her bony arm, but that wasn't what made her yell. The moment he'd grabbed her, he'd turned to look down in dismay, and she had seen the light catch on his dead eyes.

She hissed and squirmed, bracing her bare feet against his leg and trying to pull her wrist out of his hand. When it wasn't enough, she balled her free hand into a fist and began to beat against his leg and arm. He only tilted his head and looked at her with a stunned expression – that, or perhaps the deformities growing in his mouth forbade him to close it entirely, now. Regardless of his outward expression, he was ... surprised.

The guttersnipe could not have been more than eight years old. The sight of her, with her messy hair and her tattered dress, stirred a strange sort of familiarity in him. He'd never abide this sort of filth – he'd demand a bath and would not permit even a bite of supper until she could prove her hands were clean. He'd taught her to take better care of her clothes and her person than this. He'd already begun to teach her the many ways of mending, of how to keep fur and leather, and how to treat it with respect.

This street rat wriggling in his hold wasn't the girl he'd taught ... surely, she wasn't. She had blonde hair. That wasn't right. Or was it? He couldn't remember. What color had his little girl's hair been? It didn't matter the color: a familiar stripe of blue was missing. Hezekiah let the girl go, and she scurried off in haste, tossing curses back over her shoulder that a girl that age should not know.

He watched her go, eyes straining from the lamps. As his gaze followed the direction she'd run, he noticed a poster. The boy in the sketch looked familiar. He glanced up and down the alley, ensuring no one was taking an interest in him, and tore it from the wall. It was then rolled up and stuffed into his belt as he marched off toward a far more comfortable-looking darker alleyway, where he would not strain his eyes so much.

72

HILIP'S HEAD SWAM. DARK AND BLURRY, EVERYTHING seemed distant and yet utterly overwhelming. And cold. So very, very cold. Voices were chattering over him, and he wondered why the infirmary was such a noisy, dank place – that's not at all how he remembered it. He remembered sunshine and a warm hearth, fresh air and strawberry bushes growing on the windowsill. Quiet, considerate voices – even as they bickered over how to care best for a patient. If he thought hard enough, he could practically hear his uncle insisting he knew best, as he always did. It made him smile, but that little twitch of his lip made him whimper in pain. Dried blood crackled on the skin between his lips. He tasted more of it in his mouth.

The voices grew louder, perhaps closer, as he shifted weakly and groaned in discomfort. The linen sheet under his cheek felt far more scratchy than it should have. A loud bang sounded and he was suddenly wide awake as sound erupted around him. A shrill voice yelled from somewhere.

"String him up, hang him high! Let the Hunters find his rotting corpse!"

"Skin him!"

What Philip's tired mind had interpreted as a linen sheet was a rough, filthy produce sack that scratched him like sandpaper as it was ripped off his head. The sound of rushing water was distant. A river he couldn't see through the crumbling stone and thick, overgrown vines. He could barely make them out, snaking like restless spirits around what must be very ancient ruins. Vague shapes fluttered around him, too dark to truly distinguish from one another – vampires in varying states of decay. The very air rotted with the smell of the undead.

A hand that was more bone than flesh reached out and grabbed him. Another pair curled around his arms. Still another clawed into his waist. All together, they hoisted him up off the floor. Groggy, but shocked awake, Philip immediately shouted and twisted. His training and instinct flared bright, despite his injuries and the immense pain he very quickly realized he was in. Fear throbbed cold inside his chest. His heart pounded and every part of him shivered. His wrists were bound behind him. The harsh digging of claws into his arms and chest told him his cassock had been removed without needing to look down or strain his eyes in the dark to ascertain for himself.

"Oh, ho – he's a hero!"

"The young ones always are."

"Break his legs!"

Philip tried to leap upright, leaning back into the hands that held him and kicking out hard at any shape that came too near. He made some connection, a skeletal grin lost a few teeth, but rather than making any meaningful purchase toward escape, it only earned him howled laughter and a hard punch to his unprotected gut. It winded him and he groaned, unable to flex his muscles to protect himself from another jab under the ribs. Another, and another, until he gagged.

It was near impossible to tell how many vampires surrounded him – too many hands clawed and too many feet kicked at him. Bound, he was flung back and forth, shoved to the ground and trampled as the bitter dead screeched at him, kicking him and stomping on his legs as he screamed in pain.

"Where is your god now that you need her?"

A dull, metallic scrape sounded as one of the vampires brandished the only sorry excuse for a weapon they had: a rusty wheat sickle with less of an edge than a cat's claw. They could land no solid blow through the throng of creatures that surrounded the downed Hunter, but still tore a gash in his shoulder that made him yell.

"Enough," a bored voice interjected. "Bring him here."

Rather than pick him up, this time a spindly hand grabbed him by the hair, and another by the foot, dragging him across the floor like a dead animal. Philip fought to keep his breath steady, cheek bruised and eye swollen shut, blood trickling from his mouth and ear. His head rang and his throat ached from crying. He wondered if he was losing focus due to the blur of tears, or if he was losing consciousness.

Philip could not see the shattered marble base of what once had been an altar. Zemirah took some sick pride in defiling it. An ancient, long-abandoned thing – no longer consecrated – but it felt like a victory nonetheless. One of several in the underground ruins beneath the Cannoneer. She'd had an armchair set down overtop the rubble, and now languished in it. Philip could barely make out her angular face in the low light.

"Sit him up."

Philip was pulled unceremoniously upright, yanked and scratched in different directions until he awkwardly knelt in front of her. His head was held up by the rusty sickle cradling his jaw. Zemirah's upper lip betrayed her disgust. But when she spoke, it was sweet. Sickly, saccharine – it'd entice him, despite its complete contradiction, if he was not careful. *Witch*, he thought.

"We are given a way to truly understand one another, you and I."

She reached into her shirt, pulling free a generous still-sealed bottle of murky blood. Philip inhaled sharply and writhed, feet scraping into the floor to push himself away from it, to no avail. She smiled just wide enough for him to see her fangs. Zemirah then leaned in close, swirling the bottle before Philip.

"With this," she whispered, as if confiding something of great importance. "You can truly understand us. All that we endure, all that you condemn from your towers, from your steeples, you can understand. This is not merely blood, boy. No, no – this ... this is knowledge. You need but a taste, and you can be as wise as the Father himself."

Philip looked fearfully at the thick blood sloshing about in the corked bottle. It seemed such an ugly, unrepentant thing – but he could not deny it radiated power. Even from within the glass, he could feel it. A sort of smothering, oppressive presence. Cold, but comforting, like the first rain of autumn. The longer he looked at it, the weaker he felt against its draw, realizing belatedly that he was struggling to pull his eyes away. He shook his head and groaned, freeing himself from the near-hypnotic state he'd entered. Neck straining against the sickle, he hung his head and swallowed hard. A small shudder, and he spat out his reply.

"I refuse."

"I thought as much. Good." Her voice grew darker. The illusion of that comforting contradiction shattered. "You will suffer as Ambrose suffered."

With that, Zemirah sat back in her chair and spoke to her fellows. "Water, for my guest."

A clawed hand hooked into Philip's forehead, splitting skin and raking bloody lines backward as they grabbed him by the hair and slammed him onto his back. He screamed and writhed, but it did little good, only earning him a few hard blows to the ribs and belly. One of his legs was still bent underneath him from kneeling, and a boot stomped down hard on that leg while the other was leaped upon.

Fingers pressed into his cheeks, a greasy thumb and uncomfortably sharp index finger digging into his skin. He cut the inside of his own mouth on his gritted teeth, but another blow to his stomach made him gasp and his mouth was pried open. Yet another hand shoved a soiled, wadded up rag into his mouth. They pushed and pounded their fist into his mouth, loosening his teeth and making him gag on the grimy thing.

The first slosh of foul water over his face made him squeal like a trapped animal. The rag in his mouth was quickly soaked by both saliva and muddy water as a second pail was dunked over his head. It stung in his eyes and in the deep cuts on his scalp. Clumps of hair were torn from his head as he tossed about, and more hands grabbed him to hold him still, curling into bloodied hair and pulling hard on his ears. Being held still while water was slowly drizzled over his mouth was even worse. Each awful pour seemed slower than the previous. His ribs and abdomen ached from coughing. He desperately tried to expel filthy water but was forced to choke on it again, or else try to drink down what filled his mouth.

It didn't matter how he cried or writhed, or how disgusting his stomach felt, or how dirt coated his mouth and bleeding teeth – the water kept coming. Then, a loud ripple of laughter and hollering told him that awful bottle had been uncorked. He smelled it before he tasted it. It dribbled slowly over his lips, soiling the already drenched rag and smothering him. His muffled scream yielded yet more nothing. He fought to spit it out, retching and wailing out broken sounds that almost sounded like prayers. The first drop against his tongue, though, began to numb the pain.

Even if he had tried to will himself to drown rather than drink, the body had a horrible way of preserving itself. The more blood flowed, the more dripped through the rag, the more he had to swallow. Still, he fought against his own body's reflexes, summoning the newfound energy it gave him to thrash around. It trickled over his tongue and down his throat, and he realized in stunned disgust that the more he let in, the dimmer his pain became.

Suddenly the rag was ripped from his mouth. He sucked in a deep breath and immediately choked, coughing up spittle and blood. This time, the bottle was upended into his mouth. Blood gushed and glugged as the glass was shoved past his teeth, held even as he tried to flail. He gritted his teeth so hard he threatened to crack it. Pain racked hard through Philip, his jaw strained and throat tensed as he gagged on blood. Confused relief flooded his body. He subconsciously guzzled down the blood before a taunting voice seemed to snap him from his stupor.

"Go on, drink it!"

Newfound strength surged through Philip and tears streamed from his eyes. One leg managed to free itself and he kicked out hard, confusing the mob around him just enough to shake his head and spit out the loosened bottle. The moment it was gone, the pain returned in an overwhelming wave that made him cry out. His voice hoarse, eyes glowing a soft gold in the dark, he shouted his refusal, as if trying to convince himself.

"I don't want it!"

A fist across his face made him spit his own blood out this time. More hands latched onto him, holding him down, knowing very well that he'd grow stronger thus drugged. A hard kick to his ribs made an awful cracking noise. The bottle was picked up, most of it still remaining. It was pushed between his split, swollen lips again. One vampire stomped down on his knee, pushing and pushing it against the natural bend until it snapped and gave. Another one of the vampires howled in laughter, bringing both of their fists up above their head and slamming them down into

Philip's belly as he drank. Again, and again. Not even the heart-pounding, pain-numbing adrenaline being forcibly fed to him could keep him awake through the beatings.

The voices faded in Philip's ears as he vaguely felt himself being dragged along. Then it was cold. Cold, but no hands were crawling on him. Instead, a frigid puddle of rainwater and blood surrounded him as he blinked. Far above, he could just barely see clouds parting to reveal stars. With no voice, no strength, and no rosary – Philip wept. Tears streaked down his cheeks as he barely managed to whisper a precious little prayer to himself. Thunder rumbled overhead as his once blue eyes flickered gold and fluttered closed.

⬦

"FATHER?"

CYRIL SLOWLY OPENED HIS GOOD EYE, lifting his head off his hand. He glanced down at the chessboard before him. Benjamin tilted his head and gave Cyril a soft smile from where he sat opposite him.

"It's late. Would you rather not be abed at this hour?"

Cyril shook his head, picking up a knight and playing his turn. "I couldn't sleep if I tried, not now."

"What is that?" Benjamin hadn't even heard Cyril's reply. He was looking out the window behind him.

Cyril turned to look over his shoulder in curiosity.

A strange, unnatural glow shimmered in the distance. Barely a speck, though it was growing brighter and fiercer with every second. A pure white spark that crackled and dripped motes of light to the east. Cyril and Benjamin both stood at once. Cyril opened the door to the balcony and Benjamin followed behind, swatting misty rainwater from his vision. The Cleric strained in the dark to isolate the irregular spark from the warmer, more yellow gleam of the streetlamps. It didn't behave like the church's usual call for help – rather, it seemed to be thrumming and pulsing with near indignance the longer it went unanswered. Pure white, not the typical violent gold of the Order.

"What is that?" Benjamin said. "It's not a Hunter's flare."

"I am not sure," Cyril murmured, bringing up his closed fist and breathing into it. "I seek a reunion."

A golden light sparked to life and flew from between Cyril's fingers. It dove over the edge of the balcony, leaving a precious trail of fragmented light. It raced nimbly down, down to the ground and along the paved courtyard toward the gates, leaving a subtle, illuminated path to follow as it rushed to join its fellow, to rendezvous.

"Oh, my word –" Benjamin's voice broke, but Cyril was already moving.

He ran back inside, grabbing his cassock and hastily pulling it on as he snatched his cane. The doors to his chambers flew open and he rushed down the corridor, loose robes billowing about him. His voice echoed like thunder through columns and down cloisters.

"Sound the Lilian Bell!"

The Hunters standing guard below heard the order and repeated it, looking at each other in shock before sprinting off in opposite directions.

The sleeping church woke all at once. Hunters and Clerics alike leaped from their beds. Horses whinnied in the stables as half-dressed handlers rushed in, waking and saddling the swiftest and strongest among their number. Amidst this initial chaos and confusion, that particular bell began to sing. A certain note that few were privileged to hear in their lifetimes. She called out, waking even the townsfolk, many of whom rushed to their windows and flew open the shutters, painting the wet cobblestone streets with yet more brushstrokes of light.

Benjamin came rushing down the stairs, spilling from a doorway in a swish of black robes and gold chains. He blocked a handful of his sleepy fellows from reaching the window, preventing them from joining the others looking down at the hustle and bustle of the stable yard. He pointed back toward the infirmary.

"Prepare me a bed at once! I need linens, towels, and hot water. Now! Go!"

Brother Serge emerged, red-eyed and with his nightshirt only half tucked into his trousers. He stood still in stunned silence, staring out a tall window at the glimmer in the distance. It seemed to pulse and flicker in time with the tolls of the Lilian Bell. Tears welled up in his eyes at the sound, such a beautiful and cruel thing, this hope.

Brontë, too, was roused from her bed by the bell. Rubbing her eyes, she elbowed her way through the crowd of confused and curious clergy to a popular window, just in time to see Cyril and several more Hunters mount horses and race off into the night.

Coldwater was not oblivious. Domingo felt a jolt through his body at the sound of that particular bell. It pierced his heart like grief and made him cry out. A strange familiarity, far too familiar for comfort. He clutched his chest and cursed it aloud as it dragged him out of sleep by force. He instinctively fumbled about for his medals, angrily breathing the spell he knew ... only to find it made no difference. The pain pierced deeper, a pair of hands he couldn't see clutched tighter, and he could not numb it. The pain throbbed in tandem with the unfamiliar bell he heard.

He stumbled from bed to his own window to see the city practically setting itself aflame in reply. The faithful flooded the streets with torches and lanterns. Even his own knights were fleeing their barracks to answer the bell. To him, it looked like a near riot. To them, it must have looked like salvation. To the east, a strange and blindingly bright earthly star hovered above the rooftops.

The streets of Windermere flowed gold that night, with torches and twinkling trails of light painting the path that would reunite a lost Hunter with his beloved Order.

NEITHER THE CITY NOR THE CATHEDRAL WOULD SPEAK of anything else for days. But ... it was unavoidable that rumors escaped the walls. They always did. Delight at Philip's being found alive – destroyed, but *alive* – was soon overshadowed with dread. Whispers crept up necks and into ears that the Hunter had consumed vampire blood. The zealous debated the possibility loudly in the streets. The more demure bickered about it in coffeehouses. The papers wrote far too many words with far too little proof. Everyone knew the Archbishop would have a public, and difficult, decision to make – or else he'd face a riot on his doorstep. The potential of this plagued Domingo and made him write letter after letter to Cyril. Each letter was ignored. Cyril refused to speak on the matter. Not to the Guard, not to the people, not even in confession to share the burden.

Philip was curled up in the infirmary bed, clutching tight to a downy pillow and with the linens pulled up all about him. Hiding, practically, save for where the bloodied and bandaged top of his head poked out. A pail was beside him, to catch the blood and bile he constantly tried to force himself to vomit up. Now thankfully too weak to continue to mercilessly gag himself, he had collapsed into the warmth and safety of a soft bed.

He dozed fitfully, sometimes muttering or mumbling nonsense, sometimes shuddering or sobbing. Serge hovered nearby, still only half-dressed and with dark circles forming under his eyes. Philip's head had been shaved, to more easily tend to where the lacerations had torn through his skin. Claw marks ran back halfway through his scalp from his forehead. Serge patted the still-seeping, grossly infected wounds dry periodically, reapplying ointment to the stitches and carefully adjusting his pillows and blankets when he fidgeted.

Philip's inspection had been thorough, and harrowing. Far too many pages were dedicated to the number of wounds, to the evidence of foul magic, to the many breaks and blows suffered. Beyond this, too, was the horrid knowledge of his having consumed vampire blood. It lurked like a rat, scuttling about the infirmary in whispers and murmurs between Clerics. Serge would snap at them for daring to insinuate that his nephew, *his* nephew, had consumed blood. Serge, though, was no fool – he knew plenty well Philip had tasted blood.

Serge was quick to forbid any Hunter from even daring to loiter in the hallway, much less enter Philip's infirmary room. Poor Jael, so very eager to see him, had barely made it past the threshold when a horrible cry and terrifying seizure from Philip had her shooed out of the room by his uncle. Textbook symptoms, but Serge denied them still, pushing the problem out of the room the same way he did any Hunter; including Cyril.

"Don't you dare come close, Hunter!" Serge whispered fiercely and pointed an accusatory finger. "You, smelling of blood and filth. You will prompt those awful reactions from him!"

Another awful cry interrupted any further conversation as Philip lurched in his bed, wailing in pain as the muscles on one side contracted and his body curled over. His mouth filled with froth as the other Clerics, Benjamin among them, rushed to his side. Serge swiftly joined them, rapping out instructions and requests. Cyril slunk backward toward the door, mumbling Benjamin's name and motioning him to follow with two fingers.

The Archbishop was pacing in the hallway outside of Philip's room when he heard the door open. Benjamin emerged and closed the door gently behind him. A pang of sadness tugged at Benjamin's chest as he heard Philip's weeping through the door. It pulled like a taut thread hooked in his heart, begging him to return, despite knowing there was so little he could do. He folded his hands into his habit sleeves as he approached Cyril.

"Tell me everything you've observed."

Benjamin shook his head. "His injuries are many and varied. Fractures all over. We've applied stitches in his head and chest thus far. I suspect pneumonia, as well. It's a wonder he can move at all."

"And?" Cyril could tell by Benjamin's tone that, though his voice had gone quiet, he had more to say.

Benjamin took his glasses off and cleaned them, frowning as he seemed to realize the answer to his own question of why Philip, despite such horrid injuries, managed strength to move. "It's clear he ingested vampire blood, but I have no way of knowing how much."

The end of Cyril's cane thudded sharply into the ground as his hand tightened around it. "Damn. And you're certain?"

Benjamin nodded. "He was trying to make himself vomit it up, with some success. We had to stop him from carrying on, he was hurting himself."

"How much do you estimate?"

Benjamin frowned again and this time busied himself looking out the window.

"Brother?"

"Too much," he murmured. "His fractures have healed and been broken again several times. For how long he was missing, that could not have happened naturally."

Cyril hissed a curse under his breath, putting his hand over his mouth to silence himself.

"Many of the bones have already fused," Benjamin continued quietly. "Healed incorrectly, in a hurry. They need to be broken again and realigned. Even if we put him through the procedure ... he may never walk again. And he ... will inevitably suffer withdrawal from –"

"From blood, yes," Cyril finished. "And yet he seizes up in even the presence of a Hunter."

"Yes. Serge has sealed off the room to only allow Clerics access. It's like his body leaps right from withdrawal to overindulgence at the slightest exposure."

Cyril nodded. "Serge is in the right to do so. We Hunters will wear blood, no matter how we wash ourselves of it."

"But he himself is a Hunter ..."

"Aye. They're no fools. They knew his state would devolve into this. They didn't need to kill him."

Benjamin could tell Cyril's mind was already working – mulling over his knowledge of sinsickness, blood, of charms and philters and every concoction he possibly knew of that might be of use. The way he subtly shook his head and furrowed his brow made Benjamin worry. After all, if Cyril had a cure for addiction, wouldn't he have given it by now?

"I will inspect what I have that might help him, and pass it on to you to administer. I will consult the Cardinals, too. They may have some treatment or enchantment that can put him more at ease."

"And if they don't?"

Cyril looked over at Benjamin, who had wandered toward the banister, staring out over the city below.

"If they don't?" Benjamin repeated.

"Then we will think of something else."

"And what of them?"

Cyril approached the Brother and joined him in looking out over the banister. Even from the great height afforded by the cathedral, it was still plenty easy to make sense of the shapes below. Beyond her walls, beyond her closed gates, crowds gathered. Unrest bubbled outside, demanding a verdict. They could even see the Guard, the knights milling about, trying to dissuade the gathering from devolving into a plain riot.

"What about them?" Benjamin repeated.

"Let them shout themselves hoarse. We have an injured Brother to tend to, nothing more."

Benjamin nodded quietly. In a way, he was relieved. But he knew that respite was temporary. The theological question would need to be addressed. The people would demand it.

74

2A PATH WOULD BE WORN IN THE RUG AT THIS RATE. Cyril was pacing back and forth before his desk in his study. His arms folded over his chest, one hand to his mouth as he brushed his lip in that old habit of his. This was his third cigarette tonight. Or was it his fourth? He'd lost count. He glared at the documents littering his desk as he walked. The befuddling ensemble atop his desk matched the chaos in his mind. A thousand and one thoughts fought for his attention. The newspapers were already flooded with doubt and accusations. The morning copy was lying atop his desk, practically begging to be ripped apart and tossed into the fire, where it belonged.

The worst possible scenarios played out in the theater of his mind. It was bad enough to have the populace in an uproar over a sinsick member of the clergy. Demanding answers, demanding justice. The liturgical law was plenty clear: consuming vampire blood was unforgivable, damning in totality. Even worse, his own Clerics whispered it in the corridors and stairwells, where they thought he couldn't hear. He had an expectation, an obligation, to uphold.

It had been bold already to bend on behalf of the sinsick civilians. Offering some respite from the pain of withdrawal, some half-mercy in the form of medicine. That was already a step too far, to many. Not enough to shake truly the public's faith, not enough to make them doubt the Heart. But Philip would be enough. His situation was an unjust oddity, a question without a proper answer, like Brontë.

He paused. She was a distraction. *An unwelcome one, at a time like this.* Or so he told himself. The smoke from his cigarette thought itself a comedian. It mocked him, contorting into soft, round shapes reminiscent of her. He swatted his hand through it as he turned again, grinding his heel into the poor rug. Cyril moaned low in frustration and rubbed his chest, pressing his fingers beneath the cross he wore as if that'd soothe his pounding heart. His mind was so busy that he didn't hear the knock at his chamber door. Only when it came a timid second time did he snap out of his fuming. He snuffed out his cigarette and went to the door, fixing the scowl he nearly made when he found Miss Brontë on the other side.

She looked tired. Messy hair poked out from her veil, and beneath her eyes was swollen and still damp with tears she likely had only just wiped away, now valiantly attempting to restrain them in his presence.

"I am sorry to bother you so late," she whispered.

"Not at all. Come in."

Brontë wasn't really sure what to do with herself without some kind of excuse to hide behind. She so often had a crutch of some sort. She could see him under the pretense of confession, of medicine, of tending to potted plants – something, always something. But not this time. Cyril rubbed his good eye in exasperation as he led her back into his study. He gestured for her to make herself comfortable on the couch before the hearth, and busied himself with rummaging through a cabinet for his tea set.

"Are you unwell?" he asked habitually.

"No ... I am well enough. Thank you."

"What is it, then?"

Brontë felt a pang of guilt and began to regret coming to see him, on account of how practiced his tone sounded. She surveyed the mess of notes and documents all over his desk. Those countless sheets of parchments with what she recognized as his handwriting and sketches. She'd obviously interrupted his work – she knew he had plenty. *And she didn't even have a good reason to be here.* She'd been lulled here by her own insecurity, her own tempest of emotions. Seeking shelter like a ship seeks a harbor in a storm. *But it was so lonely in her little room.* She felt like a burden before she'd even opened her mouth. She sat quiet on the sofa, staring down at her shaking hands folded in her lap. Cyril glanced over his shoulder to see her, curled into herself with her head bowed and shoulders drooping. He took a quiet, deep breath and summoned his composure.

"What is it?" he repeated, this time with a voice softened through no small effort on his part. This shred of gentleness was enough to coax words out of her.

"I heard Clerics speaking in the garden. Has Philip consumed vampire blood?"

"Yes, I'm afraid so."

"Enough to become addicted?"

"... Yes."

A muffled curse fell out of her mouth as she buried her face in her hands. She could practically hear Philip teasing her and calling her a crybaby as her eyes watered again.

"Philip will know what I am now," she said after a pause, realization heavy in her chest. She looked up at Cyril, pain written clearly across her features. "He'll be able to smell my blood, won't he?"

Cyril opened his mouth to reply, but only managed a sigh. He gave a small nod.

Brontë took a deep breath and rubbed her arms. "He'll know that I'm a ..."

"You do not need to say the word, if it upsets you."

"A halfling," she settled on instead, bitterly.

"You would really prefer to be called that?"

She shrugged. "It hardly matters. I don't think Philip will care for particulars. He's a Hunter, after all."

"So am I."

"Heh." She huffed and shuffled her legs, rubbing them together beneath her skirt. "You're different. You know everything."

There was more uncomfortable silence, only broken by the crackle of the hearth and the settling of wooden beams overhead. The kettle whistled, and Cyril moved to fetch it. Brontë said nothing as he prepared a small pot of tea, not speaking again until he set the tea tray down on the table in front of her.

"Brother Serge will forbid me to see Philip, yes?"

Cyril hummed in thought as he straightened. "I am not sure. But that is a matter to be settled in future. You don't need to trouble yourself over it right now –"

"It troubles me whether I like it or not," she snapped. She clapped her hand over her eyes the next moment and mumbled an apology. Cyril moved around the table to sit beside her. She pointedly looked away from him, even as she shuffled her hips on the cushion to be a little closer to him. He poured her a cup of tea and slid it toward her on a saucer. She didn't acknowledge the proffered beverage at all, staring off into the empty distance, to the bookshelves and the furniture against the far wall.

"I'm starting to think I should never have been born at all," she whispered.

"That sort of talk does neither you nor Philip any good."

"You don't need to coddle me, Father." She glared down at the teacup. "That sort of false gentleness won't soothe me."

"I don't coddle you. It's the truth." He crossed his ankle over the opposite knee and leaned back into the sofa, setting his jaw as he mulled over his own words before saying them. "Your emotion is better spent elsewhere."

"Where? I can't ... see him. I can't go to him. So what ... *can* I do?" There was a shift in her tone as she sat up a bit straighter, as she swallowed cries and attempted – valiantly – to summon strength. "There must be something I can do for him. I cannot just ... idle away like this. Not while he is in so much pain. I must do something for him."

Cyril thought for a moment. "Philip wanted you to pray with him, didn't he?"

Brontë flinched. "He ... he did, yes."

"I recall he'd take two candles with him every morning, in the event you decided to join him."

Brontë failed spectacularly at hiding her surprise, staring at him with a perplexed look and a horrible guilt wrinkling her eyebrows.

Cyril eyed her pointedly. "Perhaps now is a good time to take up the habit on his behalf. He would appreciate the gesture, and it is likely to do you good."

Brontë leaned in closer, her mouth open, though no words came out. It was clear she was thinking very seriously about his suggestion, thinking about it as seriously as any other novitiate of the church would. Still, she was riddled with doubt. *The saints don't speak to me.* And after all, it was so easy for a priest to encourage prayer. A saint, no less, she reminded herself. Everyone knew the prayers of good men and women were worth more – that they received answers when others did not. It didn't matter how she wished to have the sort of faith that made Cyril so confident; the sort of faith that allowed him to weave magic and work miracles. She was never destined to achieve such heights. Her face fell before she'd even replied.

"What good ... would prayers from a monster like me do for him?" She swallowed, her throat sore with sadness. "Oh, Father, tell me I would not make everything worse, if I tried? What if ..." *What if I pray wrong, somehow?*

"We are all sinners. Perfection is not a requisite for prayer. It can do nothing but good."

She scoffed. "You are biased, Father. You are no sinner."

"All of us," he repeated. "Even me."

She studied his face for a long moment, and he returned the inspection – paying far more attention than was appropriate to the shape of her lips. He finally pointed with his head to the teacup before her.

"You're letting it get cold. I thought you were fond of vanilla tea. Or would you prefer I make something else for you?"

"Oh ... and you went to all that trouble ..." She took up the cup and saucer carefully. Luckily, it had cooled only slightly. She had to timidly blow steam away before sipping at it. It seemed to make her feel a little better, based on the way she relaxed and even hummed a little note of contentment. It was such an endearing sound. Another thought for him to push from his mind.

It felt wrong to send her away that night. Alone, back to her cold, drafty room, to bear the weight of her guilt and grief alone. Cyril stood in the doorway of his chambers for a long while, illuminated by the gold light from inside as it flooded the dark corridor, even after Brontë had long since disappeared down the stairs. When he finally closed the door, he leaned back against it as he clicked the latch into place.

Cyril slid two fingers between the buttons of his cassock and pulled out the kerchief he kept in his breast pocket, just beneath the cross over his heart. He had folded it in on itself, but it was still marked with Brontë's blood. Deep, dark red from when he'd held it to her leg; a rose petal of a stain. He twirled the little square of cotton around in his fingers, deep in thought.

75

WINDERMERE DEMANDED AN ANSWER. THE PEOPLE HAD overtaken the southern bridge to the point that no traffic could pass. Offerings of pity for Brother Philip were already set against the locked and guarded southern gate, as if he was already dead. Flowers, incense, lanterns, and candles might have made for a touching display, if they were not coupled with the fear, anger, and uncertainty of a disturbed crowd.

Debates had already begun between the townsfolk on the proper fate of a sinsick clergyman – the respective cries for judgment or mercy in various forms. Would Father divest the fallen Hunter of his station, his title, his rosary? Or would he continue this off-white brand of mercy he'd begun, feeding the boy partial forgiveness in tablet form the rest of his days? Still others called for a harsher judgment, to reignite the Torches and burn the sickness out. To purify both blood and spirit with that final act. That was the Heart's real use after all, wasn't it? To purge sickness.

The Royal Guard attempted to keep order, to ensure that no bonfires grew too large, to ensure the lamplighters were not accosted for their precious oil, to ensure those who pushed too far forward over the bridge were made to turn back. But there were so few crown officers, and so many Windermere knights – and those knights grew more and more impatient, too, with the Archbishop and his refusal to answer. Night after night, the streets echoed with the demand for a verdict, and night after night, Cyril made no appearance. And every night, the people sang those sorrowful hymns while the knights one by one joined in.

With so many knights dedicated to the trouble bubbling at the pyre stones, with so many pickpockets seeking to take advantage, with so many brawls one bad word away from breaking out – it wouldn't be difficult to miss a hooded cloak wandering through the crowd. A tired, perhaps wounded, man with a lantern in his hand stumbling through with the help of a rotting stave.

Another restless night was setting in, and Levi desperately wanted to sleep, but he was kept awake by the incessant shouting of the crowd. He and Sergeant Allermane were taking turns patrolling the unhappy scene on horseback. In truth, Levi also wanted an answer. His interactions with Philip had been so ... brief. And having learned that the Archbishop was above all things unpredictable, he felt even more uneasy about Philip's fate.

Levi shook his head. It was quiet. No, not quiet, only the shouts and jeers had died down. They'd been replaced by a low hum, music. Levi twisted in his saddle and looked over toward the bridge. He felt a panic climbing up his throat like a sickness, and he immediately turned his horse around to race back to Coldwater, to find Domingo. Levi had no fetters, and the knights had done nothing to stop it: a Flagellant had climbed up to one of the empty pyre stones, and he had begun to sing a different song.

The knights disregarded Allermane's orders. The crowd that had amassed upon the bridge had joined in the hymn, and smothered even her authoritative voice. They all knew the words. A choir echoed forth as the mob in the streets and the poorer folk lurking below bolstered those voices on the bridge. They could only hear the words, could just barely see the speck of a man from below. A cheer sounded as a hand from the crowd held aloft a pilfered flask of oil. Many hands passed it toward the pyre stone, and many more passed torches. Hand over hand, lifted high above heads as the song grew louder, as the voices drowned out Allermane trying to break through the crowd. Elbowing through, being pushed back, being crushed. The burst of flames and the scream that followed only made the crowd grow louder.

"Move!" Allermane yelled.

Such is the path to the firmament.

"Do not interfere, southerner!"

Such is my path to the firmament.

Domingo's horse seemed to jump off the very air itself to clear the gap. Domingo's gestures were swift and made with mathematical precision. Blue light swirled up from between the cobblestones, swelling to a torrent that splashed over the burning man and smothered the flames. The Flagellant howled in disapproval and agony – but no matter how he hollered or how the crowd sang, Domingo was louder. He whipped his horse around and shouted to Levi.

"A medic, now! Bear him back to Coldwater!"

Another quick series of movements and the burnt, smoldering husk of a man was bound at the wrists and dragged down, bowing to magic that would hear no argument. Domingo could only bid his incantation wash over the man. Perhaps the cold could numb whatever nerves were not already destroyed, but Domingo was no medic, no healer. The man's agony was palpable, as overwhelming as the stench of burning flesh.

The crowd was angry. The hymns had morphed to curses, and Domingo's stallion was too well tempered by war to do anything but trample any civilian that dared come too close, or raise a hand too high. Domingo knew this, and was quick to create space around himself and his destrier in the throng of people. More of that blue light leaped up from the ground, following the path Domingo traced about himself with his eyes. The people's superstitions and fear of the unknown served him well in this moment. They leaped back in fright from the lines he penned with his motions and his muttered spells. He pushed most of them back far enough that their staves and crosses could not reach him.

There were still the brave and foolish who would not be swayed. They leaped toward Domingo, toward the Royal Guard, fueled by rage at what they deemed disrespect to their Lady. The captain clicked his tongue in dismay, but wasted no time. Bound hands were not enough for these zealots. Each gesture Domingo made to command his bindings not only snapped about wrists, but the ribbons of light wrapped tight around heads, over eyes. Staves and swords, crosses and rosaries fell from hands as panicked civilians were restrained. Some tried to flail, some tried to pry away the conjured blindfolds, and some simply froze where they were. Like the man on the pyre, the magic dragged their arms down, forcing them to their knees – unharmed, but securely subdued.

Domingo's brow was damp with the effort, and he felt dizzy from whipping his head about in so many directions, but he shook the stars from his eyes and maneuvered his horse. The destrier too was snorting heavily with the effort of answering its rider's commands.

"Stand back from the Royal Guard! Stand aside!"

Those who did not do as they were bid were forced aside by the guards, who were spurred to action by Sergeant Allermane threatening the dungeons, or by yet more of Domingo's magic. They only needed to be parted enough to let the Coldwater ambulance rush through.

PHILIP SAT IN A WICKER WHEELCHAIR, not unlike the one the Archbishop's own mother had become so well acquainted with over the years. A quilted blanket was over his broken legs, both still held in place with metal pins and enchanted wraps of linen. Charmed bandages covered his hands, arms, and chest – all the way up to his neck, where his jaw was bruised and bottom lip still swollen. Brother Serge was beside him, keeping him propped up with a good pillow or three, and tending to any need he might have. Though he could scarcely move, there was a soft twinkle in his now gold eyes, and the smallest hint of a smile. The fresh air and peace of the cathedral grounds did him much good. Only time would tell if it would be enough.

The garden within the infirmary was a pleasant, quiet place. Strawberries grew in patches near the windowsill. Vines climbed their trellises, sometimes straying from the path to wind about the columns of the cloistered walkways. This time of year, the ivy leaves were beginning to lose their deep, dark green and instead lit themselves aflame with brilliant tones of red and orange. In the center, as was the case in most of the gardens, a fountain bubbled with clear water – often coaxing all manner of autumn-loving songbirds and thrushes to bathe and gossip in their own tongue.

Philip was feeling well enough to lean his head over and listen to his uncle read aloud to him. Another one of the Clerics brought a small dish of washed strawberries, cut into small, easy-to-eat pieces, but Philip shook his head weakly at the offering.

As Serge set the dish beside them on a table and continued to read, Philip stared at the red berries. Something stirred in his cloudy, muddled memory that made his uncle's words drift further and further away. Something about strawberries, the trickle of water, washing his hands ... The more he thought about it, the more he could swear he smelled something pleasant. Overwhelmingly pleasant. Something he'd not noticed the last time he'd had strawberries, but flooded his senses and made his tongue prickle now.

His eyes slid up, roving over the cathedral complex: beyond the steep roof of the infirmary, the towering spires adorning the Cleric dormitories, to a cut stone walkway that connected two of the larger structures. An arched colonnade where, he swore, he could see a familiar, veiled silhouette standing. Watching him. *Mocking him.* His lip curled in disgust, but the difficulty of focusing his weak eyes that far made him shut his lids and rest back against his pillow. The combination of Serge's gentle voice, the peace of the garden, and the comforting warmth of his bandages lulled him to sleep within minutes.

Brontë was leaning on the balcony railing, looking down into the garden where Philip and Serge sat. Guilt ate her inside out. She was so sure she had seen him looking at her. She of course was forbidden to see him. Forbidden to even enter the infirmary. Beyond even those old rules, she had heard the mutterings and mumblings. That he was sinsick now; plagued, bewitched. Perhaps she would never be permitted near him ever again, being what she was. She would have to avoid him, like she so often avoided Lady Mara. So many thoughts swam through her head at the injustice of it all that she didn't hear Cyril's footsteps behind her.

"He seems to be recovering well."

Brontë nodded, not even bothering to look up, much less greet him properly. Her blurry eyes were too fixed on Philip. "Yes," she whispered. "I'm glad."

Cyril watched her for a moment. She seemed oblivious to him, save for her reply. He joined her in looking down at Philip in the garden.

"I went to pray for him this morning," she whispered. "Just as you advised me."

"Good. I am glad to hear it."

Even this little sliver of praise flickered a smile at her lips, but any joy she might have felt was replaced by guilt upon feeling it at all. He saw it, and rather jealously wished she'd indulged a little while longer.

"But I do not know if it … does any good for him."

"There are some things we cannot know, but we pray all the same."

She nodded, and realized shamefully she'd been reaching for Cyril's hand on the banister when she encountered his little finger. She withdrew her hand and murmured an apology.

Cyril's trek downstairs to the infirmary was a short one. He was greeted by two Clerics. They paused in their busy housekeeping, both bowing to him as he entered the room. He nodded in acknowledgment and they returned to their task, remaking Philip's empty bed with fresh linens.

"Good morning. How is Brother Philip?"

One of the Clerics gave him a weak smile. "Better, thank goodness. He can hardly move on his own yet, but is more alert. Brother Serge took him out to the garden for breakfast."

"I see. Very good."

The two healers bowed once more and each picked up their baskets of spoiled and fresh linens, leaving to collect and refresh the next room's bed. Cyril stood quietly in Philip's room alone, looking over to the open window. Sunlight filtered into the room and distant chatter could be heard, mingling with laughter. A gentle hope, carried on the early autumn afternoon.

77

SERGE ALMOST NEVER LEFT PHILIP'S SIDE, even to his own detriment. A low cot had been erected against the wall of the infirmary room, layered with spare blankets and pillows, so he could tend to Philip with speed. Benjamin, too, was never far – though he was managing most of Serge's usual affairs as Head of Infirmary. Still, Benjamin made an effort to be near and available to Philip. And to his uncle, though Serge would deny his needing any assistance whatsoever. Finally, though, with Philip nestled comfortably in a great mountain of soft pillows, Serge's body had given in to its own weariness, and he fell asleep on his cot.

Benjamin was therefore very quiet as he shuffled about the room, careful not to disturb either of them. Only really for Philip's sake, as the sly Cleric had added a gentle sleeping draught to Serge's usual cup of afternoon tea. Thank goodness, he needed the rest.

The first sign that something was wrong was a quiet creak. These old infirmary beds and their wooden slats often settled like the beams in the roof. Another creak sounded, due to Philip twitching under the sheets. Too weak to do much else – too confined by pins and bandages – it was a small movement, but abrupt and unexpected. Benjamin heard the sharp rustle of the sheets and turned around.

Philip was sitting upright, staring ahead in terror, eyes wide and glistening with tears.

"Philip?"

He didn't respond.

"Leave me be," Philip whispered to the empty space before his bed.

Benjamin approached him slowly. He was about to say his name again when Philip yelled. He thrashed in his bed, reaching over to the table beside him. He grabbed a half-empty pitcher of water and clumsily hurled it in the direction he'd been looking.

"Get out, get out!" he cried. "Get *out!*"

The clay pitcher shattered against the wall and water splashed over the windowsill. Benjamin bit his tongue to hold back a curse and dove to Philip's bedside. He snapped a quiet incantation, setting one hand against Philip's forehead, and the other very carefully on his wounded chest. He tried to be gentle, not to put pressure on his patient's shattered ribs, but with his thrashing and yelling, some force was required.

"Please," Philip mumbled. "Send her away, Brother."

A repeat of the incantation to increase the potency had the desired effect. Philip's eyes drooped and he slowly stopped crying, his sniffles slipping away and his features relaxing as he sunk into sleep. Benjamin withdrew his hand and sat down on the edge of his bed, chest heaving at the sudden outburst and the energy drained by the spell both. He looked around, searching as hard as he could for anything – *anything at all*. The smallest hint of blood, a ripple in the air that obscured magic, anything. But his keen senses and eye for enchantments found nothing. *Who had Philip seen? His attackers?* Benjamin grew worried. Hallucinations were a known phenomena accompanying the sinsick, and once they surfaced, they rarely withdrew.

The smashed pitcher echoed throughout the infirmary as gossip. Clerics spoke under their breath about his condition, of Philip growing more unstable and unpredictable. Of how it would only grow worse, as the withdrawal plagued him. Still others were more concerned about Benjamin and Serge. They were, after all, the only two Clerics willing to be in the same room as Philip for any prolonged amount of time, especially unmasked. Were they in danger?

RONTË FELT A LITTLE WARMER THAN SHE HAD IN SOME weeks, a little hopeful. Though, she feared it was for the wrong reason. Cyril had made a point of seeking her out more often, to inquire after her well-being. Not the sort of reply from a saint one expected from prayer, but one she was selfishly happy for nonetheless. But as she lay in her bed, curled up in her nightgown and clutching her pillow, she felt an odd twinge of guilt. Over and over, she replayed each conversation in her head as best she could remember it. Cyril had been true to his statement before, he had not called her 'little one', not once. She chastised herself for rebuking his endearment and buried her face in her pillow. It was a long night of second-guessing for Brontë. Of heartache and relief, of wondering if seeking out comfort was indeed selfishness on her part.

The next morning, when the earliest of the liturgical bells began to ring, Brontë was already out of bed. In her hurry, she had done a rather poor job of putting her hair in her veil. But she was determined to find Cyril before his busy day took possession of him – and before she would change her mind a hundredth time. She had summoned courage before, to face him, and could do so again! She raced up the stairs toward Cyril's chambers and hoped she'd not missed her chance. For all her confidence, she knew herself well enough to know she must spend it immediately, or lose it.

All of that courage was almost knocked right out of her as she almost collided with Cyril, coming down the stairwell.

Luckily for the both of them, Cyril had a Hunter's reflexes, even if he was still rubbing sleep from his eye. He wrapped his arm about her, using both their momentum to swing her about and set her down on the steps above him.

"Heavens, girl! Where are you running to so early?"

He disentangled himself quickly, shifting down a step to look at her. Brontë was breathless and almost teary-eyed as she puffed nervously, clutching her heart and stammering out apologies. Cyril was two steps beneath her now, putting their faces on equal ground, for once. This close to him, she was given the rare opportunity to study his features in detail. He looked worried, at least as much as his face would ever show it.

"Are you alright? Is something wrong?"

Brontë heard herself babble some nonsense, fumbling with her hands in front of her. Half of her wanted to flee to her room right then. Only, she realized she would have to continue in the same direction Cyril had been walking. Embarrassment made butterflies battle in her belly, to say nothing of her awareness that her flushed face hovered so close to his own.

"Goodness, what is it? Speak up, now."

"I ..." Her mouth fell open, unable to say what she had spent her entire early morning working up the courage to tell him. *That she flounder like this!* She knew full well he despised her stammering, her mumbles, her whispers. Everything she had rehearsed seemed to have abandoned her, to wither under his scrutiny as usual. His one eye flicked from her lips back up to her eyes. She put a hand on her forehead and whined in frustration at her inability to admit what she wanted.

"Would ... it help to whisper it?" he offered.

"Maybe?" she breathed.

Cyril nodded and leaned over, twisting his head to lend his ear. What an offer! Such generosity from him, to tolerate her broken voice. Brontë had to catch her breath, the relief of not having him staring her down replaced with more nerves of an entirely different sort as she could nearly touch her cheek against his. She could feel his breath, soft and even and nothing like her own frazzled huffs, against her neck. He smelled wonderfully of his aftershave and incense, a warm, comforting blend that distracted her and made her words fall out of her mouth far easier than they should have.

"I see," Cyril said as he straightened. "Would you like it if I called you that?"

She nodded, and he gave her a small reassuring smile.

"Very well. In that case: good morning, little one."

"Good morning, Father."

79

The Coldwater physicians were skilled surgeons in their own right, but burns so severe as those suffered by the Flagellant were rarely survived. The man's pain could be somewhat managed, his burns somewhat treated, but his mind was beyond salvaging – likely long before he lit himself on fire. At least, thus was the opinion of the surgeon who spoke to Domingo. The two stood in a corridor just outside the hospital wing as she reported on the status of her patient.

"He's hysterical, Captain," she said, "Rambling nonsense and suffering from seizures. We have tried to sedate him for his own comfort, but it hardly stills him. And while your scribe has been most diligent in trying to record all that he says, it truly *is* nonsense."

"I see." Domingo was flexing his hand to diffuse a cramp after overexerting it in the employ of magic. "And how deep are the burns? How long does he have?"

"I would be surprised if he survives the night, sir –"

"Help me!" A pained scream from the adjacent room interrupted further conversation. Behind them the door to the hospital wing flew open with such force it bent the hinges and made the wood creak.

"Seven shoals!" The medic leaped out of her skin. "What in the world –!"

"Behind me at once, doctor!" Domingo drew his sword. "Alarm!"

The alarm bells of Coldwater were alike to the Lady's: angry, obstinate, and loud. They shouted down the halls and made the stones seem to quiver. The charred mass of the Flagellant staggered through the door, dragging linen, melted flesh, and the bespectacled head of the scribe behind him. The scrawny scribe clawed desperately at the hand that held him, but it was tight as a vice and would not give. He floundered and yelled in agony as the Flagellant tugged him along like a sack of flour.

A mix of what little blood the burnt man had left, salves, and fluid seeping from his burns soaked through the bandages and hospital gown he wore, all stuck together in uncomfortable layers. He was twitching and seizing violently, groaning with pain as he forced himself forward. One eye had been melted out of its socket, but somehow seemed to function where it clung to his cheek. It sought Domingo out, glossy with agony and rage.

"Release him at once!" Domingo pointed and magic leaped to obey. Blue coils of light raced toward the glorified corpse, but the Flagellant snickered. He held up the scribe, and Domingo had to hiss through his teeth and cut off his spell before it harmed him instead.

"Damn you to the depths of the Rotherdare!" The charred skin on the man's cheek tore as he opened his mouth too wide for it to bear. "I refuse to speak with you once." He tightened his grip on the scribe's head and the poor bloke howled. "And so you send your minion to my bedside instead?"

The scribe's feet kicked about, desperately trying to find the floor. He was thrown aside the next moment and crashed face-first into the stone wall. He went silent and slumped down against it.

Domingo didn't wait for the madman to advance further. He drew a line in the air from the man's wrist to the floor, and his own magic answered dutifully. It flashed blue and wound about the Flagellant's arm. Hurried footsteps and shouts approaching could be heard between the tolls of the alarm bell.

The Flagellant screeched and lunged forward. His shoulder clicked out of socket as Domingo's magic refused to give, but he dug his feet in and tried to move against it anyway.

"Halt, man!" Domingo shouted. "If you've a mind left, listen to me!"

"I take no orders from *you!* You are no guard of mine!" The flicker in his molten eye raged gold – the same gold the clergy brandished.

The doors at the far end of the corridor opened and knights poured into the hallway. Levi was among them, his own sword already drawn. He skidded to a halt when he saw the mess before him, and was relieved to see Domingo already restraining the … man? His relief was shattered the next moment.

The Flagellant lurched forward and tore through Domingo's tether, ripping off skin and bandage as he did so. A blessing of strength, or a dying man's last surge of adrenaline, who could say. The magic cried out like a wounded animal as it broke, and Domingo grimaced as the rebound sent pain snapping back up his arm. He would have taken a step back, but he was halted by the madman's hands curling hard into his shoulders. Blood began to darken the fabric of Domingo's doublet as the grip tightened.

"Damn you and damn your fragile god!" the Flagellant shouted. "You took our pyre! You took our *hope!* What more will you take from us?"

Domingo was still reeling from the rebound, still bewildered that it'd happened, that he only just began to feel the pain in his shoulders. He grimaced and tossed his head. The claws in his shoulders scratched deeper, closer to his throat. It was going to throttle him.

"You deny us! I curse you, southerner! The holy dark will find you, this I swear –"

Domingo's sword ran him through and silenced him. The captain gritted his teeth and regained his composure, gripping the hilt of his sword with both hands and, by a combined effort of body strength and skill, hoisted the man off himself and flung him to the floor – severing a cut straight from his heart out the side of his ribs. Filth splattered over the hallway and the madman convulsed wildly before going still.

"Sergeant," Domingo panted, holding his sword with both hands. "Get to the archives. Bring me that damn treatise, now!"

"Yes, sir!"

80

ℬRONTË WAS IN A MUCH BETTER MOOD THE REST OF THE day. Even Hugo noticed. He'd ordinarily tease her for that when he saw it. Poke fun at whatever might have her giddy as a schoolgirl. But instead, it was a refreshing change for him, too. He was glad to see her smiling again, even if it made her a touch worse at her job.

"Oh, and don't forget." He set a glass jar of foamy starter on her workstation. "I need this prepared tonight and ready to bake tomorrow morning."

Brontë was only half listening, stuffing dirty linens into a basket and lifting it onto her hip. She made a vague sound in acknowledgement, and hopped up the steps out of the bakery. She made her way toward one of the laundry rooms, up a flight of steps and through a long open-air cloister. As she passed beneath the lanterns, she noticed a familiar shape loitering in one of the smaller gardens below. It was Cyril, the cane told her that. He was lighting candles and setting them inside a small niche in the wall.

Cyril was taking comfort in these little habits. He stepped back a bit to survey his work: the small effigy of a fallen Hunter – his face gentle, his hands clutching sword and shield – was now properly flanked by candles. A smoking dish of incense and some dried flowers were laid at the effigy's feet, yet more offerings brought to this otherwise unremarkable niche.

Heavy footsteps in the gravel told Cyril who was approaching without the need to turn around. Maddoc slicked his hair back out of his face with a palm and tongued his cheek, but Cyril spoke before he had a chance.

"Anything to report?"

"That I am annoyed to have met so many worthless and dishonest people in the space of an afternoon."

"Cash rewards for information often bring out such ilk."

Brontë's curiosity had her glued to the wall. She hid from the priests' line of sight behind the column as she eavesdropped on their conversation. She thanked Hugo and his brogue for making it easier to parse Maddoc's equally thick accent. His voice carried up through the open arches of the cloister as he spoke.

"A few of the folk who live on the river did report seeing a particular woman about here and there – always with an escort, and never staying long. But the woman they described didn't match Sybil's description of the witch on the train."

"Not at all?"

Maddoc crossed his arms. "Curly hair, short, plump ... sounds the opposite of the tall, lean woman Sybil described."

"Indeed. And what of the escort?"

"Wore a cloak and covered their head, by every account. Though a few suspect the escort to have been a woman as well by their gait. She was tall, aye, but even that –"

"– is not enough to rely upon, you are right. What else?"

"Nothing else. Only Greer and his posse back and forth, as usual, but he never stopped by the river hamlets unless it was for the horses, I am told. Never went near any of the Sunderman mills, either."

"No, no, he wouldn't. He goes to their granary."

"Aye, like clockwork. And the path between the mill and warehouse is an open field. Some rocks and trees, but hardly enough to hide behind, unless you're moving at night. But the noise of a wagon or horses would be heard."

"Greer is already under investigation from the Royal Guard for smuggling, but blood trade is no criminal offense, by their standards. He must be doing something else."

"Something involving Sunderman, though?"

"It's not impossible, or it may be a front. Either way, I doubt her direct involvement. Operating a business at such a scale, with so many employees, all it would take is one snake in the grass to cause trouble. Still, she may be more aware than she lets on. Have her watched, as quietly and closely as you can. Sister Ealisaid may be good to employ to that end."

"Aye, aye."

"Did you manage to glean anything helpful from Sister Jael?"

"Ah, the poor lass. She struggles to speak of the matter yet, but told me what she could manage."

"And?"

Maddoc shrugged and shook his head. "I'm afraid what she described was not that far from what you and I saw with our own eyes. Some mess of corpses stacked together and sustained by shoddy work –"

"Shoddy," Cyril cut him off, "does not survive Immolation."

Maddoc could only chew his lip and nod. Another pair of footsteps in the gravel interrupted before their conversation could continue. To both of their surprise – and to Brontë's, who had failed to keep from peeking around the column to watch – it was Serge. Unkempt and sorely lacking sleep, he kicked up dust and gravel in his haste.

Though Maddoc dipped his head to the Bishop and gave his usual salute, Serge only glared at him. He shifted to speaking in the church's old language, much to Maddoc's dismay. Like Maddoc, Brontë couldn't make heads or tails of it from where she was eavesdropping. But she didn't need to understand what was being said to know that Serge was angry. Her heart dropped into her stomach at the thought that something had happened to Philip, that he might be dead.

"Where is she?" Serge snapped at Cyril. "Where is your little witch that you love so much?"

Even more to Maddoc's dismay, Cyril returned the archaic tongue in kind. Maddoc had to tilt his head and think hard to listen for fragments of words he could recognize.

"Your concern for Philip has run off with your head, Brother –"

"Don't patronize me! He cries out for mercy. He claims to see her everywhere. In his room, on his bed. What trickery do you allow her?"

"Brontë is beside herself with grief over his wounds." Both Maddoc and Brontë perked up at catching the sound of her name. Brontë nearly matched Maddoc in his indignance – though hers quickly gave way to humiliation, and then to fear. *What were they saying about her?*

"She has not been skulking about, eager to undo him," Cyril continued.

"That you know of."

"I do know, Brother."

"You think I'm a fool?" Serge snarled. "You think I can't tell the difference? It was horrid enough for him to endure the consequences of withdrawal. It's the overindulgence that rends him apart, now."

"And you truly think this is Brontë's doing?"

"Who else? I have sealed off his room from all Hunters. None of you blood-wearing brutes can come near him, and yet he thrashes and seizes like he's being doused in blood day and night."

"He himself is a Hunter –"

Serge's fists clenched tight. "Were you not listening? He sees *her* in his room, he begs her to leave him be –"

"And the sinsick are known to hallucinate," Cyril mumbled. "Brontë is not bewitching him."

"Why wouldn't she? She's already bewitched you. You defend her without hesitation."

"I ... would defend any of us from unjust accusations."

"Hah. To whom do you think you speak, boy?" Serge's head flicked up in a haughty manner that Maddoc disapproved of. "I *know* you. I know that little witch. Or did you forget it was my good work that spared her?" Serge curled his lip and tilted his head. His gold eyes were wild with a flame of an entirely different sort. Indignation, anger, resentment, all of these and more. "Do you forget how I corrected *your* misjudgment? Oh, you may carry Our Lady's heart, you may play at being Archbishop, but I know you to be a selfish, sadistic bastard –"

"That's enough, Brother. I know well your opinion of me, and of the girl. But your opinion does not render your accusations true. Brontë is not bewitching him."

"Why, then?" He jabbed an accusatory finger into Cyril's chest. Maddoc huffed at the trespass, even took a step closer instinctively, but knew better than to intervene without permission. Serge continued to ignore him. "*Why* is it that he suddenly declines? What reason can you give?"

"I fear that it may simply be the natural progression of his state."

"I cannot believe that," Serge snapped. "I cannot."

"You will not avoid the inevitable by ignoring it –"

All of Serge's frustration was carried in his fist as he let it fly. He caught both Cyril and Maddoc by surprise. Cyril stumbled back a pace as his head was knocked sideways, as Serge's knuckles caught him in the upper lip and base of his nose. He spluttered, more in surprise than from the Cleric's strength, and blood ran red from his nose. Brontë clapped both hands over her mouth to keep from revealing her presence. Maddoc's furious shout obscured the sound of her basket hitting the floor and the bit of her voice that escaped her fingers.

"Oi!"

Maddoc was between the two men in a heartbeat. He grabbed Serge by his cassock and lifted him right up off his two feet, shaking him and bellowing a string of unflattering words. Serge shouted back in the common tongue, grabbing at Maddoc's fists.

"Butcher's dog, unhand me!"

"How dare you! You sorry excuse for a –"

"Let him go, Maddoc."

Maddoc let out a noise between a growl and a shout, but did as he was ordered. Though, he shoved Serge away more roughly than needed. The healer staggered backward and hastened to right his garments, aching from the way they'd chafed over his skin. Maddoc may have released him, but he still stood defensively between Cyril and Serge, fists a little too high and a little too prepared to bludgeon the Bishop, if only given the word to do so.

Behind him, Cyril straightened, gingerly feeling for the stitches on the side of his face, feeling for whether they'd come undone. Blood still oozed from his nose and splattered over his cassock as he – despite his kinder words and controlled tone – glared hellfire at Serge. Such was the look in his eye that it made the Bishop step back another pace, made him clutch at his cross about his neck. Still, Serge couldn't help but sneer at the sight of the two of them: two tall, bulky, brutal men with bloody hands and black hearts, in his estimation.

"Our Lady at the whim of two rabid street dogs." Serge shook his head. "Curse that my nephew should live and die in an era such as this." Serge held his cross to his lips and took a deep breath. "I only ever had one ask of you, *Archbishop*. If you fail me, that leash will become a noose."

Without waiting to be dismissed by his superior, Serge turned on his heel and marched back toward the infirmary. Maddoc very nearly went after him, mouth agape.

"Don't you turn your back, you –"

"Leave him be, Maddoc. He is grieving."

"The boy's not lost yet!" Maddoc pointed in disbelief at the direction Serge had gone. "And what sort of excuse is that? You ought to flog him! Hell, have him whipped out at Coldwater!"

Maddoc watched as Cyril pulled out a kerchief and held it to his bloodied face. The quiet this afforded them both gave Maddoc's temper a chance to cool. He scoffed in disbelief at the whole affair.

"That was almost a proper hook. Since when does that old Cleric know how to throw one like that?"

Brontë had not heard a word of the commotion after the punch. Even from the cloister a whole floor up, even from across the garden, the smell of blood being spilled smothered her. She sunk down, her back against the wall as her legs buckled. That tug in her chest was screaming, thrashing about low in her throat to reach it, to reach him, like it would crawl up and out her mouth if she let it.

It felt like anguish, rage, compassion, helplessness – it felt like far too many things at once and she felt the urge to shout. Even with both hands over her mouth and nose, the smell suffocated her, as if she'd suffered the same wound and the blood was on her lips. A blow to the head, a blow to the heart. There had been so many bitter reminders of what she was, but this by far was the worst.

Up in the cloister and cold from the open air, she endured it alone, shaking with grief and fear and frustration as she fumbled about for her medicine in her pocket.

81

ᴮRONTË'S THROAT STILL ACHED AS THE BELLS DISTANTLY tolled half past eleven o'clock. Not even her medicine could completely cool the pain. Nestled deep beneath the scratchy wool blanket and linen sheets, only her eyes and pink nose poked out from her little cocoon. She almost groaned aloud as she remembered Hugo's evening request: that she prepare a batch of sourdough – *and* the addendum that he'd expect it to be ready and waiting for him in the morning. She kicked away at the sheets, dragging herself out of bed and patting her cheeks in exasperation.

She opened her door and poked her head out into the hallway, looking up and down the corridor to be sure no one else was sleepless, up and about, to see her prance down the hallway on her tiptoes in nothing but her nightgown and stockings, her hair haphazardly pinned up. She took her single candle with her, shielding the flame from the wind she whipped up trotting along toward the bakery.

As she walked, she felt that intense pull in her chest again. Maybe it was the incense, always hanging heavy. She had a small thought that she might go pray again, when her work was done ... not that it would do any good, for her or for Philip. Would it be selfish to pray for herself this time? To pray for relief, even if only temporary, so she could sleep? She thought this as she went down the stairs, past the small auxiliary chapel, and through the atrium. She nudged the door to the bakery open with her hip.

She at once set about lighting the candles and lanterns around her station so she could get to work. Get to work, and more importantly, get back to bed. The bakery smelled heavily of clover honey, another reminder of the work Brontë should have done hours ago. Hugo did so love to doctor his sourdough breads with lots of fresh butter, honey, and even flowers. It made Brontë's nose itch, being so sensitive, but she persevered – if not out of compassion for her nose, then for her freezing cold toes on the stone floor.

The bells were less distant in the bakery than they were in the dormitory. The Lady's voice made Brontë hop in surprise as the twelve loud chimes of the midnight hour echoed through the empty courtyard and the now only semi-abandoned bakery. As Brontë finished sealing her jars and washed her hands, she heard footsteps in the corridor outside the bakery. She shuffled to the far side of the worktable as she dried her hands on a towel, lest the nighttime passerby happen to glance in and see her state of undress. A good thing, too, as the footsteps, though very slow and perhaps quite sleepy, seemed to be approaching the bakery.

"Oh dear. Is that you, Hugo?" she said as she sorted bowls to put them away. "I swear, you have a sixth sense for when I've shirked my work, deliberately or not –"

Brontë froze in surprise to see a familiar, now terrifyingly skinny figure staggering into the bakery.

"Philip?"

Philip groaned quietly, swaying unstably on his feet. He wore the infirmary's loose, comfortable linen trousers and smock. With all the weight he'd lost, he looked more bone and linen than muscle and skin. The many bandages and stitches that covered him strained with his movements, and he held one hand to a ripped stitch in his belly that had begun to bleed. His head twitched and his breathing was ragged, but he seemed awake enough to find Brontë in the dim, flickering light of the candlelit bakery. His once brilliant blue eyes were cloudy and dull, flickering gold with faith as he glared at her.

Brontë fumbled and dropped her empty bowl. It fell, forgotten, to the floor as she rushed around the table, nearly tripping over her gown. "Why are you out of bed? Is something wrong? Philip, you're bleeding!"

The closer she was to him, the more unstable he seemed to become, holding his head and groaning aloud in pain and swaying.

"It's you," he muttered, his mouth dry and tongue swollen.

"I'll ring for a Cleric!"

Brontë picked up her skirt and rushed for the corridor, to where the closest calling bell resided. That is, she tried to. Upon passing close enough to Philip, he grabbed her by the arm and flung her back into the worktable behind her. In her surprise, she was knocked back so hard the air rushed from her lungs.

"It was you! The whole damn time!" Philip sobbed and hobbled toward her. "All along! You lied to me!"

Philip kept gesturing with his hands in that habitual manner – which, if he had been in possession of his rosary, would have brought his sabers into play. Without them, he could only grimace and cry in frustration, swiping at Brontë as she scrambled backward from him and he knocked jars and dishes from the countertops. One such swipe knocked hard against his knuckles and toppled the knife block. Kitchen knives went clattering across the floor, and Philip snatched one of them up. Brontë's eyes went wide as it flashed through the air toward her.

She yelped and kicked at him. She earned herself a shallow slice to the leg, but sent him reeling back a few paces. Any apprehension at the idea of hurting poor Philip, injured as he was, was swept aside in the interest of self-preservation.

"Philip, please!" She gasped for air. "Stop, it's me!" *It's me, it's only me!*

She kicked him again, harder this time. Back he went, crying out as her foot connected with still-healing wounds. It was just enough room. Her nails dug into the stone floor as she pulled herself to her feet. Philip was shouting now. A hoarse, broken sound as he cursed her. Cursed her for tormenting him.

The knife plunged deep into her chest and Brontë's voice failed. The scream she thought she'd make was swallowed as she instinctively gasped for air. Philip twisted the knife and ripped it out, sending red splattering over the stone floor, his hands, and her once-white linen gown. She felt the blow like heartbreak. Panic assumed total control and the pain came on quickly. It swept through her faster even than the blood gushing from the gash ripped through her chest. She fell against the table.

"What are you?" His voice was hoarse as he shouted. He raised the knife again. "I deserve to know!"

"Stop!" She gasped and her legs gave out. "You're hurting me!"

Philip twitched hard, his head twisting alarmingly far on his neck from the convulsion as he was overwhelmed by the scent of her blood, by the sensation of it on his skin. *You're hurting me!*

"That's what the other one said," he moaned. "That's what that *thing* said!"

He stabbed her again. Brontë cried out in pain and to her dismay heard a horrible, animalistic hiss from her own mouth. She sunk to the floor in a puddle of blood and tried to crawl away from him. The knife found purchase again, this time plunging through her ribs. The screech she made hurt her own ears. Her vision was failing.

There was no voice, no command, no words – only the rush of footsteps and a blurry silhouette. Cyril's cane clattered to the floor as he tossed it aside in his hurry. Philip had neither the speed nor the presence of mind to resist his senior.

Cyril's arm was looped about Philip's neck, crushing it in the crook of his elbow as he yanked the younger man back, away from Brontë. Philip yelled and flailed in confusion. Cyril grunted at the effort of holding him, and his free hand grabbed for Philip's spindly arm. With some effort, he secured a grip. Cyril held Philip's hand at the wrist and smashed the knife into the countertop. The vibration of the metal made Philip howl out in pain and drop it. The kitchen knife fell to the floor, splattering blood from the puddle it landed in. Now unarmed, Cyril held Philip's head and increased the pressure of his hold, dragging him away from both Brontë and the fallen knife.

It only took a few seconds of grappling the boy, and even fewer seconds of applied pressure to render him unconscious, to cease his flailing. Cyril did his best to carefully lay Philip down on his side, but even as he hastily muttered that old language, his focus was on reaching Brontë where she lay, wailing as she bled from her wounds.

Brontë sobbed as blood pooled beneath her. So much blood. Pain, like nothing she'd ever known. She raised her soaked hand, though it trembled uncontrollably. She reached for Philip where he lay, unconscious on the bakery floor. She whispered apologies and tried to stroke his face, as if she could reach. As if such small favors could soothe either of them now. Her hand fell limp, refusing to obey her intentions as weakness settled heavy over her. Her eyelids drooped and she felt sick, yet something deep inside of her told her she could not sleep. She must stay awake, she must.

Delirious with grief, she could only cry out in a hoarse voice as Cyril murmured an apology of his own. He picked her up off the floor. Moving her hurt, but it had to be done. She made broken, guttural noises – more from not wanting to leave Philip in such a state than a reaction to the pain of being moved. She had already bled through her nightgown, and now as Cyril hoisted her up, her blood ran down the skirts of her gown and stained his shirt.

Her head lolled to rest against his shoulder, and through the white linen of his shirt and the blurry, dark silhouette of his jaw, she could faintly see red. A Cardinal, she realized. Two of them, even? Or perhaps she was simply seeing double. She fought to keep her eyes open as they burned in protest. She caught bits of a hushed, rapid conversation. And then she was moving – Cyril was carrying her out of the bakery and away from dear Philip, leaving him behind, in the attentive care of the Cardinals. She voiced her disapproval in the form of unintelligible sobs and broken coughs. Her tongue was swollen and tasted of her own blood, and oh how her eyes burned.

Her sobs slowed only due to fatigue. Weaker and weaker fractions of her voice came spilling out as that deep, dark sleep threatened to overtake her. She was colder than she'd ever felt. Every hard shudder and shiver was an invitation, promising ice-cold relief to the fire in her eyes, if she would but give in and close them. But she mustn't! Fear kept her eyes snapping open at the last moment

"Stay awake, little one."

She moaned in acknowledgment, but her eyelids were so very heavy, and her eyes ached so bad ... she feared they would disobey his order of their own accord. Would she wake, if she dared to rest? *Just for a moment?* She whimpered, spitting blood and tears as she forced words out. Though she spoke with all her strength, it barely came out as a whisper.

"I don't want to die."

"This will not kill you. You'll be alright."

"It hurts."

"I know."

A single, violently resisted blink of her eyes made time pass alarmingly fast. The dark stone walls were a blur as she moved past them. Another blink, and she felt Cyril setting her down. Her bloodshot, tear-filled eyes could barely make out his silhouette as he leaned over her, much less make sense of the curtains and canopy that stood over her. Wherever she was, it was very soft. She sunk into the comfort of the pillow and the downy sea of blankets, tears still streaming down her face as she gritted her teeth from both pain and despair in equal measure.

Cyril moved quickly after setting her down in his bed. He practically tore through his bloodied clerical collar, removing it and his ruined shirt. He flung both into his washroom, breathing a deep sigh of relief to get it off his skin. With this done, he fished a key from his sash and opened the cabinet built into the wall just beside his dresser. He tore the Cleric's briefcase of emergency essentials from where it rested.

He set the briefcase on the foot of his bed, retrieving and opening a tin of leaves. He set the tin on the small table by the head of his bed, pulling the lit candles closer and unfastening the buttons of Brontë's nightgown. Embarrassment should have been the furthest thing from her mind, but from what little she realized was happening, Brontë still whined her disapproval. One hand rose weakly to protest, though it barely stirred in the sheets. She only smeared blood over his bed in doing so.

"Wait ..."

"You need to let me see, little one."

A weak toss of her head in disagreement, and Cyril left her side a moment. He retrieved a fresh shirt from his dresser. Clean linen destined now to be soiled by her blood. He draped it over her, and then carefully set to work wrestling her nightgown open, tearing through it when it did not comply fast enough for him. His shirt allowed for some precious privacy as he took the leaves and applied them to the area of her wounds. The leaves were soaked with blood by the time he reached the third stab wound – a horrible, deep gash on the lower left side of her belly. The herb did its task dutifully, though only to some extent, given Brontë's muddled heritage and a lack of additional enchantment. Still, her face relaxed as the pain slightly subsided. So too did the flow of blood slow as her veins constricted, a side effect of the numbing leaf.

Cyril had a needle and suture thread prepared, but as he gently moved his shirt to reveal her collarbone, he hummed a low note and mumbled. Brontë was only vaguely aware, but she recognized all too well the sound of his disappointment. Almost habitually, she inquired after the noise with a guilty tone in her voice.

"What is it?"

Cyril covered her back up, setting his intended tools aside and fetching a kerchief and a cup of water. He wiped the blood and spittle from her face gently. "Your wounds have already closed."

Brontë scoffed in disbelief. Surely not. The entirety of her chest stung horribly. She refused to move, to test it, lest she feel that horrible pain through her ribs. Had they been broken? Perhaps sliced clean through? The thought sickened her.

"They don't ... feel that way."

"Closed," he said, wiping her brow. "Not healed."

Of all things Brontë cared for in this moment, semantics was not one of them. She frowned and gave a frustrated, pained cry. "Please speak plainly to me."

Cyril carefully lifted her legs so he could pull the blanket and duvet over her. "You regenerate. The skin will stitch itself closed, to stop bleeding. The rest will settle with time."

He saw her hold back still more sobs. Of course, she needed very few reminders of what she was, in this delicate, awful moment. He adjusted the pillow behind her head.

"All it means is that you are in no danger of bleeding out. You can sleep now, little one."

"Is Philip ...?"

"He's been taken back to the infirmary, and is resting. Now so must you."

Brontë whimpered, but the permission to sleep was too enticing. Cyril watched as she succumbed to sleep. He sat back on the foot of the bed and stared at her, a bloody mess in his bed.

82

ERWIN SAT AT HIS SECRETARY AND STARED BLANKLY OUT the window. He looked down at his hands, at the shake and shudder present in them. His throat itched for blood, a rather familiar feeling. And one he rather enjoyed, if he was being entirely honest. He had taken the vials of blood and stashed them in his desk. He now turned one over in his hand. It was easily the most potent blood he'd ever held. The pleasurable tingle of normal blood on his fingertips was magnified tenfold, if not more.

He wasn't a fool; he knew better than to play about with something so obviously potent. But he was, too, a sinsick son of a bitch. He popped open the bottle and leaned back, only letting a few drops enter his mouth. They were divine. They gave immediate relief to his aches and pains. Completely stopped the tremor in his hands, too. A sort of deeply pleasant, difficult-to-describe taste. He smiled and relaxed back in his chair. He decided this would be enough, and sat up, to put it away. Despite his intentions, that isn't what his body moved to do. He blinked in confusion. Was he dreaming? He watched his hands move without his input. Worryingly enough, he could not stop them. He felt himself lean back again, holding up the vial to his mouth. He shook his head as, at the same time, he drank more.

Something's wrong. He must be dreaming. Had he hit his head one time too many, he wondered? Why couldn't he stop himself? He was a spectator in his own body, fighting for control over it.

He dropped the empty vial. He tried to stand, but fumbled as his legs, too, stopped obeying him. His chair clattered over. Aoife heard the chair hit the floor from the hallway. She knocked on the door quietly, putting her ear against it.

"Erwin? Are you alright?"

She heard only pained cries.

"Erwin!"

The door was locked. Of course it was. Aoife darted for the closest servant's corridor, picking up her skirt and yelling at her staff to get out of her way. Her butler chased after her in confusion. She shoved the servant's door open, stopping short at what she saw.

Erwin was contorting on the floor and spitting up blood. He was fighting himself, trying to stand, to get up, only to be forced back to the ground when one side of his body tensed and folded him over. He screamed at the pain, clawing into the carpet, into his hair, into his own skin. Aoife's knees buckled but she tried to reach him.

"My lady, come away!"

Darcie grabbed her arm and pulled her back. Erwin's back arched and he thrashed on the floor, his hands pulled so hard at his hair he was splitting skin and spilling blood on the rug. He rolled around, sobbing at the pain of all his muscles contracting and bending him too far. His voice was hoarse and soft, pleading.

"Aoife ... help me."

Aoife tore herself away from Darcie and ran over to him. He sobbed as blood foamed in his mouth and cut off his words. The crying abruptly stopped. Aoife rolled him over and pulled him into her lap. She wiped bloody hair out of his face, and he stared up at her, eyes wide and mouth agape, dead.

⁜

"What manner of creature," Levi said, still in disbelief, "can break through Monocerian fetters?"

"Not a creature," Domingo replied. "Still a man, even if a possessed one."

Levi had his doubts. The leaking coffins, the bubbling flesh, the yellow teeth, the immense strength – he didn't think these things were human. But Domingo was well traveled and well learned, and had his gift of sight. If Domingo saw humanity somewhere in this mess, who was he to disagree? Levi thought for a moment, and had a small realization: Domingo wore silver earrings. He remembered, then, Brontë saying silver could deafen some of the noise. But surely the silver didn't impact the sharpness of his sight, did it? And he had no freckles, no *marks*, as the people said.

Domingo was still nursing his injured arm as he fought to stay awake. The boundaries he knew. The Lord Governor's purview he knew. His own rights as Captain of the Royal Guard he knew. But he branded himself a fool for not further reading into the countless pages of history, not having Levi sit down and bore himself to tears reading through it all. His eyes burned with the effort of focusing on faded ink, page after page. Then, finally, there it was – tucked deep between unassuming lines of otherwise mundane demands listed in the treatise.

"Here," he said, and Levi sat up immediately. "Our Lady in Windermere shall bring down every one of Her Torches upon the bridge. She shall dismantle the steps to her pyre stones and leave them bare. No Lesser Vampyre may be consigned to any flame be it conjured or created."

Levi blinked at the words. *The sinsick were considered lesser vampires? And the pyre stones ...* "Pyre stones ... those empty spaces upon the bridge? Between the statues? There are tens of the things."

"Aye, all black with fire, too. Every one of them." Domingo sat back in his chair and rubbed his injured arm. "So that's it, then. That woman was recreating a ritual banned by the Empress."

"They'd burn every addict, then? Even one of their own clergy?" Even Philip? Was that what the people wanted?

"Of course they would. If they believe the Lady's fire a mercy, why wouldn't they beg for it?"

83

CYRIL PENNED A SMALL NOTE AND LEFT IT BESIDE BRONTË, should she wake up while he was away. Barely a sentence, telling her where he was, and that he would be back soon, but written and signed with all his typical formality. It almost felt cold to leave such a formal note. But after a moment of standing beside her and waffling over it with the note in hand, he realized he was being foolish. He set it down, took up his cane, and departed.

"And here I was thinking you'd forgotten all about me ..."

Mara's teasing voice faded off as she noticed a familiar floral scent as Cyril entered her room. Her jokes forgotten, she grew worried, holding out her hands for him. He hung his cane off the back of the chair and took her hands in his own.

"Are you alright?" she asked, switching to their shared language, on account of the staff still situating dinner on the table. "I smell blood on you."

"Do you?" He frowned, replying in the same language. "I am sorry. I thought I had rid myself of it. Does it upset you?"

"No, no – I do not feel ill at all. I only noticed it. But you smell as if you just felled a mark. Are you injured? Was there trouble?"

Cyril sighed as he now debated the matter of Brontë. His mother seemed to read his face far too easily, as she often did.

"There is trouble, then? Oh, my dear – you are not hurt, are you?"

"I am not," he assured her. "The matter is handled."

"And you will tell me the matter, then?"

Cyril waited until dinner was set out upon the table, and then dismissed the staff. He portioned out Mara's meal himself before sitting down.

"My son, do not keep me in suspense. Come, you must tell me. I have scarcely seen you so downcast."

"I apologize. I must be lost in thought."

"I do not doubt it. Now share these thoughts with me. My imagination creates worse and worse ordeals by the minute."

"There was an incident involving young Philip."

"Oh no. Is he –?"

"No. He's alive. But I fear for his mental state."

"What occurred?"

"Same as you noticing the way I wear blood; I'm afraid poor Philip has become too well aware of his surroundings."

"Oh, no ..." Mara seemed to already make the connection. "He has found out little Brontë?"

"He has."

"He must be heartbroken."

"It is much, much worse than that."

"Tell me."

"Whether he was dreaming or conscious, I do not know. But he pulled himself from his bed at night and attacked Brontë."

"Heavens above!" Mara was too stunned to say much else. She babbled syllables that flip-flopped between her new and old languages.

"She survived." Cyril gestured with a hand in an attempt to quiet her babbling, so he could explain. "They both did. Only just, in his case. Just being near vampire blood is enough to send him into a fit, never mind walking on his broken legs. And of course, Brontë fought to defend herself. And she is much stronger than she realizes."

"But what of her? A Hunter's weapons would burn right through her, wouldn't they? And, good god, Immolation is irreversible."

Cyril shook his head. "No, no. None of that. He does not have his rosary. He can cast no magic, not now. Good thing, too. He would sap what precious life he has left in him."

"What, then? Did he just batter the poor thing? How did he even get to her? The distance between the infirmary and the maid's apartments –"

"She was in the bakery. He took up a knife."

"My word –"

"She is recovering." Mara was still processing as Cyril continued, both of their meals growing cold on the table before them. "I am tending to her in my room. I'm afraid having her there infects the place, though." He gestured at his robes. "So, I apologize, that I may smell of her blood for a time, to you, keen as your senses are."

"Hardly deserving an apology." She looked earnestly at him. "But what of you? Being so near those open wounds? Are you ... well?"

"I am." His tone made her give up pursuing the matter further.

"May I see her?"

"I beg your pardon?"

"Miss Brontë, may I see her?"

"Why?"

She smiled. "I don't mean to say that your company or care is insufficient. But the poor girl must be reeling at the loss of her dear friend. What a tumultuous turn of events. I think she might need a friend."

"I do not think that's wise. Being near her may aggravate your condition."

"I will keep my visits short and halt them entirely if I feel any change, then," she said simply, and in an uncharacteristically serious tone. "Would that satisfy you?"

"I know that tone. I suspect I won't be able to stop you."

"Do you disagree?"

He shook his head. "No, I think you've the right of it. You know what she is, after all. That sort of kind gesture from a knowing soul would do her good, I think."

84

Bronte slept fitfully in Cyril's bed. Her mind was being cruel to her, making her relive the wounds, the noise, the fear, over and over. It made her toss, which only pained her, and then woke her up – repeating in a cycle hour after hour through the dark of the night. Every time she opened her eyes, she could see Cyril. *Did he never sleep?* One blink he'd be pacing back and forth before the hearth across from her. One nightmare later, he'd be scratching in a notebook. Only once did she ever see him actually lying down, his legs hanging over the armrest and off the edge of the sofa, as it was too short for him. Of course, that had been the one time her pain had made her cry out, and he'd immediately risen to his feet to tend to her. *Of course,* she lamented, *the one time he'd found rest, she ruined it.* She really was just a cursed thing, wasn't she?

Her cry had convinced Cyril to give her another of those more potent draughts he had on hand. It quieted her mind and soothed some of the pain. Just enough that she finally slept for a time, uninterrupted. When she finally opened her eyes again, it was only due to the odd sensation of something warm against her skin. Cyril was leaning over her and rubbing her arm. She could dimly see the pink sunrise flooding in from the window. She could see his mouth moving, too, but couldn't quite hear him, and turned her head over in the pillow toward him. He knelt down beside his bed.

"I am sorry to wake you, little one. But we must clean you up. Can you move?"

Brontë stirred a little in the sheets, stretching weakly and attempting to prop herself up on her arms. Cyril helped her sit up, and he undid the remaining buttons of her ruined nightgown. Though her hands were sluggish and slow, she still held on to the now bloody shirt he'd given her. She almost let it fall away accidentally as she awkwardly tried to reach for his hand.

"I ... I can do it."

"You cannot."

He helped her out of her nightgown, freeing one arm and then the other, each time giving her time to resituate the shirt that protected her modesty.

"Can you stand?"

Brontë shakily slipped her legs off the bed, very gingerly setting her toes upon the floor. She expected it to be cold and almost withdrew her feet instinctively, but the floors in his room were comfortably warm. A small blessing. She attempted to hoist herself up, and found some success, though she swayed precariously. A step too shaky, and Cyril hummed his disapproval.

"May I pick you up?"

Brontë clutched the shirt he'd given her so tightly she nearly ripped it in half. She stumbled into him, though not from pain, not this time. He already had one arm around her bare back as he waited for her reply.

"You may."

He nodded then and swept her up. As he carried her into his washroom, she realized he'd already drawn her a hot bath. Cyril maneuvered her carefully around the many hanging plants, ensuring she didn't bump her head or her toes. He then helped her lower into the bathtub, letting her hold on to that bloody, borrowed shirt as a privacy curtain. Once she had settled herself, he brought extra towels, folding them up and setting them beside the bath on a stool. He took one and shook it out, draping it over the tub itself, over top of her, to give her actual privacy. Having done this, she allowed him to withdraw the blood-soaked shirt. As Brontë settled back against the edge of the tub, the water began to cloud pink with the dried blood it cleansed. He wrung out the stained shirt he'd taken from her in the sink.

"Can't you ... do something more ... for the pain?" she murmured. "A spell or the like?"

Cyril set the shirt down and went back over to her. He rolled up a towel and helped her set her head back against this makeshift pillow, brushing her hair aside.

"I cannot, little one. Holy magic would only harm you, more than help you."

"Try? It could not possibly feel worse than this."

"It would." Her face contorted in disappointment and pain both, though the latter was borne from yet another reminder of what she was. He stroked her forehead apologetically. "I'll fashion you another draught. It may help to numb some of the pain."

She watched him, then, through the open door to his washroom, as he bundled up all the bloodied clothing and unmade his bed. The hot water helped to soothe the tension she had begun to recognize as her body stitching itself back together. It hurt, though not nearly as much as her heart. No matter how she tried to calm it, it beat uncontrollably fast, and every single beat struck the same horrible sore.

Cyril knew she could see him, and so dragged the basket of bloody linens out of sight. He unlocked and elbowed open the servant's entrance in one corner of his bedroom. After nudging the basket inside with a foot, he snapped his fingers at it and hissed a quiet spell. The contents of the basket went up in that usual flame, burning out only the blood. He breathed a deep sigh of relief to have that overwhelming scent out of his head, and out of his bed. Not that he'd be sleeping in it anytime soon, he realized. After he remade the bed, he dressed properly: with his clerical collar and his long hair wrapped in silk. He leaned against the doorframe of his washroom as he pulled on his gloves.

"I will not be gone long. I will fetch you fresh clothes and something to eat."

Brontë only nodded, her cheek resting against the towel on the edge of the tub.

"Shall I fetch one of your books for you, as well?"

"Oh, I … would not want to inconvenience you."

"It is not an inconvenience, I am offering. Do you have one that you would like?"

She opened her mouth, but didn't answer.

"Perhaps the one you hide beneath your pillow?"

"I –" Brontë gave a stunned squeak.

He shook his head and smiled. "I won't be long."

"Father?"

"Yes?"

"Could you … fetch me a new pair of stockings, too, please? I keep them in the top drawer of the dresser."

"Of course."

Cyril took visiting Brontë's room as an opportunity to stop by the bakery. Hugo of course had no inkling of what really had happened. He only knew his apprentice was feeling quite terrible, and would be unavailable to assist him. He had nodded sagely upon hearing this news, attributing her absence and supposed sickness to the stress of poor Philip's state. In her stead, three wide-eyed and much younger novices – *real* novices – bumbled about the bakery. The trio were trying and failing to shoulder the workload Brontë often hefted so effortlessly.

All three of them stopped short and stood to attention – two girls and one boy, to be precise –when Cyril entered the bakery. He greeted them and let them resume their work. They scrambled out to the courtyard to tend to the several ovens, almost bowling over a sleepy-eyed Hugo, who came inside wiping his hands on his apron.

"Father, good morning. How is the lass?"

"She is recovering well," Cyril said as he looked about the bakery.

There was not a single hint of blood to be seen or sensed anywhere. The Cardinals had done good work, following Cyril's orders that night. It was as if the attack had never happened. Everything was back in its rightful place, clean and organized. Or, it would be – if Brontë were here. The novices had already strewn utensils and ingredients every which way.

"How do you find your volunteers?" Cyril asked.

Hugo laughed. His usual good-natured chuckle was tinged with a little bit of sadness, a quiet note of proof that the whole unhappy situation weighed on even him.

"What they lack in skill they make up for in energy, these young ones. Alas, I wish they were half as clever as my apprentice, but I'll learn to forgive them."

As it happened, Hugo heard a small commotion outside that told him his volunteer substitutes were likely goofing off instead of following orders, and so he shuffled out into the courtyard to supervise them. Cyril looked down at the floor, the same place he'd picked up Brontë. There was nothing, not even a stain in the grout between the flagstones. He nodded to himself, pleased. The Cardinals had done good work.

85

AOIFE WAS SITTING IN A CHAIR BESIDE ERWIN'S BED. His body was still stiff, contorted in pain, and his mouth open. It was covered by a sheet, a small blessing, but she could still make out the scream lurking beneath the linen. Her grief was quiet. It fell in tears down her cheeks and onto her hands, but this was all she allowed herself, especially in the presence of others. Namely Darcie, her butler, who had a hand on her shoulder. A knock on the door made Darcie step aside. And, when she opened the door, Aoife could hear her mother in the corridor beyond.

She refused to enter the same room as Erwin. Even now, she had a perfumed kerchief over her mouth and nose. Aoife wasn't really paying attention to what was being said, only catching bits and pieces of her mother's concern that she be in the same room as the corpse for so long. The butler both reassured her mother that Aoife was well enough and encouraged her to be patient.

"It's better this way," her mother mumbled to Darcie. "She was always so preoccupied with that scrappy little knave."

"He may never have been your son," Aoife snapped. "But he was entirely my brother."

Her mother looked appalled. She came thundering into the room to assert herself, but after pushing the butler aside she stopped. The corpse on the bed was far too off-putting. Beneath the linen, it seemed to stare at her. Darcie's smile behind her mother gave Aoife enough confidence to continue speaking her mind.

"And furthermore, I intend to bury him in the family mausoleum."

Her mother's eyes narrowed. She was still dumbstruck by Aoife's sudden outburst, her sudden irreverence when she was always so composed. Dismay was evident on her face. She was disappointed that her daughter let herself be so swayed by the half-bred sorry excuse for a boy in the bed.

"Very well, bury him if you wish. On one condition: you are not to surrender him to the church."

"But –"

"I forbid it!" she yelled. "I would not sully our house by advertising a sinsick bastard within our halls! This is my price."

Aoife was about to argue, but her mother continued.

"If you give him to the church, this house will relinquish all claim to him – and he will be thrown into a pauper's grave, as he deserves."

"I will not send him to the church," Aoife said quietly.

"Then do as you will. And do it soon. I want this room rid of his stench."

With that she barreled past the butler, back toward the main hall and what she considered to be cleaner air.

⁘

BRONTË FELT MUCH BETTER IN A FRESH, clean chemise and with a few of her belongings nearby. Small comforts, but familiarity above all things was a boon. Cyril had retrieved her current book – though it mortified her to know he was aware of what she was reading: a rather graphic romance between a knight and his lady – a linen chemise, her stockings, and a few other essentials, like her hairbrush. She sat in his bed, supported by pillows and nestled between soft, silky sheets that made her want to rub her legs back and forth beneath them.

Cyril was now more regularly torn between his office and his chambers. After all, he couldn't well receive visitors, not even a late cup of tea or coffee with a Brother or Sister, with her lounging in his bed. Such social, and sometimes serious, obligations were attended to in his office.

When Cyril returned to his room from one such obligation, he found Mara had let herself in, and was busy conversing with Brontë where she sat in his bed. Mara was holding up a creamy-white nightgown from a garment box on her lap, pointing out different features like the amount of puff in the sleeve, the high collar, or the trim. Two other gowns were already laid out upon the bed.

"What's this?" he asked.

Mara looked up and smiled innocently at her son. "Miss Brontë informed me that her nightgown had been ruined, and I wanted to correct that."

"She is already wearing a perfectly acceptable chemise."

Mara turned up her nose and gave a haughty huff. "Every woman deserves a good nightgown."

Cyril held up his hands in defeat. He sunk into the sofa beside the hearth and thumbed open his sketchbook. The two ladies went back to their chatter as he filled in an already cluttered page of notes and sketches with yet more of the same.

"A wonderful choice. I think it will flatter you. What do you think?"

It took Cyril a moment to realize Mara's question had been directed at him. He looked up from the book in his lap. "Pardon?"

"Well?" Mara held up the nightgown in question. "What do you think? *I* think it suits her very well."

"It is ... hardly my place to have an opinion –" Brontë's brown eyes made his words fumble as she waited expectantly for his opinion. "Yes. I think it's lovely," he added quickly.

Cyril's outward ease did not at all match the flutter in his belly. It made a little smile appear in the corner of his mouth as he looked back down at his sketchbook. Brontë noticed it, over Mara's shoulder as she folded up the other gowns. A quick glance up from Cyril to meet her gaze and she hastened to look away.

86

"FATHER, MIGHT I HAVE A WORD?"

CYRIL LOOKED UP TO SEE BENJAMIN HALF HIDING behind the open door of his office. Beneath his rosy spectacles, his eyes were fixed on the floor. Jaw set, hands trembling with nerves where they rested, tucked into the safety of his habit sleeves. From his distance across the room, Cyril could make no such subtle observations. Benjamin was grateful for it.

"Of course, Brother. Come in."

Benjamin slipped silently inside and latched the door behind him, pausing a moment to ponder, before deciding to seal it as well. Cyril saw the seal flicker into existence as he rose to his feet, innocently picking up his cane as he meandered about the side of his desk and, with an outstretched arm, invited Benjamin to sit upon the far more comfortable sofa nearer the crackling hearth.

The Brother followed the direction, but did not take a seat. Cyril stood next to him, and Benjamin fought to avoid shriveling away from his presence in shame. He stood quietly in obvious discomfort before finally forcing his words out around his dry tongue, eyes still fixed on the floor, the flame, a stray spark in the air, anywhere but up at Cyril.

"My vow to keep the confidence of those who confess is not one I challenge lightly, Father."

A weight settled over the room, a tension that smothered the beating heart and dampened the furrowed brow.

"And you feel deeply compelled to commit this sin, Brother?"

"I do," he replied, without hesitation, inching closer and sinking to one knee. "And I will beg for forgiveness now and hope that you hear me."

Cyril let him take his own hand in both of his, and press a kiss to it. The younger man clung to him, fighting to get his words out through the guilt that was thick over his teeth.

"It was Philip, Father, who confessed to me."

"You would betray the trust of one of our own?" Benjamin flinched beneath Cyril's booming disapproval. "Our Brother, broken by the enemy?"

"I beg you forgive me, Father," he whispered hastily. "I have no choice."

"You would add lying to your insults against me?"

Benjamin's lip quivered and he gripped Cyril's hand tighter, shaking his head and resting it against the back of the Father's knuckles. "No! No, Father …"

"You have a choice, then. You must make it."

"Yes, I do." He swallowed, throat sore and voice hoarse. "This is my choice. I beg your blessing, Father. This weighs heavy upon my heart."

Cyril felt indignation like a burn in his ribs, but he stilled the flame in his heart and took a quiet breath. Gently disentangling his hand from Benjamin's, he rested it on the healer's ashy hair. Benjamin took a deep, shaky breath.

"I have heard you. You have my pardon."

Benjamin slowly let his breath go, fighting to release the tension in his shoulders as he accepted the pardon he hadn't wanted to ask for. This time, when Cyril's hand was offered, it was as equals – and he helped the Brother to his feet.

"The baker girl, Brontë – may be a vampire."

Behind his back, Cyril's grip on his cane tightened. It relaxed a moment later.

"Philip told you this?"

"Yes, Father. It took him great effort to do so."

"And he believes this because he can smell her blood, correct?"

"... Yes, Father." There was a questioning note to Benjamin's reply.

"I suspected as much. Please, do be seated."

Benjamin once again did as he was invited to do, wondering why Cyril did not seem nearly as shocked by this information as he had when he'd heard it. Could he already have known? Surely not ... He would have taken immediate action. The girl would have been dead by now.

"How much did he tell you, Brother?" Cyril asked from across the room, rummaging through a secretary desk tucked into the corner. "About the girl?"

"He spoke of being able to smell her, her blood, rather, from a fair distance."

"Yes, anything else?"

"That it was unique ...? He said he could recognize it, or at least believed that he could."

Cyril nodded and returned to the hearth with a small rucksack tucked up under one arm. He set it down on the small coffee table, sliding tomes and candles aside to make room for it. Benjamin watched curiously as he unwrapped a small handful of what looked to be simple dinner rolls. He picked up one delicately, holding it out to Benjamin and cautioning him.

"Smell, but do not taste."

Benjamin took the bread and did as instructed. The little roll was soft and relatively fresh, though in desperate want of reheating to be enjoyed at its best. It smelled plain enough, perfectly ordinary, though perhaps with a slightly floral note beneath the baked grain – a familiar aroma in sweetbreads prepared with the church's honey.

"Honey, maybe?" he said as he passed it back to Cyril's waiting hand.

"Exactly." He put the bread back and sat back in the opposite chair. He spoke nonchalantly as he offered the perplexed Brother an explanation. "The honey is masking both the smell and taste of vampire blood. It is baked in."

Benjamin looked down at the rucksack on the table in disbelief. "I beg your pardon?"

"Do you recall the morning the restraints in Philip's bed were installed?"

Benjamin's head was sent spinning as he subconsciously shrunk back into the velvety cushions of the sofa, away from what he now knew was in front of him.

"I ... his – two days ago, now. Why?"

"Three nights past – whether induced by sleepwalking or hallucination, I know not – Philip departed his bed and wandered the halls. He veered too near the kitchens, where the bread was being prepared, and clearly caught the scent of blood. Thus did he proceed to the source – and of course, found the girl."

Benjamin looked down at the rucksack again, realizing the error made. His mind then sparked a question. "How do you know this?"

"I was in the south chapel, and heard the commotion."

"Commotion?"

He nodded. "Philip attacked Brontë."

Benjamin's surprised expression did nothing to interrupt the Father's retelling of the event.

"As I said, I know not if sleepwalking or hallucinating – nor do I know his motivation. Was his thought to act as a Hunter, and dispatch her, now believing her a vampire? Or was it sinsickness driving him? I cannot say, nor do I believe he could. And I would not pain him so by asking."

"And I take it you intervened."

"Naturally. He was subdued and returned to his bed with restraints, to prevent further risk to himself or another. Brontë, poor girl, was shaken, but not severely injured."

"And the bread?"

"Is used as medicament."

Benjamin sat forward, his whole body tense. "You would feed Philip the very thing that makes him ill?"

"Calm down. No – it is not for him."

Benjamin attempted but was unable to release the tension in his body. "Then why in the world would –"

"Mara," he cut off the question.

"Your mother? But, she ... her condition is due to injuries ..." Benjamin's eyes closed as he paused to actually give thought to the matter. She was never tended to in the infirmary. She never had been; Serge never allowed the sinsick. She was always attended in private, by her son – and by his predecessor before him. Her limbs had long since begun to fail her, a textbook symptom of withdrawal ... until recently. He felt the fool indeed.

"Her affliction is comparatively mild," Cyril said when he believed Benjamin had been given enough time to think. "She is a textbook case, being weaned onto the blood, and weaned off, as much as is possible. But Philip was given no such gentle treatment."

Benjamin sunk back into the sofa as he let the vast swaths of new information process in his mind. "And she is fed this ... because the tablets have no effect? To moderate pain?"

"Yes. Though, it only postpones the inevitable."

"What do you mean, Father?"

"I do not ..." His words trailed off as he brushed his finger over his lip in thought. "I have no cure. For all my work, all my trials, all my schooling – I cannot cure her. All I can do is moderate her decline, slow it with small doses that keep the worst away."

"So, in time, she will devolve into the same state as Philip?"

"Yes." As if he himself needed to hear it twice, he repeated the affirmation: "Yes, she will."

"And Philip?"

"I do not know. All I can prescribe is that he is kept comfortable. I do not want him in pain. He has suffered enough."

87

RONTË WAS STILL IN PAIN. BUT THE WONDERFULLY SOFT fabric of her nightgown and the distraction of her book helped to soften the aches. She moved slowly, when she dared move at all. Mara was a kind companion during these longer days, when Cyril was called away and she was left alone with her thoughts for far too many hours. Mara was busy putting away the chess set the two of them had been playing, half-jokingly upset that she had lost.

Brontë was only partially listening to her as she prattled well-intentioned silliness. She grimaced a touch as she shifted slightly wrong and an arc of pain shot through her. She put her hand over her chest, huffing in frustration at her body's strange way of repairing itself. She hated the sensation, the reminder of what she was. It was unfair ... wasn't everything else enough? She'd rather be stitched up with threads, the way Philip was. Mara smiled sadly and circled around the table, fluffing the blanket over Brontë's legs.

"Chin up, my girl. You'll heal soon enough."

Brontë's lip curled into the tiniest sliver of a smile on one side. "I don't know if this will ever really heal," she muttered.

"Oh, poor dear." Mara gave her cold hands a reassuring squeeze. "Don't worry, you have a saint praying for you. You'll be alright."

Brontë nearly laughed aloud. "I don't think any of them would waste time praying for me, ma'am."

"Nonsense, I know he does. He told me so."

518

Brontë's jaw dropped and Mara gave her a smug smile, winking and putting a skinny finger to her lips. "But you didn't hear that from me. Good night, Miss Brontë."

Mara wheeled herself away, leaving Brontë to sit alone, too stunned to speak.

Brontë was precarious on her stockinged feet, leaning heavily against the bedpost as she pulled herself, aching and weak, from Cyril's bed and hastily donned a veil. *Foolish girl!* She *really* had such a voice interceding on her behalf? Suddenly, Philip's insistence that she come pray didn't feel like a coincidence. This tug she felt, this need ... Was this what it was like to feel the saints trying to speak? Had she misinterpreted their gentle voices all along, tricked by her own improper expectations?

She gritted her teeth and endured the pain of moving. The northern auxiliary chapel was a small, lonely thing in comparison to the others. Tucked deep within the cathedral, it was one of the older chapels, perhaps the first, built into the church. She stumbled through the open door and caught her breath. The chapel was not abandoned, not even at this hour, as she'd hoped. Cyril was kneeling silently on one of the hassocks. Brontë angrily held back a cry, trying not to be noticed. But Cyril turned around anyway, glancing over his shoulder in some look between worry and disappointment. *Of course he did*, she thought. He could smell her blood from down the hall. He always knew.

"What are you doing out of bed?" he whispered, rising to his feet.

"I'm sorry, I did not mean to disturb you."

"What do you need? Come along, back to bed with you."

Cyril made to turn her around but she shook her head vehemently.

"No!" she whispered. "No, please! I need … I need it."

Cyril tilted his head at her curiously. She looked up at him, brown eyes bloodshot from weeping and her lip quivering. Her stare was intense, as if meaning to say more than she did.

"I need to pray, please."

"The chapel will be here in the morning, and the next –"

"No, now. Just for a moment, please?"

He looked down at her, a little dumbfounded, before nodding his permission. He helped her to walk up toward the many, many candles. He tugged another one of the hassocks out, setting it beside the one he'd been kneeling on. She eased down onto it, wincing a bit at the effort, but managing to sit on her knees in relative comfort. She thanked him, resting her hands in her lap and closing her eyes.

Cyril then knelt beside her, standing on his knees in the proper fashion, as he always did. He had every intention of returning to his own prayers, the ones she'd interrupted. But he had trouble keeping his good eye shut, keeping it from moving to her, in that charming, sheer little nightgown. Even if he fought and fought to look away, to close his eye, he could still smell her. Like vanilla and nostalgia, heavy salted cream, and once tender connections. She loitered on him like hope of togetherness. It made his neck itch under his clerical collar.

Brontë too felt this smothering presence, in her own way. With her eyes closed and tears beading up on her eyelashes, she attributed the warmth she felt to grander things. To humility and a newfound respect, a newfound reverence. It harkened back to much younger, much more innocent memories. Back to when she, in her dirty school uniform, used to kneel beside a younger Cyril, watching him with wide eyes until he finally agreed to teach her some short prayer and help her light a candle. The world had

seemed such a simpler place. And he hadn't been quite so ...
warm, then.

Back then, he'd tolerated her with far more patience. And yet, here he was, kneeling beside her. She opened one of her eyes and, blinking away tears, managed to look up at him. His good eye was closed in a far more peaceful expression than she expected. Was he praying for her, she wondered, even now? He'd tended to her so carefully, even let her sleep in his bed. Another wave of humility, or perhaps just plain embarrassment, flooded her. Had she truly been so oblivious?

Her prayers turned into questions, and those into roving, incoherent thoughts as her head drooped and sleep began to overtake her. Thank goodness for Cyril's white shirt. It spared her cheek a harsh sting when it rested against his arm. She thought she heard him say something, but it was too distant to make out.

Finally, a little shift as she went limp told Cyril she'd fallen asleep. He clicked his tongue, looking up at the candles and mumbling aloud. "You have a sick sense of humor, my Lady. You know that?"

The candles flickered and sparked in reply to him, as if laughing. He picked Brontë up carefully, holding her to his chest. She fidgeted in her sleep, moaning some quiet approval as she nestled into the warm crook of his neck. Even her pale little hands slid up and around his neck, holding on to him with all the strength she could muster. Her hand was horribly pleasant around him, and he chastised himself for feeling some pleasure from her at a time like this. He adjusted her so that she did not bump the door to the chapel, and bore her up the stairs to his room.

Cyril lay her in his bed, cradling her head as he leaned over and gently lowered it to the pillow. Her eyelids fluttered open briefly; her cheeks went red – as if she realized the position she was in. But her eyelids were too heavy to stay open. As he pulled away, her hand about the back of his neck slipped around to his chest and clung to his shirt, reluctant to be parted.

"How cruel," he muttered to himself, stuck leaning over her. Over her, in his own bed, with a gown begging to be ripped off.

More asleep than awake, and forgetting herself because of it, Brontë's disapproval came out as a quiet moan. Cyril tried urgently to remove her hands from him, but she clawed weakly into his shirt and drew lines through the fabric against his chest in a way that made him swallow an unwelcome noise. He grumbled in defeat, gnawing his lip in thought as he looked down at her. He then unbuttoned his shirt, untucking it from his sash and working the sleeves down both his arms.

After negotiating his ordinarily pinned cross around the fabric, he pushed the garment into her waiting hands. Brontë curled over with her prize, the shirt still warm from his body and smelling of incense, and nuzzled into it. He hurried to cover her up, then, to hide the curves of her body better, beneath the blankets and the sheets.

Cyril held his loose cross to his chest as he leaned over and kissed her on the forehead. After fetching and pulling on a new shirt, pausing in the doorway to look back at her, adrift in silky white linens and appearing ... rather lonely in that big bed of his. He shook his head and closed the door, descending the stairs to make his way back to the chapel. As he walked, he rubbed at his chest; at the sore space she'd dragged her sleepy hand over. He imagined her doing it again, while awake, hard enough to leave little red lines on his skin. Cyril rubbed the back of his neck, trying to banish such things from his mind, as if he'd be able to think about anything else that night.

88

THOMASINA WOULD HAVE BEEN QUITE FETCHING, IF SHE was alive. Now she had half a face rotting off and was almost proud of it. She was efficient, but brash – far from a favorite. Her usual dull, rusty sickle hung from her belt as she stood before Zemirah's desk. Greer was eyeing that sickle nervously as he, too, stood in the office beneath the Cannoneer. He kept wondering if she'd claw him open the same way she had that Hunter boy. He was so preoccupied with the idea, he didn't hear Zemirah addressing him.

"Well?" Zemirah snapped her fingers to get his attention. "Can you do it or not, Greer?"

He apologized and stammered out his words, his eyes flicking back to the sickle, Thomasina's hideous face, and back to Zemirah.

"Do you know how *hard* it is to move anything about this damned city anymore? It was bad enough with the Royal Guard breathing down my neck, but now the Hunters are –"

"I will handle the Hunters. Just get me doctors. Living or dead, it doesn't matter. Ambrose had an apprentice, start there."

"And the Royal Guard?"

"Keep away from the lamplighter's routes, and the Guard will not trouble you."

Greer frowned. "But what about me?"

Zemirah unlocked a drawer in her desk. She fished out an oval medallion, engraved with Windermere's twin stags on it: the same trinket necessary to unlock the door in the Cannoneer's storeroom. She tossed it to Greer.

"That will buy your life once or twice. Have care where and when you spend it."

⁜

IT FELT LIKE AGES SINCE BENJAMIN had seen his own office. He stumbled across the floor, shoulders drooping from exhaustion and his eyelids feeling heavy. He had intended to retrieve a bottle from the shelf – something to keep him awake just a little bit longer – but was so tired that his searching hand was slow and sluggish. Benjamin took off his glasses, folding them and letting them dangle from the chain about his neck. He groaned and rubbed his eyes as if it would somehow soothe his dull headache, somehow help him wake up.

"Brother Benjamin?" A voice addressed him, making him straighten up and look over his shoulder to see Cyril already closing the door behind him. "Are you feeling alright?"

Benjamin busied himself cleaning his spectacles where they hung about his neck. "Yes, Father, thank you."

Cyril set his cane aside, leaning against Benjamin's desk beside him and crossing one ankle over the other. "Have you eaten yet?"

"Not yet, I asked for dinner to be brought to the infirmary. I only came to fetch something."

"And?"

Benjamin was obsessively wiping his glasses over and over pointlessly. His lips trembled as he muttered tiny phrases in the back of his throat. Cyril sighed quietly and took hold of Benjamin's hand, stopping him from rubbing a hole in the cloth.

"Ben, if you are weary, you can rest."

"I can't," he breathed. "I can't ... leave him like this."

"I know you are doing all you can for him."

"It's not enough."

"None of us could do better."

"And if I fail him?"

"No such thing. It is not your failure to bear."

Benjamin gave a small shudder that revealed the cry he'd been withholding. He then leaned into Cyril, his head resting on the gold stole draped over his shoulder. "I don't know what more to do for him, Cyril. He gets worse by the minute."

Cyril moved his arm in an invitation for Benjamin to curl into him, which he wordlessly accepted. "Has something else happened, Ben?"

"Philip refused to drink," he mumbled into Cyril's chest.

"I see."

Sinsickness, withdrawal, both had many cruel and irreversible symptoms. But they could be managed, contained, treated. Overindulgence, though, not so. Once the victim began to fear light, to fear food and drink ... there was no recovery. Never had been, not in the hundreds of thousands of years. Not in all the scriptures and records. Not with the effort of a thousand holy men and women.

"How long does that give us?" Cyril finally asked.

"Ten days, at best? It will progress swiftly."

"Does Brother Serge know?"

"I'm sure he does."

"I'll call the Chapter to decide on what should be done."

89

THE CHAPTER HOUSE HAD SURELY HEARD MANY A melancholy meeting, in its time. Still, the room was thick with grief. The Timekeeper ticked away, oblivious and yet so very aware all at once. As if that inanimate object could sense the weight of the conversation below. Serge had only slightly regained his composure, but he still glared at Cyril across the room. Murmurs about his being so near an addict without a mask for so long did very little to soothe his anger.

Benjamin was asked to speak first. He spoke quietly, simply – stating only his observations on Philip's degrading condition. The Chapter House was filled then with quiet deliberation. Posed questions of how to prevent pain, of how else he might be saved, some horrid insinuations that he was lost the moment he'd become an addict. Serge, who at one point would likely have agreed with the latter, seemed to snap at the concern being raised now.

"He is suffering!" Serge howled at the top of his lungs. "I have seen enough cowardice at his expense!" Serge sunk into his chair and buried his head in his hands, containing himself for a moment before muttering out heavy words. "If he cannot be saved, at least let him die with dignity, and not like this. Not like this."

Silence settled over the Chapter until Florence ventured to speak. "Could something be put into his food or drink?"

Benjamin was quick to dismiss the idea. "He refuses to drink and scarcely eats. It's likely he would not ingest enough to put him under quickly or comfortably. It'd be cruel."

"It could be given in an injection?"

The topic descended slowly into mumbled deliberation, until Serge stood again, speaking above the din. "Father, I ask you to let Philip die by Mercy."

A hush fell over the room at once, and every eye focused on Cyril, waiting for his reaction. The silence grew overwhelming as the Timekeeper ticked away above their heads and the Cardinals shuffled through their documents. A few mumbled words were caught here and there, between bated breaths. Cyril sat quiet. A great weight settled over his shoulders and his brow furrowed with pain as he pondered Serge's request.

"You can't ask that of him," an elder murmured.

"I can, and I will. I know it can be done. What say you, Father?"

The Cardinals in front of Cyril held up a document. He leaned down to take it, pausing to let them whisper to him, and nodded his understanding. The quiet hum of conversation and doubt amongst the Chapter quieted as Cyril stood up.

"I can only grant such a pardon if Our Lady gives it. You understand this?"

"I do."

Cyril nodded. "How long can you keep him comfortable?"

"I'm afraid we fail to do that already," Benjamin said. "Three days?"

"Five," Serge stated. "Give me five more days with him."

Benjamin opened his mouth to protest. He was of the opinion that Philip refusing both food and drink would render those additional days unnecessarily cruel. But the cracks in Serge's usually stony features made him unable to speak his mind. He closed his mouth.

Cyril nodded again. "Five days, Brother. Make good use of them."

Serge was quick to depart, to be back with his nephew. Cyril made it clear he would hear no argument. If anyone doubted, they could request the Cardinals show them the law that allowed for such a request.

Benjamin loitered in the Chapter House as the others filed out of the room. He approached Cyril, who had sunk back into his chair and was staring blankly ahead, one finger stroking his lip in thought.

"Do you believe yourself in a fit enough state to don the white again so soon, Father?"

"I do not have a choice," he said quietly. "It is the least I can do for Philip."

"And ... if no pardon is given?"

"Then I will use Immolation. Serge understands."

90

SABEL STOOD UP AT THE DESK SHE'D BEEN INHABITING AS the doors opened. Domingo barged in without waiting for the butler to introduce him properly.

"Where is Lord Sinclair?"

"His obligations have taken him to the northern border."

"Of course they have."

"You will forgive me for reminding you, sir," Isabel said coldly as she turned around to face him, "that these obligations are precisely *why* my Lord Vidal requested your presence here. My husband trusts you to handle matters in his absence with alacrity and tact. Please do not disappoint him."

"Perhaps your husband will be disappointed to learn that you seek to prevent my involvement." He eyed the cross she wore about her neck. "Your bias is clear enough. I'm sure he knows."

"Moderate your tone when in front of me, Captain –"

"I knew this would happen!" Domingo marched over to Isabel, his finger pointed in what he realized looked far too accusatory a gesture. "I warned you in every letter, and you ignored me. That damned priest is going to start slaughtering every so-called *addict* he gets his hands on! And you will do *nothing* – permit *me* to do nothing – to stop this?"

"The boy is to die to prevent his suffering. Not because of his sinsick –"

"Hah! For wanting so desperately to endear yourself to the people, you are quite ignorant of their beliefs when it suits you."

Isabel pressed her fingers into Domingo's chest, pushing him away to give herself space. It had the intended effect of making him step back. "Your frustration loosens your tongue in an unflattering way."

"I'll not soften the truth to suit Your Ladyship's ideals. I know the Archbishop's intentions."

"Do you?" Isabel held up a letter from her desk. Domingo vaguely recognized the already broken wax seal as the Archbishop's. Isabel unfolded it and shuffled to the latter page, reading it aloud. "It is with great sadness I must inform you ... that our young Brother is injured beyond repair. Our Clerics have kept him comfortable. His surviving family have requested a gentle end to his life, and I am obligated to fulfill this request –"

"How easily he paints himself a sympathetic figure," Domingo cut her off.

She frowned and lowered the letter, tossing her head in exasperation. "I know you despise the Archbishop. I do not understand why, despite my efforts to do so. But even you must admit the Brother is not to die due to his addiction. This is the request of his family. A request that we would honor, and pardon, from any hospital. The church is no different."

Domingo put his hands on his hips and shook his head. "He doesn't fool me, my lady."

"You are so eager to see him as a liar you ignore any evidence to the contrary."

"I know a charlatan when I see one!" He spun about and began pacing back and forth to vent some of his agitation. "Those filthy priests are all the same. He kills that boy to save himself further controversy in the public eye. Do you realize the precedent this sets, my lady? If the boy dies by fire, every single addict in this city will be sentenced to death, whether the law permits it or not. If the boy dies by this god's mercy, the

Archbishop solidifies himself as infallible. Do you not see this ploy for what it is?"

"It is not the Archbishop's decision," Isabel repeated sternly. "He is subject to the needs and expectations of his people, as are we."

"How naive. You let your ideals, your *religion,* blind you to reality. You believe his every word without hesitation."

"He has given me reason to believe him, Captain. Have you?"

Domingo halted his pacing and the two shared a long, intense look.

"Very well, my lady," he finally said. "I shall endeavor to be more deserving of your confidence in future."

91

CYRIL PAUSED IN THE CORRIDOR OUTSIDE of his chambers. His hand loitered above the handle, as if summoning the courage to open the door. He would be the one to tell her, of course. How cruel it would be to hear it from the executioner. He flexed his hand a few times, took a deep breath, and let himself into his chambers. He locked the door behind him.

He passed through the doorway leading into his bedroom. Brontë stood before the hearth in her nightgown and a borrowed silk shawl. She looked at him expectantly, trying to put on a brave face. Her eyes were puffy and red. She watched him quietly close the door to his bedroom. She could see the downcast tinge to his expression – a subtle observation she might have prided herself on, in any other situation.

"Please tell me," she whispered. "Is he going to die?"

"Yes."

Brontë heard the news like a crack of thunder. Her legs wobbled and failed her. Cyril hurried over to her as she collapsed. She doubled over before the hearth, wailing and curling her hands into her gown. Guilt and grief like she'd never known swallowed her up, tears splattering over the floor as she coughed and cried. She tore through her nightgown, ripping the fabric open as her voice went hoarse. Deep down, she knew it had been coming. But still, she had clung so tight to hope, so very tight, and for what? *For what?*

Cyril set aside his stole, draping it over the couch and kneeling beside her. He put a gentle hand on her shoulder, tugging her away from the fire. "Come away from the hearth. You will damage yourself."

"Good," she mumbled. "I'd deserve it."

"I'll tolerate none of that sort of talk. Come here."

"It's my fault," she whispered as he slipped his arm beneath her and pulled her up. "It's my fault!"

She fought against his arm around her, trying to push it away, even though her hand stung to touch his cassock. He hoisted her up anyway, sitting her down on the couch. He knelt in front of her, pulling her hand away from his sleeve, red and agitated from the damage even that brief touch inflicted.

"Anger at yourself will not change what has happened."

"It's my fault!" she cried. "*I* told him about the mill! And now I am the reason he cannot heal! *I* am the reason you –"

"I know."

He knows. The guilt, the blame of it all, he knows. Her voice gave out like her legs. Cyril's hands moved to hold her face. His thumbs brushed away tears from her cheeks pointlessly as more came to replace them.

"Tragedy has no rhyme or reason. None of us could have predicted the future."

Brontë tried desperately to slow her cries, shuddering and whispering out apologies. Cyril tilted his head with her movements, ensuring he could retain eye contact with her.

"I'm sorry, I'm sorry …"

"Do not be ashamed. The grief hurts as it should."

"What do I do?" she whispered. "What … am I supposed to do?"

"Grief must be allowed to run its course. To weep is not a sin. You can cry here."

She flung her arms about his neck and wept. He could feel her grief through every shudder of her chest against his own. It was enough to overwhelm even him. Cyril shifted a bit closer, resting on both knees in front of her as she held on to him. He'd heard countless others' grief, listened to sins and sorrows aplenty. He had carried more than his own fair share of misery himself. But this was different, because it was hers. So deeply and profoundly hers. She felt everything with such sincerity, such earnestness – even the most ugly things. The guilt, the grief, the loneliness, she carried it all. And now, for perhaps the first time, she shared it.

Slowly, he wrapped his arms around her in a much-needed hug. It was gentle at first, almost timid. It grew tighter with each fresh wave of tears, and she clung tighter. Her head cradled to his chest, she wailed and sunk into the comfort of his arms. His cassock stung her hands where they clung to him, but she didn't care. It bit at her cheek, but couldn't possibly feel worse than the tears. So overwhelmed that no words could convey the flurry of emotions, of precious memories and dashed hopes mingling with gratitude and humility. She had never felt such grief, nor ever felt so comforted. Would that such comfort had not come at so high a cost.

92

GERGE HAD NOT LEFT PHILIP'S BEDSIDE. His beard and hair were ragged as he cradled Philip's head in his lap, stroking what was left of his hair, rendered down to velvety peach fuzz from being shaved. The rest of the boy seemed to waste away. Occasionally he'd try to talk to Philip, but the sight of his nephew unresponsive was often too much for him to bear.

"I'm sorry, son. That I can't explain this to you. I wish I could tell you."

BENJAMIN FELT AN AWFUL feeling deep in his belly as he approached the altar in the eastern chapel. He knelt once at the foot of the altar before ascending the steps and moving past it. Tucked behind the altar, hidden from view by curtains and sculpted statues of marble, was a small semicircular space. Tall candelabras lined the wall and incense was heavy in the air. Cyril was knelt quietly in the center of the little room, cane resting on the floor beside him, involved in one of the many rituals necessary to request the death of a clergyman.

"Father –"

"Not yet," Cyril whispered sharply.

Benjamin's lip quivered and he wrung his hands beneath his sleeves.

Cyril hung his head and repeated himself. "Not … yet."

IT WAS STILL DARK when the southwest gate of Our Lady opened. Three horses emerged. One bore the black silhouette of Father

Stacy, one carried Brother Benjamin, and the last bore a blood-red Cardinal. The ambulance was driven behind them, two twinkling lanterns swaying on either side of Sister Jael as she drove alone. She had insisted upon it, despite her own still-healing injuries. Inside the ambulance, nestled in many downy blankets and propped up by pillows, lay Philip. All skin and bone, he mumbled incoherently as Serge tried, to no avail, to soothe him. Delirious and unaware of his surroundings, his eyes were milky and dull as he trembled in the cot.

Maddoc stood in the courtyard with his arms crossed over his chest, holding back his own emotions. In the stable behind him, just out of view, the hearse was already prepared. Two horses, wearing the formal black tack reserved for fallen clergy, were secured to the finer hearse in the Lady's collection. Its departure would be delayed. It was to bring Philip home after the bitter deed was done, yes – but the hearse need not mock his uncle by forcing him to look at it before it was truly needed.

The three horses kept step, steel shoes cold and unforgiving against the cobblestones. The soft bells of the censer seemed to beg anyone listening for their pity. Together, they made for a sad symphony of metallic notes that alerted the townsfolk. Murmurs and whispers floated between the walls and alleyways as the city became aware of the long-awaited procession.

Incense billowed heavily from the censer carried by the Cardinal. The wisps of smoke enveloped the whole cavalcade, making them look like specters or spirits emerging from the fog itself. From open doors streaming light into the road, faithful knelt and bowed their heads as the clergy passed, not a word said as they trod the boulevard toward the city's wall. When they had passed, the people followed.

The wind rustled, sweeping the morning fog aside as the little procession arrived at their destination. The peach and apricot sunrise had begun to stain the clouds pale pink. As if the heavens knew what was to come, and wished to make good on some promise made.

A familiar, rather lonely looking tree atop a small knoll had only lost some of its leaves. The rich coat of foliage it wore was already painted honey yellow and buttery orange. Jael had to bite her tongue to keep from spitting out a sob upon seeing it in such a beautiful state. She'd never understood why Philip was so fond of such a useless, fruitless tree. Why he'd praise it for turning so early in the season. Now she knew she'd never be so grateful for anything again as she was in that moment; grateful for the kaleidoscope of colors it bore.

Cyril stood beneath the great, gnarled tree – looking up through its branches at the very last speckles of stars in the morning sky. He shifted his cane in his hand, gripping it by the handle and stomping it down into the soil. A gold ripple like disturbed water radiated out from it, and the earth itself seemed to obey his request. Pebbles, acorn caps, and grit scurried out of his path, leaving only soft grass and sod.

Philip was so light now that even Serge could lift him. Limp and dripping white linen from every one of his spindly limbs, he was carried to Cyril's side and carefully set down beside the tree, leaning back against it as he would so often do. Though Serge did not want to see the strike coming, he could not bear to be parted from Philip. He would not separate his hand from his nephew's, not while it still held life.

Philip had refused the consecrated bread and wine, same as he would vehemently refuse any other food or drink. His eyes were crusted with long-dried tears and his throat hoarse from dehydration. But like the sunrise, Cyril had a promise to keep. And though it could not save him ... perhaps it would soften this injustice. Cyril looked at the Cardinal, who seemed to understand him without any exchange of words.

Philip tried to toss his head in defiance when the Cardinal cupped it in their hands, but was far too weak. They whispered a tearful blessing behind their mask and brushed their gloved thumbs gently over Philip's closed eyelids. Scales seemed to flake and fall from Philip's eyes, the awful poison eating away at them temporarily undone, to keep that precious promise. Philip blinked. Only blurry, confusing colors greeted his ruined eyes. Then, as the Cardinal stepped away, the rolling wheat fields that stretched on and on came into focus. Gold and glistening, they caught the morning sun like waves on the ocean, stalks rustling in the breeze.

With the smallest bit of energy he had, Philip sat forward, helped by his uncle supporting one arm. A tiny smile played on his cracked lips, to realize where he was. He propped himself up as he stared out over the wheat field, no matter how his body trembled and strained at the effort. Philip opened his mouth, but only broken sounds fell out. His once wonderful voice destroyed by all that he'd endured. Fragments of a prayer, or perhaps a hymn. Only the heavens would truly know.

Benjamin approached Cyril and removed the rings and glove from his right hand. He then bowed and stepped back a pace. Beneath his sleeves, he gripped the leather glove with all his might, as if that gesture would subdue his tears.

From the shelter of a cypress tree opposite the hill, Domingo and Levi sat astride their horses, watching. The townsfolk filled the roads, and each man, woman, and child had a candle in hand. The Flagellants had congregated around the ruins atop a hill. All present awaited the verdict.

Cyril made the familiar gesture on his chest. This time, the gesture did not finish with his hand lowered, with two fingers poised to deliver judgment. Instead, he lifted his bare hand heavenward, open. He spoke in the old language, a prayer both Benjamin and Serge could interpret.

"I seek a pardon," he whispered.

There was a tense moment as all three of the priests waited, while all onlookers waited.

A white spark materialized in the palm of Cyril's hand. White hot and eight-pointed, the same mark of mercy that had revealed Philip to them, not all that long ago. It hummed to life, singing that eerily familiar note in reply. It flickered and settled against Cyril's skin, marking it with the glowing, white-hot image of the same cross he wore on his breast. As it did so, a thin ring of gold crackled to life about Cyril's head. A pardon granted, an addict – and his murderer – excused. Serge cried out at the confirmation. He clapped one hand over his mouth to silence it, lest he disturb his nephew, as tears flooded his eyes. The crowd murmured and a few even shouted. Levi heard an ungodly noise shatter down from the heavens and covered both ears. Domingo grit his teeth and shielded his eyes to spare them from being blinded.

The color of mercy drenched Cyril from head to toe, pouring over him like water and fluttering his cassock in a nonexistent breeze. One featherlight touch did the deed. Philip slumped over with a quiet, contented sigh into Serge's waiting arms as his uncle wailed. Thus did Brother Philip – the Hunter and addict – die.

93

Cyril stood motionless, staring down at the now empty infirmary bed Philip had inhabited the past weeks. The linens had been changed. Clean and crisp, the bed lay vacant, ready for another patient in their moment of need. The room seemed a bit darker without him, like he'd taken that little bit of sunshine with him. One of the Clerics making her rounds restocking towels jumped a little in surprise to find the room occupied. She stood a moment in the doorway, debating simply closing it again, but decided to address him, even if it was an empty gesture.

"Are you alright, Father?"

Of course, she knew the answer, but it seemed unkind to say nothing. There was no reply for a moment.

"Yes." His voice was hardly a whisper. "Thank you, Sister."

She thought it best to leave the man to his grief, and so quietly closed the door behind her as she shuffled down the hall. A deep quiet settled over the infirmary room, with only the slight whistle of the wind outside and the settling of beams overhead disturbing the silence. Cyril dwelt in this silence for some time, before slowly, wordlessly leaning his cane against the bedframe and kneeling beside the unoccupied bed.

His gloved hand slid underneath the frame, between the supporting slats of old splintered wood. His fingers felt about carefully until they encountered what they were looking for. Cyril very nimbly worked the downy cotton kerchief free from where he had tucked it, so many days ago now.

Brontë's blood had done its task well. A little too well, in driving Philip from his bed that night to attack her, but then Cyril had known that was a possibility. He knew the constant exposure to even this tiny amount of blood would break what was left of Philip's mind, that it'd make his words untrustworthy and his accusations unfounded. Her blood was more potent than she realized, than he ever intended to let her know; a dried drop was enough to undo an addict. A steep price to keep his own secrets, and one cruelly extracted. But then, the end justified the means.

Oh, how he'd missed this little companion. As he rose to his feet, brushing splinters from the cotton, he couldn't resist a smile to have it back in hand again. He folded it in on itself properly, planting a small kiss against the bloodstain. A slow, deep breath – to enjoy the subtle way it swept over him, far too delicate a scent for anyone other than himself, or a hopeless addict, to notice. Bliss like a sugar cube dissolving on his tongue, like vanilla and myrrh. He slipped it back between the buttons of his cassock, nestled lovingly against his heart where it belonged.

THE END OF VOLUME I

Immolation

Volume II

VISIT **DIASTREFO.COM** FOR UPDATES

Glossary of Terms

LOCATIONS

VISIMUND A province situated along the northernmost border of the Monocerian Empire. Previously a sovereign city-state, annexed by Monoceria c.300 years past. Topographically known for its dense forests, craggy plateaus and sheer cliffs at the shoreline – Visimund has a reputation for being a harsh, cold land... a land allegedly haunted by the undead.

WINDERMERE Capital city of Visimund, home to Our Beloved Lady, Coldwater Keep, and Dunrior. A holy city sick with sin, she remains in the grip of a centuries-long vampire panic, even long after being conquered by her empirical neighbor to the south. Though suffused with superstition, she remains a well-traveled trade route and her rivers flow fast with goods and silver both.

OUR BELOVED LADY Grand cathedral situated in northwest Windermere, houses the Order of the Sacred Heart. The oldest structure within city walls, estimated to be several thousand years old, though her exact age is unknown (and really, it's impolite to ask). Considered by many to be the original heart of the city, Windermere branches out from her and all paths lead back to her gates.

DUNRIOR Palace and primary residence of the Lord Governor of Visimund, located in the southwest of Windermere. Surrounded by acres of parkland and often used to host events, both public and political.

COLDWATER KEEP Primary defensive fortress of Windermere, situated in the center of the city on a man-made island where the twin rivers converge. Ceded to Monoceria upon annexation, it now houses the Royal Guard and is overseen by a Monocerian officer of the crown.

PARRVON A historic and dense town several days' travel south of Windermere, one of many formalized stops along the pilgrim's path, now also connected to Windermere via the rail line.

MELI A small village between Parrvon and Windermere, tucked into the woods alongside the rail line. An informal stop on the pilgrim's path, but a welcome one.

HAMLETS Farms and homesteads situated between the two rivers to the immediate west of Windermere. Filled with mills and granaries, and almost exclusively owned by Sunderman Farms.

THE CHURCH

CHURCH OF SORROWS A strict, traditional church that worships an unknowable Mother, a god that relieves followers of sorrow and bestows knowledge in exchange for faith and adherence to law. Referred to simply as Our Lady or My Lady, their god has no name, no form, and only manifests in the gold stars in the heavens that make up the church's symbol. A cross-shaped constellation that, when viewed from the ground, aligns with the steeple of the cathedral in Windermere.

THE SACRED HEART The Order's titular relic: an undying, supernatural flame that selects a living vessel in the form of Our Beloved Lady's Archbishop. The only thing capable of permanently killing a vampire. Some believe it a fallen star, a fragment of the constellation, some believe it a literal flame. The church has many such mysteries, and welcomes this one like it does all the rest.

CLERIC Dedicated pacifists and healers, Clerics are capable of using Our Lady's many mending and protection spells. Clerics cannot summon armaments, nor can they cast Immolation. Clerics endeavor never to interface with the undead, and leave vampires to the Hunters.

HUNTER Protectors and executioners, Hunters are oath-bound and uniquely equipped to slaughter the vampires that infest Visimund. Hunters summon armaments for battle, and can cast Immolation – but cannot use Our Lady's mending or protection spells.

BISHOP An elevated rank of clergy that is eligible to hold a seat in the Chapter. Requires elevated knowledge of theology and liturgy, demonstrated ability in the church's magic, as well as years of service to the Lady. Either Hunters or Clerics may become Bishops, but history favors Clerics. The word "bishop" has long been construed by external parties as the church's dedicated term for "mage".

CARDINAL Archivists and advisors, the Cardinals directly serve the Archbishop, researching and procuring knowledge as requested. Upon becoming a Cardinal, these clergy members lose access to all previous spells and also lose all identity; shirking their names, genders, and voices. In exchange for this, they gain unique abilities and unfettered access to all knowledge kept in the church's archives. Unlike the Archbishop, who is forced into their role, Cardinals are given a choice, and can decline the role if not willing to surrender their individuality.

ARCHBISHOP OF WINDERMERE Gender-neutral title, seat of religious authority in Visimund and bearer of the Sacred Heart. Unique to the Order, a role that is not elected by the Chapter. The Archbishop may be man or woman, but history favors women. Additionally, the Archbishop of Windermere has always been a Cleric, until now. Akin to the term "bishop", the term "archbishop" has been construed by external parties as "archmage".

MOTHER/FATHER SUPERIOR Second in command to the Archbishop, the Mother (or Father) Superior of Windermere serves as the administrative heart of the complex. An operational superintendent rather than a spiritual figurehead, this role oversees day-to-day ongoings on. Unlike the Archbishop, this role is elected by the Chapter.

Addendum: Cathedrals always, clergy roster permitting, have one Mother and one Father serving, with one of the two taking on the role of Archbishop. The remaining will take on the additional "Superior" title. This title is given to distinguish that Mother or Father as serving at a cathedral, rather than a church.

CHAPTER An elected council of Bishops that serve as an advisory body to the Archbishop of Windermere, as well as voting on matters impacting the church. The Chapter can be called at any time by the Archbishop or can request to convene if a situation requires attention. The Chapter historically favored Clerics but now sees a handful of Hunters included.

CHAPTER HOUSE Ancient, octagonal room set beneath a dome, the interior of which charts the stars and storms that plague the heavens. Suspended inside this dome is the church's Timekeeper. The Chapter meets here to discuss, debate, and hold votes when necessary. In the center of the Chapter House is the basin in which the Sacred Heart resides when without a human vessel.

TIMEKEEPER A grand astrological clock that keeps the church's time, and is used to study the position of stars both past, present, and future. The Cardinals are tasked with the upkeep and maintenance of the clock, and are the only clergy with the spells available to manipulate the Timekeeper to research certain dates or events via the clock.

SECOND TABLE A document, penned on cloth, that allows for any Bishop of adequate rank to perform a spell on the Archbishop's behalf. Acts as an extension of the author, granting both authority and the required power to execute a myriad of spells and tasks.

BELT ROSARY An item unique to the clergy, distinguished from the mundane rosaries worn by the faithful and novices by its composition and magical power. Not a source of magic itself, but a conduit, the belt rosaries carried by Clerics and Hunters allow them to cast spells. Like any conduit, if a rosary is separated from its master, it becomes useless as

a magical tool – and without it, a member of the clergy can cast no
magic.

CONFESSION A ritual by which grief and guilt are surrendered to the
Lady, with a Cleric acting as intermediary. Forgiveness is then rendered,
irrespective of the crime committed. Confessions are binding and
entirely confidential, even if law-breaking guilt is admitted. With the
exception of the current Archbishop, only Clerics can hear confessions.

CLEMENCY A name rarely whispered, instead referred to as "wearing
white". Pure mercy given form. An ancient spell that cannot simply be
cast, but must be invoked – must be requested, and only succeeds Our
Lady grants it. Physically alters the condition of the caster and of
blessed material, causing blessed robes to turn white and blessed metal
to glow. Only Bishops who have attained a seat on the Chapter can be
taught the requisite prayer. Mercy has a price and always comes to
collect.

IMMOLATION A new spell, born by a sacrifice to the Sacred Heart
from a desperate Hunter. A tongue of flame that, when touched to a
vampire, will purify vampiric body and spirit both. A reimagining of
the more ancient spell: Torch.

TORCH An ancient ritual and associated spell used to purify all
vampires by burning. Used at the pyre stones that line the bridges
leading to Our Beloved Lady. Monoceria banned this practice upon
annexation of the province c.300 years past.

PYRE STONES Flat stones blackened by flame, identical to the bases
upon which statues of saints stand. The location of the old Torch ritual,
now fallen into disrepair and disuse, mostly.

REUNION An ancient spell, a flare and call for help. Creates a
temporary earthly star of pure gold that marks a location directly above
the caster. If line of sight to the star is not broken, another clergy

member may cast the same spell to create a second star that will navigate to the first, providing a path to follow.

CHOIR The long-dead chorus of saints and sinners that echoes in the halls of Our Beloved Lady. Accepted as an immutable part of the cathedral, most go their whole lives without hearing a single note, while others claim to hear the sound in barely-discernable whispers and chimes during prayer – and still others, those with the look of a Listener, hear it like a crash.

WATERWAYS

ROTHERDARE The narrower and faster flowing of the two rivers. Flows from the north and splinters off via man-made canals both within and without the city limits. Conjoins with the Lusefil and carries on east through Windermere, retaining its name.

LUSEFIL The wider of the two rivers, meanders into the valley from the west. Also diverted via canals throughout the farmland until routed through the walls of Windermere. Upon merging at Coldwater, the river carries on east as the Rotherdare.

THE EMPIRE

MONOCERIA Conquering nation hailing from the far south. A knowledge-hungry empire expanding its influence by both trade and conquest. Annexed the province of Visimund c. 300 years past. Responsible for the installation and management of the rail line, as well as other infrastructure throughout the province.

FETTERS A Monocerian spell, what the empire often calls equations, taught to all officers of the crown, intended for humane restraint and subjugation of criminals and rowdy civilians alike. Like most Monocerian magic, it prefers straight lines and precise points, taking the form of newly drawn constellations when commanded by a caster. Painless and typically cool to the touch, this magic can temporarily bind, blind, and bear down on any target – be it man or monster.

VAMPIRIC

VAMPIRE A creature born of heresy, a blight upon Windermere and her people. Undying and unaging, they feed on both blood and flesh, and insult the natural order by stirring the dead from their graves. Capable of bewitching humans and stitching spells with threads of blood, these heretics have plagued the province of Visimund since time immemorial. Not all vampires are created equal. Some carry a potent blood and wield it well, while many are just shambling corpses plucked from earth. But all are unfit in the eyes of Our Lady, and must be put down.

DHAMPIR A half vampire, half human hybrid. While vampires can pull the dead to their feet, they cannot commit a partial sin – there is no partial vampiric transformation process. A dhampir must be born rather than made. A child born in this condition is a contradiction and cannot exist, and as such stillbirth is an inevitability. Due to the instability and incompatibility of the resulting hybrid, in all Our Lady's long years keeping watch, only one dhampir is known to have survived.

VAMPIRE BLOOD Liquid money, liquid courage, liquid strength. Remarkably addictive, vampire blood bolsters the mortal body and numbs sensitivity to pain. Those who partake of blood experience temporarily sharper sight, heightened awareness, and an unnatural swiftness of motion. While even the smallest amount will numb pain, a more substantial amount will begin to heal the human body. The healing provided, though, disobeys the natural order and can lead to an overproduction of scar tissue, bulging bones, and other such abnormalities.

SINSICK Addiction to consuming vampire blood, an unforgivable sin in the eyes of the Lady. That it alters the mortal body is an absolute. The sinsick are the most susceptible to the influence of vampires, and often develop a heightened sensitivity to the smell of vampire blood. Such is the strangeness of the changes engendered that the sinsick are known to, on occasion, forfeit all food and drink, and survive on blood alone. After death, the sinsick are suspected to make the most willing puppets.

OVERINDULGENCE Overconsumption of vampire blood beyond what the mortal body can bear. Violent convulsions, foaming at the mouth, hallucinations, confusion, and paranoia are all indications of overindulgence. While not inherently fatal, once symptoms surface, the chance of survival is markedly low. The body is irreparably damaged, torn between the unnatural healing of vampire blood and the destruction of inhuman power alien to itself.

WITHDRAWAL The inevitability that awaits any who consume even a drop of vampire blood. Once tasted, the body develops an insatiable need. What begins as a dull ache, a tremor in the hands, a foggy mind and a poor memory progresses, if not indulged, into a complete failure of body and mind. The tremors turn to stiffness as limbs shrivel, the mind frays and cannot be trusted, and wounds both mental and physical fail to heal.

FLAGELLANTS Sinsick addicts enduring withdrawal of their own volition as a self-inflicted penance. A cult of fiercely devout faithful, devout to the point of madness. This semi-organized cult of excommunicated sinsick surfaced after the province's annexation by the Monocerian empire, after the Torches were torn down.

MISCELLANEOUS

REJECTION Not a spell but a medical condition wherein the body rejects blood during a transfusion. Rejection can be avoided by receiving unblemished blood from a direct relative. If no relative can provide, any compatible donor may instead give blood, but some amount of rejection will inevitably occur and must be monitored. Blood transfusions, if handled incorrectly, can result in rejection that kills the recipient. The Church of Sorrows is renowned for their knowledge and handling of blood transfusion, having discovered the phenomenon of Rejection and how best to assuage it – a knowledge they attribute to being bestowed by their Lady.

WATCHERS Every culture has some label for those possessed of this unique ability: an ability to visually discern magic. Often simply referred to as "sight", this ability is inborn and appears at random, with no discernable pattern present in individuals who have the ability. Though an innate ability, it must be honed through intense practice – a practice that has blinded many in their pursuit of clearer glimpses.

LISTENERS A local phenomenon to Visimund and considered a superstition by those not from the region, Listeners are similar to Watchers in that an inborn ability allows them to hear what the church refers to as the Choir: the resounding echo of long-dead faithful. The church claims this ability is discernible by the placement of freckles on the cheek and brow, indicating a constellation that interacts with the Lady's. While emphasis is placed on what these individuals hear, some Listeners have also experienced various visual phenomena. Alas for the Listeners, hearing Our Lady with such clarity also makes them susceptible to the interfering voices of vampires, who seek to deceive and pull astray.

LAMPLIGHTERS GUILD One of Windermere's oldest guilds, responsible for keeping the paths lit at night in the unnatural pitch of Visimund. Bound by contract with Our Lady since her founding, the clergy bless the oil that the Lamplighters use to light the lamps, lending them a half-holy flame to keep both the way, and the Lamplighters themselves, safe from vampires. While not sacred, this fire burns hotter, warmer, and longer than mundane oil.